OXFORD WORLD'S CLASSICS

====

PIERRE CHODERLOS DE LACLOS

Les Liaisons dangereuses

====

Translated and edited by
DOUGLAS PARMÉE

Introduction by
DAVID C

OXFORD
UNIVERSITY PRESS

OXFORD

UNIVERSITY PRESS

Great Clarendon Street, Oxford OX2 6DP

Oxford University Press is a department of the University of Oxford.
It furthers the University's objective of excellence in research, scholarship,
and education by publishing worldwide in

Oxford New York

Athens Auckland Bangkok Bogotá Buenos Aires Calcutta
Cape Town Chennai Dar es Salaam Delhi Florence Hong Kong Istanbul
Karachi Kuala Lumpur Madrid Melbourne Mexico City Mumbai
Nairobi Paris São Paulo Singapore Taipei Tokyo Toronto Warsaw

with associated companies in Berlin Ibadan

Oxford is a registered trade mark of Oxford University Press
in the UK and in certain other countries

Published in the United States
by Oxford University Press Inc., New York

Translation, Note on the Text, Bibliography, Chronology, Explanatory Notes
© Douglas Parmée 1995
Introduction © David Coward 1995

The moral rights of the author have been asserted

Database right Oxford University Press (maker)

First published as a World's Classics paperback 1995
Reissued as an Oxford World's Classics paperback 1998
Reissued 2008

British Library Cataloguing in Publication Data

Data available

Library of Congress Cataloging in Publication Data

Laclos, Choderlos de, 1741–1803.
[Liaisons dangereuses. English]
Les liaisons dangereuses / Pierre Choderlos de Laclos; translated
and edited by Douglas Parmée; introduction by David Coward.
p. cm.—(Oxford world's classics)
France—Social life and customs—18th century—Fiction. 2. Aristocracy (Social
class)—France—Fiction. 3. Man-woman relationships—
France—Fiction. I. Parmée, Douglas. II. Title. III. Series.
PQ1993.L22L53 1995 843'.6—dc20 94–30781

ISBN 978–0–19–953648–1

1

Printed in Great Britain by
Clays Ltd, St Ives plc

LES LIAISONS DANGEREUSES

PIERRE-AMBROISE-FRANÇOIS CHODERLOS DE LACLOS, born at Amiens in 1741, trained as an artillery officer at the military school at La Fère. His hopes of active service were frustrated in 1763 by the Treaty which ended the Seven Years War. For twenty-five years he was a peacetime soldier in garrison towns in the French provinces where, as was expected of army officers, he socialized and dabbled in literature. His only novel, *Les Liaisons dangereuses*, was begun during a posting to Besançon in 1778 and completed in Paris by the end of 1781. The scandal which greeted its publication in 1782 led his superiors to banish him to La Rochelle. In 1788 Laclos became secretary to the Duke of Orléans and acquired an undeserved reputation as a sinister political schemer. After the collapse of the *ancien règime* in 1789, he accompanied the Duke to London, returning to Paris in June 1790 when he joined the Jacobin Club and soon emerged as one of its leading spokesmen. A convinced but moderate revolutionary, he played a crucial role in preparing the French defences for the battle of Valmy in 1792. But as the political climate deteriorated, he was arrested more than once and narrowly avoided the guillotine in 1794. On his release, he devoted himself to his family but remained sufficiently in touch with events to play a part in the coup of 18 Brumaire (1799) which brought Napoleon to power. He died at Taranto in 1803 of fever and exhaustion.

DOUGLAS PARMÉE studied at Trinity College, Cambridge, the University of Bonn, and the Sorbonne. He later served in RAF Intelligence before returning to teach in Cambridge, where he was a Fellow and Director of Studies at Queens' College. He now lives in Adelaide, South Australia. He has written widely on French Studies and is a prize-winning translator from French, German, and Italian.

DAVID COWARD is Senior Fellow and Emeritus Professor of French Literature at the University of Leeds. He is the author of studies of Marivaux, Marguerite Duras, Marcel Pagnol, and Restif de la Bretonne. For Oxford World's Classics, he has edited eight novels by Alexandre Dumas, including the whole of the Musketeer saga, and translated Dumas *fils*'s *La Dame aux Camélias*, two selections of Maupassant short stories, and Sade's *Misfortunes of Virtue and Other Early Tales*. Winner of the 1996 Scott-Moncrieff prize for translation, he reviews regularly for the *Times Literary Supplement*.

OXFORD WORLD'S CLASSICS

*For over 100 years Oxford World's Classics have brought
readers closer to the world's great literature. Now with over 700
titles—from the 4,000-year-old myths of Mesopotamia to the
twentieth century's greatest novels—the series makes available
lesser-known as well as celebrated writing.*

*The pocket-sized hardbacks of the early years contained
introductions by Virginia Woolf, T. S. Eliot, Graham Greene,
and other literary figures which enriched the experience of reading.
Today the series is recognized for its fine scholarship and
reliability in texts that span world literature, drama and poetry,
religion, philosophy and politics. Each edition includes perceptive
commentary and essential background information to meet the
changing needs of readers.*

CONTENTS

INTRODUCTION

A few days after the publication of *Les Liaisons dangereuses* in April 1782, Mme Riccoboni, a family friend and herself a novelist, administered a sharp rebuke to its author: 'I am not surprised that a son of Monsieur de Choderlos should write well. Wit is hereditary in his family. But I cannot commend him for employing his talents, his invention and his elegant pen to furnish foreigners with so appalling a notion of the manners of his nation and of the taste of his compatriots.' Berlin was shocked when Laclos's novel was translated into German in 1783 and, greeting the appearance of *Dangerous Connections* (4 vols., priced 10s.) in London in 1784, the *Monthly Review* issued the predictable warning. Though 'conducted with great art and skill', the story is quite 'diabolical'. Moreover,

the pretence of 'instruction' is an insult to the understanding of the Public, as the work itself is a daring outrage on every law of virtue and decorum . . . The scenes of seduction and intrigue are laid open with such freedom, that for one who will be 'instructed' by the catastrophe, a thousand will be corrupted by the plot . . . Actions of so atrocious a nature as are here delineated, devised by cunning, attended in their formation by a contexture of dark and disguised villainies, will not admit of particular description. When we read them, it is not enough to say we are disgusted at such complicated crimes; but we are actually chilled with horror. For aught we know, such characters may exist as are here described, not only in France, where the scene of action is laid, but in other countries, whose religion and customs may be more favourable to religion and virtue. However, let them exist where they will, instead of being exposed to the eye of the Public, they should be consigned to that *outer darkness* to which they belong.

But it was not only foreigners who were appalled. The first French reactions were equally fierce: 'a tissue of horrors and infamies', said the *Mémoires secrets*. 'However poor an opinion you might have of society in general and of Parisian society in particular,' observed the Baron de Grimm in the *Correspondance littéraire*, 'I do not think it possible for a young person of the fair sex to encounter any connections as dangerous as a perusal of

Les Liaisons dangereuses.' A 'diabolical' novel exuding fumes of sulphur which outraged the moral majority could not fail to be a commercial success. The first printing of 2,000 copies sold out in the middle two weeks of April 1782. A second followed immediately and about fifteen pirated editions had appeared by the end of the year. 'No novel of recent times', wrote Grimm, 'has enjoyed such spectacular success.' Notoriety was heaped on its author, an obscure artillery officer who was suspected of being every whit as wicked as his book. Whether he had imagined such villainy, or (as was widely believed) had merely stitched together a *roman à clef* out of an authentic correspondence, was not the question: either way, the man was a 'monster'. Marie-Antoinette ordered a copy but, before allowing it into her library, took the precaution of ensuring that neither the title nor the author's name appeared on the binding. The Marquise de Coigny (hardly a model of propriety) is reported to have closed her doors to Laclos on the grounds that were she left alone with him she would be terrified. The anecdote is probably apocryphal but it fairly captures the general reaction of the public which felt it had been caught in the cold, fascinating stare of a reptile. Yet despite the scandal, *Les Liaisons dangereuses* continued to be reprinted at regular intervals without interference from the authorities. Laclos never reoffended: the sequel promised on the last page of the book did not materialize. *Les Liaisons dangereuses* was the first and only novel of one of the most enigmatic authors in French literature.

Pierre-Ambroise-François Choderlos de Laclos was born at Amiens in 1741. His family had only recently been ennobled and, in the caste-ridden society of the *ancien régime*, occupied a lowly place in the aristocratic hierarchy. He was sent to military school and trained in an artillery regiment which not only offered the prospect of a technical career but was known to recruit from the bourgeoisie and *petite noblesse*: the more glamorous regiments were staffed almost exclusively by nobles having the requisite number of quarterings in their escutcheons. In 1762, at his own request, Sub-Lieutenant Laclos was attached to the new Brigade des Colonies then forming at La Rochelle to oppose the English in India and Canada. But Laclos's hopes of seeing action abroad collapsed the following year when the Treaty of Paris ended both the Seven Years War and French imperial ambitions. Thwarted by the persistent peace, Laclos spent the next quarter-century kicking his heels in provincial garrison towns. His superiors regarded him as an able and conscientious officer of regular habits and he progressed slowly but steadily, but was not promoted beyond the rank of captain. Like many military men serving in a peacetime army stationed outside Paris, Laclos wrote a quantity of verse, most of it unremarkable except for an 'Epistle to Margot', published in 1770, which, when it circulated clandestinely in Paris in 1774, was read as a lampoon of Madame Du Barry, Louis XV's mistress (see note to p. 375).

Laclos was then approaching the end of a six-year posting in Grenoble. There, as was expected of officers stationed in provincial towns, he fraternized with local society. Little is known of his activities at this time—certainly there is no trace of a proto-Valmont at work—and he later wrote to his wife that he had left behind there no 'true affections', merely 'agreeable acquaintances'. He spent his leaves in Paris, where he kept in touch with his family and gained a foothold in the literary world. He wrote a play, *The Matron*, which he probably destroyed, and in 1777 provided the libretto for *Ernestine*, an opera based on a novel by Mme Riccoboni, which closed after one, quite disastrous performance. Laclos was then stationed at Besançon and it was there that he began writing *Les Liaisons dangereuses* in 1778.

The following year, he was seconded to the service of the Marquis de Montalembert who had been given the task of for-tifying the Île d'Aix, off La Rochelle, where the French, who had sided with the insurgents against the British in the American War of Independence, saw the threat of a landing by the Royal Navy. Montalembert left Laclos—who would have much pre-ferred the chance of seeing action in America—to supervise the work which was successfully tested by French guns in 1781, but not by the English fleet which never came. In off-duty hours and during spells of leave in Paris, he continued working at his novel and it was there that he completed it. When the scandal broke in April 1782, Laclos's superiors took the view that he had brought the army into disrepute and, to limit the damage, ordered him out of the limelight and back to the Atlantic coast. At La Rochelle he met Marie-Soulange Duperré, the daughter of a well-to-do official. At a time when girls were normally married by the age of 18, Marie-Soulange was a spinster of 23. When she became pregnant, Laclos, instead of deserting her as any self-respecting libertine owed it to his honour to do, asked for her hand. But he was rejected by the family who had no wish to be connected with a man of such unsavoury reputation. Laclos persisted, however, and he and Marie-Soulange were married in 1786. They later had two other children and lived very happily together.

Meanwhile, Laclos had not abandoned his pen which he devoted to a number of causes, some of which surprise by their eccentricity. In 1783 he began the first of three very modern essays on the education of women, none of which he completed. Rousseau had argued that the native goodness of natural man had been corrupted by society. Laclos, who shared his contemporaries' admiration for the author of *La Nouvelle Héloïse*, said as much of natural woman who had been enslaved by a society dominated by men. As long as women remain slaves, they cannot be educated. And until such time as there occurs 'a great revolution', which only women can bring about, they will remain in ignorance and bondage. The following year, he wrote a rambling review of Fanny Burney's *Cecilia*. While other critics expressed reservations and drew attention to its cosily happy ending, Laclos commended the book for its faithfulness to life, its defence of sentiment, and its moral purity. In 1786 he published an ill-advised attack on Vauban, then regarded in official military circles as the presiding genius of France's defensive strategy. Laclos pointed out that the forts which Vauban had built on France's north-eastern frontier were vulnerable, rather as de Gaulle in 1925 cast doubt on the effectiveness of the Maginot Line. For his impertinence, he was again banished to the provinces. There he devised a rather earnest scheme for numbering the streets of Paris which he submitted to the *Journal de Paris*, the first French daily newspaper.

Laclos had been paid 1,600 *livres* for his novel and was now bringing up a family on his captain's pay of 2,700. He still hoped to make his way in the army and in 1788 applied for a military attachment to the French embassy in Turkey. His application was unsuccessful, but later the same year he obtained leave to serve as secretary to the Duke of Orléans who, with an income of 3 millions, was the richest man in France. Laclos received a salary of 6,000 *livres*: it will be remembered that Cécile de Volanges would bring her husband 60,000 a year. Orléans, the king's cousin, though weak and vacillating, carried the hopes of liberal opinion which would have wished him on the throne instead of Louis XVI. It was a view apparently shared by Laclos, though exactly what role he played in events remains unclear. But as time passed and public unrest grew, the 'Machiavellian' author of *Les Liaisons dangereuses* emerged as the sinister power behind Orléans who quickly came to be known as Philippe-Égalité, the people's choice. When the women of Paris marched on Versailles in October, eye-witnesses swore that Laclos, scattering his master's gold, had led the protest, wearing a dress. When tension mounted further, Philippe-Égalité removed himself to London, taking his secretary with him.

In London, Laclos pushed the Orleanist cause harder than the Duke himself was prepared to do. His disillusionment with his indecisive employer increased after his return to France in July 1790 and, as a moderate, constitutional revolutionary, he gravitated towards the Jacobin Club which appreciated his talents and made him editor of its journal. By the summer of 1791 (when he retired from the army on a pension of 1,800 francs) he firmly believed that Louis XVI should abdicate and that Philippe-Égalité should rule as Regent. But he was compromised over the wording of the petition which led to the massacre of the Champ de Mars in July and subsequently withdrew from the Jacobins which by now had ceased to be a club of lawyers and had begun its long lurch into extremism. He lived quietly with his family, but kept an eye on events.

After Louis XVI virtually decided the future of the monarchy by attempting to flee the country in June 1792, Laclos re-emerged from the shadows and, protected now by Danton, was sent to Châlons-sur-Marne to organize French defences against the imminent arrival of the Prussians. His crucial role in Kellerman's victory at Valmy in September 1792 was duly noted and he was redrafted into the army with the rank of Brigadier-

General. He was appointed Chief of Staff to the War Minister
and Commander-in-Chief of French forces in the Pyrenees
where, for want of an enemy, he was unable to contribute further
signal services to the Revolution. But the political mood of Paris
was volatile and he was jailed in the spring of 1793 with a number
of other Orleanist supporters. He was freed in May. Though
placed under house arrest, he was allowed to conduct field tests
of a new type of shell which he had invented. He was rearrested
in November and remained in prison, narrowly escaping the
guillotine, for thirteen months. When he was finally released
in December 1794, his application to rejoin the army was rejected and for the next four years he lived modestly as a public
functionary. Somehow, he managed to keep in touch with events
and personalities and proved useful, in ways which remain obscure, in bringing about Napoleon's *coup d'état* in November
1799. For services rendered, he was reinstated in the army and at
last heard shots fired in anger in Germany and Italy in the second
half of 1800, to the extent of having a horse killed under him.
When peace was signed with Austria in February 1801, Laclos
returned to Paris where he was given a number of postings,
finally being sent, as a full General, to Italy where he died of
dysentery, malaria, and exhaustion in September 1803.

In a decade accustomed to violent death of men great and small,
the passing of Laclos the soldier was little remarked. Laclos the
novelist left more definite traces, though he was not remembered
with advantage. During his lifetime, his unsavoury reputation
had been reinforced by his image as a dark, revolutionary con-
spirator and his novel had been kept alive by the many pirated
editions which had continued to appear. Plays based on its
characters had been staged and novelists exploited its notoriety
by including the words 'Danger' or 'Liaison' in their titles. By
1800, however, the Laclos vogue was more or less over. When the
conservative order was restored after the fall of Napoleon,
Laclos was identified as one of the dangerous rakes and revol-
utionaries who had brought down the *ancien régime*. *Les Liaisons
dangereuses* was banned by a Paris court in 1823 'for outrage to
public morality' and among Romantic writers, only Stendhal
held it in any esteem. Laclos's name continued to be associated

with 'systematic licentiousness' and 'the most odious immorality' and, in 1865, the courts which had prosecuted Flaubert's *Madame Bovary* and Baudelaire's *Les Fleurs du mal* extended the same treatment to *Les Liaisons dangereuses*. In Great Britain, its author was unknown to all but Francophiles like Swinburne, and Ernest Dowson's translation, the first in over a century, was privately printed when it appeared in 1898.

But by the end of the century, Laclos was beginning to find defenders on both sides of the Channel who looked beyond the 'second-rate Machiavelli' and 'consummate immoralist' of academic criticism. His Essays on Women, his verse, and his correspondence were published and they showed a new side to him. He found an influential champion in Paul Bourget, while the publication in 1903 of Baudelaire's enthusiastic notes for a study of *Les Liaisons dangereuses* added considerably to his stature. His biography was written and, after the horrors of the Great War had taught Europe to look on human nature with a cooler eye, Laclos seemed to articulate very modern concerns. The Surrealists saw him as a paler version of Sade the Liberator; André Gide included *Les Liaisons dangereuses* in his list of the ten greatest French novels; and André Malraux, novelist and man of action, saw in Laclos a triumphant demonstration of the 'eroticization of the human will'. The English began to discover him at about the same time, in spite of the arch pronouncements of the critic George Saintsbury who called Valmont and Merteuil 'prosaic and suburban' and relegated *Les Liaisons dangereuses* to an 'outhouse' of his *History of the French Novel* (1917). Laclos was admired by writers as different as Arnold Bennett, Virginia Woolf, and Aldous Huxley, and Richard Aldington's translation, first published in 1924, made him available at last to a wider Anglo-Saxon audience.

Yet the rehabilitation of Laclos proceeded slowly and his rise to greatness since 1945 provides an interesting lesson in the making of literary reputations. The nineteenth century, for all its doubts, had expressed broad confidence in social and moral values which, if properly managed, could yet make men good. In such an age, a writer like Laclos, who showed such scant belief in the prospect of human goodness, spoke with a discordant and disturbing voice. But by 1920 the war had destroyed the old world order and Marx and Freud were shaking the established verities by showing that social justice and the distribution of power were unrelated, and that behaviour is the product of subconscious motivation, most of it far from admirable. In this new intellectual climate, Laclos appeared more honest than scandalous. Subsequently, the Nazi terror and the Holocaust revealed new depths to which the human spirit could sink, and in their aftermath, which brought the cold war, the threat of global destruction, the increased use of torture, and the apparently unstoppable rise of new dictators, it became increasingly difficult to argue that the health of societies could be maintained on the basis of the old ethical values which seemed irksome, ineffective, and irrelevant. Attempts were still made to hold the old moral pass. In 1957, exactly one hundred years after the prosecution of *Madame Bovary* and *Les Fleurs du mal*, a new edition of Sade was banned. In 1960 Roger Vadim's screen version of *Les Liaisons dangereuses* was challenged in the courts and, though his film was granted a certificate, it was denied an export licence, a ruling which would have delighted Mme Riccoboni.

By this time, the literary critics had ensured for Laclos a measure of intellectual and artistic respectability. But their efforts were much less significant in promoting his cause than was the liberalization of attitudes which took place in the 1960s. Thus when Vadim's film was shown on network television in 1974, it caused no outcry among the French who were by then accustomed to material so explicit that the government introduced measures to limit the growing sexploitation of screens small and large. In this new, more liberal climate, Laclos's novel finally dislodged Rousseau's *La Nouvelle Héloïse* as the greatest of eighteenth-century French novels, and it became widely available in many forms: unexpurgated, bound or paper-covered, annotated or left to speak for itself. 'Classic' status was confirmed when Laclos became a prescribed author for French university students. And, more significantly, Laclos passed an essential modern test: it was discovered that his book transferred well to other media.

The stage adaptation of *Les Liaisons dangereuses* by Paul Achard in 1952 and Vadim's film had merely paved the way. In 1974 Claude Prey turned Laclos's novel into an 'epistolary opera', with recitatives doing duty for the exchange of letters, and two years later Vadim extracted from the book a second film entitled *Une Femme fidèle*, set in 1826, which proved much less stylish and went unnoticed. In the same year Alberto Cesare Alberti freely transposed the text for the stage as *Amor di guerra, guerra d'amore*, which makes use of the characters (including Laclos himself) to dissect the relationship between men and women which is seen as sexual warfare. In Germany, Rudolf Fleck's play *Gefährliche Liebschaften* (1979) was followed by Heiner Müller's *Quartett* (1981), which again cast Laclos's characters in roles designed to convey an avant-garde and highly personal view of the war of the sexes. But it was Christopher Hampton's stage version, first performed at Stratford-upon-Avon in 1985, which turned Laclos into an unlikely star, even in Paris. The process was completed by a film, *Dangerous Liaisons* (1989), directed by Stephen Frears from Hampton's script, which pleased both reviewers and the general public. Milos Forman's *Valmont* (1991), though less well received, served to maintain the momentum. After a decade of exposure to unaccustomed limelight, Laclos has taken his place alongside Alexandre Dumas and Victor Hugo (and ahead of even Racine and Balzac) in the ranks of classic French authors who travel well.

But on what passport does the revamped Laclos travel? It is rare that adaptations and continuations, like fakes and forgeries, do not show their age sooner or later. The postface added to the German translation of 1798 follows Mme de Merteuil to Holland where she reforms and devotes herself to the pursuit of Virtue, a projection of her character which tells us more about the reaction against eighteenth-century libertinism than about *Les Liaisons dangereuses*. Attempts to modernize Laclos invariably repaint his face in colours which fade, in some cases rather badly. Vadim's first film now seems rooted in its period. His Valmont and Merteuil belong to the international set and they stalk their prey in the swinging Paris and fashionable ski-resorts of 1960, but their cynicism now seems as dated as the jazz on the soundtrack. Alberti made Laclos rather more aphoristic and systematic than he was, while Müller shows, with an explicitness of language quite foreign to *Les Liaisons dangereuses*, the squalor that lies at the heart of desire. Even Hampton's brilliantly executed play ends with an evocation of tumbrels which imposes a political reading: the decadent behaviour we have observed is a prelude to the destruction of a society ripe for the revolution to come. On the other hand, his film restores Laclos's ending and leaves the ambiguities intact: indeed, *Dangerous Liaisons* is by far the most faithful in letter and spirit of all attempts to re-create the novel. In comparison, Forman's *Valmont* is an altogether jokier affair which sacrifices the subtleties to the requirements of drama and action. Laclos's modern mouthpieces must, of course, be judged on their own merits, for they do not pretend to be faithful translators or guardians of the sacred memory. Nevertheless, Laclos has been reprocessed many times, gaining here, losing there, but always manicured to suit the taste of passing fashions. Laclos in the 1990s is a manufactured product, all style, gloss, and cynicism.

But while Laclos might seem to cast a strikingly modern eye on manners and morals, he was very much a product of the French Enlightenment which, in the last two decades of the eighteenth century, meant the often uncomfortable fusion of the barbed wit of Voltaire and the soaring, passionate idealism of Rousseau. It involved speaking of Vice and Virtue and assuming that men of goodwill were committed to the Happiness both of society and, increasingly, of the individual. For those who had lost their faith in the God of the Roman Catholic Church, the philosophic movement provided a comfortable substitute: through the application of Reason to social and moral problems, mankind could set its feet upon the road of Progress at the end of which lay the Ideal City where Ignorance, Poverty, Superstition, and Injustice would be finally vanquished. In 1789 many felt that the promised land was nigh. Like his contemporaries, Laclos thought in words that began with capital letters.

But unlike Rousseau, whom he admired greatly, Laclos was not given to making confidences. He was a very private man and, though much in the public eye, made no attempt to correct his public image as a monster of depravity and political manipulation. He had allies and enemies, but no friend to speak unambiguously in his defence. His actions provide no clear endorsement of his character, and little of what he wrote for publication both before and after *Les Liaisons dangereuses* yields reliable glimpses of the man. 'Cold', 'taciturn', and 'methodical', Laclos remained tightly buttoned inside his soldier's tunic and grew no more visibly human when he exchanged his uniform for the no less concealing black frock-coat in which he picked his way through the Revolution.

Fortunately, letters he wrote to his wife from prison and from his tours of duty have survived and they reveal him in warmer colours. He proves to have been surprisingly uxorious. He sent his wife a lock of his hair to remember him by and when she confessed she had grown stout in his absence, he rejoiced with heavy good humour: the more there was of her, he said, the better. He worried about his children's health and recommended walks in the country, though he issued stern warnings against venturing into woodland after sunset when emanations of carbonic gas reach dangerous levels. If his children were to occupy an honourable place in society, they should certainly receive a solid formal education. Yet a Feeling Heart was more desirable than a well-stocked, well-trained Mind. True contentment was ultimately the product of 'the Affections'. So convinced was he that Love yields the only riches worth having that, towards the end of his life, he considered writing another novel which would show that 'there is no Happiness outside the family'. He faced disappointment and adversity with resignation and did not believe that there was a Divine Plan: in his tidy world-order, death was no more than the cessation of life. But he did take highly moral attitudes. He despised the self-seeking leaders of successive regimes and based his own conduct on stern principles of Duty and Service.

He was a methodical man of fastidious, even ponderous inclinations: he was not above correcting his wife's spelling. He had little visual sense: as a traveller, he was much more interested in his Affections than in Views. He was unimpressed by the Alps which left all true Rousseauists gasping at Nature's finest handiwork. Nor did he care much for man-made beauty: the *palazzi* of Milan and Genoa in which he was billeted were uncomfortable and draughty and he would have much preferred something less gorgeous and more sensible.

Laclos's letters show him to have been disappointingly dull, a conforming, methodical, and very upright man. Although the first of his letters to his wife were written more than a decade after *Les Liaisons dangereuses*, it is clear that the man who had courted Marie-Soulange had not been turned by the Revolution into a political schemer or a sour cynic. He never disowned his political writings but on the contrary stood by his principles which reflect far more earnest idealism than opportunism. Nor did he ever regret having written his novel, though it had harmed his reputation. He rarely mentions it, though he did make a point of noting rather proudly that two Italian bishops, on separate occasions, had commended it as a moral work and well suited to the instruction of the young. His stray comments on writers and writing also suggest that he had not changed his opinion, expressed in his review of Fanny Burney's *Cecilia* in 1784, that while the duty of the novelist is to observe, feel, and describe, a feeling heart is far more important in an author than all the talent in the world. Nor does he seem any less attached to an argument which he had used in his correspondence with Mme Riccoboni and which he illustrated with the example of Tartuffe. At the end of Act IV of Molière's play, Tartuffe has succeeded in his ambition to gain control over Orgon, his family, and his property. Legally, he is unassailable, for he has taken care that all the necessary papers are in order. But this does not prevent his being a rogue and Molière, in the last Act, ensures that right prevails. Tartuffe, then, is not punished by law but by a higher authority.

I make this remark because it seems to me that the rights of the moral writer, whether he be playwright or novelist, begin at the point where the law is powerless to intervene. Once they have formed a society, citizens are entitled to see that justice is done only in the case of misdemeanours which the government has decided do not fall within its jurisdiction. This public justice consists of heaping ridicule on those who have faults and indignation on those who have vices.

Tartuffe is punished not for what we have seen him do but for what he is. Laclos believed that this is precisely what he had achieved in his novel: he had mobilized the 'healthy indignation of the public' by drawing attention to those who, like Valmont and Merteuil, exploit the no man's land between what is legal and what is right.

Such an argument is clearly a reflection of the moralizing tendency of all Enlightenment literature which required vice to be punished and virtue rewarded. If Laclos was a man of his times, then his novel is no less the product of a specific literary convention.

By its tone and subject-matter, *Les Liaisons dangereuses* belongs to the 'libertine' tradition of fiction. In common parlance, 'libertinage' meant no more than sexual depravity. It was the term adopted by the police to categorize offences which 'outraged public morality'. It was also widely used to describe the notorious debauches of aristocrats like the Duke de Richelieu, who once burned down a house in pursuit of an amour, or the Prince de Conti, who boasted a collection of 2,000 rings, each a token of an abandoned mistress. But in 1782 'libertinage' still retained something of its old sense of 'free-thought' which, around 1700, had meant the revolt of a group of radical intellectuals against the Church and established morality. By the 1730s the 'free-thinkers' had been absorbed by the more generalized rational spirit of the Enlightenment, but not entirely. The word had attached itself to the spectacular rakes of the Regency (1715–23) which spawned a new social type, the *roué*, of which Valmont, according to Mme de Merteuil, is a worthy exemplar (letter 2). But 'libertinage' survived happily in the novel where it raised opposition to the civil and ecclesiastical Establishment and promoted the cause of liberty (implicit in 'libertinage') in the specific context of sexual mores. The 'libertine' novel, therefore, formed one strand of the philosophical novel. Its uniqueness lay in its exploitation of the shock value of eroticism.

Of course, some novelists simply seized on the tradition to peddle cheap pornography. But others, from Crébillon *fils* in the 1730s to Sade in the 1790s, used it to call into question accepted social and ethical standards. At a time when it was dangerous to criticize Church and State openly, 'libertine' literature constituted a useful form of contestation which, because it dealt boldly with the private relationships on which public values were based, contained the threat of anarchy. This means that the first rumblings of the Revolution to come were sexual, not overtly political. 'Libertinage', therefore, meant far more than sleaze. Its purpose was to provoke and disturb. Some authors drew back from the brink. Samuel Richardson's *Clarissa* (1748), which caused a sensation when it was published in France, pressed the libertine tradition into the service of Virtue: the cynical Lovelace ends up a Rake reformed by Love. But if in the case of *Clarissa* (which Mme de Tourvel is reported as reading in letter 107 and Laclos considered to be 'a masterpiece') the theme of seduction was turned into an instrument for promoting morality, most 'libertine' novelists continued to explore the implications of free-wheeling eroticism in a variety of bolder registers, precious, satirical, philosophical, and gross. The pornographers merely showed pictures and were happy to titillate. But the elegant *libertins* dealt in ideas, were highly verbal, and sought to per-suade. But all, though ostensibly concerned with sex, were subversive agents of change and their scabrous tales acts of sabotage.

Now there is nothing coarse about Laclos's 'libertinage' which is cerebral rather than physical. Eroticism is reduced to a secret game which can only be won by players who ignore the com-monly accepted rules of decency and honesty. Manipulation replaces fair dealing, sex is power and love a form of weakness. But does *Les Liaisons dangereuses* criticize or promote such attitudes? Is freedom to be achieved by abandoning the moral ideals and social constraints which stand in the way of personal gratification? Or does true self-fulfilment lie in subordinating the self, respecting the feelings of others, and accepting the rules of civilized conduct? Most 'libertine' novelists set themselves the task of pushing back the frontiers, of demolishing the old taboos, in the name of freedom. It may be that the bishops Laclos met in Italy believed that he had denounced the immorality he describes. Yet most of his contemporaries read the book as though it were a user's manual for aspiring seducers, a view endorsed after 1789 by those who were convinced that what Merteuil and Valmont had done for sex, Laclos, the 'monster of intrigue', had acted out in politics.

Situating Laclos in the 'libertine' tradition amply confirms our impression that *Les Liaisons dangereuses* says rather more than it appears to. Yet it does not give us the key to the novel. Laclos never provided a satisfactory explanation of what he had set out to do or what he had achieved. True, in his letters to Mme Riccoboni he claimed that the reaction of readers showed that he had succeeded in rousing 'the healthy indignation of the public' against sexual predators like Valmont and Merteuil. But there, it could equally be said that, like his protagonists, Laclos did not much care for losing and would have used any means to win the argument. And if he never disowned his novel, it is far from clear what he kept faith with.

But he had certainly every reason to be pleased with his performance as the author of a work which even his sternest critics have admired unreservedly. *Les Liaisons dangereuses* is an epistolary novel, and belongs to another eighteenth-century tradition which did not survive much beyond 1800. Tales told in letters were immensely popular in an age of correspondence: the two most influential novels of the period, *La Nouvelle Héloïse* and *Clarissa*, were both written in epistolary form. But neither Rousseau nor Richardson was alive to the dramatic possibilities of the genre. They allow their correspondents to analyse their feelings in tedious detail and expatiate, at inordinate length, on moral and social questions. The tension drops and the voice of the author intrudes. Laclos never allows the pace to slacken and he is as firm with his correspondents as a sergeant drilling recruits. They march to his orders.

He removes himself almost entirely from the conduct of events and maintains only a minimum presence as the self-effacing 'editor' of a supposedly authentic correspondence. He does not address the reader and is completely hidden by his characters, each of whom has a distinctive voice. Cécile is immediately recognizable by the skittishness of her style and the inaccuracy of her grammar, which is so clumsy that Mme de Merteuil feels obliged to give her a few much-needed lessons. Danceny's youth and inexperience are detectable in his first letters which borrow pompously from the eloquent poets he admires; only when he has been disillusioned by events does he find a voice of his own. Mme de Tourvel's letters invariably begin defensively and end defiantly. Mme de Volanges clucks

and fusses, Mme de Rosemonde is wearily resigned, and
Azolan's sullen snobbishness is made all too clear in the way he
expresses himself. And although both seducers are on the same
side, they write in quite different inks: Valmont's letters are full
of male condescension and self-satisfied banter while Merteuil
has a sharper ear and a steelier manner. To others, they write
pastiche—Valmont posing to Mme de Tourvel as the contrite
lover, or Mme de Merteuil reading suitable pages by Crébillon
fils and La Fontaine in letter 10 so that she can strike the right
note with her Chevalier. Yet their style does betray something
of their natures: Valmont is given to using military images to
describe the 'tactics' which will enable him to notch up another
'conquest', while Mme de Merteuil favours metaphors drawn
from the theatre: she plays 'roles' and wears 'masks'.

Indeed, the whole novel is highly theatrical. Not only are
situations stage-managed and roles played to the hilt, the letters
are monologues which form a dialogue of sorts, but with this
difference: the written word is more effective than any conversational exchange. It allows time to reflect, to react, and to re-
group: policy replaces spontaneity and the struggle is removed
to terrain which favours those who practise finely contrived
deceit. Of course, not all the characters weigh their words as
carefully as Valmont and Merteuil, but all read and ponder the
letters which are written to them, Cécile fondly perusing
Danceny's notes, say, or Mme de Tourvel agonizing over
Valmont's. Laclos orchestrates this dialogue with the precision
of an engineer. He gave considerable thought to the order in
which letters should be placed. Thus Mme de Tourvel's letter 22
originally preceded Valmont's account of how he planned his
philanthropic rescue of the family threatened with eviction: by
putting it afterwards, her gullibility and Valmont's cynicism
emerge much more forcefully. Laclos's irony is fierce, and it is
always dramatic.

He organizes the letters in such a way that the reader acquires
a three-dimensional view of character and incident. In letter 145,
Mme de Merteuil informs Valmont that she does not know when
she will be in Paris, while in the next, she tells Danceny she will
arrive the following day—and the implications for her relationship with Valmont are clear. The three accounts of how Mme de

Tourvel sees Valmont in a carriage with Émilie (letters 135, 137, 138) show how events are interpreted—and misinterpreted. For letters contain only the truth which their reader finds in them. When Valmont, losing patience, returns to Paris and a night with Émilie, he keeps up the pressure on Mme de Tourvel. The result is letter 48, which is read by Émilie, who laughs; by Mme de Tourvel, who will be moved by his despair; and by Mme de Merteuil, who is invited to admire his skill. But the letters are not merely a vehicle for irony but hinges on which the plot hangs. Mme de Tourvel's fate is sealed by a terse note, and Mme de Merteuil's social persona, carefully cultivated in the privacy of her correspondence, cannot survive the light of exposure.

Laclos's handling of the epistolary form is responsible for some of the most memorable moments in the novel. The arrangement of the letters generates drama, irony, and a generous measure of black comedy. Their distribution and juxtaposition make character and event stand out in sharp relief and provide the pivots on which the action is articulated. Laclos controls his material with the technical skills of the professional engineer that he was. He is also a master of illusion who shows that few things are what they seem and that the words people speak, like the roles they play, are elements of a performance designed both consciously and unconsciously to replace spontaneity with artifice. But the engineer who plans and the puppeteer who pulls the strings remain frustratingly invisible. By removing himself so completely from the world he creates, he denies us any opportunity of hearing his own voice and consequently any way of knowing, or even of sensing, where his own loyalties lie. He is a supremely absent author who abandons his creation to the reader.

Not surprisingly, Laclos's readers are left staring at a puzzle and cannot even agree about what happens in *Les Liaisons dangereuses*. Most are convinced that Valmont loves Mme de Tourvel and is loved by Mme de Merteuil. It is through jealousy, then, that Mme de Merteuil shames him into ending his affair with the Présidente. Valmont despairs, is mortally wounded in the duel and, as he dies, provides Danceny with the means to ruin the Marquise. But others take a different view. They argue that Valmont does not love Mme de Tourvel any more than Mme de Merteuil loves him. The climax is the logical outcome of the dangerous game they play: their mutual annihilation is as predictable as the harm done to casual bystanders like Mme de Tourvel and Cécile.

Nor is there any agreement about the death of Valmont. Is it really plausible that he, who is omnicompetent and must surely be one of the finest swordsmen in France, should die at the hands of the callow, harp-playing Danceny? Of course, a lucky thrust cannot be ruled out, but the probabilities would suggest that Valmont allows himself to be killed, that his death is therefore an honourable form of suicide, and that he allows himself to die because he cannot live without the woman he has wronged. Support for this view is drawn from a note, mentioned by Mme de Volanges in letter 154 but suppressed by the 'editor' (it survives in the manuscript), in which Valmont makes a despairing attempt to rescue the dying Mme de Tourvel: the knowledge that he loves her will surely heal the wound which he so callously inflicted. But others interpret it, on the contrary, as yet another move in his battle with Merteuil. He plunged a dagger into Mme de Tourvel's heart, he says, and only he can pluck it out again. Pulling her back from the very jaws of death would be his finest hour, a triumph which would eclipse the Marquise's greatest exploits and restore his superior status in their partnership. And so against those who believe that Valmont has a better side to his nature and exchanges games for True Love, are ranged those who reject the possibility that a rake can ever reform: Valmont is a burnt-out case, a man who has spent too much time denying his feelings to be capable of feeling anything except the exultation of triumph and the anger of defeat.

Readers are no less divided about the ending of the book. Some view it as hurried, as though Laclos had suddenly lost interest. With Valmont gone, Mme de Merteuil is brought low with unseemly haste: she suffers public humiliation in the foyer of the Comédie-Italienne, financial ruin, and physical disfigurement. Now, while the first of her punishments is the outcome of the publication of her letters, the supplementary punishments appear, to say the least, arbitrary. The lawsuit has no roots in the plot and the attack of smallpox, though statistically plausible (about two-thirds of the population were likely to catch it, it has been estimated), seems gratuitous and may have been designed to allow Laclos to place his splendid comment that Merteuil now wears her soul upon her face. But many accept that the denouement, from the death of Valmont to the flight of Merteuil, emerges logically from the nature of their relationship, and find nothing arbitrary or gratuitous in the way Laclos brings down the final curtain.

If *Les Liaisons dangereuses* wears the smile of the Mona Lisa, that smile was put there by Laclos. The ambiguity begins even before events start to unfold. The 'Editor's Preface' states that the correspondence we are about to read is authentic and makes the standard eighteenth-century case for moral usefulness. Yet the 'Publisher's Foreword' denies both claims: what we are about to read is a novel which is unlikely to produce any moral effect whatsoever. Both were written by Laclos, and both are heavily ironic. By the time the first letter reaches us, the author has locked himself inside his stoutly defended novel and never reappears. How should we read *Les Liaisons dangereuses*?

In the last thirty years or so, a great deal of ingenuity has been expended on Laclos's secret novel and a number of interpretations have been advanced. Readers make different assumptions and set out from different starting-points. Some believe *Les Liaisons dangereuses* should be approached in eighteenth-century terms, set in its historical context and judged as the product of a specific literary and philosophical tradition. Others insist that the text escapes the narrow confines of its epoch and should not be subjected to antiquarian standards but considered in the light of modern cultural values and ideologies: Laclos is a suitable case for analysis by Freudians, Marxists, feminists, and exponents of various breeds of philosophy and divers brands of critical theory. Another broad division is formed by those who tackle the novel as a self-contained artefact, without reference to what is known of its author's life: the meaning of the text will emerge from its autonomous logic, economy, and architecture. Against them are ranged those who insist, on the contrary, that books have authors and see no reason why Laclos's biography and opinions should not be used to illuminate his book. A range of answers is now available but they have not, either singly or collectively, quite succeeded in wiping that enigmatic smile from Laclos's face.

To begin with, the possibility that Laclos was not a novelist at all but the 'editor' of a genuine correspondence has never quite been laid to rest. Models for his characters have been suggested, never convincingly, but hope is now fading that a secret family archive in Savoy will one day disgorge the original letters. *Les Liaisons dangereuses* is a *roman à clef* only in the general sense that novelists feed their own experience into the characters and situations they invent. In spite of what his contemporaries believed (a minor poet named d'Anceny publicly claimed to be the original of Cécile's admirer), it is an epistolary novel and not a collection of epistles.

More interesting have been the many attempts to tease a political message from the book which is universally accepted as an accurate picture of high society in the last years of the *ancien régime*. But Laclos does not give blanket coverage, and while there are glimpses of the world that lies outside Mme de Rosemonde's house and Mme de Volanges's *salon*—the appearance of the occasional shoe-maker or priest helps to focus the foreground against a wider setting—all we are actually given is a snapshot of a small and intimate circle composed mainly of women. Adult male figures are noticeable only by their absence: we never meet Gercourt or Monsieur de Tourvel or any of the standard financiers and churchmen who normally drew the heaviest satirical fire. If the atmosphere is claustrophobic, the social net is correspondingly small and makes it difficult to sustain the view that Laclos is in some way criticizing society at large.

Yet this is precisely what has been many times proposed. It has been argued that Laclos, who was denied promotion because he lacked the requisite noble quarterings, finally turned in frustration on those who barred his route to professional advancement. His novel was therefore the revenge of a man thwarted in his ambition. The Marxist view widens the argument to suggest that the victimization of Mme de Tourvel, a *bourgeoise*, by the aristocratic Valmont and Merteuil expresses the class struggle waged in a decadent society ripe for revolution.

This view rests on the erroneous assumption that a clear distinction existed between the upper-middle classes and the old aristocracy. On the contrary, generations of intermarriage had blurred the old class divisions to the point where they had virtually disappeared. Azolan may be reluctant to wear the Tourvel livery which he regards as beneath his dignity, but his reservations are not shared by his betters: not even Mme de Merteuil, who makes unflattering remarks about Mme de Tourvel's appearance, ever remotely suggests that she has risen above her station. And even if it is allowed that Laclos had no cause to like the aristocratic circle he so graphically describes, it would be quite wrong to see him in any sort of democratic light: the fate of the family Valmont so cynically rescues generates no social comment whatever. Nor are there any impertinent servants (a staple of the comedy of manners from Molière to Beaumarchais) to state the case for social justice or intimate that the world of Mme de Volanges or Mme de Rosemonde had in some way run its course and was due for a revolutionary change. Indeed, their world may be characterized by complacency, but only Valmont and Merteuil are shown to be wicked.

In fact, the impression many readers have that Laclos is in some way attacking society stems less from his picture of one small corner of the aristocratic world than from the way his two scheming protagonists abuse their privileges. It is they who are at fault, not the system. Only in one area does Laclos generalize from the particular. He takes marked exception to the way in which society treats women. Not only does the narrow education received by Cécile and Mme de Tourvel leave them ill-prepared to deal with the likes of Valmont, but their social horizons are dominated by the marriages which are arranged for them, as even Mme de Volanges eventually concedes. Laclos is consistent in his criticism of convents and the *mariage de raison*. Even Mme de Merteuil, who was privately educated and deliberately remains a widow, is marked by the pressures which lead her to overcompensate. Letter 81, in which she explains to what lengths she has been driven to preserve her feminine identity, is a fierce and compellingly stated defence of the way in which she has moulded her image, and it recalls the case for 'natural woman' made by Laclos's essays on female education. If *Les*

Liaisons dangereuses is not an outright satirical or political novel, then might we perhaps agree that it is an early feminist text?

Alas, few feminist critics acknowledge it as such. Mme de Merteuil may in some respects be a liberated woman, born to avenge her sex. But she is hardly an advertisement for female emancipation. She shows no solidarity with her sisters in bondage and deceives them with as little compunction as she dupes Danceny, Prévan, Belleroche, and even Valmont himself. Moreover, Laclos's feminist sympathies become suspect when his treatment of the Marquise is set against his greater sympathy for the Vicomte. Never quite as ruthless as Merteuil, Valmont is granted something approaching an honourable death in a masculine passage of arms. Furthermore, as he lies dying, he recruits Danceny to the male cause: now that war has been declared, his true loyalties resurface. It is a matter of honour that Prévan's good name be restored and his rehabilitation can be achieved only by the destruction of the expendable Merteuil. This in itself is a measure of the limits of Laclos's feminism, but there is more. If Valmont is in a sense redeemed in death, Merteuil is hounded without mercy and punished comprehensively, even vindictively. It is as though Laclos, finally wearying of this brawling woman, at last breaks cover, rejoins the men, and restores the dominant masculine order. At bottom, he is no more sympathetic to women than Lord Chesterfield who regarded women 'as children of a larger growth', or Dumas *père* who equated Milady with evil, or Zola who was simply afraid of the female sex.

The argument about the degree of Laclos's feminism has largely displaced the venerable view of *Les Liaisons dangereuses* as an acutely observed skirmish in the eternal War of the Sexes. According to this older and simpler reading, Laclos shows with considerable finesse that the relationship between men and women is never more than an armed truce which invariably breaks down because each sex operates quite different functional systems. This interpretation is still perfectly valid but it has been further upstaged by attempts to insert Laclos, not unreasonably, into the history of Don Juanism: after all, *Les Liaisons dangereuses* predates Mozart's *Don Giovanni* by only five years. While most 'libertine' writers had used sex to discredit conventional morality, some had taken the further step of arguing that since morality is based on the teaching of the Church, then the libertarian argument was not with society but with God. Laclos gives us two Don Juans, one in petticoats and one in breeches. But whereas Merteuil merely despises religion, Valmont brandishes his fist at heaven in true Donnish fashion. He does not set out simply to vanquish Mme de Tourvel or even to cuckold her dullard husband: his triumph will be complete only when he has made her, of her own free will, love him more than the God she worships (letter 6). His ambition is thus blasphemous, for he lays claim to the power of the Almighty. A cheap trick turns him into the 'image of God' in the eyes of the family he saves (letter 21); it costs him no more to perjure himself before God to Father Anselme (letter 120). Valmont takes on God, as Don Juan takes on the Commendatore. In choosing pride over humility, he tests the power of free will against the laws of heaven. Thus Laclos, a lifelong rationalist, is projected into the realm of metaphysics, and his novel shows, not a social or political conscience, but a concern for the spirit.

This view at least has the merit of catering for the 'chill of horror' felt by the *Monthly Review*. Valmont and Merteuil place themselves beyond the pale because neither acknowledges any power, human or divine, greater than themselves. In this sense, *Les Liaisons dangereuses* may be seen as an illustration of the 'spiritual poverty' which, according to Pascal, the seventeenth-century divine, is the inevitable, unenviable lot of the unbeliever. It is a novel, therefore, about evil. But is the evil really ontological, an inescapable part of the fabric of the universe? The book may seem 'diabolical' as the *Monthly Review* put it, but neither the Devil nor any other supernatural power plays any noticeable role in the demythologized struggle which we observe. On the contrary, evil here seems much more earthbound. It is the result of human failings—pride, selfishness, contempt, and indifference for others—and of social pressures. Human society is so constructed that it requires its members to choose between deceiving or being deceived: it is on this basis that its prizes are awarded. Valmont's Don Juanism thus leads us up another trail which disappears in the tangle of ambiguity. Perhaps we should see *Les Liaisons dangereuses* less as a metaphysical tale of evil than as a practical fable about winning and losing.

Many readers have wondered why Valmont and Mme de Merteuil, who have youth, wealth, wit, and social position, all of which might have been put to better uses, settle for so little. Valmont devotes himself to seducing women who, as he observes, are frequently all too ready to be seduced, while Mme de Merteuil fills her time by manipulating people whom she obviously despises. One answer is that they are both drawn to the exercise of power: in this sense, they are ancestors of the Nietzschean 'superman'. Another is that they hone skills and techniques whose perfect execution is its own reward: they are, in other words, artists of a very perverse kind. A further possibility is that, despising society and having outgrown God, they exist in a world which has no values except those which they give it. They can therefore seem like primitive existentialists who overcome the absurdity of life by asserting their individual identity against a godless universe which is arbitrary and without meaning. Such a view gives Laclos's 'libertinage' a very twentieth-century philosophical slant and, by denying his novel a metaphysical dimension, it allows us to see how the decadent world of the *ancien régime* is not so very different from our own.

Yet it is clear from his refusal to allow Valmont and Merteuil to succeed that Laclos ultimately disapproves both of them and of whatever philosophy directs their actions. Of course, it would be perverse to deny that he respects and perhaps even admires them. He was a soldier trained in the tactics of defence, not attack. But he was enough of a professional to appreciate the contemptuous ease with which they make their conquests. Valmont and Merteuil exhibit effortless superiority. Audacious, intelligent, and lucid, they reduce human relationships to a set of strategies and their control of the campaigns they initiate is absolute. Their battle plans are implemented with military precision and they have nerves of steel. Moreover, they have style in abundance and wit to squander. Yet they have one weakness. Their self-confidence does not quite disguise their need to be admired. This explains why they throw caution to the winds and, against their policy of not writing down anything that might possibly be used against them, maintain a correspondence with each other which leaves their flanks supremely vulnerable. The war they wage is undeclared, covert, and secret. They cannot have allies nor do they seek disciples. But they do need an audience. As lone operators constantly at battle stations, they are denied true intimacy and all human contact. When each at last discovers a worthy opponent, equal in skill and capable of fighting to a draw, both eagerly grasp the opportunity of having an ear which they can fill with tales of their own cleverness. The need for applause is, of course, vanity, and vanity proves their undoing. When their plans clash, as must happen sooner or later, one must prevail and the other will not yield. Whether or not Valmont loves Mme de Tourvel, whether or not Mme de Merteuil loves Valmont, the Marquise cannot accept losing control of the Vicomte, nor can the Vicomte tolerate being outmanœuvred by the Marquise. When Titans clash, the whole earth shakes. Perhaps, then, they might be seen as tragic heroes, fatally flawed and doomed by the fate that is character.

Now, while Laclos might well have respected their ruthless efficiency and style, he nowhere suggests that they are victims. On the contrary, they are persecutors, the Enemies of innocence, and, unlike many 'libertine' writers who connived at the triumph of life's predators, Laclos does not allow them to succeed. To some extent, his disapproval of them may be accounted for in social terms. Valmont and Merteuil are upper-class bullies who prey on the weak and the gullible, spoilt brats who squander their intellectual gifts on mean acts of petty destruction, beautiful people guilty of the abuse of power and social privilege. They represent the decline of the old aristocratic ideal of honourable conduct and its corruption by the newer, vulgar ethic of success at any price.

And yet their failings are not those of their caste. Their vices are personal, the result of conscious choices for which they alone must be held accountable. In the process of acquiring their iron discipline, they have turned themselves into emotional cripples. Their lucidity and self-control have been achieved at the expense of stifling their inner, affective being which they regard as a source of weakness. When their egos finally collide, they may (according to the interpretation which the reader puts upon events) feel the power of love or the pain of jealousy or they may simply lose their tempers. But however we interpret their reactions, it is clear that their judgement is clouded by their feelings and they make mistakes. If this is indeed the case, then Laclos's novel seems to be less a criticism of named individuals or even of a social group, and begins to look like a wider comment on the spirit of the age. Valmont and Merteuil are products of the Enlightenment which claimed to show the road to the millennium. The philosophic spirit associated Reason with right and Emotion with error. The first would unravel the mysteries of nature; the second encouraged prejudice, superstition, and fanaticism. However, Rousseau, the *antiphilosophe*, had already demonstrated the structural weakness of this position: a man is not merely another cog in a clockwork universe, a machine to be programmed, but a wayward bundle of needs and desires. In this context, *Les Liaisons dangereuses* expresses cogent reservations about the philosophic spirit itself. It shows what the intellect can achieve, but it also reminds us that mere effectiveness detached from feeling is barren. Reason guides the hand; but the hand labours in vain which is not guided by a compassionate heart. The irony of Laclos's novel is Voltairean, but its sympathies are Rousseauistic.

What we know of Laclos's private attitudes—he was not averse to 'Glory' but set a higher value on 'the Affections'—lends some support to this view. If he did indeed see the point of Rousseau's suspicion of the whole ethos of the Enlightenment, it follows that his novel might well express what he took to be proper moral and spiritual priorities. Not that *Les Liaisons dangereuses* is a moralizing tract. Nor is it even a very moral book by eighteenth-century standards. Vice is not convincingly punished, nor is virtue rewarded. Indeed, if there is a moral lesson at all, it seems to be that clever people should not underestimate their feelings and that the innocent and well-intentioned should tread warily and not assume that everyone is as honest and decent as they are.

If this is what Laclos intended, it is a banal lesson. Yet it fairly echoes the 'libertine' debate on the relative merits of Head and Heart in the production of Happiness. But Laclos does add an important rider. In expressing his condolences, Bertrand, Mme de Rosemonde's steward, humbly points out that feeling hearts exist at all levels of society. It may be therefore that Laclos does not think in class terms at all, but divides men and women into those who judge and do not feel and those who feel and judge not. Mme de Rosemonde clearly belongs to the latter category and, for some readers, she holds the moral centre of the book. She is neither censorious nor sentimental but resigns herself to accepting what cannot be avoided. There is even something in her of the stoicism with which Laclos spoke to his wife of his dashed career hopes. But Bertrand and Mme de Rosemonde are bystanders who observe from afar, unlike the reader who occupies a seat in the stalls and is made privy to every piece of villainy, every drop of suffering. Knowing what we know, we find it difficult to accept the moralizing Preface at its face value. If Laclos indeed intended it to be taken literally, then he is far more effective as a novelist than as a moralist. Valmont and Merteuil soar and cast their cynical glow over the reader who finds it difficult to believe that the clear-eyed, ironic Laclos demanded no more of his reader than a tepid acceptance of the way of the world. Surely, he intended something profounder, something of a stature commensurate with the intricate whorls of his novel, some kind of political or moral or philosophical message . . . But this is where we came in.

Laclos's novel is as stoutly defended as the forts he built on France's western approaches. Every attempt to scale its heights meets with a rebuff. At different moments and to different readers, *Les Liaisons dangereuses* seems to change shape and direction. It is a novel (if it is a novel) written by a man with a personal grudge against the society which blocked his career prospects. Or it may be just an exercise in realism, a faithful picture of one corner of society painted without prejudice, a kind of documentary exposure of manners presented without bias. Yet it feels more like an indictment of the values of a group of individuals and the general mood of privileged corruption. But if it is not overtly revolutionary, we might believe that it criticizes the fate of women in a male-dominated society, were it not for the fact that Laclos proves, on closer inspection, to have been rather more anti-feminist than he at first seems. If we cannot agree on the precise object of his social strictures, perhaps we can say that he defends a coherent set of values against the cerebral excesses of the Enlightenment. But are these values metaphysical, philosophical, moral, or spiritual? Or is Laclos really no more than an eighteenth-century sceptic, caught in the crossfire between Voltaire and Rousseau? A pre-Romantic, who recommends Sensibility against Reason? A libertine writer raking dutifully through the relative merits of Head and Heart?

It goes without saying that none of the many interpretations which Laclos's admirers have proposed is either right or wrong. *Les Liaisons dangereuses* lays many trails which turn out to be false when they are not liberally strewn with red herrings. But the fact that so many possible routes are worth pursuing is a fair measure of its greatness as a work of art. As we read, our sympathies fluctuate between admiration for the style and brilliance of Valmont and Merteuil and dismay at their utter contempt for ordinary decency. They tempt us to despise their victims until we reach the point where the game turns dangerous and deadly. The ironies are rich and we are given marvellously sustained high comedy which runs from glorious farce to the blackest humour. But we always have a disturbing sense that Laclos is being ironic at our expense too, that we are included in his line of fire, that our own values are targeted. The safest starting-point is to assume that the author of this sardonic book was the earnest, upright, and uxorious eighteenth-century man revealed by his letters. But it is not necessarily the most rewarding approach to a book which burns, as Baudelaire said, like ice.

NOTE ON FRENCH TEXTS

The translator's reference text was the invaluable Pléiade edition (Paris, 1979) of Laclos's complete works, edited with exhaustive expertise by Professor Laurent Versini to whose outstanding scholarship every student of *Les Liaisons dangereuses* owes a debt impossible to pay but here gratefully acknowledged. The other main text used was that of the Classiques Garnier edition (Paris, 1961) edited with a long introduction, including detailed examination of the individual voices of the correspondents. Other texts consulted were: the two-volume edition (Paris, 1981) edited for Lettres françaises by René Pomeau, who also introduced the Garnier-Flammarion edition (Paris, 1964); the Livre de Poche edition (Paris, 1987) with a preface, commentary, and notes by Béatrice Didier; and the older but still interesting Textes français edition (Paris, 1943) for the Société des Belles Lettres edited with an introduction by Édouard Maynial. However, in any case of a doubtful reading, Versini prevailed.

SELECT BIBLIOGRAPHY

There is a vast amount of Laclos criticism in French. The following list is minimalist.

Pomeau, R., *Laclos* (Paris, 1975).
Seylaz, J.-L., *'Les Liaisons dangereuses' et la création romanesque chez Laclos* (Paris and Geneva, 1958).
Todorov, T., *Littérature et signification* (Paris, 1967).
Versini, L., *Laclos et la tradition* (Paris, 1968).
——— *Le Roman épistolaire* (Paris, 1979).

There are two excellent French biographies of Laclos:

Dard, E., *Le General de Laclos, auteur des 'Liaisons dangereuses', 1741–1803* (Paris, 1908, new edns., 1920, 1936).
Poisson, G., *Choderlos de Laclos ou l'obstination* (Paris, 1985).

The following list is a select bibliography of Laclos criticism in English:

Alstad, D., *'Les Liaisons dangereuses*: Hustlers and Hypocrites', *Yale French Studies*, 40 (1968).
Brooks, P., *The Novel of Worldliness* (Princeton, 1969).
Byrne, P., *The Valmont/Merteuil Relationship: Coming to Terms with the Ambiguities of Laclos's Text*, Studies on Voltaire and the Eighteenth Century 266 (Oxford, 1989).
Coward, D. A., 'Laclos and the "Dénouement" of *Les Liaisons dangereuses*', *Eighteenth-Century Studies* (1972).
Crocker, L., *An Age of Crisis* (Baltimore, Md., 1959).
Cruickshank, J. (ed.), *French Literature and its Background*, iii, *The Eighteenth Century* (Oxford, 1968), esp. chs. 4, 9, 10, 12.
Davies, S., *Laclos, Les Liaisons dangereuses* (London, 1987).
Free, L. R. (ed.), *Laclos, Critical Approaches*, Studia Humanitas (Madrid, 1978).
Greshoff, C. J., *Seven Studies of the French Novel* (Cape Town, 1974).
Grimsley, R., *From Montesquieu to Laclos: Studies on the French Enlightenment* (Geneva, 1974).
Hill, E. B., 'Man and Mask: The Art of the Actor in *Les Liaisons dangereuses*', *Romanic Review*, 1972.
Hughes, P., and Williams, D. (eds.), *The Varied Pattern: Studies in the Eighteenth Century* (Toronto, 1971).

Mason, H., *French Writers and their Society (1715–1800)* (London, 1982).

Miller, N. K., 'The Exquisite Cadavers: Women in Eighteenth-Century Fiction', *Diacritics*, 5 (1975).

—— 'Female Sexuality and Narrative Structure in *La Nouvelle Héloïse* and *Les Liaisons dangereuses*', *Signs*, 1 (1976).

—— *The Heroine's Text: Readings in the French and English Novel, 1727–1782* (New York, 1980).

Minogue, V., '*Les Liaisons dangereuses*: A Practical Lesson in the Art of Seduction', *Modern Language Review*, 67 (1972).

Munro, J., *Studies in Subconscious Motivation in Laclos and Marivaux*, Studies on Voltaire and the Eighteenth Century 89 (Banbury, 1972).

Mylne, V., *The Eighteenth-Century French Novel: Techniques of Illusion* (rev. edn., Cambridge, 1981).

Perkins, J. A., *Irony and Candour in Certain Libertine Novels*, Studies on Voltaire and the Eighteenth Century 56 (Banbury, 1968).

Picard, R., *Two Centuries of French Literature (1600–1800)*, trans. J. Cairncross (London, 1969).

Rosbottom, R. C., *Choderlos de Laclos*, Twayne's World Author Series (Boston, Mass., 1978).

Showalter, E., jun., *The Evolution of the French Novel 1641–1782* (Princeton, NJ, 1972).

Thelander, D. R., *Laclos and the Epistolary Novel* (Geneva, 1963).

Thody, P. M. W., *Les Liaisons dangereuses* (2nd edn., London, 1975).

Turnell, M., *The Novel in France* (New York, 1950).

Wagner, G., 'Madame de Merteuil: Women as a Sexual Object', in his *Five for Freedom: A Study of Feminism in Fiction* (London, 1972).

Wohlfarth, I., *The Irony of Criticism and the Criticism of Irony: A Study of Laclos Criticism*, Studies on Voltaire and the Eighteenth Century 120 (Banbury, 1974).

For further bibliographical guidance consult:

Coward, D. A., *Laclos Studies 1968–1982*, Studies on Voltaire and the Eighteenth Century 219 (Oxford, 1983).

Michael, C. V., *Choderlos de Laclos: The Man, his Works and his Critics. An Annotated Bibliography* (New York and London, 1982).

A CHRONOLOGY OF
CHODERLOS DE LACLOS

1741	18 October: Pierre-Ambroise-François Choderlos de Laclos born in Amiens, the capital of Picardy, where his father was a senior official; the family had had the status of nobility without a title since 1725.
1759	Became officer cadet in the artillery school of La Fère, in north-east France.
1762	Posted at his own request to the Colonial Brigade forming at La Rochelle, on Atlantic coast.
1763	End of Seven Years War ruins France's colonial aspirations in India and Canada as well as Laclos's hopes for foreign travel. Posted to Toul in eastern France.
1765	Posted to Strasbourg; starts writing verse (see Appendix 3 and note); at this time probably becomes a lifelong Freemason.
1769	Posted to Grenoble in south-east France, a provincial capital and important judiciary and legal administrative centre; it had the reputation of possessing an elegant and cultivated upper-class society.
1771	Received acting rank of captain.
1775	Posted to Besançon, near the Swiss frontier.
1776	Mentioned on the roll of the Military Masonic Lodge of his regiment Toul-Artillery.
1777	Made full captain. Seconded to set up an artillery school at Valence on the Rhône, where Napoleon was one of the first pupils. Comic opera *Ernestine*, with libretto by Laclos, adapted from a novel by Mme Riccoboni received a single performance.
1778	Posted back to Besançon. Starts work on *Liaisons*.
1779	Seconded for fortification work on the Île d'Aix (near La Rochelle) under the Marquis de Montalembert. Work on *Liaisons* interrupted in May until June of following year.
1780–2	Various leaves in Paris to continue work on *Liaisons*.
1782	Early April: *Liaisons* published in edition of 2,000; receives 1,600 *livres* (see note to p. 3); second edition appeared almost immediately. Scandal aroused by the novel leads to the order to return to unit at Brest, on Atlantic coast of Brittany; but

quickly allowed to return to La Rochelle to continue fortification work on Aix. Starts affair with Marie-Soulange Duperré (b. 1759), daughter of a former senior official of petty nobility who had died in 1775.

1783 Begins but fails to complete his first essay on women's education, followed shortly afterwards by a second essay, also uncompleted, on the same subject.

1784 Review in the *Mercure de France* of a French translation of *Cecilia*, an epistolary novel by Fanny Burney. Birth of Étienne-Fargeau, his son by Marie-Soulange.

1785 Elected to the Academy of La Rochelle.

1786 Publishes a letter addressed to the French Academy questioning the competence of Maréchal de Vauban (a sacred cow of the military Establishment) as a builder of fortifications. In disgrace, yet again ordered to return to unit in Metz, then La Fère. 3 May: marries Marie-Soulange.

1787 Made Knight of the Order of Saint-Louis, a nominal entitlement based on seniority.

1788 Dissatisfaction with his treatment by the army authorities grows when he fails to obtain military attaché's post at French embassy in Turkey. Applies for indefinite leave from the army and moves to Paris, joining the staff of the Duke of Orléans, cousin of Louis XVI. The Duke's residence was becoming the centre of political intrigue and revolutionary agitation, in which Laclos became heavily involved. Frequents one or two Parisian *salons*.

1789 Frequents various revolutionary clubs but is forced to leave hastily for London, with the Duke, under suspicion of being involved in organizing riots against the king in Versailles; Orléans, plotting to supplant his cousin and become Regent, adopts the title of Philippe-Égalité.

1790 On return to Paris in July joins the Jacobin Club, at that time a moderate club; its original title was Society of Friends of the Constitution. As secretary to the Jacobins, drops his aristocratic title to become Citizen Choderlos. Resigns his commission. Proposes Philippe-Égalité as Regent but shortly afterwards, as the Jacobins become increasingly violent anti-monarchists, he resigns as secretary and ceases regular attendance.

1792 Despatched by War Minister to French army HQ in Châlons-sur-Marne to help organize the army against invading Austro-

Prussian forces but leaves before the battle of Valmy which causes them to withdraw. Rejoins the army as Brigadier-General in the infantry, appointed Chief of General Staff of the army in the Pyrenees, but immediately recalled; appointed Governor-General of the French settlement near the Cape of Good Hope; this appointment too is cancelled almost immediately.

1793   Arrested with other supporters of Philippe-Égalité; imprisoned, released, rearrested, again released. For some weeks conducts experiments with his brilliant invention of the hollow artillery shell to replace the solid cannon-ball. 5 November: rearrested and imprisoned. 7 November: Philippe-Égalité executed. Expecting the same fate, Laclos sends a lock of his hair to his wife as a memento and consoles himself by reading Seneca.

1794   5 April: Laclos's protector Danton executed. 1 December: Laclos released; lives in Paris.

1795   Appointed Secretary-General of Mortgages, a post held till 18 Brumaire (9 November) 1799, when Napoleon seizes power as First Consul.

1799   Applies to be recommissioned as Brigadier-General in the artillery.

1800   Application approved; posted to Rhine Army as second-in-command of the artillery reserve; present but not actively involved at battles of Biberach and Memmingen. Moved to second-in-command of Royal Army Service Corps (Mines) at Grenoble, and ordered to Italy. 15 December: placed in command of the reserve artillery of the French army in Italy.

1801   Peace signed between French and Austrian forces in Italy; again frustrated, Laclos leaves Italy and returns to Paris.

1802   Appointed Inspector-General of Artillery. Posted as Artillery Commander in Saint-Domingue (Haïti); posting rescinded two days later.

1803   Appointed Artillery Commander of the French Army of Observation in the States of Naples, an appropriate, relatively important, command at last. 14 July: arrives in Taranto, southern Italy. 5 September: dies from the effects of dysentery and malaria.

LES LIAISONS
DANGEREUSES

PUBLISHER'S FOREWORD

We feel in duty bound to warn our readers that, despite the title and the editor's comments in his preface, we cannot guarantee the authenticity of these letters. We even have strong reasons to suspect that this is a work of pure fiction.

Furthermore, it seems to us that although the author claims to be trying to achieve credibility, he has himself crassly vitiated his own claim by his choice of the period in which these events are set. A number of his characters are so immoral that it is impossible to imagine them living in this century, this philosophical century in which, as we all know, universal enlightenment has made all men so honourable and all women so modest and reserved.

In our view therefore, if the adventures here related have any basis in truth, they can only have occurred at other times and in other places. We strongly condemn the author, no doubt misled by the hope of making his work more interesting by situating it closer to our times, for having had the audacity to portray people with morals so foreign to our own in modern dress and with our social customs.

In order at least to protect, as far as lies within our power, any over-gullible reader from being hoodwinked in this way, we support our contention with this argument, put forward with every confidence since it seems to us decisive and indisputable: although it is certain that identical causes would produce identical effects, we never see, in this day and age, any girl with a private income of sixty thousand francs* a year taking the veil nor the young and pretty wife of a presiding judge dying of grief.

EDITOR'S PREFACE

Although our readers may perhaps find this work, or rather this collection of letters, still somewhat lengthy, it nevertheless represents a very small proportion of those included in the total correspondence from which they have been extracted. When I was commissioned to collate these letters by the persons into whose possession they had come and who, as I was aware, were intending to have them published, my only request in return for my effort was to be allowed to prune anything which I considered superfluous.

In fact, I have retained only those letters which seemed to me necessary for the understanding of the events or the development of the characters. Apart from this straightforward task, I classified the letters which I had selected almost without exception in chronological order,* and finally provided a few brief notes, chiefly with the aim of indicating the source of a few quotations or justifying some of the excisions I had ventured to make. This was all that I was required to do and I played no further part in the production of this work.*

I had suggested making greater changes, very largely relating to correctness of style or turn of phrase which, as can be seen, leave much to be desired. I should also have welcomed the opportunity to be allowed to abridge some excessively long letters, a number of which deal, almost without any transition, with separate, quite unconnected matters.* This suggestion, which was rejected, while doubtless not adequate to make this a work of real value, might at least have removed some of its imperfections.

It was pointed out to me that it was the letters themselves which it was intended to make public and not just a work based on them and that it would be unlikely, as well as misleading, for all the eight or ten people involved in the correspondence to write equally correctly. When I replied that this was anything but the case and that not one of the writers had failed to make crass mistakes which readers would be bound to criticize, I was told that any sensible person would naturally expect to find errors in a collection of letters written by ordinary people, since in all similar collections by different, highly regarded authors, not even excluding some Academicians,* none would be entirely exempt from such criticism. These reasons did not succeed in convincing me; I considered and still consider them easier to put forward than to accept; but since the matter was beyond my control, I did not persist, merely reserving my right to protest and make it quite clear that this was not my view, as I now wish to place on record once again.

It is perhaps no business of mine to discuss the possible value of this work since my opinion neither can nor will influence anyone else's. However, those who like to know more or less what they can expect before they begin may read on; the others will do better to start reading the text straight away; they do not need any further explanation.

First of all, may I say that, while admitting that I advised publication of this correspondence, I am very far from expecting it to be a success. This is an honest opinion which must not be seen as false modesty on the part of an author, for I must state equally frankly that, had this work not seemed to me worth publishing, I should not have become involved in it. Let us try to resolve this apparent contradiction.

The value of a work lies either in its usefulness or in the pleasure it gives or even in a combination of the two, if it is capable of providing them. But its success, which is not necessarily a proof of its value, depends more often on the choice of subject than on its realization, on its general content rather than on the way it is handled. Now since this collection comprises, as its title* indicates, letters from a whole social group, it represents a diversity of interests which weakens the interest of the reader. Moreover, since almost all the feelings expressed in it are contrived or disguised, they cannot even arouse anything more than curiosity which is always inferior to true feeling and which above all leads us to be less indulgent and makes us all the more aware of its particular faults inasmuch as the latter constantly undermine our only motive for wishing to read it.

These weaknesses can be redeemed to some degree by a quality inherent in the nature of the work, its diversity of styles,* a quality which an author finds it difficult to achieve but which here occurs naturally and which at least rescues it from boring uniformity. More than a few readers may also find some interest in the not inconsiderable number of observations,* novel or unfamiliar, scattered throughout these letters. To my mind, even looking at these letters in the most favourable light, this is also the sole enjoyment which a reader can hope to find.

However, the work's usefulness, which may perhaps be even more strongly challenged, appears to me easier to establish. It seems to me, at least, that morality is served by unmasking the methods used by those with bad morals to corrupt those whose moral standards are high, and I think that these letters can contribute effectively to this aim. They also contain examples and proofs of two important truths which, seeing how poorly they are applied, we must suspect of being little known: first, that any woman who agrees to consort with an immoral man will end up as his victim; secondly, that any mother who allows anybody but herself into her daughter's confidence is, to say the least, unwise. Young people of both sexes could also learn that any friendship which persons of loose morals seem so ready to offer them is never anything but a fatal trap, as disastrous for their happiness as for their moral welfare. However, the fact that goodness is separated from its abuse by such a narrow margin creates grave dangers and, far from recommending young people to read this book, I consider it most important to keep all such works away from them. The age at which such works may stop being dangerous and become useful seems to me to have been very well defined, as far as her sex is concerned, by one good mother, not only intelligent but sensible, who said to me: 'Having read this correspondence in manuscript, I should think that I was doing my daughter a real service by giving her this book on her wedding day.' If all mothers with families think the same, I shall be eternally glad to have published it.

But though I maintain this favourable view, I still think that few people are likely to enjoy this collection. Depraved men and women will consider it in their interest to discredit a work which may do them harm and since they are no fools, they may be astute enough to enlist the support of strict moralists alarmed by this fearless portrayal of immorality.

So-called free-thinkers will have no interest whatsoever in a pious woman since they will consider her a namby-pamby, while the pious will be annoyed to see a virtuous woman's downfall, and protest that religion is depicted as lacking in strength.

For their part, fastidious readers will find the over-simple and incorrect style of some letters not to their taste while the ordinary reader, persuaded that anything printed is the result of a certain effort, will imagine that in some of the other letters they can detect the laboured style of an author who is visible behind the character he is portraying.

Finally, it will perhaps be fairly widely remarked that there is a time and a place for everything and if an over-polished literary style would indeed normally deprive private letters of some of their charm, slovenly writing leads to outright errors which are quite unacceptable in print.

I frankly admit that these strictures may all be justified; I also believe that it would be possible for me to reply to them, even within the limited space of a preface. But people are bound to think that if it seems necessary to provide an answer to everything, the work must be inadequate to provide any answer itself; and that if I had held that view, I would have dispensed with this preface and the book as well.

LES LIAISONS DANGEREUSES

PART I

I

Cécile Volanges to Sophie Carnay at the Ursuline Convent* of ——
Paris, 3 August 17—

Well, Sophie dear, as you see, I'm keeping my word and not spending all my time on bonnets and bows, I'll always have some to spare for you! All the same, I've seen more frills and furbelows in this one single day than I ever saw during the whole four years we spent in the convent. I think that stuck-up Tanville girl* will be more peeved on my first visit to you—and I'm certainly going to ask for her!—than she thought she made us when she used to call on us *in fiocchi*.* Mummy's consulting me about everything, she's not treating me half as much like a schoolgirl as she used to. I've got my own maid, a room and a study for my own use, and I'm sitting writing this letter at a very pretty secretaire—they've given me the key and I can lock away anything I like. Mummy's told me I can come and see her every morning while she's getting up and that I don't need to put my hair up properly till dinner-time* because we'll always be on our own and then she'll tell me every day when I'm to come and see her in the afternoon. The rest of the time I'm free to do whatever I like and I've got my harp, my sketch-pad, and my books, just like at the convent, only Mother Perpétue won't be there to tell me off and it's up to me whether I want to spend all day doing nothing; but as I haven't got you to have a chat and giggle with, Sophie dear, I'd as soon be doing something.

It's not five o'clock yet and I'm due to see Mummy at seven so there's lots of time if there's anything to tell you! But nobody's said anything yet; and apart from all the preparations I can see being made and all the dressmakers who keep coming just

A room of her own [handwritten marginal note]

for me, I wouldn't guess they're thinking of finding a husband for me and would think that it's just another bit of dear old Joséphine's* nonsense. However, Mummy's told me so often <u>that a girl ought to stay in the convent till she gets married that</u> <u>as they've taken me away Joséphine must be right</u>.

A carriage has just stopped in front of the gate and Mummy's sent a message telling me to come and see her straight away. Suppose it's *Him*! I'm not dressed and my hand's shaking and my heart's beating so fast! I've asked my maid if she knows who it is with my mother. 'It's really Monsieur C———,' she said and she was laughing! Oh, I think it *is* him! I'll certainly let you know what's happened as soon as I come back. Anyway, you know his name now. Goodbye, I'll be right back.

Here I am again and you're really going to laugh at me! It's ever so embarrassing but you'd have been taken in just as much as me. When I went up to Mummy's there was a gentleman dressed in black standing beside her. I did my best curtsey and just stood there frozen to the ground. You can imagine how closely I examined him! 'What a charming young daughter you have, Madame,' he said and gave me a bow, 'and I appreciate your kindness even more.' These words were so plain that I started trembling so much that I couldn't stay on my feet so I made for an armchair and sat down all red and flustered. And then there was this man on his knees in front of me! Poor me! I lost my head completely, as Mummy said, I was scared out of my wits and I leapt up with a scream, you know, just like that time there was that thunderclap. Mummy burst out laughing and said to me: 'What on earth's the matter? Sit down and let the gentleman have your foot.' And in fact, Sophie dear, this *gentleman* was actually the bootmaker! I can't tell you how ashamed I felt . . . Fortunately, only Mummy was there. When I'm married, I don't think I'll use that bootmaker any more.

Well, you must admit we girls really are *very* clever, aren't we? Goodbye, it's nearly six o'clock and my maid's just told me it's time to get dressed. Goodbye, Sophie darling, I still love you just like I did in the convent!

PS I don't know who I can find to get this letter to you so I'll wait till Joséphine comes.

2

The Marquise de Merteuil to the Vicomte de Valmont
at the Château de ———
Paris, 4 August 17—

My dear Vicomte, you must come back to Paris, you really must! What are you up to? What on earth can you be doing down there with an old aunt when you're due to inherit everything she's got anyway? You must pack your bags at once, I have need of you. I've dreamed up a really wonderful scheme and I'm ready and willing to let you put it into practice. These few words should be quite enough for you to feel so honoured that my choice has fallen on you that you'll rush to fall at my feet, panting to receive my instructions; but you're still taking advantage of my kindness of heart even now you've stopped taking any advantage of my kindness in other directions, leaving me with no alternatives but implacable hatred or sublime forgiveness. Luckily for you, my kind heart has prevailed and I'm willing to tell you my plan, but you must give me your word, as a perfect gentle knight, not to embark on any other adventures until you have brought this one to successful completion. It's a task worthy of a hero: you'll be serving the cause of Love and of Revenge; and it will indeed be one *rakery** more to put in your memoirs*—I'm determined they'll be published one day and I undertake to write them myself. But let's leave that for the moment and come back to what I have in mind.

Madame de Volanges has unearthed a husband for her daughter; it's still a secret but she told me about it yesterday. And who do you think is the lucky man? None other than the Comte de Gercourt. Who'd ever have guessed I'd be de Gercourt's cousin? I'm positively livid . . . And you still can't see why? What an obtuse fellow you are! Have you forgiven him for that affair he had with the wife of that *intendant*?* And haven't I even stronger reasons for complaint, you monster!* All right, all right, I'll calm down and comfort my soul with the hope of getting my revenge . . .

Like me, you've been bored times without number by Gercourt's inordinate concern regarding his future wife and his fatuous presumption that he alone will be spared the common fate; you know his ridiculous prejudice in favour of convent-bred girls and his even more ridiculous conviction that blondes are modest and reserved. In fact, I bet that in spite of the Volanges girl's private income of sixty thousand a year,* he'd never have agreed to marry her if she'd been a brunette and not been educated in a convent. So let's give him proof that he's cheating himself. He'll be cheated on sooner or later, I've no worries on that score, but it would be such fun if he was cheated from the start. How wonderful it would be to hear him bragging the morning after! And brag he certainly will . . . What's more, once you've set that little girl off on the right track, it'll be bad luck indeed if that fellow Gercourt doesn't become the talk of Paris, like anyone else.

Incidentally, the heroine of this new romance merits your close attention; she's very pretty; only fifteen years old, the rosebud.* True, she's awkward—incredibly so—and completely unsophisticated, but you men aren't put off by that. In addition, there's a sort of soulful look that really is most promising. And what's more, she comes with my recommendation. All you're asked to do is to thank me and do as you're told.

You'll be getting this letter tomorrow morning and I require you to present yourself here at seven o'clock sharp tomorrow evening.* I'll not be in for anyone else till eight, not even to my current knight: he's not quite bright enough for such important business. I'll release you at eight and you are to come back at ten for supper with the beautiful object, because mother and daughter are to be there then. Goodbye. It's after twelve noon and very shortly you'll be far from my thoughts . . .

3

Cécile Volanges to Sophie Carnay at the Ursuline Convent of ——
Paris, 4 August 17—

I'm still in the dark, dear Sophie. Yesterday Mummy had a lot of people to supper. I realize it was worth my while to take a good look, especially at the men, but I was dreadfully bored. The men and the women were all watching me a lot and then whispering to each other and I could see they were talking about me, which made me blush. I just couldn't stop myself though I wished I could have because I'd noticed that when other women were looked at they didn't blush. Or perhaps it's all that rouge they wear that prevents you seeing if they go red when they're embarrassed, because it must be jolly difficult not to go red if a man's staring at you.

The thing which made me feel most uncomfortable was not knowing what people were thinking about me. Though I do believe I heard the word *pretty** a couple of times and I definitely did hear the word *awkward* and I know that's true because the woman saying it is related to Mummy and a friend of hers. She even seems to have taken to me straight away. She was the only one to speak to me at all the whole evening. We're going to supper at her's tomorrow.

I also heard after supper a man who I'm sure was talking about me and saying to another man: 'We'll have to let it ripen up a bit and see what happens this winter.' Perhaps he's the one who's going to marry me but in that case it wouldn't be for another four months! I'd love to know what's actually going on.

Here's Joséphine and she says she's in a hurry but I'd still like to tell you one of the *awkward* things I did. Oh, I think that lady was quite right!

After supper, people started playing cards. I sat near Mummy and I don't know how it happened but I dropped off to sleep almost at once. I was woken up by a loud burst of laughter. I don't know if they were laughing at me but I think they were. Mummy gave me permission to go off to bed which I was very glad to do, it was after eleven o'clock! Goodbye, Sophie dear, please don't stop being fond of your Cécile. I promise you society isn't half as much fun as we used to think it would be.

4

The Vicomte de Valmont to the Marquise de Merteuil in Paris

From the Château de ——, 5 August 17—

Your commands exude charm, dear lady, and the way you issue them is even more charming; you'd make a really lovable dictator. As you know, this isn't the first time I've felt sorry I'm no longer your humble and obedient slave, and however much a monster I may be—your own words—I always look back with pleasure on the time when you bestowed less unfriendly names on me. Indeed, I often have the desire to earn them again, thus finally providing, with you, an example of constancy* in love for all the world to see. But there are more important matters to engage our attention: we are fated to be conquerors and we must follow our destiny;* perhaps at the end of our career we shall meet again, because, with all due respect, most lovely Marquise, you are following in my tracks at a pace at least equal to mine, and ever since, for the greater good of mankind, we set out on our separate paths to preach the good word each in our own way, it seems to me that as a missionary of love, you have made more converts than I. I know your proselytizing eagerness, your burning zeal, and if that particular God judged us according to our works, you would one day have risen to be the patron saint of some great city whereas your humble friend would be at best a local village saint. You find my choice of language surprising, don't you? But it's the only language I've been using and hearing for the last week and it's because I'm anxious to hone my skills that I find myself compelled to disobey you.

Don't be cross and listen to me. As you are the faithful trustee of all my heart's secrets, let me unveil to you the most ambitious scheme I have ever devised. What were you proposing for me to undertake? To seduce a girl who's seen nothing of life, who's completely ignorant and who, to put it bluntly, would be handed to me on a plate; who'll lose her head at the first compliment she receives and be impelled more by curiosity than by love. There are a dozen men as competent to do that job as I and my present campaign is very different; if I can pull it off, it'll be not only a triumph but a pleasure. Even Cupid, now busily preparing the crown to honour my victory, is hesitating between myrtle and laurels* or perhaps a combination of the two. You yourself, lovely lady, will be stunned into respectful reverence and proclaim enthusiastically: 'Here is a man after my own heart!'

You know Madame de Tourvel, the judge's wife; you know her religious fervour, her conjugal love, her strict principles.

She's my objective, an adversary worthy of my steel; I'm hoping
for a bull's-eye.

> *Et si de l'obtenir je n'emporte pas le prix,*
> *J'aurai du moins l'honneur de l'avoir entrepris.*

We're allowed to quote bad poetry when it comes from a great
poet.*

I must inform you that the judge has gone off to conduct an
important case in Burgundy (I have in mind to make him lose a
more important one). His better half is inconsolable; she's having
to spend the whole of her heart-breaking grass-widowhood here.
Mass every day; a few charitable calls on the local poor; prayers
night and morning; lonely walks; pious chats with my old aunt
and an occasional dreary hand of whist; these were to be her only
distractions. I'm arranging some rather more active ones for
her . . . My guardian angel has guided my steps here to consummate her happiness and my own! And to think I was quite
disconsolate at having to sacrifice twenty-four hours of my life to
fulfil a social duty! How idiotic! What a penance it would be for
me to have to go back to Paris at the moment! Fortunately you
need four people to play whist and as there's only the local parish
priest, my indestructible aunt made an urgent appeal to me to
sacrifice a few days for her sake. As you may guess, I didn't say
no. You can't imagine how genial she's been towards me ever
since and especially how edifying she finds my regular attendance at her Masses and prayers. She's got no idea of the divinity
I'm worshipping . . .

So for the last four days I've been in the grip of a total passion.
You know how sharply my desire flares up, how I take every
obstacle in my stride; what you don't know is how strongly it's
fuelled by solitude. I've only one idea in my head; I think of it by
day, I dream of it by night. I've got to have that woman or else I'll
make a fool of myself by falling in love with her. Who knows to
what lengths frustrated lust can't lead? Ah, the bliss of gratified
desire! May it be granted me for the sake of my happiness and
above all of my peace of mind. How fortunate we are that women
are so bad at defending themselves, otherwise we'd become their
abject slaves! And so I thank God for women of easy virtue and
this naturally leads me to fling myself at your feet and humbly

crave forgiveness, thus bringing this excessively long letter to an
end. Goodbye, very lovely lady. No hard feelings?*

5

The Marquise de Merteuil to the Vicomte de Valmont
Paris, 7 August 17—

Do you know, Valmont, your letter was so remarkably impertinent that I very, very, nearly lost my temper? But it showed that
you're stark raving mad and that alone spared you from my
wrath. So, with my usual generosity, sensitivity, and friendliness,
I'll overlook your offence and concern myself solely with your
parlous situation; and though bringing people to their senses is
frightfully boring, your present plight is so parlous that I can't let
you down.

You, have that judge's wife? You, Vicomte de Valmont in
person? It's absurd, a typical fancy of your perverse nature,
wanting only the impossible. What sort of woman is it we're
talking about? Well, quite decent features, that I'll grant you,
even if lacking expression. A reasonable figure, though gawky;
and always hilariously dowdy, draped in layers of fichus and
corseted up to the chin! Here's a bit of friendly advice: a couple
of women like that would be more than enough to cost you your
whole reputation. Have you forgotten the day she was taking the
collection at Saint-Roch's,* when you told me how grateful you
were to me for providing you with such a sight? I can still see her,
giving her hand to that long-haired beanpole of a man, stumbling
every time she took a step, continually smothering people under
her enormous hoop-skirt and blushing scarlet each time she
genuflected. Who'd have guessed then that you'd be casting
libidinous eyes on that woman? Come, come, Vicomte, you
ought to be covered in blushes yourself. You must come to your
senses and I then promise never to breathe a word.

And just think of all the various vexations involved! And
who are you competing against? A husband! Don't you feel
humiliated at the very thought? And if you were to fail, what a
disgrace! Even if you succeed, it'll be nothing to boast about!

What's more, don't expect to get any pleasure out of it: how can you expect a prude* to provide pleasure? I mean the ones who really are prudes; even their pleasure will be carefully doled out, they'll never be able to offer you anything but strictly limited rapture. Letting yourself go completely, without restraint, so that pleasure is refined into ecstasy because it's pushed to excess, delights such as these are a closed book for prudes. Let me make a prophecy: even if everything turns out as you hope, your judge's wife will imagine she's doing her best for you by treating you like her husband; and in the most loving duet between married couples, they always remain two separate persons. In this case, it's even worse: your prude is a pious prude and with an old womanish sort of simple piety that condemns her never to grow up. That sort of obstacle can be overcome but don't delude yourself that you'll ever destroy it; when you've won the battle against love of God you'll still not have won it against Satan; when you feel your mistress's heart pounding as you hold her in your arms, it'll be for fear, not for love. Perhaps if you'd got to know her earlier on you might have made something of her; but this woman is twenty-two years old and has been married for nearly two years. Take it from me, Vicomte, that sort of *stick-in-the-mud* must be abandoned to her fate; she's never going to be anything but small fry.

And yet it's for this splendid object that you are refusing to obey me, burying yourself in your aunt's graveyard, and throwing away the chance of an absolutely delightful adventure and one likely to do you credit. Why should Gercourt be fated always to get the better of you? Look, speaking quite dispassionately, at the moment I'm tempted to think you're falling far short of your reputation, and more specifically, I'm tempted not to continue letting you enjoy my trust: I could never bring myself to telling Madame de Tourvel's lover all my secrets.

Let me inform you meanwhile that the little Volanges girl has already turned one man's head: young Danceny's mad about her. He's been singing duets with her and indeed she sings better than any convent girl ought. They must spend a lot of time rehearsing their songs together and I suspect she'd not be averse to singing to his tune. But young Danceny's still wet behind the ears; as a lover, he's a dead loss, he'll never see anything through to the end. For her part, the little miss is rather coy and in any event it'd be far less fun for her than it would be with you, if you were willing. So I'm in a foul mood which I shall certainly take out on my knight when he arrives. I'd advise him to be very meek because at the moment I wouldn't think twice about sending him packing. I'm sure that if I were sensible enough to leave him now he'd be in despair, and there's nothing quite so funny as a lover in despair. He'd call me false and faithless and I've always had a weakness for those two words; next to cruel,* they're the nicest words for a woman to hear, and not so hard to earn. I must definitely start thinking about getting rid of him. Just look at the things you're making me do! I hope it gives you bad dreams. Goodbye. Get your Madame de Tourvel to put me in her prayers.

6

The Vicomte de Valmont to the Marquise de Merteuil
From the Château de ——, 9 August 17—

Sexist remark

So you're no exception to the rule: once they've established their authority, all women abuse it! Even you, the one I've so often called the most tolerant of all my women friends, have changed your tune and had the impertinence to attack me through the object of my affection! How dare you describe Madame de Tourvel like that! Show me the man who wouldn't have paid for such impertinence with his life! And any other woman but you would have been at least in serious trouble! I do beg you, never submit my patience to that sort of trial again; I couldn't guarantee to take it lying down. In deference to our friendship, if you do feel like making beastly remarks about that woman, at least wait until I've actually had her. Didn't you know that it's not until after enjoying its delights that Love can stop being blind?

But why am I talking like this? As if Madame de Tourvel needed to blindfold her admirers! She's just adorable as she is! You called her dowdy and it's quite true her beauty is best unadorned and the more you can see of her, the lovelier she is. In her négligé she looks utterly ravishing. Thanks to the sultry weather we've been having, I've been privileged to see her lithe round figure in a simple linen gown with only a wisp of muslin over the entrancing curves of her breasts, which I've already managed to explore out of the corner of my eye.* Her face lacks expression? And why should it have expression when her heart has nothing to express? No, of course she hasn't got that come-hither look of some women, a look which may sometimes flatter but only to deceive. She doesn't prettify a vapid remark with a bogus smile and she laughs only when she's really amused, even though she has the loveliest teeth you ever saw. But you should see her when she's feeling playful, a picture of innocent, honest fun; or see the light of pure joy and genuine sympathy in her eyes when she's anxious to help some poor unfortunate person! You should see the touchingly embarrassed look of real modesty on her heavenly face, particularly at the slightest hint of praise or flattery! So you think, just because she's pious and prudish, that she's bound to be cold and unresponsive? Well, I think quite differently. How amazingly sensitive must she be to extend her love even to her husband and continue to love someone who's never here? Would you like more convincing proof? I've managed to gather some.

I arranged a walk that forced us to cross a ditch—although she's very nimble, she's even more timorous: as you can imagine, a prude is scared of taking the plunge!* This modest young woman had to place herself in my hands; I've held her in my arms! Getting ready and then carrying my old aunt across had sent this playful pious young woman into fits of laughter but as soon as I'd picked her up, as clumsily as I could, our arms somehow became entangled ... I pressed her breasts hard against my chest and for a few seconds I could feel the throbbing of her heart. She blushed delightfully and her bashful expression told me well enough that her heart was *pounding with love and not with fear*.* However, my aunt made the same mistake as you and began saying: The poor girl was afraid; but the *poor girl's* disarming honesty didn't allow her to lie and she said innocently: O no, it's not that but ... This told me everything I wanted to know. From now on, my misgivings have given way to quiet anticipation: I'm going to get this woman. I shall take her away from her husband who is desecrating her and I shall even snatch her from the bosom of the God she worships. What a delightful thought: to be the cause and the cure of her remorse! Far be it from me to try to break down the prejudices which worry her! They'll merely help to increase my happiness and my reputation. I want her to have these high principles—and to sacrifice them for my sake! I want her to be horrified by her sins yet unable to resist sinning; to suffer endless terrors which she can overcome and forget only in my arms; then I'll agree to let her say: 'I adore you!' She'll be the only woman in the world really worthy of uttering those words. I shall truly be the God whom she loves best.

Let's be frank: in our mutual accommodations which are as cold-blooded as they are casual, our so-called happiness can hardly be described as pleasure. Shall I tell you something? I thought my heart had quite dried up. I had the feeling I could enjoy only physical pleasures and was miserable at the prospect of growing prematurely old. Madame de Tourvel has brought back the charming illusions of my youth. With her I'm happy without my senses being involved. The only thing which frightens me is the length of time this affair will require. My earlier swashbuckling exploits are irrelevant; I can't bring myself to use those methods. For me to be really happy, she must give herself and that's no easy matter.

I'm sure you'd admire my circumspection; I still haven't mentioned the word love but we're already talking about trust and common interests. Not wishing to be more dishonest than necessary and above all to cover myself against any gossip which might come to her ears, I have myself told her, more or less self-accusingly, about some of my more notorious affairs. You'd laugh to see how innocently she sermonizes me. 'She wants', she says, 'to convert me'; she still doesn't realize the price she's going to pay for attempting to do that. She has no idea that, in her words, 'by pleading the cause of the unfortunate women whom I've ruined', she's pleading her own cause, in advance. This thought came to me yesterday in the middle of one of her lectures and I couldn't resist the pleasure of interrupting has to tell her that she was speaking like a prophet. How ironic!

Goodbye, dear lady. You will notice that my plight isn't entirely parlous . . .

PS By the way, did this forlorn knight actually do away with himself in despair? You know, you're a far better bad lot than I am and if I were conceited, I'd feel humiliated.

7

Cécile Volanges to Sophie Carnay*
7 August 17—

[handwritten: Ealers Danceny]

I haven't said anything about my marriage because I'm as much in the dark as ever. I'm getting used to not thinking about it now and quite enjoying the sort of life I'm leading. I spend a lot of time practising my singing and my harp and I think I'm enjoying them more now I haven't got a teacher or rather because I've got a better one. Monsieur Danceny, the gentleman I mentioned who I sang with at Madame de Merteuil's, has been kind enough to come every day and spend absolutely hours singing with me. He's such a nice man. He's got a heavenly voice and can compose very pretty tunes and write the words to them as well! What a dreadful pity he's a Knight of Malta! It seems to me that if he got married, his wife would be very happy!* He never seems to be paying compliments yet everything he says seems flattering. He keeps ticking me off all the time, for my music as well as other things, but he seems so interested and cheerful while he's doing it that it's impossible not to feel grateful to him. Even when he's just looking at you he seems to be saying something nice. He's very obliging, too. Yesterday for instance he'd been invited to some grand concert and he preferred to spend the whole evening at Mummy's. That was very nice for me because when he's not there nobody talks to me at all and I get bored, but when he's there we sing together and have a chat. He's always got something to tell me. I think he and Madame de Merteuil are the only two nice people I know. But I must sign off now, Sophie dear, I've promised that by today I shall learn a little aria which has a very tricky accompaniment and I don't want to let him down. I'll go back to my practising till he comes.

8

Madame de Tourvel to Madame de Volanges
From the Château de ——, 9 August 17—

I'm so touched by your confiding in me, dear Madame. No one could be more interested in your daughter's future than I am and I wish her with heart and soul all the happiness which she surely deserves and which I'm sure your wisdom will guarantee. I do not know Monsieur de Gercourt personally but I can only have the highest opinion of him now that you have singled him out to be your son-in-law. I need only express the hope that her marriage is as happy and successful as my own, for which you were also responsible and for which I'm more grateful to you than ever. I hope that your daughter's happiness is the fitting reward for the happiness you have provided for me and that my best of friends becomes the happiest of mothers.

I'm truly sad that I shan't be able to come and offer my heartfelt good wishes to the bride in person and make her acquaintance as soon as I should have liked. Having enjoyed your truly motherly affection, I feel justified in hoping to find true sisterly love and friendship with your daughter. Please ask her, dear Madame, to share with me that feeling until such time as I am in a position to show that I'm worthy of it.

I'm expecting to stay on in the country for as long as my husband is away. I'm spending this time enjoying and benefiting from the company of Madame de Rosemonde, such a highly respected and ever charming lady who shows no signs of her advanced age; she has kept all her memory and all her sprightliness; her body may be eighty-four years old, her mind is still twenty.

Our cloistered existence is being enlivened by her nephew, the Vicomte de Valmont, who has kindly sacrificed a few days of his time to spend them in our company. I knew the Vicomte only by reputation, which gave me no desire to get to know him any better. But I think his reputation does him some injustice. Down here, where he is freed from the whirligig of society, he talks surprisingly sound good sense and admits the error of his ways with an unusual frankness. He talks very openly to me and I preach him very stern sermons. You know him and you will agree that converting him would be a feather in anyone's cap;* but in spite of his promises, I've no illusions—a fortnight in Paris will drive all my preaching out of his head. His stay here will at least have provided a break from his normal activities and my belief is that, with his way of life, the best thing for him to do is to do nothing at all. He knows I'm writing to you and has asked me to send you his kindest and most respectful regards. I send you mine as well, to the safe keeping of your unfailing kindness. With sincerest good wishes, yours, etc.

The true moral nature of
✗ 9 *Valmont is revealed here*

Madame de Volanges to Madame de Tourvel
11 August 17—

My dear young friend, I've never doubted the genuineness of your friendship or of your concern with everything regarding my affairs and this answer to your *reply** is not to elaborate on this point, which I trust can never be in any doubt for either of us. But I do feel that I cannot refrain from raising with you the question of the Vicomte de Valmont.

I must confess that I never expected to read that name in any letter of yours. What indeed can you and he have in common? You don't know the man; where could you have gained some insight into the mind of a rake? You mention his *unusual frankness*; yes indeed, any frankness from Valmont must be very unusual. He's even more deceitful and dangerous than he is pleasant and attractive. From his earliest youth he has never made the slightest move or uttered a single word without having some evil or criminal intent. Dear friend, you know me and you're well aware that, of all the qualities I strive after, tolerance is the one which I consider most precious. So if Valmont was a man dominated by the violence of his passions or, like thousands of others, powerless to resist the temptations of his age, though I would deplore his conduct, I should feel sorry for him and quietly wait for him to reform his ways and win back the respect of decent people. Valmont's not like that: his despicable behaviour is a matter of principle. He calculates precisely how far he can pursue his abominable conduct without compromising himself; and to gratify his cruel and wicked nature without any risk, he's chosen to prey on women. I'm not thinking of those he may have seduced but of who knows how many he has ruined. You live a chaste and sheltered life and such scandalous adventures never reach your ears; yet I could tell you some that would make you shudder with horror; but your eyes are as pure as your soul and would be defiled by such insights. You feel confident that Valmont can never be a danger to you, so that you've no need of any such warning to defend yourself. I'd like to tell you just one thing: of all the women to whom he has paid his attentions, whether successfully or not, not one has failed to regret it. The Marquise de Merteuil is the sole exception; she is the only woman who has managed to resist him and frustrate his evil designs; indeed, her exemplary conduct in this compensated in everyone's eyes for certain regrettable indiscretions of hers which occurred shortly after her husband's death.*

However that may be, dear, dear friend, my age and experience and above all my friendship for you entitle me to draw your attention to the fact that people are beginning to take notice of Valmont's absence and if it becomes known that he may have formed part of a threesome with you and his aunt, your reputation will be in his hands, which is the ultimate misfortune for any woman. I advise you to urge his aunt to cut short her invitation to him and if he persists in wanting to stay, I think you should not hesitate to leave yourself.

But why should he want to stay? What is he doing tucked away in the country anyway? If you got someone to keep an eye on his comings and goings, I feel sure you'd find that he's chosen his aunt's place merely as a convenient cover for carrying out some nefarious scheme in the neighbourhood.* And since there's no remedy for evil, we must do what we can to protect ourselves from it as far as possible.

Goodbye, my dear young friend. My daughter's marriage will now have to be postponed for a while: we were expecting the Comte de Gercourt to be arriving any day but he has now sent word that his regiment has been ordered to Corsica* and as there is still talk of war, he can't possibly be free before winter. This is tiresome but it gives me hope that we shall have the pleasure

of seeing you at the wedding. I was annoyed that it might have
taken place without you. So, goodbye once more from your ever
faithful and ever sincere friend, yours, etc.

PS My kindest regards to Madame de Rosemonde, with all
the affection which I feel, as ever, she richly deserves.

✳ 10

The Marquise de Merteuil to the Vicomte de Valmont
12 August 17—

Are you sulking? Or dead, possibly? Or are you living only for
your judge's wife—much the same thing, by the way? This
woman, who's given you back your *youthful illusions*, will soon be
giving you back its absurd prejudices as well. You're already
timid and submissive; you might just as well be in love. So you're
saying goodbye to your *swashbuckling exploits*? In other words,
you're behaving in a completely unprincipled manner and relying purely on chance or rather, on the whim of the moment.
Have you forgotten that, like medicine, love is nothing but *the art
of giving Nature a helping hand*? As you see, I'm fighting you with
your own weapons but I'm not going to crow over it because I'm
fighting someone who's already bitten the dust. *She must give
herself*, say you. Of course she must and she'll give herself like all
the others, except that it'll not be willingly. But for her ultimately
to give herself, the best way is to start off by having her. Such a
laughable distinction really is an aberration of love! And I use the
word love because you are in love and if I told you otherwise I'd
be misleading you and preventing you from seeing what your
trouble is. So tell me, my faint-hearted swain, do you really think
that all those women you've had were raped? Nevertheless,
however keen we are to give ourselves and however quickly we'd
like it to happen, we still need some pretext. And can you tell
me a more convenient one than seeming to submit to force?
Let me be honest: for me one of the most gratifying things is
a sharp, well-conducted assault in which everything takes place
in the proper order but smartly, so that we're never placed in
the tiresome and awkward predicament of having to overlook
certain technical weaknesses which we ought really to have taken

advantage of; which retains a semblance of violence even when we've given up the fight, and is skilful enough to satisfy our two favourite passions, a glorious resistance followed by a pleasurable defeat. I agree that such a gift, rarer than most people think, has always afforded me gratification, even when it hasn't made me lose my head, so that at times I've given in purely in recognition of a good performance. Rather like the tournaments of olden days when Beauty awarded the prize for skill and valour.

But you're not the man you were, you're behaving as if you don't really want to succeed. Since when have you enjoyed travelling in short stages and on byroads? My dear man, when people are keen to get somewhere, they travel post-haste and on main roads! But let's drop the subject, which is all the more boring because it's depriving me of the pleasure of your company. At least write more often to keep me up to date with your progress. Do you realize that you've been engaged on this absurd amorous enterprise for more than a fortnight and that you're neglecting us all?

And speaking of neglect, you're like those people who regularly ask for news of their friends and never bother about getting an answer. You ended your last letter by enquiring if my knight was dead. I didn't answer your question and you've shown no further interest. Have you forgotten that my lover is your born friend. But don't fret, he's not dead or if he were it would be through an excess of bliss . . . Poor fellow, how tender-hearted he is! Just made for love! So sensitive! I'm quite losing my head! But seriously, being loved by me is making him so blissfully happy that I'm becoming really quite fond of him.

On that very same day when I was looking for an opportunity to drop him, I made him such a happy man! Yet when he was shown in I really was thinking how I could drive him to despair. Then, for some reason, good or bad—just a whim, perhaps?—I thought he'd never looked so handsome, though I still treated him badly. He'd been hoping for a couple of hours with me alone before anyone else called. I said I had to go out. He asked me where. I refused to tell him. He persisted. *Somewhere without you*, I snapped. Luckily for him, this reply petrified him, because if he'd uttered a word, a row would have inevitably ensued and that would have led to the break I'd been planning. When he didn't reply, I looked at him in surprise, with no other idea in mind, I promise you, than to see his reaction. And his charming face had that crestfallen look, tender and heartfelt, which you yourself admit is well-nigh impossible to resist. The same cause produced the same effect; I was hooked again and from that moment onwards my only concern was to avoid giving him any reason not to like me. 'I'm going out on a matter of business,' I said, looking rather less fierce, 'and in fact, it's something that concerns you but you mustn't ask me anything more now. I'll be back for supper, so come here and I'll tell you all about it.' At this he recovered the use of his tongue but I didn't give him a chance to speak. 'I'm in a great rush,' I went on. 'I'll see you this evening but now you must go.' He kissed my hand and left.

To make amends to him and perhaps even to myself, I decided on the spot to introduce him to my little house* that he knew nothing about. I called my trusty Victoire; my migraine sets in and my servants are all told I've gone to bed. Finally, left with just my maid, my *old reliable*, I myself dress up as a lady's maid while she disguises herself as a footman. She then arranges for a cab to pick me up at my garden gate and off we go. Having arrived at this temple of love, I select my most fetching négligé, a delectable lacy thing designed by myself, extremely revealing but with minimum exposure. I'll let you have a pattern of it for your judge's wife when she's proved a fit person to wear it.

Thus armed, leaving Victoire to look after the other details, I read a chapter of *Le Sopha*, one of Eloïsa's letters and a couple of tales of La Fontaine,* so as to make sure I had all my various roles by heart. My lover meanwhile, champing at the bit as usual, turns up at the door of my house, is refused admission by my major-domo and told I'm not well: episode one. At the same time, he is handed a note from me but not written by me, in accordance with the Merteuil principle of absolute discretion. He opens it and reads these words, in Victoire's handwriting: 'Nine o'clock sharp, on the boulevard in front of the cafés.'* He betakes himself thither to be met by a small footman whom he doesn't know or thinks he doesn't know—once again, it's Victoire—who tells him to send his carriage away and follow her. These romantic* proceedings inflame his already heated imagination—there's never any harm in a heated imagination. And finally, here he is and truly spellbound by wonder and by love. To give him time to recover, we took a short stroll under the trees and then I took him back to the house. The first thing he saw was a table laid for two; next, a bed, already made up; then we went through into my boudoir, decked out in all its splendour. Once there, impelled partly by design and partly by emotion, I flung my arms around him and slid to my knees at his feet. 'Oh, my dear, dear man,' I said, 'I've been very naughty and pretending to be angry with you. It was only to give you this surprise but it was wrong of me to hide my real feelings from you even for a second. Please forgive me and let me make amends by proving to you how much I love you.' You can imagine the effect of this sentimental set-piece. The happy lover picked me up and consummated my forgiveness on that very ottoman where you and I consummated in similar style our joyous decision to part for ever.*

Since we had six hours to spend together and I was determined that each one was to be equally enjoyable for him, I damped his ardour down a trifle and lovemaking was succeeded by a little gentle dalliance. I think I've never taken such trouble to be agreeable before nor ever been so pleased with my performance. After supper, I enjoyed pretending he was a sultan and by being alternately girlish and sensible, sentimental and impish, and now and again even lascivious, I took on the roles of various favourites in his harem, so that while each of his amatory efforts was addressed to the same woman, it met with a response from a different mistress.

At daybreak, it was time to stop. He needed a rest; his spirit was willing but the flesh . . . As we were leaving, as a parting gesture I handed him the key of my little love-nest. 'I only got it for you,' I said, 'so it's only right that you alone should have charge of it. The temple of love belongs to the one who performs the sacrifices.' This subterfuge should forestall any misgivings he may have at my owning a little house, always something rather suspect. I know him well enough to be sure he'll use the key only for me; in any case, should I ever need it for my own use, I've got a spare. He was very keen to arrange a return visit but I'm too fond of him to wish to wear him out so quickly. We must only over-indulge with people we don't want to keep too long. He doesn't understand this but luckily for him I'm clever enough for both of us.

I see it's three o'clock in the morning and I've written whole screeds when I only intended to write a short note! That's the result of having such a charming and trusted friend. And that's why you're still the man I'm fondest of, though, to be frank, I get more pleasure out of my knight.*

11

Madame de Tourvel to Madame de Volanges
From the Château de ———, 13 August 17—

Your stern letter would have scared me, dear Madame de Volanges, if, fortunately, it hadn't contained more to reassure than to frighten me. Before coming to the château, that reputed terror of the ladies, Monsieur de Valmont, seems to have laid down his deadly weapons. Far from hatching plots he couldn't be more unassuming, and those winning ways which even his enemies are prepared to grant him have almost disappeared and been replaced by pure and simple friendliness. It must be the country air which has brought about this miraculous transformation.* I can assure you that although he is in constant attendance on me, and apparently even enjoying it, not one word even remotely connected with love has crossed his lips, not a single remark of the kind men seem unable to refrain from passing even when, unlike him, they have none of the necessary qualities to justify it. He never forces me to be on my guard, as every decent woman needs to be these days to ensure respect from the men around her. He understands how to avoid taking advantage of the good humour which radiates from him. He is perhaps a trifle too ready to pay compliments but he does this with a delicacy that would not bring a blush to the cheek of the most modest of women. In fact, if I had a brother, I should be delighted if he were like Monsieur de Valmont, as I see him here. Many women might perhaps like him to pay them more marked attention but I must confess that I am extremely grateful to him for not mistaking me for that kind of woman.

So my description of him is very different from yours, but I suspect the two can be reconciled if we look at the periods concerned: he himself admits to behaving badly on many occasions in the past and society is likely to have credited him with a few extra scandals. But I know few men who speak with greater deference, I'm tempted even to say with greater enthusiasm, of respectable women. Your letter confirmed that on this point at least he is not being deceitful: his attitude towards Madame de Merteuil proves this. He has mentioned her a good deal, always singing her praises and with such transparent affection that until you told me, I thought that what he described as their friendship was in fact love. I feel guilty at having judged him over-hastily, especially as he himself often made a point of speaking up on her behalf. I confess I thought he was being disingenuous when in fact he was merely being honest and straightforward. I cannot be sure but it seems to me that a man capable of such devoted friendship for so well-respected a woman cannot be an out-and-out libertine. I am not in a position to judge if, as you surmise, his impeccable behaviour is due to anything he may be plotting in the neighbourhood. There are certainly a few agreeable women living around here but he goes out very little except in the mornings when he tells us he is going shooting. It's true he doesn't often bring back any game but he freely admits to being rather a poor shot. In any case, I'm not greatly concerned by what he may do outside; if I did want to find out, it would only be in order to discover some further reason either to persuade me to accept your opinion of him or to convert you to my view.

As for your suggestion that I make an effort to curtail Monsieur de Valmont's stay here, I would find it very awkward to request his aunt to dispense with her nephew's company, especially when she is so fond of him. However, purely in deference to you, although I don't think it necessary, I promise to find an opportunity of making this request, either to her directly or to him. As for me, Monsieur de Tourvel knows of my plans to stay here until he returns and he would be justifiably surprised were I to be inconsiderate enough to change them.

Well, dear Madame de Volanges, I've taken up a good deal of your time with my explanations but I felt that, in the interests of truth, I ought to show Monsieur de Valmont in a more favourable light since it is plain that he badly needs it in your eyes. But please do not think that I am unappreciative of your friendly advice nor of the nice things you were saying about me to your daughter. However, I would willingly sacrifice the very great pleasure which I look forward to enjoying during my stay with you to my hope that Mademoiselle de Volanges's happiness will not be too long delayed, even if she can surely hardly ever be happier than she is with a mother who so greatly deserves her love and respect, which I also share and which fill me, dear, kind Madame de Volanges, with such affection for you.

With sincerest regards, etc.

12

Note from Cécile Volanges to Madame de Merteuil
13 August 17—

Dear Madame de Merteuil, Mama is a trifle indisposed and not well enough to go out, so I have to stay here and keep her company. I'm afraid I shan't be able to go to the Opéra with you, though I'm much more sorry to miss seeing you than at missing the performance. Please believe me, I'm so fond of you! And would you please tell Monsieur Danceny that I haven't got the selection he mentioned and that I shall be delighted if he can bring it along with him tomorrow? If he calls today, he'll be told we're not at home, because Mama doesn't want to see anybody. I'm hoping she'll be better tomorrow.

Very faithfully, etc.

13

Madame de Merteuil to Cécile Volanges
13 August 17—

My dear girl, I'm really so vexed at being deprived of your company as well as by the reason for it. I do hope we may have another chance. I'll deliver your message to the Chevalier Danceny, who will certainly be very upset to hear that your Mama is not well. If she will be fit enough to see me tomorrow, I shall call on her. She and I will jointly take on the Chevalier de

Belleroche* at piquet and while relieving him of his money we shall enjoy the additional pleasure of hearing you sing with your pleasant young music master; I'll suggest it to him. If that suits your Mama, I can answer for my two knights. Goodbye, dear girl; my regards to Madame de Volanges. Affectionately yours, etc.

14

Cécile Volanges to Sophie Carnay
Paris, 14 August 17—

Darling Sophie, I didn't write to you yesterday, not because I was having a nice time, I promise you, but because Mummy wasn't well and I spent all day with her. When I went up to my room last night, I didn't feel like doing anything so I went to bed straight away so as to be sure that the day really was over. It's the longest day I've ever spent, not because I'm not fond of Mummy, I don't really quite know what it was. I was meant to be going to the opera with Madame de Merteuil and the Chevalier Danceny was coming with us. You know they're the two people I like best. When the time came when I'd have been there, I felt so depressed and everything was so beastly and I cried and cried and couldn't stop. Luckily Mummy was in bed and couldn't see me. I'm sure the Chevalier Danceny was sorry too but he's had the pleasure of going to the opera and seeing all the people there and that's not the same thing at all.

Fortunately Mummy's feeling much better today and Madame de Merteuil is coming with the Chevalier Danceny and somebody else but she never comes till late and when you're all alone for such a long time, it gets jolly boring. It's only eleven o'clock. It's true I've got my harp and it will take me quite a while to get dressed because I want my hair to look really smart tonight. I think Mother Perpétue is right when she says going into society makes a girl vain. I've never wanted to look pretty as much as I have recently and I don't think I'm actually quite as pretty as I used to imagine; and we girls are at a great disadvantage compared to women who wear rouge. Take Madame de Merteuil for instance, I can see men think she's prettier than me, though I'm not really bothered because she's fond of me and anyway she says the Chevalier Danceny thinks I'm prettier than her. Isn't it jolly nice of her to tell me that? She even seems quite pleased at the idea. My goodness, now that's really something I can't understand. It's because she's so fond of me! And as for him . . . oh, I was so glad! And I reckon that even just looking at him makes you better-looking. I'd never stop looking at him if I wasn't scared of meeting his eyes because every time that happens, I get embarrassed and I feel rather miserable; but that's not really important.

Goodbye, Sophie dear. I'm going to start getting dressed. Lots of love as always.

15

The Vicomte de Valmont to the Marquise de Merteuil
Still from the Château de ———, 15 August 17—

How very kind of you not to abandon me to my sad fate! My life here is really quite exhausting because it's extremely inactive, monotonous, and dull. As I read your letter with its charming blow-by-blow report on your daily round, I was often tempted to invent some business in town and come and fling myself at your feet, asking you to be unfaithful to your knight for my benefit; after all, he doesn't really deserve your bounty. Do you realize you've made me feel jealous of him? And what do you mean by *our joyous decision to part for ever*? I hereby recant that pact, obviously the product of a moment of delirium; were we to stick by it, that would prove that we were not fit persons to have made it. Oh, if I can only one day get my revenge for the pique that lucky man has quite inadvertently caused me! I confess I'm outraged by the thought of his enjoying, effortlessly, without a second thought, merely by following the natural urgings of his heart, a bliss inaccessible to me! Oh, I'm going to put a spoke in that wheel! Promise that you'll let me! Don't you feel humiliated yourself? You go to enormous lengths to deceive him and yet he's happier than you! You think he's under your thumb? In fact, you're under his. He's peacefully dozing while you have to keep on the alert, for his good pleasure. What more would any slave be expected to do?

Hark ye, fair lady: as long as you distribute your favours, I'm not jealous in the least; I perceive your lovers purely as the successors of Alexander the Great, incompetent joint rulers of an empire where I once ruled supreme. But I cannot tolerate your surrendering completely to just one of them, thereby making another man as happy as I used to be. Nor must you expect me to tolerate it. Either take me back or at least take someone else. Don't violate our mutual pact of friendship by frivolously settling on one single lover.

It's surely bad enough for me to have to suffer the pangs of love. You see, I'm accepting your judgement and admitting my errors. Indeed, if being unable to live without possessing the object of our desires—sacrificing our time, our pleasures, and our life to her—amounts to love, then I am in love. I've made little progress and I'd have nothing to report at all if something hadn't just happened to give me food for thought, though I still don't know if it's a reason for fear or for hope.

You know my manservant, a prime intriguer, a valet straight out of a comedy,* and you may be sure that he'd received orders to fall in love with the maid and to get her servants drunk. The wretch has been luckier than his master: he's already made her. He's discovered that Madame de Tourvel has told one of her servants to obtain information as to my behaviour and even to shadow me when I go out in the morning, as well as he can, without being seen. What's she up to? Here we have a woman who's the soul of modesty taking reckless risks which even we would scarcely like to take! I swear that . . . But before thinking of how to retaliate for such feminine skulduggery, let's work out how we can turn it to our own advantage. Up till now, these outings of mine which are arousing such suspicions haven't had any special purpose. I must see if I can give them one. As this will require my whole care and attention, I must leave you and ponder over it. Goodbye, fair lady.

16

Cécile Volanges to Sophie Carnay
Paris, 19 August 17—

Oh, Sophie dear, I've got some news! Maybe I shouldn't say but I've absolutely got to tell someone, I just can't stop myself!

Chevalier Danceny . . . I'm so confused I can hardly write, I don't know where to start . . . Since writing* to you about that nice evening party at ours, with him and Madame de Merteuil, I haven't mentioned it again, because I didn't want to talk about it with anyone. But I still kept thinking about it all the time. Since then he's begun looking so sad, so really and truly miserable that I felt sorry for him, yet when I asked him why, he said he wasn't but I could see he was. Anyway, yesterday he looked even sadder than usual. That didn't prevent him from being kind enough to sing with me as he always does but each time he looked at me I felt really miserable. After we'd finished singing, he took my harp away to put it in its case and when he came back with the key, he asked me to play it again that evening when I was alone. I didn't suspect anything and wasn't even very keen to do it but he was so pressing that I agreed. And he certainly had his reasons! After I'd gone to my room and my maid had left, I went and fetched my harp. In the strings there was a letter, not sealed, just folded, and it was from him! Oh, if you only knew what he said to me! Ever since I've read it, I'm so pleased that I can't think of anything else. I read it four times straight off and then I locked it up in my secretaire. I knew it by heart and when I'd gone to bed, I kept repeating it so often that I couldn't get to sleep. As soon as I closed my eyes I could see him there himself repeating what I'd just read. I didn't drop off till it was very late and as soon as I woke up (it was still very early), I went and fetched the letter so as to read it again at my leisure. I took it back to bed with me and I kissed it as if . . . Maybe it's naughty to kiss a letter like that but I just couldn't help it.

And now, Sophie dear, although I'm very pleased, I'm also very embarrassed because I certainly ought not to reply to that letter, I know it's not really the right thing to do, but he does ask me to and if I don't, I'm sure he'll be miserable again. It's really bad luck for him! What do you think I ought to do? But you don't know any more than I do. I'd love to ask Madame de Merteuil about it as she's so fond of me and I'd love to cheer him up but I shouldn't want to do anything wrong. We're always being told to be kind-hearted and then they tell us it's wrong to do what our heart tells us to do when there's a man involved! It's just not fair! Isn't a man just as much our neighbour as a woman is, perhaps even more so? After all, we've got our fathers as well as our mothers and brothers as well as sisters. And there's our husbands, too. But if I did something that wasn't right, maybe Monsieur Danceny himself would have a bad opinion of me. Oh dear, in that case I'd rather he went on being miserable and then I'd always have time later on anyway. Just because he wrote yesterday, I'm not bound to reply today. And I'll be seeing Madame de Merteuil this evening and if I can pluck up courage I'll tell her everything. If I only do what she tells me, I shan't have anything to blame myself for. And anyway, perhaps she'll tell me I can let him have just a teeny reply and he won't be so sad! Oh, my head's in such a whirl!

Goodbye, darling Sophie. Tell me what you think anyway.

17

The Chevalier Danceny to Cécile Volanges
18 August 17—

Dear Mademoiselle, the pleasure I feel in writing to you and my need to reveal my feelings towards you have become too strong for me to resist. So I beg you to forgive my audacity and to hear me to the end. It's true that there would hardly be any point in asking for your forgiveness merely to justify my feelings for you because all I am doing in fact is to reveal the overpowering effect you have had on me. And what can I say that hasn't already been expressed by my eyes, my embarrassment, my every action, and even by my silence? So why should you be offended by a feeling that you have yourself inspired? And since you have caused it, surely it is right for me to offer it to you: it is as ardent as my soul and as innocent as yours. Was it a crime to admire your entrancing features, your fascinating gifts, your graceful charm, and the touching candour of your mind which adds so immeasurably to your other priceless qualities? No, surely not; but being not guilty is no bar to being unhappy and that will be my fate if you reject my offer of love and devotion. You are the first person ever to touch my heart so deeply. But for you, I should be, if not happy, at least at peace. Then I saw you and in a flash my peace was shattered and my happiness in jeopardy. And yet you are surprised that I look sad and you ask me why; at times, I even half-thought that you were unhappy yourself because I was. Ah, one word from you will make me blissfully happy! But before you speak, remember that one word can also plunge me into the depths of despair. It is for you to decide my fate. Through you, I shall be for ever* happy or unhappy. And in what dearer hands can I place any matter of greater concern to me?

I shall conclude as I began by begging your forgiveness and indulgence. I asked you to hear me to the end; and now I'll be even bolder and beg you to grant me a reply. If you refuse, I shall think I have offended you, yet my heart is my pledge that I respect you as much as I love you.

PS For your reply, you can use the same method as I have used to send you this letter. I think it's safe and convenient.*

18

Cécile Volanges to Sophie Carnay
Paris, 20 August 17—

Really, Sophie! So you're telling me off in advance for what I'm going to do! I'm already worried enough without you adding to my worries. It's obvious, you say, that I mustn't reply. It's all very well for you to talk and anyway you don't really understand the situation, you're not here to see how things are. I'm sure that in my place you'd do the same. Certainly in theory one ought not to reply and you saw quite well from my letter yesterday that I didn't want to either. But the fact is that I don't think anyone has ever been in a situation like mine.

And now I've got to decide what to do all on my own! I was expecting Madame de Merteuil yesterday evening but she didn't come. Everything's conspiring against me, it was through her that I got to know him, she's almost always there when I see him and speak to him. It's not that I bear her a grudge but she is leaving me rather in the lurch just at an awkward time. Oh, I'm in such a fix!

Just imagine, he came to see me yesterday as usual. I was so confused that I didn't dare look at him. He couldn't say anything to me because Mummy was there. I felt pretty sure he'd be put out when he saw I hadn't written to him and I couldn't think what I could possibly do. A moment later he asked me if I'd like him to go and fetch my harp for me. My heart was beating so hard that I could only just manage to say yes. When he came back it was even worse. I only took a quick peep at him and he didn't look at me at all but his face had the sort of expression as if he wasn't feeling very well. It made me feel very sorry for him. He began tuning my harp and when he handed it over to me he said: 'Oh, Mademoiselle . . .', just those two words but in such a way that I was quite upset. I started running my fingers over the strings without knowing what I was doing.

Mummy asked weren't we going to sing something. He excused himself, saying he wasn't feeling very well, so as I didn't have any excuse, I had to sing. I wished I'd never been able to sing at all. I deliberately chose a tune I didn't know because I was quite sure I wouldn't be able to sing anything properly and it would have been noticed. Luckily for me a visitor called and as soon as I heard a carriage pulling up I stopped and asked him to put my harp away. I was terribly afraid he wouldn't come back, but he did.

While Mummy and the lady who'd called were chatting, I tried to take another quick peep at him. Our eyes met and I couldn't look away. A moment later I saw tears in his eyes and he had to turn away so as not to be seen. So then I couldn't bear it any longer and I felt I was going to start crying myself. I went out of the room and quickly wrote on a bit of paper: 'Please don't look so sad, I promise I'll write to you.' Surely you can't say there's anything wrong in that? And anyway I just couldn't help myself. I put my note between the strings of my harp, like his letter, and came back into the drawing-room. I was feeling calmer and very anxious for our visitor to go. Fortunately she had other calls to make and left soon afterwards. As soon as she'd gone, I said I'd like to have my harp again and asked him to go and fetch it. I could tell by the way he looked that he didn't suspect anything. But didn't he look happy when he came back!

When he put the harp down in front of me, he placed himself so that Mummy couldn't see and took my hand and squeezed it . . . but in such a way! . . . It was only for a second but I can't tell you the pleasure it gave me. All the same, I took my hand away, so I've nothing to be ashamed of.

So now you realize, Sophie dear, that I can't possibly not write to him because I've promised. And anyway, I'm not going to make him miserable again because it makes me unhappier than him. If it was for something wrong, I'd certainly not do it, but what harm can there be in writing, particularly if it's to stop someone being unhappy? What does worry me is I don't know how to write a proper letter but he'll understand that it's not my fault. And anyway I'm sure the fact that it's from me will be enough to make him glad.*

Goodbye, dear, dear Sophie. If you think I'm wrong you must tell me but I don't think I am. It's nearly time for me to write to him so you can imagine how fast my heart's beating. But I'll have to go ahead with it now I've given my word. Goodbye.

19
Cécile Volanges to the Chevalier Danceny
Paris, 20 August 17—

Dear Chevalier Danceny, yesterday you looked so sad and made me feel so sorry for you that I couldn't stop myself from promising to write to you though today I feel that I ought not to. However, as I've given my word I don't want to break it, which must show how friendly I feel towards you. Now that you know that, I hope you will not ask me to write to you again. I hope too that you won't tell anybody that I did write to you because I would certainly get told off and that would make me very unhappy. Above all, I hope you will not think badly of me, that would make me unhappiest of all. I promise you I would never have agreed to do something like this for anyone else but you and I hope you can now do something to oblige me and stop looking so sad, because that completely spoils my pleasure at seeing you. You see, Monsieur Danceny, that I am speaking very frankly. I should like nothing better than for us always to remain good friends but please don't write to me again. Yours truly, etc.

20

The Marquise de Merteuil to the Vicomte de Valmont
Paris, 20 August 17—

Ah, you're trying to get round me, you naughty man, because you're afraid I shall make fun of you! All right, I'll let you off; you've been writing such dotty things to me that I suppose I shall have to forgive the good behaviour imposed on you by your judge's wife. I doubt if my knight would be so forbearing; he's not the sort of man likely to approve any renewal of our lease; he'd be positively unfriendly towards your mad idea. All the same, it gave me a good laugh and I was really sorry I couldn't share the joke with anyone else. If you'd been there, I can't imagine what my good humour might not have led to . . . But having had time to think it over, I shall harden my heart. Not that I shall always say no but I shall play a delaying action. And I'm right: my vanity might become involved and once my blood's up, we could never be certain where things might end. I'm the sort of woman who'd get you under her thumb again and make you forget your judicial wife; and if an unworthy woman like me were to spoil your taste for virtue, what a scandal that would be! To obviate such a risk, here are my conditions:

As soon as you've had your pious beauty and produced proof of it to me, come into my arms, I'm yours. But as you are aware, in matters of consequence, proof is required *in writing*. This arrangement means that, in the first place, I shall be a reward rather than a consolation prize and I prefer it that way; in the second place, your success will have the added zest of paving the way for your infidelity. So do come as soon as you can, bringing with you a warrant testifying to your conquest, just as gallant knights of yore laid their shining trophies of victory at their ladies' feet. But seriously, I'm really curious to see what a prude can write after such an event, what sort of language she can clothe it in when in other respects she's been left rather bare . . . I leave it to you to judge whether you think I'm setting too high a price on my favours, but I must warn you, I'm not offering any discounts. Until such time, my dear Vicomte, you must be content for me to remain true to my own knight and beguile my time making him happy even if it means leaving you a trifle disgruntled.

Incidentally, were I a less moral woman than I am, I think my knight would at the moment be facing a dangerous rival: the little Volanges girl. The child is adorable and I'm quite infatuated. Unless I'm mistaken, she's shaping up to become one of our very smartest women. I can see her little heart starting to open up and it's a delight to watch. She's already madly in love with Danceny, without realizing it. Although he's very much in love himself, he's young and still shy and can't pluck up the courage to tell her. They both worship me. The girl in particular is keen to confide in me, especially during the last few days which have really been weighing her down and I'd have done her a great kindness by offering her a little help. But I remember that she's still a child and I mustn't compromise my position. Danceny has spoken to me rather more openly but I've made my mind up as to him and I'm refusing to listen. As for the girl, I've often been tempted to give her a few lessons; I'd enjoy doing Gercourt that favour. He's giving me the chance to do it because he's stuck in Corsica until October. I have a mind to take advantage of that opportunity and we can deliver him a properly house-trained young woman and not his innocent convent girl. And the sheer impertinence and conceit of the man to be sleeping the sleep of the just when a woman he has wronged is waiting to settle her account with him! You know, if that girl were here at this very moment, I don't answer for what I wouldn't tell her!

Goodbye, Valmont; goodnight and good hunting. But for Heaven's sake, do get on with it. Don't forget that if you don't have that woman, your other women will feel ashamed at having had you . . .

21

The Vicomte de Valmont to the Marquise de Merteuil
From the Château de ——, 20 August 17—

Fair lady: At last I have made a step forward and even if I'm not yet home and dry, I can see that at least I'm heading in the right direction and have removed my fear of being on the wrong track. I have finally declared my love and though greeted by a very dogged silence, I did obtain perhaps the least ambiguous and most gratifying admission. But let's not anticipate. To start from the beginning:

You will remember that my comings and goings were being spied on. Well, I decided to turn this scandalous proceeding into an edifying experience for all concerned. This is how I set about it. I got my man to rout out for me some poor wretch in need of help. It didn't prove difficult. Yesterday afternoon he informed me that this morning the whole of a family's furniture was due to be seized for non-payment of taxes. I made sure that the family concerned didn't have any daughter or wife who by her age or looks might have raised any suspicions concerning the purity of my motives and having gained all the necessary information, during supper I declared my intention of going shooting next day. And here I must be fair to Madame de Tourvel. No doubt she had qualms as to the instructions she had given, and even if she was too weak to resist her curiosity, she did at least have the strength to try to dissuade me: it was going to be frightfully hot; my health might suffer; I wouldn't shoot anything and I'd be tiring myself out for nothing. During this exchange her eyes, which were perhaps saying rather more than she would have liked, were telling me pretty plainly that she wanted me to accept her reasons, poor though they were. As you may imagine, I took good care not to be intimidated and even refrained from responding to a minor diatribe against game-shooting and those who practise it, as well as to a slight shadow of disapproval which clouded the beauty of her heavenly features for the rest of that evening. For a moment I was afraid she might countermand her instructions and foil my plans by being too scrupulous. I was mistaken: I'd underestimated her feminine curiosity. My man was able to reassure me that very night and I went to bed at peace with the world.

I got up at dawn and left the château but I'd hardly gone thirty yards before I caught sight of my spy following me. I set off carrying my gun and struck out across country towards the village I'd been told of. On the way my only pleasure was keeping the rascal following me on his toes because as he didn't dare leave the tracks he was often forced to run hard to keep up, covering three times the distance I had to walk. Giving him all this exercise made me extremely hot too, so I sat down under a tree. Do you know, the fellow had the colossal cheek to slip behind a bush less than a dozen yards away and sit down as well? For a second I was tempted to take a pot-shot at him, which, although I was only using birdshot, would have taught him a salutary lesson on the dangers of being inquisitive. Luckily for him, I reminded myself that he was a useful and indeed indispensable part of my plan, so he got off scot-free.

Meanwhile, here I am at the village where I observe an uproar; I enquire what's happening; I'm told the situation; I send for the tax-collector and, yielding to my compassionate and generous heart, I magnanimously pay over fifty-six francs for which amount five people were being condemned to destitution and despair. This very simple gesture gave rise to a chorus of blessings which you can't imagine, showered on me from all sides! The tears of gratitude streamed from the eyes of the venerable head of this unhappy family, transfiguring the old patriarch's countenance which a moment before had been hideously distorted by frantic grief! I was contemplating this sight when another younger yokel, holding a woman and two children by the hand, flung himself towards me, saying to them: 'Let us all give grateful thanks to this living image of God!' And before I knew where I was, I was surrounded by this whole family prostrate at my knees. I must confess to a moment of weakness: my eyes filled with tears and in spite of myself I felt a delicious emotion stirring inside me. I was amazed at the pleasure a good deed can produce and I'm tempted to think that those so-called virtuous people don't deserve quite as much credit as we're invited to believe. Be that as it may, I thought it was only fair to repay those poor folk for the pleasure they'd just given me. I'd brought ten louis* with me which I now handed over to them. They began thanking me all over again but this time it was less touching: their heartfelt response had been when they saw the necessaries of life provided; the rest was merely expressing their surprise and thanks at my superfluous generosity.

All the same, in the midst of this family's garrulous blessings, I did look somewhat like the hero in the final scene of a drama.*

Please note particularly the presence, in the crowd, of my faithful shadow. My goal was achieved; I tore myself away from them all and returned to the château. All things considered, I have reason to feel pleased with my scheme. Certainly that woman is well worth my trouble;* it will stand me in good stead one day. And since I shall, so to speak, have paid for her in advance, I needn't feel any scruples about disposing of her as I think fit.

I was forgetting to tell you that in order to ensure the greatest possible benefit, I asked all those good folk to pray God to help me in all my doings. And you are now about to hear whether their prayers have to some extent not already been answered . . . But I've just been told that supper is served and if I left this letter unfinished until I came back, it would miss the post. So *the rest by the next post*. It's a nuisance because the rest is the best part . . . Farewell, dear lady: you're depriving me of several moments of the pleasure of her company.

22

Madame de Tourvel to Madame de Volanges
From the Château de ——, 20 August 17—

Dear Madame de Volanges, I am sure you will be more than pleased to hear of an action by Monsieur de Valmont which seems in stark contrast to everything else that other people have told you about him. It is so horrible to think badly of anyone, so distressing to see nothing but viciousness in people who would have every quality to make virtue attractive! And after all, you are so fond of showing forbearance that you can only be glad to have a reason to reverse too stern a judgement. Monsieur de Valmont seems to me to have grounds to hope for this forbearance, I'm tempted to say, this act of redress. Here are my reasons.

This morning he went out on one of those expeditions which might lead to the suspicion that he was plotting something in the neighbourhood, as you surmised; a surmise which I feel guilty of having taken up too eagerly. Fortunately for him and, above all, for us, because we have been spared from committing an injustice, one of my servants was due to be going in the same direction and it's through him that my curiosity, for which I blame myself, has turned out to be providential. This man reported to us that Monsieur de Valmont, discovering that in the village of —— an unfortunate family was about to be dispossessed for non-payment of taxes, not only immediately settled those poor people's debts but even gave them quite a considerable sum of money. This most charitable act was witnessed by my servant and he reported in addition that the villagers had revealed, during talks with him and with each other, that a manservant whom they described and who my man thinks is Monsieur de Valmont's, had been enquiring yesterday which of the local inhabitants might be in need of help. If this is true then this is not just a casual act of pity, resulting from chance, but a deeply charitable concern, a deliberate intention to do good, that most noble quality of noble souls. But whether by chance or by intent, it is still an honourable and praiseworthy act; merely hearing about it moved me to tears. Let me add, since I still wish to be fair, that when I spoke to him about his action, which he'd not once mentioned himself, he at first denied it and when he finally confessed, his modesty was even more admirable as he seemed to view it as something quite trivial.

Now tell me, dear, respected friend, if Monsieur de Valmont actually is a hardened libertine and nothing more, yet behaves in this way, what is there left for decent people to do? Can evil people really share with the good the saintly pleasures of charity? Would God allow a virtuous family to receive help from the hands of a scoundrel and offer up thanks for it to His Divine Providence? Would it please Him to hear innocent lips calling blessings down on the head of a sinful man? Of course He would not!* I prefer to believe that evil actions, however long they continue, do not last for ever and I cannot conceive that a man who does good can be an enemy of virtue. Perhaps Monsieur de Valmont is just a victim of the danger of certain acquaintances. And this is a pleasant thought indeed on which to end this letter. If it can help to justify him in your eyes, it will surely serve to make my lifelong friendship and affection for you even more precious.

Ever most truly, etc.

PS Madame de Rosemonde and I are setting off this very moment to see for ourselves this honest and unfortunate family and belatedly to add something to the help already received from Monsieur de Valmont. We shall take him with us. At least we shall provide these good folk with the pleasure of meeting their benefactor again, even if, as I suspect, he has left us with little more to do.

23

The Vicomte de Valmont to the Marquise de Merteuil
From the Château de ——, 21 August 17—, 3 a.m.

We'd reached the point where I'd gone back to the château. I take up my tale from there.

I just had time to change before going down to the drawing-room where my beauty was working at her tapestry while the local parish priest was reading the Gazette* to my old aunt. I went and sat down beside the frame. The looks cast in my direction, even softer than usual, indeed verging on the affectionate, soon led me to guess that the servant had already reported on his mission. And in fact my dear prying lady was unable to keep to herself any longer the secret she had wrested from me and, intrepidly interrupting the venerable cleric whose tone of voice suggested he was delivering a sermon, she announced, 'I have some news of my own', and launched into an account of my exploit with an accuracy which does credit to the competence of her informant. You can imagine the great show of modesty which I put on; but what can possibly stop a woman who, all unsuspectingly, is praising the object of her affections? I decided to let her have her head. You would have imagined that she was eulogizing a saint. Meanwhile, I was examining, not without optimism, all the promising signs of love in the sparkle in her eyes, the greater freedom of her gestures and, above all, the marked change in her tone of voice which betrayed the depth of her emotion. As soon as she had come to an end, my aunt exclaimed: 'Nephew, come here, I must give you a hug!' I immediately perceived that my charming spreader of the Word could not escape her turn; she tried to evade my grasp but was quickly held in my arms and far from resisting, she barely had the strength to hold herself upright. The longer I observe this woman, the more desirable she becomes. She hurriedly retreated to her frame, ostensibly to start her tapestry work again; I alone could plainly see that her hand was trembling too much for her to do so.

After dinner, the ladies were anxious to go and see the unfortunate villagers whom I had so piously helped; they took me with them. I'll spare you the boring details of this second scene of acclaim and thanksgiving: my heart is burning to hurry back to the château, driven on by a delicious memory. As we drove back, my lovely judicial lady was more meditative than usual and uttered not a word. I too remained silent, running over in my mind ways and means of exploiting the impact of the day's events. Only Madame de Rosemonde had anything to say but found us unresponsive. I intended her to find us boring and I succeeded. As a result, as soon as my aunt got out of the carriage, she went up to her quarters, leaving my beauty and me alone in a dimly lit drawing-room; a subdued half-light, encouraging for a timid lover.

I had no difficulty in leading the conversation round to where I wanted. The zeal of my charming sermonizer came to my aid far better than any wiles of mine could have done. She had a soft look in her eyes. 'When someone is capable of such good works,' she began, 'how can he spend his life doing wrong?' 'I'm afraid I don't deserve either your praise or your blame,' I replied, 'and I can't understand how someone so highly intelligent as yourself hasn't yet found me out. Even if what I'm going to confess may harm me in your eyes, nobody deserves to be told the truth more than you, so I must tell you. The key to my behaviour lies in my character which unfortunately is extremely weak. Being surrounded by people with no morals, I've come to imitate their vices and through vanity and conceit even tried to outshine them. Similarly since I've been here I've been captivated by virtuous examples and even if I could never hope to match them, I have at least made an effort to follow in your footsteps. And perhaps my action which you find so praiseworthy would lose all its value for you if you knew the real motive behind it.' (Please note, fair lady, how close I came to telling the truth!) 'Those unfortunate people I helped,' I went on, 'owed me nothing. What you considered an act of charity was merely my way of trying to please you. Since I'm determined to be frank, let me say that I was merely the frail instrument of the Divinity whom I worship' (and here she tried to cut me short but I didn't give her the chance). 'Even now,' I continued, 'it's nothing but my weakness which is making me reveal my secret. I'd promised myself not to say anything, I was happy to worship your goodness and your charms with so pure a devotion that you would have never become aware of it. But seeing your own sincerity, how could I deceive you? At least I shan't have to feel guilty at living a lie. Please don't think I have any sort of hopes, that would be an insult and a crime. I know my plight is hopeless, I'm doomed to be unhappy, but I'll accept my misery gladly because it will prove how deeply I'm in love. I shall kneel at your feet and throw myself on your mercy to comfort me in my sorrow and to find new strength to go on suffering. You will be kind and compassionate and I shall feel consoled because you've shown me pity. Oh, how I adore you! Hear me and pity me and help me!' By now I was down at her feet, clasping her hands but she suddenly pulled them free and held them crossed in front of her eyes with a look of despair. 'Ah, poor me, poor me!' she exclaimed and burst into tears. Luckily I'd talked myself into such a state that I was crying too, so I clutched her hands again and bathed them in my tears.* This was a highly necessary precaution because she was so preoccupied with her own troubles that if I hadn't brought mine to her attention she wouldn't have noticed them; it gave me the added advantage of leaving me more time to scrutinize her lovely face, made even lovelier by the potent charm of tears. I was becoming roused and in such poor control of my feelings that I was sorely tempted to exploit the situation.

How feeble can you be? What a poor victim of circumstances I'd have been if I'd forgotten my plans and, by making her surrender too quickly, risked forfeiting the delights of a long-drawn-out struggle and the niceties of an agonizing defeat? If I'd been led astray like some lecherous youngster and, by seducing Madame de Tourvel then and there, had merely gained a dreary reward for all my efforts by chalking up yet one more name on the list? Certainly she must surrender but she must offer resistance; an opponent too weak to win but not too weak to put up a struggle. She must be given time to savour her weakness to the full and be forced to admit defeat. Any piddling poacher can lie in wait for a stag and shoot it unawares; the true sportsman brings it to bay. Don't you think my plan's divine? All the same, I might perhaps now be feeling sorry not to have followed it if chance hadn't intervened to support my caution.

We heard sounds; people were coming towards the drawing-room. Madame de Tourvel sprang to her feet, picked up a candelabra and left the room. It was impossible to stop her. It was only a servant. As soon as I was sure of this, I followed her but hardly had I gone a few steps when, either because she recognized me or because she was afraid, I heard her quickening her stride and go or rather rush into her room, locking the door behind her. I went up to it but the key was inside. I carefully refrained from knocking: that would have provided her with a far too easy way of resisting. I hit on the bright idea of quite simply peeping through the keyhole* and I could see this adorable woman on her knees, her face streaming with tears and praying hard. What God was she daring to pray to? Is there any God strong enough to resist Love? It's useless for her to seek help from outside; I'm the one who'll decide her fate now.

Thinking I'd done enough for one day, I went straight back to my room and started to write this letter. I'd been hoping to see her at supper but she sent a message that she wasn't feeling well and had gone to bed. Madame de Rosemonde wanted to go up and see her but the sly little invalid alleged she had a headache which prevented her from seeing anyone. You can imagine that I didn't linger after supper and quickly developed a headache of my own. As soon as I got to my room I wrote a long letter protesting against her harshness towards me and went to bed, intending to hand it to her this morning. As you can see from the date of this letter, I slept badly. On getting up, I reread my missive to her again and realized that I hadn't been sufficiently circumspect and that it was passionate rather than loving and petulant rather than disconsolate. I'll have to rewrite it but I've got to be calmer.

The sun's just coming up: I hope the cool of dawn will enable me to get some sleep. I shall go back to bed and I promise that however strong that woman's power over me may be, it'll not be too strong to prevent me from finding time to think of you a very great deal. Goodbye, dear, lovely lady.

24*

The Vicomte de Valmont to Madame de Tourvel
20 August 17—

For pity's sake, Madame, relent and relieve my troubled spirit; relent and tell me what I may hope or fear.* I'm tortured by uncertainty: do I face happiness beyond my dreams or calamity? Why did I speak out? Why was I overwhelmed by your charm and forced to open my heart to you? As long as I was content to worship you in silence I could at least indulge my feeling of love; my happiness was untroubled by the sight of your distress and this chaste feeling was joy enough. But ever since I saw you crying, this joy has turned to despair; ever since I heard you utter those cruel words: '*Ah, poor me!*', which will long re-echo in my heart. Why does Fate seem to have ordained that love, that gentlest of feelings, fills you only with fear? But I misread your heart: you're not made for love; I am the only one with a loving heart, even though you constantly misrepresent it. Indeed, your heart is pitiless; how else would you be able to refuse someone a word of comfort when he'd revealed the extent of his misery; you wouldn't have hidden yourself away from him when his only pleasure is to see you; you wouldn't have had the cruelty to play on his anxiety by announcing that you were unwell and then refusing to let him visit you to enquire after your health; you would have sensed that last night, which for you meant merely twelve hours' rest, would become for him an eternity of anguish.

Tell me the crime I've committed to deserve such a crushing sentence. I'm not afraid to ask you to judge me, just tell me what I have done, apart from giving way, against my will, to feelings inspired by your beauty and sanctioned by your spotless reputation, feelings never exceeding the bounds of respect, feelings which I confessed, innocently and in all good faith, without hoping for any gain. Are you now prepared to betray that trust which you seemed to place in me and to which I responded so open-heartedly? No, Madame, that I cannot believe; were I to believe it, it would suggest that you are capable of behaving badly and the mere hint of such a thought makes me sick at heart; I take back any reproaches I may have made against you, I may have written them but I never believed them. Please, please don't destroy my belief that you are perfect! That is now the only pleasure remaining. And you must prove it is true by being generous and helping me! Have you ever known an unfortunate with a greater need for help than mine? Don't desert me, don't leave me in the state of madness into which you've thrown me! Since you've taken my good sense away from me, help me with your own! Discipline me and then complete your charitable work by telling me what I am to do.

I cannot deceive you: you'll never succeed in driving out my love but you will teach me to keep it under control, you'll guide my steps, you'll dictate what I may say and at least save me from the horror of incurring your displeasure. That particular fear you must relieve me of, by telling me I'm forgiven and that you feel pity for me. Promise to be forbearing; you will never have all the forbearance I should like but I beg you at least to let me have all I need. Will you refuse me that?

Goodbye, Madame de Tourvel. Be kind and accept the wishes I offer you, knowing that they can never weaken the deep respect in which I hold you.

25

The Vicomte de Valmont to the Marquise de Merteuil
22 August 17—

Here's yesterday's situation report:

11 a.m.: I went to see Madame de Rosemonde and under her watchful eye was admitted into the bedroom of the bogus invalid. She was still in bed, with big rings round her eyes; I do hope she slept as badly as I did. I took advantage of a moment when Madame de Rosemonde was otherwise engaged to hand her my letter, which she rejected. However I left it lying on the bed and very politely went over and fetched my old aunt's

armchair up beside the bed as she wanted to sit near to her 'dear child'; to avoid scandal, the letter had to be secreted away. The patient was ill-advised enough to say she thought she had a temperature and Madame de Rosemonde called upon me to feel her pulse, expressing great confidence in my medical skills. My beauty thus had the double mortification of letting me take hold of her arm and of having her little stratagem exposed. In fact, I took her hand and squeezed it while I ran my other hand over her cool, plump arm; the naughty girl did not have the slightest reaction, which prompted me to say, as I let go: 'No trace of fever at all; the heart seems sluggish.' I suspected she was looking daggers at me so I avoided her gaze, as a punishment for her behaviour. A moment later she said she'd get up and we left her. She came down to dinner, which was not a cheerful occasion. She announced she would not be taking a walk, which was her way of letting me know that I wouldn't have any chance of speaking to her. I realized that it was up to me to throw in a sigh or two and a grieved look; no doubt she was expecting me to do so for that was the only time during the day when I succeeded in meeting her eye. Chaste she may be but she has her sly little ways like any other. I grasped the opportunity to ask her *if she had relented enough to let me know my fate* and was somewhat surprised to hear her reply: *Yes, Monsieur, I have written you a letter*. I was very eager to receive it but either because she was being sly again or awkward or shy, she didn't let me have it until it was time for her to retire. Here it is, together with a draft of mine. Read it and judge for yourself what an arrant hypocrite she is to deny that she feels any love for me when I'm certain that it's not true. And then later on she'll complain if I deceive her when she's had no qualms at all in deceiving me now. Fair lady, the cleverest of men can just about hold his own with the most truthful woman. Yet one has to pretend to believe all this rubbish and become haggard with despair because the lady is pleased to play at being hard to get! How can we resist retaliating against such vicious conduct! Ah, we must remain patient . . . And now, goodbye, I've still a lot of writing to do.

And by the way, please send back that heartless woman's letter. It may be that later on she might think that such trivia have some sort of value. We must make sure everything's in order.*

I haven't mentioned the Volanges girl; we'll come back to her at the first available opportunity.

26
Madame de Tourvel to the Vicomte de Valmont
21 August 17—

You would certainly never have received this letter from me, Monsieur de Valmont, if my stupid behaviour of yesterday evening hadn't forced me to embark on an explanation today. Yes, I admit I was crying, I may even have let slip the couple of words which you quote so accurately; you clearly missed nothing, either of my tears or my words, so I must give you an explanation of everything.

Up till now I have never been accustomed to arousing any but honourable feelings or hearing anything that might make me blush; as a result I have enjoyed a sense of security which I like to think I deserve and so I'm unable either to conceal or restrain my emotions. The surprise and embarrassment caused by your actions, a vague fear prompted by a situation into which I should never have been placed and perhaps the horrible suspicion of being mistaken for one of those women whom you despise and treated with the same lack of respect, all this combined to give rise to my tears and may have made me commiserate with myself out loud. But the words 'Poor me!', which you seem to consider so strong, would surely have been quite inadequate if they and my tears had been caused by something else and, instead of expressing my disapproval of your feelings which could only offend me, had expressed my fear of sharing them.

No, Monsieur de Valmont, I have no such fear; if I had I should quickly take refuge in some faraway exile to rue the sad day that I ever met you. Perhaps, in spite of being certain of not loving you, of never loving you, I should even have been wiser to follow my friends' advice and never let you come near me.

I believed—and this is my sole mistake—I believed that you would respect the feelings of a decent woman who asked for nothing better than to find the same decency in you and to treat you fairly, who spoke up in your defence, whereas you were secretly insulting her with your criminal intentions. You do not know me, Monsieur de Valmont, you do not know what I am like; otherwise you would never have thought you had the right to take advantage of your disgraceful conduct. Merely because you dared speak to me in terms I should never have listened to, you should not have considered yourself entitled to write me a letter that I should never have read. And you ask me to *guide your steps, dictate what you may say*. Very well then: leave me alone and forget me: that's the proper advice for me to give and for you to follow. If you do so, you will indeed have some claim to be forgiven and it would rest entirely with you even to earn my gratitude. And yet . . . No, I refuse to ask anything from anyone who has shown me such disrespect; I shall not offer any token of trust to someone who has undermined my peace of mind. You are forcing me to be afraid of you and even to hate you. I didn't want that; I wanted to regard you merely as the nephew of my most respected friend; I was a friendly voice challenging that of public opinion which saw you as a reprobate. You have destroyed all that and I can foresee that you will be unwilling to make any amends.

So I shall confine myself, Monsieur de Valmont, to informing you that your sentiments are offensive, that it was outrageous to confess them and that above all, far from persuading me to share them, you will force me never to see you again unless you undertake to preserve absolute silence on the subject, as I am entitled to expect and even, it seems to me, to demand. I enclose with this letter the one which you wrote me.* I hope that you will similarly let me have this one back, for I should be greatly concerned if any trace ever remained of an incident which should never have occurred.

I have the honour, etc.

27

Cécile Volanges to Madame de Merteuil
23 August 17—

My goodness, you really are being so kind to me, Madame de Merteuil! And how clever of you to guess that I'd find it easier to write to you rather than speak! You see, it's because what I have to tell you is very hard! But you're my friend, aren't you, yes, really and truly a friend! I'm going to try not to be afraid. And I do need you and your advice so badly. At the moment I feel so miserable, I think everyone can read my thoughts; and particularly when he's there, I blush every time anyone looks at me. When you saw me crying yesterday, it was because I wanted to speak to you and then something seemed to stop me and when you asked me what was wrong, I just couldn't help crying. It just wasn't possible to say anything. And but for you, Mama would have noticed and what would have happened to me then? Yet that's what my life is like at the moment, especially the last four days.

That was the day, yes, I've got to tell you, that was the day when the Chevalier Danceny wrote to me. Oh, I promise you that when I found the letter I didn't know what it was at all but I mustn't tell a fib, I can't pretend I wasn't very pleased when I read it. You see, I'd sooner be miserable for the rest of my life than not have had that letter from him. But of course I realized that I oughtn't to tell him that and I promise you, really and truly, that I even told him I was annoyed by it but he said he couldn't stop himself and I believe him, because I'd made up my mind not to write to him and I still couldn't help doing it. Oh, I only wrote to him once and even that was partly to tell him not to write to me again but in spite of that he still keeps on writing and as I'm not replying, anyone can see he's sad and that makes me even sadder so I don't know what to do or what's going to happen and I feel very sorry for myself.

Please, dear Madame de Merteuil, can you tell me, would it be very wrong of me to reply to him once in a while? Only just until he promises to agree not to write to me himself and to remain as we were at the start, because, as for me, I don't know what will become of me if things go on like this. You know, as I was reading his last letter, I just couldn't stop crying and I'm absolutely certain that if I still go on not answering him, it'll make us both too miserable for words.

I'm going to send you his letter too, or rather a copy of it so you can judge for yourself. You'll see he's not asking for anything wrong. All the same, if you think it's not right then I promise not to do it, but I do believe that like me, you will think there's nothing wrong in it.

And while I'm on the subject, will you forgive me if I ask one more question: I've been told it's wrong to love someone but why should that be? The reason I ask is that Monsieur Danceny claims that there's nothing wrong in it at all and that everybody loves someone and if that's true I don't see why I'm to be the only person to stop myself doing it. Or is it only wrong for young ladies? Because I heard Mama herself say that Madame D——loved Monsieur M——. She wasn't talking about it as something all that wrong yet I'm sure she'd be cross with me if she even suspected that I felt friendly towards Monsieur Danceny. Mama still treats me like a little girl and doesn't tell me anything at all. When she took me away from the convent I thought it was to get me married but now that doesn't seem to be true, not that it troubles me, I assure you. But as you're such a good friend of hers, perhaps you know what the situation is and if you do, I do so hope you can tell me.

What an awfully long letter but as you gave me permission to write to you, I've taken the opportunity of telling you everything, relying on you as a real friend.

Yours very faithfully, etc.

28

The Chevalier Danceny to Cécile Volanges
23 August 17—

So you really still don't want to reply to my letters, Mademoiselle! Oh, how hard-hearted you are! Every morning my hopes rise and every evening they're dashed to the ground! You say that we are friends but what sort of friendship is it that isn't even strong enough to make you realize how miserable I am; that leaves you cold and indifferent while I'm burning with a love which I find impossible to quench; that doesn't even extend to trust, let alone pity? Your friend is suffering and you won't lift a finger to help him! He asks you for one little word and you refuse to give it to him! You expect him to be satisfied with such a lukewarm feeling and even that feeling you won't dare to put into words a second time!

Yesterday you were saying you didn't want to seem ungrateful yet believe me, trying to offer friendship in exchange for love doesn't mean that you're afraid of being ungrateful, merely that you're anxious not to appear ungrateful. But I don't dare to come back to a subject which you're bound to find tiresome if it doesn't interest you. I shall have to shut up my love inside me at least until I've succeeded in overcoming it. I can feel how hard that will be and I realize that I'll need all my strength. But I shall keep trying in every possible way and the one which I'll find most heartbreaking will be to have to tell myself over and over again that you have a heart of stone. I'll even try seeing less of you and I'm already looking round for an excuse to do that . . .

But how terrible to have to give up that pleasant habit of calling on you every day, as a friend! At least I shall always be able to treasure that as a sad memory! So my love and devotion will be rewarded by a lifetime of misery and it will be all your making because that's how you've wanted it! And I can feel that I shall never, never recover the happiness that you are taking away from me, for you were the only girl in the world I could love! How happy I should be to swear to live only for you! But your ears are closed, your silence tells me quite plainly that your heart has nothing to say to me and that is the surest proof of your indifference as well as the cruellest way of letting me know. Farewell, Mademoiselle.

I've no delusions about getting a reply from you: a lover would have been longing to write, a friend would have been glad to, a kind person would have written out of pity but in your heart there's no room for pity, friendship, or love.

29

Cécile Volanges to Sophie Carnay
24 August 17—

Didn't I tell you, Sophie, that in some cases it was right to write? And I blame myself a lot, I promise you, for having followed your advice, which made Chevalier Danceny and me so miserable. The proof that I was right is that Madame de Merteuil, who's certainly a woman who knows all about that sort of thing, has finally come round to my view. I confessed everything to

her. At first she said the same as you but after I'd explained it all
to her, she agreed it wasn't the same thing at all. The only thing
she wants is for me to show her all my letters as well as all
Chevalier Danceny's so as to be sure I'm not saying anything
I oughtn't. So now I've no more worries. My goodness, what
a nice lady Madame de Merteuil is! She's so kind and she's
such a respectable person, too! So there's nothing more to be
said.

And what a letter I'm going to write to Monsieur Danceny and
how pleased he'll be! He's going to be even more pleased than he
thinks because up till now I've only mentioned 'friendship' and
he always wanted me to say 'love'. I reckon it's really the same
thing, but anyway I didn't dare and he wanted so badly for me to
say it! I told Madame de Merteuil about it and she said I was
right and you should only admit to feeling love when you
couldn't hide it any longer. And I'm quite sure I shan't be able to
hide it much longer; after all, it's the same thing and he'll like it
much better.

Madame de Merteuil told me as well that she'd lend me some
books on the whole subject which would teach me how to behave
and also to write better than I do. You see, she tells me about all
my faults which is a proof that she's fond of me. But she's
recommended me not to mention anything about these books to
Mummy because it would look like hinting she hasn't brought
me up properly and that might make her cross. Oh, I'm certainly
not going to mention them.

All the same, it's really extraordinary that a woman who's
hardly related to me, or even not at all, is looking after me better
than my own mother. Aren't I a lucky girl to have met her!

She's also asked Mummy to let her take me to the Opéra the
day after tomorrow, in her own box. She's told me we'll be all on
our own and we can talk all the time without any danger of being
overheard. I'll enjoy that much better than the opera itself. We'll
talk about my marriage too, because she said it's really true that
I'm going to be married; but we didn't have a chance to say
anything more about it. Well now, isn't that quite amazing too,
that Mummy hasn't said a word about it to me?

Bye-bye, Sophie dear, I'm going to write to Chevalier
Danceny now. Oh, I'm so thrilled!

30

Cécile Volanges to the Chevalier Danceny
24 August 17—

I've finally decided to write to you, Monsieur, to promise you my friendship, my love, because otherwise you will be unhappy. You say I'm heartless but I assure you that you are mistaken and I hope that I have now removed your doubts. If you were sad because I didn't write to you, don't you think that I was sorry too? The reason was that I wouldn't ever want to do anything wrong, not on any account, and I certainly would not have admitted my love if I had been able to hide it. But I felt so sorry for you. Now I hope you'll not be sad any longer and that we're going to be very happy.

I'm very much looking forward to seeing you tonight and I hope you'll come early; it will never be too soon for me. Mama is having supper at home and I think she'll be inviting you to stay on for it. I do hope you haven't another engagement like you had two days ago. I suppose the supper party you were going to must have been a very nice one because you left very early to go to it. But don't let's talk about that and now you know I love you, I hope you'll stay with me as much as you can, because I'm only happy when I'm with you and it would be very nice for me to think that you feel the same.

I'm very sorry that you're still unhappy at the moment but it's not my fault. I'll ask to play my harp as soon as you come so you can get my letter straight away. That's the best I can do.

Goodbye, Monsieur. With all my heart, I'm so, so fond of you and the more I say it, the happier I feel. I do hope you'll be, too.

31

The Chevalier Danceny to Cécile Volanges
25 August 17—

Oh yes, there's no doubt we're going to be happy! I'm sure to be, because you love me and if your happiness lasts as long as the love you've inspired in me, it will never, never end . . . How wonderful it all is! You love me, you're not afraid of telling me of

your *love*! *The more I say it the happier I feel!* And after reading
that charming 'I love you',* written by your own hand, I heard it
from your lovely lips! I saw your charming eyes, made even more
wonderful by their expression of love, looking deep into mine. I
heard you swear to live always for me and now you shall hear my
vow to dedicate my whole life to making you happy! Believe me,
you can be sure that's a vow I shall never break.

What a happy day we spent together yesterday! Oh, why can't
Madame de Merteuil find secrets to tell your mother every day?
Why are the delicious memories that fill my mind spoilt by the
thought of the obstacles that stand in our way! Why can't I clasp
that pretty hand which wrote *I love you* and smother it in kisses,
to compensate for your refusal to grant me any greater favours?

Tell me, dear Cécile, weren't you sorry when your Mama
came back and we had to start pretending to be indifferent to
each other and you couldn't go on promising to love me, as a
consolation for not being able to give me any proof of it? Didn't
you say to yourself: 'He'd have been happier with a kiss and I've
deprived him of that pleasure'? Do promise me, dear, dear
Cécile, that at our next opportunity you'll not be so strict. If you
do promise, I can bear with all the dreadful frustrations of our
situation and at least have the consolation that you're suffering
from them as well.

Goodbye, charming Cécile. It's time for me to come and see
you and I couldn't possibly say goodbye to you now unless I was
on my way to see you. Goodbye, dear Cécile, I love you so much
and I'm going to love you more and more, for ever!

32
Madame de Volanges to Madame de Tourvel
24 August 17—

So you are trying to convince me that Monsieur de Valmont is a
man of high principles? I must confess that I can't bring myself
to be persuaded. From the single instance you mention I should
find it as difficult to consider him an honourable man as I should
to think that a man well known for his goodness was vicious
merely because he'd once behaved badly. Mankind is never per-

fect, in good or in evil. Scoundrels have their good points just as men of honour have their failings. This truth seems all the more important to believe since it leads to the need to be indulgent towards those who are evil as well as those who are good; it stops the latter from becoming arrogant and the former from losing heart. You will no doubt be thinking that at the moment I'm not displaying much of the indulgence which I've been preaching but I consider it nothing but a dangerous weakness when it leads us to treat vicious and good people on an equal footing.

I shan't presume to scrutinize the motives of Monsieur de Valmont's actions; I'm prepared to accept that they are as praiseworthy as the actions themselves. But hasn't he nevertheless spent his life spreading confusion, disgrace, and scandal in many homes? By all means, listen to the voice of that poor unfortunate man whom he helped but don't close your ears to the cries of a hundred women who have been his victims. Even if he were, as you say, just an example of the danger of certain acquaintances, would that make him less of a dangerous acquaintance himself? You say he could reform his ways? Let's look ahead and assume that this miracle has taken place. Wouldn't he still have public opinion against him and isn't that enough to guide your conduct? Absolution belongs to God alone at the moment of repentance; He can read inside people's hearts, men can only judge thoughts from their effects on action and no man who has lost the esteem of his fellow men has any right to complain of the inevitable distrust which makes it so hard to redeem that loss. And above all, dear young friend, never forget that to forfeit public esteem it is sometimes sufficient merely to appear to treat it lightly; and don't accuse such an attitude of being unduly strict and unfair because, quite apart from the fact that we are justified in assuming that no one is willing to forfeit such a precious thing if they think they have a claim to it, the person who is no longer held back by this powerful deterrent is in fact all the more likely to do wrong. Yet that is how people would regard you if you seem to have been too closely acquainted with him.

Your warm advocacy of Monsieur de Valmont makes me so frightened that I must answer your likely objections without delay. I can hear you quoting Madame de Merteuil, whose relationship with him has been forgiven; you'll be asking me why

I allow him into my house; you'll tell me that far from being ostracized by decent people, he's admitted and even warmly welcomed in what is known as 'good society'. I think I can answer all those objections.

First of all, Madame de Merteuil, though indeed a woman highly regarded, has perhaps only one fault: she overestimates her ability; she's a skilful driver who enjoys guiding her chariot between rocks and precipices and whose sole justification is that she remains unscathed. We can certainly praise but it would be unwise to follow her; she agrees with that view herself and condemns herself for it. With greater insight she has developed stricter principles, and I have no hesitation in assuring you that she would support my judgement.

As far as I'm concerned, I shan't try to justify myself more than anybody else. Certainly, Monsieur de Valmont comes to my house and he is accepted everywhere. This is one more absurdity to add to the thousand and one others condoned by society. You know as well as I do that we spend our lives noticing them, complaining about them, and committing them. Monsieur de Valmont has an honoured name, great wealth, and many likeable qualities and he recognized early on that to acquire social prestige two things only were required: to be equally adept at flattery and ridicule. No one possesses this double gift better than Valmont: he uses the first to charm, the second to intimidate. People don't think highly of him but they indulge him. This is how he exists in a world which is prudent rather than courageous and which prefers to humour him rather than stand up to him.

But one thing is certain: not even Madame de Merteuil, let alone any other woman, would be rash enough to go off and shut herself away in the country, almost on her own, with such a man. It was left to the most chaste and modest of women to offer an example of such an absurdity—you must forgive the expression, it is one which, as your friend, I could not avoid. Dear, dear friend, it is your own high principles that are leading you astray because they give you a sense of security; but you must reflect that you will be judged on the one hand by the frivolous who'll refuse to believe in such principles because they don't exist amongst themselves, and on the other hand by mischief-makers who'll pretend not to believe in them in order to punish you for holding them. Just consider that, at this moment, you are doing things that even some men wouldn't risk doing. Indeed, amongst the younger set with whom Monsieur de Valmont has established an all too powerful reputation as an oracle, I have noticed that the most sensible of them are chary of appearing to be too closely associated with him—and yet you're not afraid of him! Oh, I do entreat you to come back to Paris now and if my reasoning doesn't convince you, let me appeal to you as a friend. It's my friendship which is my justification for continuing to urge you to leave. I expect you'll be thinking that these friendly warnings are too stern and I do sincerely hope they're unfounded; but I'd prefer you to complain that I'm too concerned rather than uncaring.

33

The Marquise de Merteuil to the Vicomte de Valmont
24 August 17—

My dear Vicomte, as soon as you start being scared of succeeding, as soon as you plan to arm your opponent against yourself and seem less keen on winning than on just waging war, then there's really nothing more to be said. Your conduct shows either exemplary caution or else exemplary stupidity. To be blunt, I'm afraid you're pulling the wool over your own eyes.

Not that I'm blaming you for failing to take advantage of the right moment; for one thing, I'm not at all certain in my own mind that it was the right moment;* for another, I'm perfectly well aware that, contrary to conventional wisdom, opportunity always knocks more than once whereas a false step can never be retraced.

But your real howler was to embark on letter-writing. I defy you to foresee now where that may land you. Do you, perchance, hope to prove to that woman that she's got to give herself to you?* It seems to me that's something which has to be felt, not proved, and to convince anyone of it you must appeal to the heart, not the head; but what's the point of softening a heart by correspondence when you're not there to take advantage of it?

Even assuming your fine phrases manage to whip her into a frenzy, do you flatter yourself that she won't have time to pull herself together and stop herself from admitting it? Just consider how long it takes to write a letter, how long it takes to reach her, and see if a woman, particularly a pious high-principled woman like yours, can persist over such a long period in wanting to do something she's trying hard never to do anyway. That sort of thing may work with children who when they write 'I love you' don't realize that they're saying: 'Take me.' But Madame de Tourvel is virtuous and argumentative and seems to have a pretty good grasp of the exact value of words, so, in spite of the advantage you gained over her while talking, in her letter she beats you hands down. And do you know what happens next? The very fact of arguing means that you refuse to give in. You cast around for good reasons, you find some, you put them forward and then stick by them not because they're good but to avoid having to contradict yourself.

And there's something else I'm surprised you haven't noticed: there's nothing harder than writing something you don't really feel, I mean doing it convincingly; it's not that you don't use the proper words but they're not arranged in the proper way or rather, they obviously are arranged and that's quite enough. Just reread your letter: it's organized in such a way that every sentence gives the game away. I'm willing to believe that your judge's wife isn't sophisticated enough to notice it but what does that matter? The effect is still obvious. It's the weakness of novels; while the author works himself up into a passion, the reader remains unmoved. *Héloïse** is the only possible exception; and though the author of that book is very gifted, this observation has always led me to think that the novel was based on fact. Talking is quite different. With practice, you can make your voice tremble with emotion and that can be enhanced by a few well-placed tears; eyes can express a blend of tenderness and desire; and finally, a few broken words help to reinforce the air of bewilderment and agitation which is the most eloquent proof of love. Above all, the presence of our lover prevents women from thinking and makes us want to surrender.

Take my advice: you've been asked to stop writing; take advantage of this to correct your mistake and wait for a chance to speak. D'you know, that woman's stronger than I thought? Her defences are first-rate; there were only two things which gave her away: her letter was too long and she expressed her gratitude, thereby offering you a pretext to return to the charge.

There's one other factor which promises well for your campaign: she's committing too many forces in one operation; I predict that she'll use them up in the war of words and won't have any in reserve to defend herself when it comes to deeds.

I'm sending you back your letters and if you're wise, they'll be the last you write before victory is yours. If it wasn't so late I'd tell you about the Volanges girl who's coming along nicely. I'm highly satisfied with her. I reckon I'll get her past the finishing post before you and you must be feeling very ashamed at that.

Goodbye for now.

34

The Vicomte de Valmont to the Marquise de Merteuil
25 August 17—

You talk admirable good sense, fair lady, but why make such an effort to prove what every schoolboy knows? In love, rapid progress is achieved by talking rather than writing: that, I think, just about sums up your letter. Really, my dear! That's the most elementary principle of the game. But may I point out that you allow only one exception, whereas there are two: in addition to children who follow this primrose path through timidity and come to grief through ignorance, you must include clever women who allow themselves to become involved through conceit and are brought down by their own vanity. For instance, I'm quite sure that the Comtesse de B——,* who found no difficulty in responding to my letter, felt at the time no more love for me than I for her and merely saw the chance of talking about a subject that would increase her prestige.

However that may be, a lawyer would say that in this case the question is *ultra vires*. You are in fact assuming that I have the choice between writing and speaking. This is not the case; ever since that business on the 20th, my heartless lady has remained on the defensive and thwarted any manœuvre to see her with masterly skill. It's reached the stage where, if this continues, she'll force me to give serious thought to finding means to regain my advantage, since I'm certainly not prepared to be outmanœuvred by her in any way. Even my letters have become the subject of a minor war: she's not content to leave them unanswered, she's refusing to accept them. Each letter requires a fresh stratagem and they're not all successful.

You'll recall how simply I managed to get the first one to her. The second one was equally easy: she had asked me to return her letter; quite unsuspectingly, she got mine instead. But either because she resented being taken in or from some whim or other or even the voice of conscience—I'm being forced to take that voice seriously—she stubbornly declined to accept the third one. However, I have hopes that the embarrassment which nearly resulted from that refusal will make her think twice next time.

I wasn't really surprised that she didn't accept this third letter when I merely tried to hand it to her: that would have meant climbing down, and I'm anticipating a more spirited defence. After this attempt, made purely on the off-chance, I put my letter into an envelope and seizing the opportunity as she was dressing for dinner in the presence of Madame de Rosemonde and her maid, I got my man to take it in to her, instructing him to say it was the document she'd been asking for. I'd assumed, quite rightly, that she'd be scared of the scandal involved in having to explain should she refuse it, and she did, in fact, accept the letter. I'd told my emissary to watch her closely; he has quite a sharp eye and failed to detect anything more than a faint flush in her cheeks, embarrassment rather than anger.

I was naturally congratulating myself that she would either keep the letter or if she wanted to return it, would have to see me alone, giving me the chance to speak with her. About an hour later, one of her servants comes into my room and on behalf of his mistress hands me an envelope, different from mine, addressed in the handwriting which I was longing to see. I tore it open. It was my own letter, unopened and merely folded in half. I suspect that this diabolical trick was inspired by her fear that I'd be less scared of any scandal than she would.

You know what I'm like and I don't need to tell you that I flew into a rage. However, as I've got to find other ways, I've now calmed down. This is the only idea I could come up with.

Every morning they go and pick up the mail at the post, which is just over a mile from here. They use a box, something like a church offertory box; the postmaster has one key, Madame de Rosemonde the other. Everybody puts their letters in this box any time they like during the day, then they're taken to the post every evening and letters that have come in are collected every morning. The servants, including the guests' servants, take it in turns to operate this system. It wasn't my man's turn but he volunteered to do it, pretending he had business nearby.

Meanwhile I wrote my letter, disguising my handwriting for the address and producing a reasonably good imitation of the Dijon stamp on the envelope. I chose Dijon because I felt it was more fun, since I was soliciting the husband's rights, to write from that town and also because my lovely lady had been talking all day about how much she was looking forward to getting letters from Dijon. I felt it was up to me to gratify such conjugal concern.

Having arranged all this, it was child's play to slip my letter in with the rest. This subterfuge gave me the added advantage of enabling me to watch her receive it, as it's the practice here to congregate at breakfast-time and before going our own ways, wait for the post to arrive, which it finally did.

Madame de Rosemonde unlocked the box. 'One from Dijon,' she said, passing my letter to Madame de Tourvel. 'That's not my husband's writing!' the judge's wife said anxiously and quickly slit open the envelope. One glance sufficed and her face was so transfixed that Madame de Rosemonde noticed and asked: 'What's the matter?' I went over to her as well and said: 'Is it really such distressing news?' The saintly woman was hanging her head in embarrassment, not trusting herself to say a word; she pretended to run her eyes over the letter which she was hardly in a fit state to read. Enjoying her confusion and welcoming the chance to goad her a little, I added: 'You seem less upset . . . I trust that means that your letter contained just unexpected news, not bad news.' At this her anger got the better of her discretion. 'It contains things that are grossly offensive,' she retorted, 'and I'm amazed that anyone could presume to write such a letter.' 'But who . . . ?' Madame de Rosemonde interposed. 'It's not signed', the lovely lady replied angrily, 'but I consider that the letter and its author are both equally contemptible. I don't want to say anything more on the subject.' So saying, she tore the shameless epistle up, stuffed the pieces into her pocket, sprang to her feet and left the room.*

She may be angry but she's still got my letter and I'm quite content to leave it to her curiosity to peruse it right through.

A detailed account of my day would take me too far. Here are drafts of my two letters,* so now you're as well informed as I am. If you want to be kept up to date with this correspondence, you must get used to deciphering my scribble: copying them out would be too excruciatingly boring for words. Goodbye, lovely lady.

35

The Vicomte de Valmont to Madame de Tourvel
21 August 17—

I must obey you, Madame; I must prove that for all the faults you like to credit me with, I still have enough delicacy of feeling not to lay myself open to reproach and the courage to accept the most grievous sacrifices. You order me to leave you alone and to forget you. So be it: I shall force my heart to be silent and I shall forget, if I can, how cruelly you have treated it. Certainly my longing to please you gave me no right to succeed in doing so, nor did my need for your indulgence entitle me to obtain it. But you call my love offensive, forgetting that however wrong it might be, you were its sole cause and justification. You forget too that, as I had become accustomed to baring my innermost soul to you, even though my frankness could do me harm, I had lost the ability to conceal the feelings which were overwhelming me, so that what you consider my impudence was nothing but my good faith. And so your reward for my most true, most tender, and most respectful love is to banish me. You even speak of hating me . . . Who else would not complain at such treatment? But I shall not complain, I shall submit and suffer in silence; you strike me down, I worship you. Your power over me is unimaginable, you control my feelings absolutely; and if my love is able to resist you and you are unable to destroy it, this is only because this love is of your making, not mine.

I am not asking for your love in return; I have never deluded myself on that score. I don't even expect the compassion which your earlier interest in me might at times have led me to hope for. But I confess that I do think I may appeal to your sense of justice.

You tell me that people have been trying to poison your mind against me and that had you taken your friends' advice to heart, you would not even have let me hear you: those were your very words. Who are these busybodies? Surely such stern judges, with such rigid principles, will not refuse to be named? Surely they would not wish to take refuge in secrecy and behave like any low gossipmonger? I shall then no longer be left in ignorance of their names and of their accusations. I would ask you to remember, dear Madame, that since you are passing judgement on me on their testimony, I have the right to know both these things. No one finds a man guilty without telling him his crime or naming his accusers. That is the only favour I ask of you and I undertake in advance to justify myself and force them to retract.

If I may have displayed too openly my contempt for the empty babble of public opinion for which I've no great respect, your good opinion of me is quite another matter; and since I intend to dedicate my life to obtaining it, I shan't stand idly by and let anyone deprive me of it. And it is all the more precious to me inasmuch as it is your good opinion of me which will no doubt allow you to make the request that you are afraid to make and which, you say, might even allow me *to enjoy your gratitude*. Ah, far from demanding your gratitude, I shall feel that I owe gratitude to you for giving me the chance to please you. So start treating me more fairly: don't keep hiding from me what you wish me to do. Were I able to read your mind, I should spare you the trouble of having to tell me. And if with the pleasure of meeting you I have the added good fortune of serving you, I shall be even better rewarded by your forgiveness. What could hold you back? I hope that it's not your fear that I might refuse, that's something I couldn't forgive. My failure to return your letter wasn't a refusal; I'm even more anxious than you that I shall have no further need for it. You see, having become used to thinking that you have such a gentle soul, it's only in that letter that you appear as you wish to appear. Whenever I feel the desire to soften your heart, it tells me that rather than let me do so, you would take refuge far away from me; when everything about you strengthens and justifies my love, it is your letter that informs me that my love is *offensive*; and every time I see you and my love for you seems a blessing from Heaven, I only need to read it to realize that it is just a cruel martyrdom. As you see, nothing would make me happier than to return this horrible document; and for you to ask me for it once again would justify me in thinking that I need no longer believe in its contents. I hope you have no doubts as to my eagerness to hand it back to you.

36

The Vicomte de Valmont to Madame de Tourvel
(*postmarked from Dijon*)
23 August 17—

You are growing stricter every day, Madame, and, dare I say it? you seem less afraid of being unfair than of showing indulgence. After condemning me unheard, you must indeed have concluded that it would be easier to leave my arguments unread than to reply to them. You stubbornly refuse to accept my letters and send them back with contempt. At the very time when my sole aim is to convince you of my good faith, you are forcing me to stoop to deceit. My need to defend myself against you is surely sufficient to excuse my methods. In any case, I am so convinced of the sincerity of my feelings, so convinced that I need only to explain them fully to you in order to justify them in your eyes, that I thought it permissible to employ this slight subterfuge. I'm hopeful that you will forgive me and not be greatly surprised that love is more ingenious in revealing itself than indifference in brushing it aside.

So allow me, dear Madame de Tourvel, to bare my heart completely. It belongs to you and it is right for you to learn its secrets.

When I arrived at Madame de Rosemonde's I had not the remotest idea of the fate awaiting me. I did not know that you were here and may I add, with my usual bluntness, that even had I known, I should not have felt in any way apprehensive; not that I failed to give due credit to your beauty but having fallen into the habit of feeling nothing but desire and only following those desires where I could hope to succeed, I knew nothing of the agony of love.

You yourself saw how strongly Madame de Rosemonde urged me to stay on for a while. I had already spent one day with you yet I merely gave way, or thought that I was giving way, to the very natural and legitimate pleasure of showing my regard for a relative whom I respect. The style of life here was certainly very different from what I was accustomed to; I found no difficulty in fitting in with it and without trying to probe into the reasons for the change taking place within me, I attributed it solely to my easy-going nature which I believe I have already mentioned to you.

Unhappily (why has it to be unhappily?), as I got to know you better, I quickly realized that your entrancing face, which was your only feature which had struck me, was the least of your charms; my soul was stirred and bewitched by your heavenly spirituality. From admiring your beauty, I came to worship your virtue. Without any hope of winning you, I made an effort to be worthy of you. By asking you to forgive my past, I was eager to obtain your future approval. I tried to read it into your words, I watched for it in your eyes!—in those eyes which were sending out a poison all the more insidious because it was being unwittingly discharged against an unsuspecting target.

And so I learned the meaning of love. But no thought of complaining ever remotely crossed my mind! I was resolved to bury it in silence for ever and I had no fears in plunging whole-heartedly into this delightful emotion. Its power over me grew stronger every day; soon the pleasure of seeing you turned into a necessity. If you were away for a second, my heart sank; when I heard you coming back, it pounded with joy. I existed only through you and for you. Yet I call on you yourself to bear witness: during all our games and light-hearted fun or our serious conversations, did I ever let slip a single word to betray my secret love?

Finally the day came which was to usher in all my misfortunes and by some unbelievable mischance it was an act of generosity which gave rise to them. Yes, it was while I was with those unfortunate folk whom I had helped and you were displaying that admirable tender-heartedness which makes beauty all the lovelier and virtue even more precious that you finally threw my heart, already drunk with love, into a frenzy. Perhaps you may remember how preoccupied I was as we drove back? I was struggling to resist an emotion that I felt threatening to overwhelm me.

When my strength had become exhausted in this uneven struggle, I found myself, by some unforeseeable chance, alone with you. And then, I admit, I succumbed: my heart was too full to hold back my words and my tears. But is that a crime? And if it is, has it not been punished enough by the agonies I've been suffering?

I am ravaged by a hopeless love; I am pleading for compassion and you offer me only hatred. Seeing you is my only joy and in spite of myself I constantly look in your direction even though I'm terrified that our eyes may meet. You have reduced me to the frightful plight of spending my days concealing my sorrows and my nights tormented by them, whilst you remain calm and peaceful and know nothing about my miserable state, except that you're the cause of it; and that gives you great satisfaction. Yet it's you who are complaining and I who am apologizing . . .

So there you have, Madame de Tourvel, the true account of what you describe as my offensive conduct, which might more fairly be called my misfortunes. Love, sincere and pure, unfailing respect, utter obedience: those are the feelings you have inspired in me. I should have felt no qualms in offering them to the Divinity Himself. Ah, dear Madame, you are His finest creation, follow His example of infinite mercy! Do not forget my sufferings and, above all, do not forget that, poised as I am between the pinnacles of happiness and the depths of despair, the first word that you utter will decide my fate for ever.

37

Madame de Tourvel to Madame de Volanges
25 August 17—

I intend to defer to your friendly advice, Madame. I have become so used to accepting your judgement in everything, in the belief that it is always based on good sense. I'll even admit that this Vicomte de Valmont must indeed be dangerous in the extreme if he can pretend to be what he seems to be here while still remaining the man you have described. But anyway, since you insist, I shall send him away or at least do all that I can to achieve that result: things that should be very simple in theory turn out to be very embarrassing in practice.

To my mind it still seems impracticable for me to ask his aunt to take any action; it would be invidious both for her and for him. I should also be somewhat reluctant to agree to leave myself because, apart from the reasons I've already given with regard to my husband, if my departure were to run counter to Monsieur de Valmont's ideas, which is not impossible, wouldn't it be quite easy for him to follow me to Paris? And wouldn't his return, prompted or apparently prompted by mine, seem stranger than our having met in the country, in the house of someone known to be his relative as well as a friend of mine?

So there's no other possibility open but for me to prevail on him to have the kindness to leave himself. I have the feeling that it will not be easy to make that suggestion but as he seems to be keen to prove to me that he's more honourable than his reputation implies, I have some hope of success. In fact, I shall not be loath to make the attempt; it will give me the chance of seeing if, as he repeatedly claims, really respectable women never have had nor ever will have cause to complain of his behaviour. If he does fall in with my request, it will indeed be out of consideration for me, since I have no doubt that he's planning to spend a large part of the autumn here. If he refuses and insists on staying on, then it will be time for me to leave myself and I promise you to do so.

So there we have, I think, everything that, in your friendly concern for my welfare, you wanted me to do. I shall lose no time in doing it and prove to you, dear Madame de Volanges, that the warmth I may have shown in defending Monsieur de Valmont doesn't in any way hinder me not only from listening to but even from following my good friend's advice.

With kindest regards, I am, etc.

38

The Marquise de Merteuil to the Vicomte de Valmont
27 August 17—

Your massive packet has just arrived, my dear Vicomte. If the date on it is correct, I ought to have received it some twenty-four hours ago. Anyway, if I were to spend my time reading it now, I shouldn't have any left to reply to it, so I prefer merely to acknowledge it and we'll chat about other things now. It's not that there's anything much to tell you about myself; with autumn on its way, there's hardly any identifiably human male left in Paris so for the last month I've been devastatingly good and anyone but my knight would be thoroughly sick and tired of my constancy. So having nothing to do, I'm whiling away my time with the Volanges girl and I'd like to talk to you about her.

Do you know, you've missed more than you think by not taking on that little girl? She's absolutely scrumptious! vapid and unprincipled: just imagine what a sweet, easy-going partner she'll make! I don't think she's ever going to be strong on sentiment but she promises to have lots and lots of temperament. Lacks intelligence and subtlety but she has a sort of natural deceitfulness, if you can understand me, which sometimes amazes even me and will make her a great success, particularly as her face is a picture of innocence and candour. She's got an extremely affectionate nature and now and again I have fun leading her on: her little brain sparks off on the slightest provocation and then she's all the more comic because she's got no idea, not the vaguest inkling, of what she's so anxious to know. She becomes so impatient that she's really funny: she laughs, gets upset, starts crying and then asks me to tell her all about it with an innocence which is utterly entrancing. To tell you the truth, I'm almost jealous of the man who's destined to have that pleasure.

I forget if I told you that for the last four or five days she's been taking me into her confidence. As you can guess, at first I made out to be very strict but as soon as I realized that she thought she'd persuaded me with her bad arguments, I pretended they were good ones and accepted them: she's fully convinced that she owes her success to her powers of persuasion. I had to be cautious to avoid compromising myself. I allowed her to write and say *I love you* and that very same day, without her realizing it, I arranged for her to be alone with Danceny. But can you credit it? He's still so wet behind the ears that he didn't even manage to obtain a kiss! Yet that young fellow writes very charming poetry! God, aren't brainy people obtuse! And this one's quite embarrassingly so! After all, it's not up to me to guide *his* steps.

It's now that you'd be so useful to me. You know Danceny well enough to gain his confidence and once you'd got that, we could go ahead like a house on fire. So do despatch your judge's wife double-quick because I really do not want Gercourt to get away with it. And incidentally, I told the little body about him yesterday and painted such a pretty picture of him that she'd have a job to hate him more even after ten years of married life. However, I read her a long lecture on a wife's duty to be faithful: there's nobody stricter on that topic than me. Doing this will enable me on the one hand to restore my reputation as a woman of impeccable morality which might be damaged if I appeared too broad-minded; and on the other to make her hate him more, which is precisely the wedding present I wish to give to the groom. And finally, by making her think that she'll be free to indulge in love only for the short time before her marriage, she'll be quicker to make up her mind not to waste a second.

Farewell, my dear Vicomte. I shall now read your weighty tome while getting dressed.

39
Cécile Volanges to Sophie Carnay
Paris, 27 August 17—

Sophie darling, I'm worried and miserable. I've been crying nearly all night. It's not that for the moment I'm not very happy but I can't see it lasting.

Yesterday I went to the Opéra with Madame de Merteuil. We talked a lot about my marriage and what she told me wasn't very nice. I'm meant to marry Monsieur le Comte de Gercourt. He's rich, he's got a title, and he's colonel of the ——th regiment. So far so good. But first of all, he's positively ancient! Just imagine, he's at least thirty-six!!! And then Madame de Merteuil says he's glum and stern and she's afraid I shan't be very happy with him. In fact, it seemed quite plain to me that she's sure of it and she just didn't want to tell me so, so as not to make me miserable. She scarcely talked of anything else the whole evening but a wife's duty towards her husband; she agrees that Monsieur de Gercourt isn't a bit agreeable but she still says I've got to love him. And didn't she also say that once I'm married I shall have to stop loving Chevalier Danceny? As if that was possible! Oh, Sophie dear, I swear I'll always love him. Do you know, I'd sooner not get married at all! Monsieur de Gercourt can do what he likes, I didn't ask for him! At the moment he's in Corsica which is a long way from here and I only hope he stays there for ten years. If I wasn't scared of going back to the convent, I'd jolly well tell Mummy that I don't want that man as a husband. But that'd be even worse. I hardly know which way to turn. I feel that I've never loved Monsieur Danceny so much as I do now and when I consider that I've only got one month to stay as I am, I can feel tears coming to my eyes straight away. My only comfort is Madame de Merteuil's friendliness, she's so kind-hearted and when I'm miserable she's as miserable as me and then she's so nice that when I'm with her, I always forget my troubles. And she's very helpful to me as well, because I don't know much and all that I do know comes from her and she's so kind that I can tell her all my thoughts without feeling bashful at all. When she thinks they're a bit naughty, she sometimes tells me off but quite nicely and then I give her a big, big hug until she's stopped being cross with me. At least I can love her as much as I like without it being wrong and I'm very pleased at that. But we've agreed that I wouldn't appear to be so fond of her in public and specially in front of Mummy so that she doesn't suspect anything about Chevalier Danceny. I promise you that if I could go on living all the time like I am now, I think I'd be very happy. There's only nasty old Gercourt . . . But I don't want to talk about him any more, it'd make me miserable again. Instead I'm going to write to Chevalier Danceny. I'll only talk to him about my love, not about my troubles, because I don't want to make him sad.

Goodbye, dear, dear Sophie. You can see that you oughtn't to grumble and though I'm occupied,* as you put it, I can still find time to love and write to you.*

40

The Vicomte de Valmont to the Marquise de Merteuil
27 August 17—

Not content with refusing to answer my letters, refusing even to take them, that fiendish woman wants to stop me from seeing her, she's insisting I go away. What will surprise you even more is that I'm prepared to bow to her harsh decision. You're going to tell me off. However, I thought that I shouldn't miss the opportunity of being ordered about by her, as I'm convinced, first, that someone who delivers orders also accepts a commitment, and secondly, that letting a woman apparently exercise fictitious authority over us is one of the pitfalls they find most difficult to avoid. What's more, her skill in managing not to be left alone with me was placing me in a dangerous predicament which I realized I must escape from at all costs: by being constantly with her yet unable to keep her aware of my love, there was a fear that she might eventually become used to being in my company without feeling uneasy—and I don't need to tell you that is an attitude very hard to shake off.

Moreover, as you may guess, I didn't submit unconditionally. I even made sure that one of my conditions was impossible to accept, thereby retaining the option of either keeping my word or breaking it, as well as entering into a dialogue with my beauty, either orally or in writing, at a time when she seems rather more kindly disposed towards me and needs me to be in similar mood; and let's not forget that I'd be extremely inept not to be able to find some way of obtaining compensation for waiving my claim, however indefensible.

After this long preamble explaining my reasons, let me begin the chronicle of these last two days; I include the dear lady's letter and my reply as documentary evidence. You must agree that there are few more conscientious historians than I.

You'll recall the impact of my Dijon letter a couple of mornings ago? The remainder of the day was very stormy. The pretty prude only appeared when dinner was just about to start and reported that she had a bad sick headache: a pretext to cover one of the most violent attacks of feminine foul temper ever; she looked really savage and the gentleness you know so well had been replaced by a defiant look which gave her quite a different style of beauty. I made a mental note to exploit this discovery on some future occasion and now and again have the defiant mistress as a change from the tender one.

I anticipated a dreary afternoon and to escape this boring prospect, I took myself off on the plea of having some letters to write. I came down to the drawing-room around six o'clock. Madame de Rosemonde suggested going for a drive and we agreed, but just as we were getting into the carriage, the bogus invalid, with truly diabolical malevolence, perhaps getting her own back for my earlier defection, herself pleaded a worsening headache and ruthlessly abandoned me to the tender mercies of my old aunt. I don't know if the curses I called down on this she-devil's head were answered but on returning from the drive we discovered she had gone to bed.

Next day at breakfast she was a woman transformed. Her natural gentleness had returned and I had grounds for believing that I was forgiven. Hardly was breakfast over than this gentle creature casually stood up and went off into the park. As you may imagine, I quickly followed her. 'Why this sudden urge for exercise?' I enquired as I caught up with her. 'I did a lot of writing this morning,' she replied, 'and my head is a trifle tired.' 'I suppose I'm not the lucky man who's to blame for your tiredness?' I said. 'I did write to you,' she replied, 'but I can't decide whether to give it to you. It contains a request and till now you haven't given me much encouragement to hope for any success.' 'Oh, I give you my word, if it's at all possible . . .' She cut me short: 'There's nothing easier and though you ought really to agree to it out of a sense of justice, I'm willing to accept it as a favour.' She held out her letter and as I took it, I grasped her hand which she drew away, not angrily or even brusquely but with embarrassment. 'It's warmer out than I thought,' she said. 'Let's go in.' She turned to go back to the château. I tried unsuccessfully to persuade her to continue our walk and if I hadn't remembered that we could be seen from the house I'd have resorted to other means than persuasion. She went in without another word and I realized that this alleged 'walk' was purely a scheme to hand me the letter. When we got back, she went straight up to her room and I went to mine to read the following missive which I recommend you to read too, as well as my reply, before we proceed further.

41

Madame de Tourvel to the Vicomte de Valmont
25 August 17—

It would seem, Monsieur de Valmont, that your conduct towards me has the sole aim of adding daily to my grievances against you. Your persistent harping on a feeling which I neither ought nor wish to hear mentioned; your ruthlessness in exploiting my good faith or my confusion in order to pass me your letters; above all, the device, which I venture to suggest was dishonest, that you employed to send me your last one, quite regardless of the possibility that my surprise could have compromised me—such behaviour clearly deserves my strong condemnation. However, rather than going over past grievances, I shall merely make one simple and fair request and if you agree to it, I am willing to let bygones be bygones.

You yourself said that I need have no fear of being refused and though, by the odd sort of logic which seems to be one of your peculiarities, that statement was followed by the only refusal which you could make,* I'm prepared to believe that you will nevertheless stick to your word, as you formally agreed only a few days ago.

I want you to have the kindness to go away, to leave this house where, if you stay any longer, you will be increasingly exposing me to the disapproval of a society always ready to think ill of people and which has all too often been prompted by your conduct to keep a sharp eye on any women who admit you into their company.

I had already been warned long ago of this danger by my friends but had disregarded and even defied their views as long as your conduct towards me could persuade me that you were kind enough not to mistake me for one of that host of women, all of whom had cause for complaint against you. Now that you are treating me like them and that I can no longer close my eyes to the fact, I owe it to society, to my friends, and to myself to take the necessary action. I may add that you will gain nothing from refusing to agree to my request since, should you persist in staying on, I am determined to leave myself; however, as I have no desire to underrate my obligation to you if you do me this favour, I should like you to know that by forcing me to leave, you would be seriously disrupting my plans. So prove to me, Monsieur de Valmont, that, as you have so often asserted, decent women will never have reason to complain of your treatment of them; at least prove to me that when you have behaved badly towards them, you are prepared to make amends.

If I thought my request required any justification, I would need only to point out that, though you have spent your life proving it necessary, had it depended on me, it would never have been made. But let us not go back over events which I prefer to forget and which would lead me to judge you harshly at a time when I am offering you the chance to earn my sincere gratitude.

Goodbye, Monsieur; it is now your conduct which will tell me in what sense I may consider myself your very humble, etc.

42

The Vicomte de Valmont to Madame de Tourvel
26 August 17—

Harsh though your conditions may be, Madame, I cannot refuse to accept them. I feel it impossible to oppose any wish of yours. Having agreed to that, I venture to hope that you will allow me, in return, to make a few requests, much easier to meet than yours, but which I want you to grant only because I am submitting to your wishes unconditionally.

The first of these, which I hope will appeal to your sense of justice, is that you will be good enough finally to tell me the names of those who have accused me; it seems to me that the harm they are doing me is sufficient to entitle me to know who they are. The second, which I hope to receive as proof of your forgiveness, is that you be willing to allow me from time to time to express to you my love which now more than ever will deserve your pity.

I ask you not to forget, Madame, that my eagerness to obey you comes at the cost of my happiness and even in spite of my strong belief that you want me to leave because you find the sight of the victim of your injustice too painful to bear. For you must agree, Madame, that you are not so much afraid of the opinion of society, far too accustomed to show you respect to venture to criticize you, as you are embarrassed by the presence of a man whom it is easier to punish than to condemn. You are banishing me from your sight in the same way as people turn their eyes away from any unfortunate wretch whom they do not wish to help.

But while absence is going to add immeasurably to my misery, where else can I turn to express it but to you? From whom else but you can I hope to receive the solace I shall so desperately need? Can you refuse me this when it is you who are the sole source of my suffering?

You will surely not be surprised, either, to know that before leaving I am anxious to justify to you in person the feelings you have inspired in me and that I can find the courage to leave only if I hear the order from your own lips.

These reasons encourage me to ask you to grant me a short interview. It would be useless to hope to replace this by letters: one can write whole screeds and still not properly express what could be covered in a mere quarter of an hour's conversation. It should not be difficult for you to find the time for our meeting since, however eager I may be to obey you, Madame de Rosemonde, as you are aware, knows that I was planning to spend part of the autumn here and I shall have to wait at least to receive a letter before being able to plead urgent business requiring me to leave.

Farewell, Madame de Tourvel: never have I found that word so painful to write as I do at this moment: it reminds me that we must part. If you could imagine the immense grief which that causes me, I venture to think that you would feel some gratitude towards me for obeying you. May I at least hope that you will show greater understanding for my most tender and respectful love?

I am, Madame, yours, etc.

Letter 40 (contd.)

The Vicomte de Valmont to the Marquise de Merteuil

And now, my dear, let's analyse the situation. You will feel, with me, that our scrupulous and respectable Madame de Tourvel can't possibly grant the first of my requests and betray her friends' trust by letting me know the names of my accusers; ergo, by making all my promises dependent on that one condition, I'm committing myself to absolutely nothing, but you will also feel that this inescapable refusal will entitle me to get everything else and that by going away I earn the right to enter, with her consent, into a regular correspondence with her. I don't attach a great deal of importance to the interview I'm asking her for, which is really nothing but a preliminary softening-up process so that she'll not be able to deny me others later on, when they become really necessary.

The only thing left for me to do before leaving is to discover who are these people who are so busy damaging my reputation.

I presume it's her pettifogging husband; I hope it is: apart from the fact that a husband's veto adds spice to one's appetite, once my beauty agrees to write to me, I'll be sure of having nothing further to fear from her husband as she'll already have been obliged to deceive him. But if there happens to be a close woman friend who is in her confidence and has her knife in me, it'll be necessary to break up their friendship. I'm pretty sure I can manage that but I do need the information.

Yesterday I thought I was actually going to get it but that woman never behaves like other women. We were in her room when we were told that dinner was served. As she had only just finished dressing, while she was hurrying to get ready and apologizing, I noticed that she'd left her key in her secretaire and I knew she habitually left her room unlocked. This kept running through my mind over dinner and when I heard her maid come downstairs, I took a quick decision, pretended I'd got a sudden nose-bleed, left the table, and quickly made for the secretaire only to find all the drawers had been left open and there was not a document in sight. Yet at this time of year there's no possibility of burning them. What's she doing with the letters she receives? And what a lot she's getting! I checked everything; nothing was locked up and I looked everywhere, but all I succeeded in doing was to convince myself that she must be hoarding those precious letters in the pockets of her clothes.

How can I get at them there? Ever since yesterday I've been vainly trying to find a way but I'm still hoping to find some solution or other. What a pity I'm not a pickpocket! Training in that valuable art should surely form part of the education of any man keen on the fair sex. What fun it'd be to steal a rival's letter or portrait or to abstract from a prudish woman's pocket something that'd show her up in her true colours! But our parents have just no idea and though I myself am brimful of them, I can only recognize how clumsy I am—and with no hope of improving . . .

Be that as it may, I went back to table extremely put out. However, the lovely lady mollified me somewhat by showing interest in my pretended indisposition and I availed myself of the opportunity to inform her that recently I'd been in a terribly agitated state of mind which had been seriously affecting my health. Since she's convinced that she's the cause of this, shouldn't she in all conscience do something to relieve it? But though she's very godly, she's not very charitable; she's unwilling to include love in her donations and that to my mind justifies me in obtaining it by stealth. But now I must go; all the while I'm chatting with you, I keep fretting over those damned letters.

43

Madame de Tourvel to the Vicomte de Valmont
27 August 17—

Why are you doing your best to make me feel less grateful? Why are you prepared only to half-obey me and trying somehow to bargain over what is the honourable thing to do? Aren't you satisfied merely to know how much I appreciate your action? You're not just asking a great deal, you're demanding something impossible. If my friends did in fact tell me about you, their only motive could have been their concern for my welfare; even if they were mistaken, their intentions were still good. And you are suggesting that I should reward them for that proof of their affection by betraying their secret! It was wrong of me to mention the matter to you in the first place and you have brought this home to me very plainly. With anyone else, it would have been seen as frankness, with you it was clearly a miscalculation. Granting your request would be grossly improper on my part. I appeal to your own sense of decency: did you imagine that I was capable of such an action? Ought you indeed ever to have suggested it to me? Certainly not, and I am sure that on reflection you will never put forward such a request again.

Your other request, to write to me, is not much easier to agree to and in all fairness you can scarcely blame me for that. With the greatest respect, in view of your past reputation which, on your own admission, you have at least in part deserved, what woman could admit to being in correspondence with you? And what decent woman can agree to do something she would feel obliged to hide?

And then again, if only I was able to be sure that your letters would never give cause for complaint, if only I could always feel justified, in my own eyes, in receiving them! If that were the case, perhaps my wish to prove to you that I was acting fairly and not out of hatred would allow me to disregard these powerful considerations and go far beyond what I ought to do by letting you write to me occasionally. If you in fact want this as much as you claim, you will be willing to submit to the only condition which will permit me to agree to it; so if you feel some gratitude for what I am doing for you at the moment, do not delay your departure any longer.

And may I point out that you received a letter this morning but failed to seize that opportunity of informing Madame de Rosemonde that you were leaving, as you had promised. I hope that nothing will now stand in the way of your keeping your word. In particular, I am relying on you first of all not to delay your departure until you have had the interview with me for which you ask, since I am firmly determined not to grant it; and secondly instead of waiting for the order which you seem to feel is required, to be satisfied if I merely repeat the earnest request which I have already made.

Goodbye, Monsieur de Valmont.

44
The Vicomte de Valmont to the Marquise de Merteuil
28 August 17—

Let us rejoice together, fair lady: she loves me; I have conquered that defiant heart. Try as she may, she cannot hide the fact any longer: my brilliant skill and persistent energy have uncovered her secret and told me all I need to know. Since last night—ah, happy night!—I've found myself once again in my element, I've started living! I have unveiled a dual mystery of love and villainy: the first, I shall enjoy; the second, I shall exact retribution for; I shall flit from pleasure to pleasure! The very thought is throwing me into a rapture of delight which is making it rather hard for me to restrain myself and perhaps even to give a coherent account of all the events. Let me try nevertheless.

Only yesterday, after writing to you, I got a letter from my pious angel which I enclose. You can see that she gives me, with the minimum embarrassment possible, permission to write to her but as she keeps urging me to leave, I felt that I couldn't delay much longer without harming my cause.

But I was still fretting about not knowing who could have written attacking me and wasn't quite ready to take a final decision. I tried to persuade the maid to let me have the contents of her mistress's pockets, which she could easily have laid hands on overnight and replaced next morning without arousing the slightest suspicion. For this piddling service I offered two hundred francs but she proved to be a prim girl, either too scrupulous or else too scared, who couldn't be persuaded or bribed. My eloquent exhortations were cut short by the supper bell. I had to leave her, only too glad that she agreed to stay mum, which, you may imagine, I hardly dared expect. I've never been more annoyed in my life. I felt compromised and spent the whole evening cursing myself for my foolhardiness.

When I went back to my room, still not easy in my mind, I had a word with my valet who, as the lucky lover, is bound to have a certain influence with the girl. I wanted him either to get her to do what I'd asked or else to make quite sure she'd keep her mouth shut. He, however, normally so self-confident, seemed doubtful of succeeding in this negotiation and made a comment which struck me as very profound.

'I'm sure your lordship knows better than me,' he said, 'that going to bed with a girl only means getting her to do something she wants to do, but from that to getting her to do what *we* want is often quite another story.'

*Le bon sens du Maraud quelquefois m'épouvante.**

'I'm all the more doubtful about her,' he went on, 'because I've a strong suspicion she's got a boyfriend and that I only made her because there's not much else to do in the country. If I hadn't wanted to oblige your lordship, I'd've only had her once' (what a gem this young fellow is!). 'As for keeping her mouth shut,' he added, 'what's the point of getting her to promise when she's nothing to lose even if she did let us down? Mentioning it again would only make her realize its importance and make her want to suck up to her mistress even more.'

His remarks made good sense and that increased my embarrassment. Luckily the rogue was in a chatty mood and as I needed his help, I let him go on. In the course of telling me all about his doings with the maid, he informed me that as the girl's bedroom was separated from her mistress's only by a thin partition and any suspicious sound could be heard next door, she spent every night in his room. I had a sudden inspiration, explained my plan to him and we've succeeded in carrying it out.

I waited until two o'clock in the morning and then, as arranged, made my way, carrying a candle, to the said room, pretending that I'd rung for him several times without result. My accomplice, who acts his parts superbly, put on a little scene of surprise, dismay, and penitence which I cut short by pretending to need some hot water and sent him off to heat it up. Meanwhile, the scrupulous maid was all the more embarrassed because the rogue had improved on my scenario by getting her to strip off to a state of undress perfectly appropriate to the season but hardly justified by the weather alone.

Feeling that the more I could humiliate her, the greater my chances of getting her to do what I wanted, I refused to let her move or cover her charms and having instructed my man to wait in my room, I sat down beside her on the bed, which was in a state of great disarray, and started my little homily while maintaining perfect control over my feelings that wouldn't have disgraced Scipio* himself; I needed to retain the hold over her so providentially provided by her predicament. So without taking the slightest liberty with her (something which, incidentally, her situation and youthful beauty might have led her to hope for), I got down to business with her as calmly as if I'd been talking to my attorney.

My conditions were that I would observe complete discretion so long as she, at roughly the same time on the following day, would let me have the papers in her mistress's pockets. 'Moreover,' I added, 'yesterday I promised you ten louis and that offer still stands. I don't want to take unfair advantage of your situation.' As you may imagine, she agreed to everything* and I withdrew, leaving the happy couple to make up for lost time.

I spent my time sleeping and when I woke up, as I needed some excuse for not answering my lovely lady's letter until I'd gone through her correspondence, which I couldn't do until the coming night, I decided to spend the whole day shooting.

I returned to a cool reception. I get the impression that feelings had been hurt by my qualified rapture in failing to take full advantage of the short time left to me, particularly in view of the rather friendlier letter which I'd received. This impression stems from the fact that when Madame de Rosemonde gently rebuked me for staying out all day, my beauty said rather acidly: 'Oh, we mustn't blame Monsieur de Valmont for indulging in the only sport available to him here.' I protested against such an unfair comment and took the opportunity of assuring the ladies that I enjoyed their company so much that I was forgoing the chance of writing a most interesting letter for their sakes. I added that having been unable to sleep for the last few nights, I wanted to see if thoroughly tiring myself out might do the trick; and my eyes explained pretty clearly both the subject of the letter and the cause of my insomnia. Throughout the evening I took care to maintain a gently melancholic mood which seemed to go down rather well and enabled me to conceal how impatiently I was waiting for the key which would at last unlock the mystery which was being so stubbornly kept from me. We broke up at last and a few moments later, true to her word, the maid brought me the price agreed to ensure my discretion.

Once I had this precious hoard in my possession, I set about making an inventory of its contents, in accordance with my cautious habits which you're familiar with: it was important to put everything back in its proper place. First up were two of the husband's letters, an indigestible mish-mash of court proceedings and flatulent ranting about conjugal love which I had the patience to read right through without finding a single mention of myself.* I angrily put them back but my anger melted when I came upon the torn-up pieces of my famous Dijon letter carefully pasted together. I felt a sudden urge to read it again and it was lucky I did: imagine my delight on detecting the very distinct stains of this saintly woman's adorable tears. I confess that

I gave way to youthful impulse and kissed the letter with a rapture I thought I'd lost ages ago. I continued my lucky dip and found the whole series of my letters arranged in order of their date; even more pleasing was the discovery of the first letter of all, which I thought had been so ungraciously returned to me, carefully copied out in her own hand, in shaky characters quite unlike her normal writing and proof enough of her disturbed state of mind whilst doing it.

Till now my thoughts were all of love; but it was soon replaced by rage. Who do you think is trying to ruin my reputation with the woman I adore? What fiend in woman's shape is evil enough to weave such an abominable plot? You know her, it's your friend and relative, Madame de Volanges. You cannot imagine the tissue of horrors that obnoxious old hag has written about me. It is she and she alone who has been disturbing my angel's peace of mind; it's her views and her pernicious advice that are forcing me to leave; in a word, it is she who has victimized me. Oh, there's no doubt about it, her daughter has got to be seduced; no, that's not enough. That woman must be smashed and since the old trout is too long in the tooth to be attacked directly, she must be made to suffer through someone she loves.

So she wants me to come back to Paris! She's forcing me to do so! Very well, I shall. But how I shall make her suffer for having to return! I'm sorry Danceny's the hero of this adventure; he's basically a decent young chap and that may prove awkward for us. However, he's in love and I often see him; we may be able to make use of that. I'm so angry that I'm letting my thoughts run wild and forgetting that I owe you an account of today's events. Let's go back.

This morning I saw my tender-hearted prude. Never had she seemed lovelier. That was inevitable: a woman's finest hour, the only time when she can arouse that spiritual ecstasy that people talk so much about—and experience so seldom—comes when we are sure she loves us but not yet sure whether we can enjoy her favours; and that's exactly the situation I'm in. Perhaps the thought that I was going to be deprived of the pleasure of seeing her also made her more beautiful. Finally, when the post arrived I was handed your letter of the 27th and as I read it I was still hesitating whether to keep my word or not; but I caught the eyes of my beauty and it would have been impossible to refuse her anything.

So I announced my departure. A moment later, Madame de Rosemonde left us alone but I was still four steps away from the coy young woman when she sprang to her feet. 'Please, Monsieur de Valmont, please leave me alone,' she exclaimed in a frightened voice. 'In God's name, don't come near me!' Such a frantic plea which betrayed her emotion could only spur me on; in a second I was by her side and had seized her hands which she was holding clasped with an intensely touching expression; but just as I was launching into protestations of my devotion some evil spirit brought Madame de Rosemonde back. The timid God-fearing woman—she's got good reason to be afraid—seized her chance and made for the door.

However, I offered my hand to escort her and she accepted it. Encouraged by this amiability which she hadn't displayed for a long while, I tried to squeeze her hand while continuing my protestations. At first she tried to draw it away but when I pressed her, she consented, not ungraciously though without responding to either my action or my words. When we reached the door of her suite, before releasing her hand I tried to kiss it. At first she firmly resisted but a tender whisper, *Don't forget I'm leaving*, left her flustered and uncertain. Hardly had the kiss been given than my lovely lady recovered and snatched her hand away to escape into her room and join her maid. So ends my story.

I assume you'll be at the Maréchale de B——'s tomorrow; as her house is definitely one where I'll not be coming to look for you and as I suspect we shall have more than one matter of business on the agenda at our first meeting, notably the Volanges girl, which I'm keeping well in mind, I've decided to send this letter on ahead, and though it's so long, I won't seal it until I'm ready to post it, because at this particular juncture all could depend on some opportunity turning up. I'm now off to see if I can find one.

PS 8 p.m. All quiet on all fronts; not a single free moment, in fact studiously avoided. However, at least as much melancholy as decency permitted. Another event that may have some relevance is that I've been asked by Madame de Rosemonde to pass on an invitation to Madame de Volanges to come and spend a little time down here in the country.

Goodbye, dear lady, I'll be seeing you tomorrow or the day after at the latest.

45

Madame de Tourvel to Madame de Volanges
From the Château de ——, 29 August 17—

Monsieur de Valmont left this morning; I felt I ought to inform you, Madame, since you seemed so anxious for him to do so. Madame de Rosemonde is extremely unhappy to see her nephew go and indeed it must be said that he is pleasant company; she spent the whole morning talking about him in the warm-hearted way you know so well; she could not stop singing his praises.* I thought it was only polite not to contradict her, particularly as it must be conceded that, in many ways, she was right. I felt more and more guilty at having been the cause of separating them and I have little hope of making amends for the pleasure I've deprived her of. As you know, I'm not a very lively person by nature and the sort of life we shall be leading here is not calculated to make me any more so.

Had it not been on your advice, I should have been concerned at having acted perhaps a trifle thoughtlessly. I was really unhappy to see that dear old lady so miserable and in tears and I wasn't far from shedding some myself.

Now we're living in hopes that you will be accepting the invitation which Monsieur de Valmont is due to convey to you from Madame de Rosemonde to come and spend some time here with her. I am sure you have no doubts as to how pleased I shall be to see you. I'll be delighted to make an earlier acquaintance with your daughter and to be in a position to convince you even more of the deep respect with which, etc. etc.

46

The Chevalier Danceny to Cécile Volanges
Paris, 29 August 17—

What has come over you, my adorable Cécile? What can have caused such a sudden cruel change in your attitude? What has become of your pledge never to change, which you repeated to me only yesterday and with such pleasure? What has made you forget it today? I have examined my conscience without finding any cause in myself and it is dreadful to have to look for it in you. Oh, you certainly aren't frivolous or deceitful and even in this moment of despair I shan't demean myself or insult you by letting any such suspicion cross my mind. Some trick of fate must have made you different, for you are different! The tender-hearted Cécile, the Cécile whom I adore, would never have avoided catching my eye, would never have refused the lucky chance that had placed me close to her. Or if for some reason which I can't comprehend she was obliged to treat me so unkindly, she would at least have condescended to tell me why.

Oh, Cécile, you don't realize, you can never realize how much you made me suffer, how much I'm still suffering. Do you imagine I can go on living without your love? Yet when I asked you for a word, one single word, to calm my fears, instead of answering you made the excuse, which wasn't true, of being afraid of being overheard and immediately made it come true by choosing to go over and join the others. When I was obliged to leave and asked you what time we could meet tomorrow you pretended not to know and it was left to your mother to tell me. And so the pleasure of being with you which I always look forward to with such joy has been ruined and the thought of seeing you which is such a comfort to me will be replaced by the fear of not being welcome.

Already I can feel that fear gripping me and preventing me from mentioning my love to you. But if you really have changed, the words *I love you*, which were so wonderful just to repeat over and over again when I could hear you echoing them, three words which were all I needed to make me blissfully happy, will only make me feel doomed to eternal despair. Yet I can't believe that those words have lost all their magic charm, so I shall still try to use them: yes, Cécile, *I love you*. So please, please, darling Cécile, repeat these words with me, for they comprise my whole happiness. Don't forget that it's you who've got me used to hearing them and that depriving me of them will condemn me to a torment which, like my love, will end only with my death.*

47

The Vicomte de Valmont to the Marquise de Merteuil
P——, 30 August 17—

I still shan't be able to see you today, fair lady, for the following reasons, for which I crave your indulgence.

Yesterday, instead of returning directly, I stopped off at the château of the Comtesse de —— which was more or less on my way and asked if I could stay for dinner. I didn't arrive in Paris till about 7 p.m. and called in at the Opéra in the hope of seeing you.

After the opera, I looked up my actress friends in the green-room where I met my old flame Émilie surrounded by a large circle of admirers, women as well as men, whom she was going to entertain in P—— that very night. Hardly had I joined them than they invited me, by general acclaim, to go along with them. I was also invited by a little dumpling of a man who issued his invitation in a sort of French double Dutch and in whom I recognized the real hero of the party. I accepted.

On the way there I learned that the house we were going to was Émilie's price for her favours contracted with this repulsive little man and the supper was truly a wedding feast. The little fellow could scarcely contain himself for joy in anticipation of the bliss in store for him. He seemed to me so smug that he gave me the desire to put a spoke in his wheel, which I in fact managed to do.

My only problem was getting Émilie to agree; the burgo-master's wealth was giving her a few scruples. However, after a little humming and hawing, she agreed to the plan which I proposed of filling this little beer-barrel up with wine and so putting him out of action for the rest of the night.

Our exalted conception of the capacity of a Dutch toper led us to employ every known method, with such success that by dessert he was already incapable of holding his own glass; but the charitable Émilie and myself vied with each other in topping him up. Finally he rolled under the table, so paralytic that it'll take him at least a week to recover. We decided to get him carted back to Paris and as he'd dismissed his own carriage I had him stowed into mine. Meanwhile I took his place, receiving the congratulations of the assembled company. Shortly afterwards they all departed, leaving me in undisputed possession of the field. All this fun and games and perhaps the cloistered life I'd been leading made Émilie so eminently desirable that I promised to stay with her until the Dutchman's resurrection.

This generous offer of mine is in return for hers in agreeing to let me use her as a writing-desk for a letter to my pious beauty which I've just finished: I thought it would be rather fun to send her a letter written in the bed, in the arms, almost, of a tart* (I broke off in the middle to commit an act of gross infidelity), in which I give an accurate account of my situation and my activities. Émilie's read it and it sent her into fits of laughter; I hope it'll make you laugh too.

As the letter in question has to bear the Paris postmark, I'm sending it to you, unsealed. May I ask you to read it, seal it, and see that it's posted? Be careful not to use your own seal or even any emblem relating to love; just a head. Goodbye, lovely lady.

PS I've opened this letter: I've persuaded Émilie to go to the Italians* . . . I'll take advantage of this to come and see you. I'll be there by six at the latest and if it's convenient, we'll go on to Madame de Volanges's together around seven o'clock. It would be hardly polite to delay delivering Madame de Rosemonde's invitation any longer; and I'm looking forward very much to seeing the Volanges girl, too.

Goodbye, fairest of the fair: I intend to embrace you so pleasurably that it will make your knight jealous.

48

Vicomte de Valmont to Madame de Tourvel
(*postmarked Paris*)
30 August 17—

After a stormy night during which I never closed an eye, after being in a constant state of restless, ravaging passion or in utter annihilation of every faculty of my soul, I come to find peace with you, Madame, a peace which I sorely need but which I cannot hope to enjoy. Indeed, the situation in which I find myself as I write makes me more aware than ever of the irresistible power of love. I have difficulty in retaining my self-control or putting some order into my thoughts. I can already feel that I shall not finish this letter without being obliged to break off. Oh, can I really not have some hope that one day you will share the troubled emotions which I am feeling at this moment? And yet I dare hope that were you really to know them, you would not remain entirely unmoved. Believe me, Madame, cold composure, the stagnation of the soul, a foretaste of death, these do not lead to happiness; ardour and passion offer the only path and in spite of the agony of suffering to which you are subjecting me, I'm not afraid to assert that I am happier than you. Your harshness is devastating and relentless but that does not prevent me from surrendering completely to love and in the frenzy it inspires, I can forget the despair into which you have plunged me. This is my way of trying to expunge the exile into which you've banished me. Never have I enjoyed writing to you so much; never have I felt whilst doing so such a tender, yet keen emotion. Everything seems to add to my delight: the air I am breathing is full of joy and pleasure; even the table on which I am pressing as I write, which has never before been devoted to such a purpose, has been turned into a holy altar of love in my eyes: and how much lovelier will it look later on! I shall have written down on it my pledge to love you for ever! I must beg you to forgive me: my senses are in disarray. Perhaps it is wrong for me to abandon myself so utterly to delights which you cannot share yourself. I must leave you a moment to relieve the frenzy which is overtaking, nay, overpowering me . . .

I come back to you, Madame, certainly with unabated eagerness but my happiness is gone and I am left with a feeling of cruel frustration. What point can there be in talking to you of my feelings if I cannot succeed in convincing you of them? After so many vain attempts, my confidence and my strength are both deserting me. If I now let my mind dwell on the pleasures of love it is in order to savour more keenly my sadness at being deprived of them. I can see no help but in your understanding and I feel at the moment all too conscious how much I need it to have any hope of obtaining it. Yet never was my love more respectful, never ought it to be less offensive to you; I venture to say that it is in a state such as the most virtuous woman should not be afraid of. But I am myself afraid of taking up too much of your time in telling you of my troubles. Since I am sure that the person who is causing them doesn't share them, I must at least not take advantage of her kindness as I should be doing were I to spend any longer painting you this unhappy picture. I shall merely use my remaining time to beg you to answer this letter and never to doubt the genuineness of my feelings.*

49

Cécile Volanges to the Chevalier Danceny
31 August 17—

I am neither frivolous nor deceitful, Monsieur. All I needed was to be enlightened as to the error of my ways to realize that I must change them; I have promised God to make this sacrifice until I feel capable of making Him a similar sacrifice of my feelings for you, which your religious status makes even more criminal. I realize that this will make me deeply unhappy and I won't even hide the fact that ever since the day before yesterday, every time I've thought of you, I've burst into tears. But I hope that God's grace will give me strength to forget you as I pray to Him to do night and morning. I even hope that as a friend and an honourable man you will make no attempt to shake the good resolution which I have been inspired to make and which I shall strive to keep. Consequently I am asking you to have the kindness to stop writing to me, all the more so as I must warn you that I would not reply and that you would be forcing me to warn Mama of everything that is happening; and that would deprive me completely of the pleasure of seeing you.

Nevertheless I shall still continue to feel towards you all possible affection, as long as it is not wrong; and I really do wish you every kind of happiness with all my heart. I quite realize that you won't love me as much now and perhaps you'll soon find yourself loving someone else better than me. But that will be one more cross to bear to punish me for the wrong I have done in giving my heart to you when it belongs only to God and my husband, when I have one. I hope that God, in His divine mercy, will have pity on my weakness and that He will not punish me beyond my endurance.

Farewell, Monsieur Danceny, I can certainly assure you that if I was allowed to love anybody, it would not be anyone but you. But that's the very most I can tell you and perhaps even that's more than I ought.

50

Madame de Tourvel to the Vicomte de Valmont
1 September 17—

So this is how you fulfil the conditions I laid down when I agreed to let you write to me occasionally? And how can I not *have grounds for complaint* when in your letter you speak to me of a feeling which I would still be afraid of giving way to even were I able to do so without flying in the face of my duty.

In any case, if I needed further reasons to reinforce this salutary fear, it seems to me that I could find them in your last letter. In fact, at the very moment when you think you are justifying love, you are instead merely showing me its storms and perils. Who can wish for a happiness which involves sacrificing reason, when its short-lived pleasures lead at best to regret, if not to remorse?

And even although you are so much at home in this dangerous frenzy that you are bound to be less affected, weren't you yourself forced to admit that it can overpower you? Aren't you the first to complain of the uncontrollable agitation into which it throws you? How devastating its effect would be on an untried, sensitive heart and all the more overpowering because of the immense sacrifices it would entail!

You think, or appear to think, that love brings happiness; but I am so convinced that it would make me unhappy that I should prefer never to hear the word. The mere mention of it seems to me unsettling and so it is not only out of a sense of duty but for my own happiness that I appeal to you to be so good as never to use the word again.

After all, this must be a very easy request for you to grant at the moment. Now that you're back in Paris, you'll have ample opportunity to forget a feeling that perhaps arose from your habit of concerning yourself with such matters, reinforced by having nothing better to do in the country. Aren't you now back in those places where you used to take no notice of me whatsoever? Can you take a single step without coming across some evidence of your fickleness? Aren't you surrounded by women, all more attractive than me, who have a greater claim on your attentions? I lack the vanity attributed to our sex. Even less do I have that false modesty which is merely a subtle form of pride. So it is quite sincerely that I tell you that I can see little in myself to attract anyone and even if I had everything, I should still not have enough to hold you. So asking you to stop concerning yourself with me is merely asking you to do today something you have done before and would certainly do again in a short while, even if I were to ask you not to.

This is a truth that I will never forget and is in itself a sufficiently strong reason for me not to listen to you. There are a thousand and one others but to avoid embarking on a long discussion, I shall confine myself to repeating my request never again to mention a feeling to which I must neither listen nor, even less, respond.

PART II

The Marquise de Merteuil to the Vicomte de Valmont
2 September 17—

Vicomte, you're really quite unbearable. You're treating me as casually as if I were your mistress. You know, I'm going to get cross and at the moment I'm in an absolutely foul temper. So you're seeing Danceny tomorrow? And you are aware how important it is for me to talk to you before this meeting? Yet completely unconcerned, you keep me waiting all day to go gallivanting off God knows where. You are to blame for making me arrive *obscenely* late at Madame de Volanges's so that all the old crones thought me phenomenal. I had to butter them up all evening to pacify them; you must be careful not to vex old ladies: they're the ones who decide young women's reputations.

It's now one a.m. and instead of being able to go to bed, which I'm dying to do, I've got to write you a long letter which will make me sleepier still because it's so boring. You're damned lucky I haven't time to go on ticking you off. And don't take that to mean that I'm letting you off; it so happens I'm in a hurry. So pay attention while I get on with it.

You won't need to be a genius to learn all Danceny's secrets tomorrow. It's the psychological moment for soul-baring: he's in a mess. The little girl went to confession and like a child, bared hers. Since then she's been so tormented by fears of hell fire that she wants to break off with him completely. She explained all her little qualms to me with a fervour that showed me plainly enough how worked up she was. She produced a letter she's written him breaking it off: a real pulpit piece. She nattered on for a whole hour without once talking sense. All the same, she still embarrassed me because, as you realize, I couldn't risk speaking openly with such a perverse young girl.

But amidst all this claptrap I could see that she still loves her Danceny; I even noticed one of those ingenious little ruses which love always has up its sleeve and which the child has rather amusingly fallen for. Agonized by her longing to go on thinking of her lover, and her fear of damnation if she does, she has hit on the idea of praying God to make her forget him and as she keeps on making this prayer every minute of the day, she's found a way of never letting him out of her mind.

With anyone more sophisticated than Danceny this little hiccough would have been more of an advantage than not; but the young man is such a Céladon* that unless we lend him a hand, he'll take so long to tackle the slightest obstacles that we'll be left with no time to bring our plan to fruition.

I agree that it's a pity and I'm just as sorry as you that he's the hero of this adventure; but what can we do about it? What's done can't be undone; and I blame it on you. I asked to see his reply:* it was pitiful. He puts forward endless arguments to prove that *a feeling you aren't able to control can't be a crime*; as if it didn't stop being uncontrollable the minute you give up trying to control it! This is such an elementary idea that even the little girl thought of it. He's rather touching when he complains how miserable he is; but he's so meek and his suffering is so genuine and deep that it seems to me scarcely possible for any woman who is offered such a golden chance—with so little risk—to reduce a male to despair could resist indulging in such a treat. Finally he explains that he isn't a monk, as the girl thought. That was definitely his best point, for if you do decide to go in for monks, our Knights of Malta would assuredly not be top of the list.*

Be that as it may, instead of wasting my time in arguments which might perhaps have been unconvincing and could have been compromising, I agreed to her decision to break with Danceny, adding the proviso that in such cases it was more honourable to explain one's reasons in person rather than in writing; also that it was usual to give back letters and any other little objects one might have received. So, while apparently falling in with the little person's views, I got her to give Danceny a rendezvous. We arranged the details on the spot and I undertook to persuade her mother to go out without her daughter; the moment of truth is to be tomorrow afternoon. Danceny's already been informed but if you get a chance, for God's sake do urge our handsome swain to wake up, and since he's got absolutely everything to learn, teach him that the best way of overcoming scruples is to leave those who have them with nothing more to lose.

Furthermore, in order to avoid any repetition of this ridiculous scene, I did not fail to sow certain seeds of doubt in the mind of the little creature as to the discreetness of confessors; and I can assure you that at the moment she's paying for the fright she caused me by her own fear that her confessor may go along to her *Mummy* and reveal all. I hope that after I've had a few more chats with her she'll stop blabbing about her silly conduct to all and sundry.*

Goodbye, Vicomte: take Danceny in hand, guide his steps. It would be too mortifying for words if we couldn't manage to get two children to do what we wanted. And if it's proving more difficult than we first envisaged, never forget there are two things to spur us on: for you, that it's Madame de Volanges's daughter who's involved; and for me, that it's Gercourt's future wife.

Goodbye.

52

The Vicomte de Valmont to Madame de Tourvel
3 September 17—

You forbid me to mention my love to you, Madame, but also fail to tell me where to find the courage to obey you. Constantly obsessed as I am with an emotion which should be so gentle and which you are making so cruel; languishing in an exile to which you have banished me; living as I do in frustration and sorrow, with my heartache made even more painful since it is a reminder of your indifference: must I then lose my only remaining consolation? For what other consolation can I find but baring my soul to you now and again—a soul which you are filling with bewilderment and bitterness? Will you turn your eyes away to avoid the sight of the tears which you are forcing me to shed? Will you even prevent me from offering you the sacrifices you are demanding from me? Would it not be more fitting for you, decent and gentle soul that you are, to take pity on an unhappy wretch whose unhappiness is of your making, rather than to increase his misery even more by a veto which is not only harsh but unfair?

You pretend to be afraid of love and you refuse to see that you yourself are the only cause of the harm of which you are accusing it. Yes, of course it is a sad emotion when it is not shared by the person inspiring it; but where is happiness to be found if not in mutual love? Cordial friendship, gentle trust—the only trust which knows no limits—sorrows soothed and pleasure enhanced, the charm of hope and of remembrance: where else can you find all these but in love? You are slandering it, whereas in order to reap its bounty you yourself need only to stop rejecting it; and by spending my time defending it, I can forget my own misery.

And you are also forcing me to come to my own defence because though I spend my life worshipping you, you spend yours finding fault with me. You've already assumed that I'm frivolous and deceitful and by drawing unfairly on a few lapses which I myself admitted, you take pleasure in confusing the man I once was with the man I now am. Not content with banishing me into miserable exile, you indulge in cruel banter at my expense for pleasures which, because of you, have, as you know, become indifferent to me. You won't believe my promises or my pledges. Well, there is still one witness I can ask to vouch for me whom at least you won't be able to suspect: yourself. Let me ask you merely in all good faith to question yourself: if you don't believe in my love, if you have a moment's doubt as to your unchallenged power over my soul, if you are not certain of having finally anchored that heart which till now was indeed too wayward, I agree to bear the punishment for that error. I shall grieve but I shan't appeal against your sentence. If, on the other hand, in fairness to both of us, you're forced to agree in your heart of hearts that you neither have nor ever will have a rival, then I entreat you not to force me to fight these figments of your imagination and let me at least have the comfort of knowing that you no longer doubt that my feeling for you will and can end only with my life. Allow me to ask you, Madame, to give me a specific answer to this question.

Yet if I turn my back on that period of my life which seems to be damaging me so grievously in your eyes, it is not because, if need be, I am short of reasons to justify it.

After all, what was I doing but failing to resist the whirligig into which I'd been plunged? I'd gone into society as a young man without any experience; been passed, so to speak, from hand to hand by a horde of women relying on the speed of their capitulation to forestall any reasoned judgement which they sensed would certainly be unfavourable. Was it for me to offer any resistance when I never met any myself? Or was I supposed to go on suffering for a momentary error, which had often been provoked, by remaining faithful, which would certainly have been pointless and made me look ridiculous? How else do you think I could have freed myself from a dishonourable commitment except by breaking off as soon as possible?

But I am able to say that this intoxication of the senses, even perhaps this frantic vanity, never penetrated into my heart. My heart was born to love and however much it was misled into amorous intrigues, they never succeeded in satisfying it. I was surrounded by attractive but despicable persons and none of them touched my heart; I was being offered pleasure whereas I wanted virtue, so that eventually I came to think of myself as fickle whereas I was merely fastidious and sensitive.

But when I saw you my eyes were opened. I soon realized that the charm of love depends on the noble qualities of the soul which alone could give rise to and justify its excesses. I felt in fact that it was as impossible not to love you as to love anyone but you.

So now you can see, Madame, the true heart to which you are so afraid to lend your trust and whose fate lies in your hands. But whatever that fate may be, you will never be able to weaken the bonds that hold it to you; they are as unshakeable as the virtues which gave birth to them.

53

The Vicomte de Valmont to the Marquise de Merteuil
Evening of 3 September 17—

I've met Danceny but only got part of the truth out of him. In particular, he persisted in withholding the name of the Volanges girl, merely saying she was a very proper young woman, even a trifle pious. Apart from that he talked pretty openly about his affair and above all of the recent incident. I egged him on as much as possible and teased him for being so sensitive and scrupulous but as he appears set on sticking to that attitude, I can't accept any responsibility for him. Anyway, I shall be able to report more fully the day after tomorrow. I'm taking him with me to Versailles* tomorrow and I'll try to get to the bottom of him during the journey.

I'm also fairly optimistic about his meeting with the Volanges girl, which is due to take place today. It might well be that everything has gone according to our plan and perhaps it only remains for us to force him to confess and gather the necessary evidence. It will be easier for you to do this than for me: the little body is more confiding than her wary sweetheart, or more of a chatterbox, which amounts to the same thing. However, I'll do what I can.

Goodbye, fair lady. I'm in a great rush. I shan't see you tonight or tomorrow. If you learn anything on your side, drop me a line for when I return. I'll certainly spend the night in Paris.

54

The Marquise de Merteuil to the Vicomte de Valmont
4 September 17—

Oh yes, there's something to be got out of Danceny, I don't think! If he said there was, he was boasting. I don't know of anyone so stupid in love and I'm getting more and more annoyed with myself for all the trouble we've been taking over him. Do you know that because of him I very nearly found myself compromised? And that it was a complete waste of time as well? Ah, I'm going to get my own back on that young man, I promise.*

When I went to pick up Madame de Volanges, she didn't want to go out: she didn't feel very well and it needed all my powers of persuasion to induce her to do so. I could see Danceny arriving before we left, which would have been all the more tricky because Madame de Volanges had told him yesterday that she wouldn't be at home. Her daughter and I were both on tenterhooks. We finally went off and as we left, the girl squeezed my hand so affectionately that in spite of her plan to break off with Danceny—which she was still genuinely intending to do—I could foresee wondrous things happening that evening.

My worries weren't over yet: we'd barely been at Madame de ——'s half an hour when Madame de Volanges was in fact taken ill, really quite ill and reasonably enough wanted to go home, which I on the other hand was most anxious not to do, particularly as there was every chance of catching the couple of love-birds by surprise and she would inevitably suspect my motives in having urged her to go out. I decided the best plan was to scare her by being solicitous about her health—luckily not frightfully difficult—and I managed to keep her there for a whole hour and a half by pointing out the risks involved in being jolted about in a carriage before eventually agreeing to see her home. So in the end we didn't get back till the stipulated time. From the shame-faced look I observed when I arrived, I confess that I had hopes that there might at least be some return for my efforts.

Intrigued to discover what had happened, I stayed with Madame de Volanges when she went to bed straight away and after having supper at her bedside, we left her very early, on the pretext that she needed a good night's rest and went off to her daughter's room. She'd done everything I'd expected: exeunt scruples, on with fresh pledges of eternal love, etc. etc.; in a word, she'd performed impeccably but that blockhead Danceny hadn't shifted one inch from his previous attitude. Oh, one need never worry about falling out with him: making it up offers absolutely no dangers.

However, the girl assured me that he did want to go further but she was able to defend herself. I bet she's either bragging or trying to find excuses for him. I even managed to make fairly sure of that point myself as I suddenly took it into my head to find out in person what sort of defence she actually was capable of putting up: with one thing leading to another, I got that girl *so* worked up—and that's by a mere *woman* . . . Anyway, take it from me, you can't imagine anybody easier to arouse: what an adorable, sweet little thing she is! She deserved a better lover; at least, in me she'll have a good friend because I feel genuinely attached to her. I've promised myself to educate her and that's a promise I think I will keep. I've often felt the need for a confidante and I'd sooner have her than anyone else. But I can't do a thing about her until she's done . . . what she's got to do . . . And that's another reason for my grudge against Danceny.

Goodbye, Vicomte. Don't come and see me tomorrow unless it's in the morning. I've yielded to Belleroche's urgent plea to spend a night at my little house.

55
Cécile Volanges to Sophie Carnay
4 September 17—

Sophie dear, you were right. Your prophecies are better than your advice. As you forecast, Danceny beat my confessor, you, and even me. So we're back to exactly where we started. I don't feel any remorse and if you tell me off, it's because you've no idea how wonderful it is loving Danceny. It's all very well for you to say what ought to be done, there's nothing to stop you. But if you'd actually experienced how dreadful it is when someone you love is miserable and how difficult it is to say no when you want to say yes, you wouldn't be surprised at anything any more. For instance, do you imagine I can see Danceny crying without wanting to cry myself? I assure you, it's definitely impossible for me. And when he's pleased, I'm as happy as he is. You can say what you like, what people say doesn't change the way things are and I'm certain that's how it is.

I'd just like to see you in my place . . . No, that's not what I really mean, because I'd certainly hate to give up my place to anybody; but I would like you to love someone as well, not only because you'd understand me better and not keep on telling me off so much but also because you'd be happier or perhaps I should say, it's not until then that you'd start being happy.

You see, all our fun and laughter and larking about was really only childish. Once it was over, there wasn't anything left. But love, O Sophie, love! . . . a word, a look, just knowing he's there, well, that's what happiness is. When I see Danceny, I don't want anything more; and when I can't see him, I don't want anybody else. I don't know how it is but it seems that everything I like looks like him. When he's not there I think of him and when I can concentrate on thinking of him without anything to distract me, for example when I'm completely alone, I'm still happy. I just close my eyes and I can see him straight away. I remember what he said and I seem to hear his voice. I start longing for him and then I get all hot and excited and restless and just can't keep still, it's agony but it's so wonderful, I just can't tell you!

I even think that once you've experienced love, it spreads to friendship as well. My friendship for you hasn't changed, of course, it's still just like it was in the convent, but what I'm talking about is my feelings towards Madame de Merteuil. I seem to love her more like I do Danceny than you and sometimes I wish she was him. Maybe that's because it's not a childhood friendship like ours or else because I see them so often together that I tend to mix them up. Anyway it's certainly true that the two of them together make me feel very happy and after all I don't think there's any great harm in what I'm doing. I'd really rather like to stay just as I am. The only thing that worries me is the thought of getting married because if Monsieur de Gercourt is the sort of man I've been told, and I feel sure he is, I don't know what will happen to me. Goodbye, Sophie mine, from your as ever very affectionate and loving Cécile.

56

Madame de Tourvel to the Vicomte de Valmont
5 September 17—

What would be the point of answering the question you ask me? Wouldn't believing in your feelings be a further reason for being afraid of them? And without either doubting or defending their sincerity, mustn't it be sufficent for me and for you to know that I neither will nor ought to respond to them?

Assuming that you did indeed love me—and it's only to avoid ever coming back to this subject that I make this assumption— would the obstacles standing in our way be any less insurmountable? And would there be anything else I could do but hope that you would quickly succeed in overcoming that love and, above all, do everything in my power to help you by removing any hope of it as soon as possible? You agree yourself that *it is a sad emotion when it is not shared by the person inspiring it.* You are by now quite well aware that I cannot possibly share it and even if such a misfortune were to befall me, I should be the more to be pitied, without your being any the happier. I hope that you have a sufficiently high opinion of me not to doubt that for one second. My heart has great need of peace and quiet and I appeal to you to stop trying to unsettle it. Don't force me to regret having known you.

I enjoy the affection and esteem of a husband whom I love and respect, in whom my duty and my pleasure are both combined. I am happy, I am bound to be happy. If there are more intense pleasures, I do not want them and I have no wish to indulge in them: is there any purer pleasure than being at peace with oneself, enjoying tranquil days and restful nights, to wake up with a clear conscience? What you call happiness is a turmoil of the senses, a storm of passion dreadful to watch even from the safety of the shore. How could anyone face such frightful squalls? How could one dare to embark on a sea scattered with the flotsam of thousands and thousands of shipwrecks? And in what company? No, Monsieur, I shall stay on firm ground; I value the links that bind me to it. Even if I could break them, I should never want to do so. If I did not have them, I should make every effort to forge them as quickly as possible.

Why are you dogging my footsteps? Why do you persist in pursuing me? Your letters were to have been written occasionally; they are coming thick and fast. They were supposed to be sensible and they talk of nothing but your mad love. Your obsession is hemming me in even more than your presence. After having been banished in one form, you have been reborn in another. Having been asked not to say certain things, you merely find other ways of saying them. You enjoy tying me up in quibbles; you avoid answering my arguments. I no longer want to reply to you and I intend to stop doing so. And what a way to treat the women you've seduced! The scorn with which you refer to them! I'm prepared to believe that some of them deserve it but are they all so contemptible? Oh, surely they were, since they were false and faithless and succumbed to guilty love. From that moment, they lost everything, even the respect of the man to whom they had sacrificed everything. It is a savage punishment and a fair one: but the very thought sends a shudder through me.*

In any case, what importance has all this for me? Why should I concern myself with them or with you? What right have you to disturb my peace of mind? Leave me alone, stop seeing me and writing to me, I beg you. I demand it. This letter is the last you will receive from me.

57

The Vicomte de Valmont to the Marquise de Merteuil
5 September 17—

Your letter was awaiting me when I got back yesterday. I was delighted to see how angry you were. You couldn't have reacted more spiritedly to Danceny's shortcomings if they had been deliberately aimed at you. I imagine that you are inculcating in his mistress the habit of being unfaithful, just slightly, to him, in retaliation? What a real bad lot you are! Yes, you're charming and I'm not surprised that you're less easy to resist than Danceny.*

I've finally got to know him thoroughly well, this wonderful hero of romance!—he no longer has any secrets from me. I kept dinning into his ears so relentlessly that honourable love was the supreme good, that one genuine emotion was worth a dozen petty intrigues, that for the moment I became a timid lover myself; in fact he found my way of thinking so congenial and was so delighted by my candour that he told me all and promised me his unconditional friendship. It hasn't furthered the progress of our plan very much.

First of all, I gathered that his idea is that a girl deserves to be treated with far greater consideration than a woman since she has more to lose. In particular, he feels that nothing can justify a man's placing a girl in a position where she has either to marry him or face public disgrace, when that girl is infinitely better off financially than the man, which is the case with him. The mother's vigilance, the girl's own trusting nature, both combine to intimidate him and make him hesitate. The problem isn't how to refute his arguments, justified though they may be: a sly word or two and a little help from youthful passion could soon make nonsense of them, all the more easily as they're open to ridicule and the weight of custom is on our side. But we're prevented from having any hold over him by the fact that he's perfectly happy as he is. Indeed, if our first loves seem generally more honourable and, as they say, purer, or in any case, if they proceed more slowly, it's not, as people think, because of shyness or scruples; it's because the heart is surprised by an unfamiliar emotion and halts, so to speak, at every stage to enjoy the charm of the experience; and for a young man's heart this charm is so powerful that it fills it to the point of excluding every other pleasure. This is so true that from the very moment a rake falls in love, assuming a rake can be in love, he becomes less eager to consummate his pleasure and in fact, between Danceny's behaviour towards the Volanges girl and mine with the prudish Madame de Tourvel, there's only a difference of degree.

To spur our young man on, he would have needed to face more obstacles than he has done; in particular, more mystery was required, for mystery fosters boldness. I'm almost tempted to think that you've done him a disservice by giving him so much help. With a sophisticated man feeling nothing but desire, your activity would have been admirable; but you should have been able to foresee that an honourable young man in love values his sweetheart's favours primarily because they are the proof of her love for him and consequently the more certain he is of being loved, the less enterprising he becomes. What's to be done now? I've no idea but I don't see any chance of the girl's being had before her marriage and we'll have taken all our trouble for nothing; it's tiresome, but I can't see any way round it.

And while I'm laying down the law in this letter, you're doing far better things with your knight. Which reminds me that you promised me a little deviation from constancy in my favour. I've got your promissory note in writing and I shouldn't like to see it turned into one of *La Châtre's*.* I agree that it isn't yet due to be honoured but it would be an act of generosity on your part not to wait till then. I'd be happy to arrange a discount on the interest. What do you say, fairest of the fair? Aren't you getting tired of remaining so constant? Is this knight so phenomenal? Oh, just

leave that to me, I intend to force you to admit that if you thought
he was quite good, it was because you'd forgotten me . . .

Goodbye, dear lady: I embrace you as ardently as I desire you
and I defy any kisses of your knight's to match mine.

58

The Vicomte de Valmont to Madame de Tourvel
7 September 17—

What have I done to deserve such rebukes, such anger? The
deepest yet most respectful affection, the most complete subser-
vience to your slightest desire, these few words sum up all my
feelings and my behaviour towards you. In his distress, your
unhappy lover had only the consolation of seeing you, which you
ordered him to forgo and he obeyed without daring to utter a
word of complaint. To reward me for this sacrifice you allowed
me to write to you and now you want to deprive me of even this
one pleasure. Can I let you rob me of it without a fight? Certainly
not! How could I fail to treasure it in my heart? It's the only thing
I have left and it was you who gave it to me.

You accuse me of writing to you too often! I would ask you to
reflect that since you exiled me ten days ago, I've not stopped
thinking of you for a single second, yet you've only had two
letters from me. In them, I talk of nothing but my love! Can you
tell me what I am to say if I cannot say what I think? The only
thing I have succeeded in doing is restraining my expression of it
and I promise you that I have only told you that part of it which
I found impossible to hold back. You conclude by threatening to
stop answering me, the man for whom you mean more than
anything in the world, who respects you even more than he loves
you! You're not content to treat him harshly, you intend to spurn
him with contempt. And why do you threaten me? Why are you
so angry? Do you need to do such things when you can be sure
I shall obey your every command, even if they are unjust? Is it
possible for me to refuse you anything? Haven't I already abun-
dantly proved that? After making me miserable, after behaving so
unfairly towards me, will you find it so easy to enjoy that peace
of mind which you claim to find so necessary? Won't you ever

have to say to yourself: he placed his fate in my hands and I destroyed him? He pleaded for help and I showed him no mercy? Do you know to what lengths despair can drive a man? No. And to plumb the depths of my misery you would need to know how great my love is. You do not know my heart.

To what are you sacrificing me? Preposterous fears! and who is causing these fears? A man who worships you, a man whom you will never cease to have at your mercy. What is there, what can there be to fear from a feeling which you will always have the power to control absolutely as you think fit? But your imagination is conjuring up monsters and you blame the terror they are causing you on love. Show a little more trust and these spectres will vanish.

A sage has said that to cure one's fears it is nearly always sufficient to investigate their source.* This truth is particularly applicable to love. Just love and your fears will melt away. Instead of these frightening apparitions, you'll discover a delightful emotion, a devoted and submissive lover, and as one blissful day follows another, your only regret will be for those you lost through your indifference. Ever since I repented of my errors and have lived only to love, I myself have come to regret my past life, when I imagined I was living only for pleasure. I feel in my heart that only you can make me happy. But I beseech you not to spoil the pleasure I feel in writing to you by making me frightened of incurring your displeasure. I do not want to disobey you but I fling myself on my knees and beg you at least to let me continue to enjoy the only happiness you have left me and which you wish me to forgo. I plead with you: see my tears, hear my prayers. Ah, Madame, have you the heart to refuse me?

59

The Vicomte de Valmont to the Marquise de Merteuil
8 September 17—

Do tell me if you can make head or tail out of this gibberish of Danceny's. What's happened to him? What's he lost? Has his beloved got fed up with his unshakeable respect for her? Let's be fair to the girl, that would be more than enough. What am I to say to him tonight when we meet, as he's asked me to and which I've agreed to do, just in case? I'm certainly not going to waste my time listening to him moaning if it's not going to get us anywhere. Lovers' laments are only worth listening to as an instrumental recitative or as a big arietta.* So do please let me know what it's all about and what I'm supposed to be doing or else I shall abscond to avoid the boredom which I can foresee. Can I have a word with you this morning? If you're occupied,* at least drop me a line and give me the cues for my part.

Where on earth were you yesterday? I never manage to see you these days. To tell you the truth, it wasn't worth getting me to stay on in Paris for September. But make up your mind because I've just received a pressing invitation from the Comtesse de B—— to go and stay with her in the country. And, as she informs me rather engagingly, her husband has the finest preserve imaginable 'which he keeps in prime condition for his friends' sport'. Well, as you know, I have certain shooting rights over that preserve* and if you haven't any use for me, I'll go down and shoot over it again. Goodbye, don't forget Danceny's going to be here about four o'clock.

60

The Chevalier Danceny to the Vicomte de Valmont
(enclosed with the previous letter)
8 September 17—

Ah, Monsieur, I'm in despair! My life's shattered. I'm afraid to tell you the tragic details in a letter but I absolutely must unburden my heart to some sympathetic and trusty friend. When can I see you? I need your comfort and advice. How happy I was that day when I opened my heart to you. But how different everything is now! My own unhappiness is the least of my troubles; what is unbearable is my anxiety for a person far dearer to me. You are luckier than I, you can go and see her, and I am relying on you as my friend not to refuse me this kindness; but I need to talk to you and tell you all about it. You must take pity on me and help me; you're my only hope. You are a man of feeling, you know what love is and you are the only one to whom I can speak freely. Don't refuse me your help.*

Goodbye, Vicomte: the thought that I have such a friend as you is my only relief for my sorrows. I beg you to tell me at what time I can come and see you. If it's not possible this morning, please make it early in the afternoon.

61

Cécile Volanges to Sophie Carnay
7 September 17—

O Sophie, dear, dear Sophie, pity your poor Cécile, she's so miserable! Mummy's found me out!! I just can't imagine how she came to suspect me but she's discovered everything. It's true that yesterday evening she did seem a bit grumpy but I didn't pay much attention and even while I was waiting for her to finish her game of cards I was chatting very cheerfully with Madame de Merteuil who came to supper and we talked a lot about Danceny, but I don't think anyone could have overheard us. Then she left and I went up to my room.

As I was getting undressed, Mummy came in and sent my maid away. She asked me for the key to my secretaire in a tone of voice that made me tremble so much that I could hardly stay on my feet. I pretended I couldn't find it but in the end I had to do what she asked. The very first drawer she opened was the one where I keep Chevalier Danceny's letters! I was so confused that when she asked me what they were, I couldn't think what to say except that it wasn't anything. But when I saw her start reading the one on top, I felt so bad that I only just had time to get to an armchair before fainting. When I came to, my mother, after sending for the maid, told me to go to bed and then went away, taking all Danceny's letters with her. I get a cold shiver down my back every time I think that I'm going to have to face Mummy again. I cried all night.

I'm writing this letter very early in the morning in the hope that Joséphine will be coming. If I can get to speak to her alone I'll ask her to hand Madame de Merteuil a little note I'm going to write her, otherwise I'll put it in with this letter to you and I'll

ask you please to send it on to her as if it's from you. She's the
only one I can hope for any comfort from at the moment. At least
we shall be able to talk about him, because I can't hope ever to see
him again. Poor me! I'm so miserable! Perhaps she'll be kind
enough to agree to take a letter to Danceny. I daren't trust
Joséphine for something like that and certainly not my maid
'cause it may even be her that told Mummy that I'd got some
letters in my secretaire.

I won't write any more now because I want to leave myself
time to write to Madame de Merteuil as well as to Danceny so
that my letter is absolutely ready, if she's prepared to take it.
After that, I'm going back to bed, so that I'll be there when they
come into my room. I'll say I'm not very well so I shan't have to
go and see Mummy. It won't really be a big fib, I'm sure I'm
feeling a lot worse than if I had a temperature. My eyes are
burning because I've been crying so much and I've got a heavy
feeling in the pit of my stomach which makes it hard for me to
breathe. When I think that I'm never going to see Danceny
again, I wish I was dead. Goodbye, Sophie dear, I can't write any
more, I'm crying so much I can't breathe properly.

Note: *Cécile Volanges's letter to the Marquise de Merteuil has been
omitted as it contains, in less detail, the same information as letter 61.
The letter to the Chevalier Danceny is missing; the reason for this
will be revealed in letter 63.*

62

Madame de Volanges to the Chevalier Danceny
7 September 17—

Having grossly abused a mother's trust and the innocence of a
child, you will scarcely be surprised, Monsieur, that your presence is no longer welcome in this house where you have repaid
the most genuine friendship by showing utter disregard for decent behaviour. Rather than having to give orders to my servants
not to admit you, I prefer to ask you to cease your visits and thus
avoid compromising us all equally by the observations they
would not fail to make. I have the right, therefore, to hope that

you will not force me to ban you from the house. Furthermore, I warn you that should you make the slightest attempt to persist in leading my daughter astray, she will be removed from your unwelcome attentions to spend the rest of her days in the strict reclusion of a convent. It will be for you, Monsieur, to see if you are as reluctant to bring about this calamity for her as you were to try to dishonour her. For myself, my choice is made and I have informed my daughter accordingly.

I enclose herewith a packet containing your letters, in return for which I expect you to let me have all those which you have received from my daughter and to ensure that no trace is left of an occurrence that I should be unable to recall without indignation, she without shame, and you, Monsieur, without remorse.

I have the honour, etc. etc.

63

The Marquise de Merteuil to the Vicomte de Valmont
9 September 17—

Yes indeed, I can shed light on Danceny's letter to you. The event which has led him to write to you is my doing and, if I may say so, my master-stroke. Since your last letter, I haven't been letting the grass grow under my feet and like the Athenian architect* I said: 'What that man said, I'll do.'

So this splendid hero of romance needs obstacles, does he, and he's drifting along in a blissful daze! Don't worry, he can rely on me to provide him with something to do and if I'm not much mistaken, his daze is not going to be blissful any more. He really had to be taught the value of time and I flatter myself that at this moment he's regretting all the time he's wasted. You also said he needed more mystery. Well, from now on he's not going to be short of that, either. One good thing about me is that you have only to draw my attention to my faults and I then never rest until I've remedied them all. Here's what I've done.

When I got home two mornings ago, I read your letter: it was positively brilliant. So, thoroughly convinced that you had put your finger on the sore spot, I devoted my whole attention to curing it. However, first of all I went to bed; for my indefatigable knight hadn't let me have a wink of sleep, and I thought I needed some. However, I was quite wrong. Engrossed as I was with Danceny and with my desire to jerk him out of his lethargy or else make him pay for it, I just couldn't drop off and it wasn't until I'd worked out my plot in detail that I was at last able to snatch a couple of hours' beauty sleep.

That very evening I called on Madame de Volanges and in accordance with my plan informed her *in confidence* that I felt sure that a dangerous relationship existed between her daughter and Danceny. While extremely clear-sighted in her hostility to you, this woman is so blinkered that at first she replied that I must surely be mistaken, that her daughter was only a child, and so on and so forth. I couldn't tell her everything I knew but I mentioned instances of remarks and glances that *had shocked my moral principles and my friendship*. In fact, I put on almost as good an act as any Devout Woman and to clinch the matter I went so far as to say that I thought I had seen letters change hands. 'Which reminds me,' I added, 'that one day I saw her open a drawer of her secretaire where I caught a glimpse of lots of papers that she must be keeping. Do you know of any correspondence she might be conducting?' Here Madame de Volanges's expression changed and I saw a stray tear come into her eyes. 'Thank you,' she said, clasping my hand. 'You are a good, kind friend. I shall look into the matter.'

After this short conversation, too short to arouse any suspicion, I went over to talk to the girl for a second and then came back to her mother to ask her not to compromise me in her daughter's eyes, which she promised all the more readily as I pointed out how fortunate it was that *the child* had sufficient trust in me to open her heart, thus putting me in a position to give her *my wise advice*. And I'm confident she'll keep her word because I've no doubt that she's anxious to claim credit for her perspicacity with her daughter. This will authorize me to remain on friendly terms with the girl without appearing deceitful in Madame de Volanges's eyes, something I want to avoid. It gives me the further advantage of spending as much time with the damsel with all the secrecy I might need without the mother's taking offence.

I availed myself of this privilege that very evening: when we'd stopped playing cards, I cornered the girl and brought the conversation round to Danceny, always an inexhaustible source of chatter with her. I enjoyed whipping her into a frenzy of anticipation at the thought of her pleasure when she saw him next day and I egged her on to make all sorts of quite outrageous remarks. I was determined to give her a foretaste of the pleasures I was preventing her from enjoying in reality: that's bound to make the shock even worse. I'm convinced that the more she suffers now, the keener she'll be to make up for lost time at the first opportunity. And anyway, it's an excellent thing for someone being groomed for grand adventures to become accustomed to grand occasions.

After all, what are a few tears compared to the pleasure of having her Danceny; she's crazy about him. Well, I promise her she'll have him even sooner than she would have done without this intervening storm. It's a bad dream with a delicious awakening; and all things considered, I think she should be grateful to me. Even if I have been a trifle mischievous, we're entitled to our bit of fun:

*Les sots sont ici-bas pour nos menus plaisirs.**

I finally left, well pleased with my mission, saying to myself that either Danceny, spurred on by these obstacles, will become even more passionate and if so, I'll lend him a hand in every possible way; or else, as I'm sometimes tempted to think, he's just dim and I give up in despair; in which case, I'll at least have settled my score with him as well as I could and meanwhile I'll have reinforced the mother's good opinion of me, my friendship with the daughter, and the trust of both. As for my prime target, Gercourt, I should feel I'd been extremely unlucky or excessively clumsy if, dominating his wife as I do and intend to do even more, I didn't find a thousand and one ways of making him become what I want him to become. With these comforting thoughts I went to bed and slept like a log. When I woke up, very late, I found two letters waiting for me, one from the mother, the other from the daughter, each containing, literally, the identical words: *You are the only one I can hope to comfort me.* I laughed till I cried. Isn't it really funny to be a well-wisher both for and

against and to be the only go-between of two people diametri-
cally opposed? So here I am like the Divinity, with blind mortals
vying in their prayers to me while I never change my immutable
decrees. However, I abandoned this august role in favour of that
of consoling angel and in accordance with that mandate, went to
call on my friends in their tribulation.

I started with *Mummy*. I found her in such a state of misery
that it must already provide you with some compensation for all
the unpleasantness she's caused you with your lovely prude.
Everything had gone like a dream. My only worry had been that
Madame de Volanges might have seized the opportunity to gain
her daughter's confidence simply by treating her in a gentle and
friendly way and making her reasons sound and seem affectionate and forgiving. Fortunately she'd taken a firm line, in fact
she'd behaved so badly that I could only applaud her. True, she
nearly spoilt all our plans by deciding to send her daughter back
to the convent. I warded that off by persuading her to threaten to
do that only if Danceny persists in pursuing her daughter: this
will force the pair of them to tread warily; I think that is necessary to ensure our success.

Next I went on to see the daughter. You wouldn't believe how
much better looking her sorrows have made her! Once she's
learnt how to flirt just a little, I guarantee she'll be shedding
many a tear; however, this time it was in good earnest. Struck by
this new and unfamiliar charm which I found most agreeable to
the eye, my first efforts to console her were ineffectual, the sort
that make people more rather than less miserable, so much so
that she was actually having to fight for breath. She had stopped
crying and I was afraid she might become hysterical. I advised
her to go to bed. She agreed; I acted as her maid. She wasn't
dressed to go out and soon her hair was floating round her bare
shoulders and bosom. I gave her a kiss and a hug; she snuggled
into my arms and her tears started flowing again with no trouble
at all. God, she looked lovely! If Mary Magdalen looked like that
she must have been much more dangerous as a penitent than as
a sinner . . .

Once the forlorn beauty was in bed I started to offer her
genuine consolation. First of all, I set her mind at rest over the
convent. I raised hopes of seeing Danceny in secret and sitting

down on the bed, I began by saying, 'Now if he were here . . .',
and embroidered on that theme, dangling one distraction after
another in front of her eyes until she'd quite forgotten she was
miserable. We'd have parted perfectly happy with each other if
she hadn't wanted me to take a letter for Danceny from her,
which I refused to do, for the following reasons which you'll
undoubtedly approve.

First and foremost, it would compromise me with regard to
Danceny and though that was the only reason I could put forward to the girl, for you and me there are many more. Wouldn't
giving our two love-birds such an easy means of solving their
problems put the outcome of all my good work at risk? And
moreover, I shouldn't be averse to forcing them to involve a few
servants in their transactions, for if their affair succeeds in the
way I hope, it must be brought to light immediately after the
wedding and there are few more reliable ways of spreading news;
or if by some miracle the servants didn't give the game away, we
should have to do it ourselves and it'll be very handy to have
them to blame for the leak . . .

So you must suggest this idea to Danceny this very day and as
I'm not sure about the Volanges girl's maid, whom she seems to
distrust herself, put him on to mine, my trusty Victoire. I'll see
to it that the operation's successful. I find this idea especially
attractive since keeping this matter dark will benefit us and not
them: you see, I've still got something up my sleeve.

So: all the time I was objecting to taking the girl's letter, I was
afraid she might suggest that I put it in the local post* for her,
something I could hardly have refused to do. Fortunately, in her
confusion or else through ignorance, perhaps even owing to the
fact that she was less interested in the letter than in his reply,
which she couldn't have received through the post, she didn't
mention it; but to prevent her from getting that idea or at least
from putting it into practice, I took a lightning decision and
when I went back to her mother I persuaded her to take her
daughter away for a short while and go with her down into the
country. And where do you think they're going? To your aunt's,
old Rosemonde! Doesn't your heart leap for joy? She's going to
let her know today: and then you'll be free to go and see your
saintly lady who'll no longer be able to put forward the bogy of

being alone in your company; so thanks to my kind attentions, Madame de Volanges will herself have made good the harm she's done you.

But listen to me and don't become so involved in your own affairs as to lose sight of this one: bear in mind my interest in it. I want you to become the confidential agent and adviser to those two young people. So inform Danceny of this trip and offer your services. Suggest that the only difficulty will be to deliver your credentials into the hands of his beloved and remove that obstacle on the spot by putting him on to my maid. There's no doubt he'll agree and as to reward for your trouble you'll win the trust of the heart of a novice, which is always interesting. Poor little thing! How she'll blush as she hands you the first letter! To tell you the truth, this job of go-between, which has given rise to certain prejudices, seems to me a delightful relaxation when one's occupied elsewhere, which will be the case with you.

So the outcome of this imbroglio lies in your hands. Take care. Calculate the right moment to bring the protagonists together. Country life offers a thousand and one opportunities and Danceny will certainly be ready to come down as soon as you say the word. A dark night, a disguise, an unfastened window? . . . How can I judge? But anyway, if that little girl comes back in the same state as she left, I shall blame you. If you feel she needs some encouragement from me, let me know. I think I've given her a sharp enough lesson on the dangers of hoarding letters to feel safe in writing to her now; I still have a mind to make her my pupil.

I think I forgot to mention that at first she suspected her maid of having revealed her secret correspondence but I diverted her suspicions on to her confessor. Two birds with one stone.

Goodbye, Vicomte, I've spent such a long time writing to you that I've held up my dinner. But my letter was dictated by vanity and friendship, two very talkative characters. Anyway, it'll reach you by three o'clock and that's all you need.

So complain about me if you dare and if it tempts you, do go and shoot over the Comte de B——'s preserve. You say he keeps it for his friends' sport? And what a lot of friends he's got, hasn't he? So long, I'm starving.

64

The Chevalier Danceny to Madame de Volanges
(*draft enclosed with letter 66*)
9 September 17—

Dear Madame, without trying in any way to justify my actions or complain of yours, I can only feel deeply distressed at an event which has brought unhappiness to three people who deserved a better fate. Ever since yesterday I have made many attempts to avail myself of the honour of replying to your letter, but feeling even more grieved at having caused than having suffered this misfortune, I have been unable to summon up the strength to do so. Yet I have so many things to say to you that I must force myself and if this letter is somewhat disjointed and incoherent, you will surely understand the painfulness of my situation well enough not to judge me too harshly.

But please allow me in the first place to appeal against the first sentence of your letter. I venture to say that I have never abused either your trust or Mademoiselle de Volanges's innocence: I can be held responsible only for my acts and no act of mine has ever shown disrespect either to you or to your daughter. But even should you wish to hold me responsible for my feelings, which were beyond my control, I am not afraid to add that my feelings towards your daughter are such that though they may cause you displeasure, they cannot cause offence. On this point, on which I feel more strongly than I can say, I shall be happy to submit to your judgement, offering my letters as evidence.

You forbid me to visit your house in future and I shall comply with every order you choose to make in this regard; but might my abrupt and total absence not expose you to similarly unwelcome observations as the order not to admit me, which you were reluctant to give for that very same reason? I particularly stress this since it affects Mademoiselle de Volanges more than myself. I do beg you therefore to weigh these matters most carefully and not to let severity prevail over prudence. I am sure that your final decision will be governed only by the best interests of your daughter and I shall await your fresh instructions.

However, should it happen that you do allow me from time to time to pay my respects to you, I promise you, Madame, on my word of honour, never to take advantage of any such occasion to attempt to speak to Mademoiselle de Volanges in private or to pass her any letters. The pleasure of seeing her sometimes will be my compensation for this sacrifice I am required to make in order to avoid endangering her reputation.

The above paragraph is also the only reply that I am able to make to what you tell me regarding the fate you are reserving for your daughter, which you intend to make dependent on my actions. To promise you anything more would be to mislead you. An unprincipled seducer can adapt his schemes to the circumstance and exploit a situation; my love has room for only two feelings: courage and constancy.

Agree to let Mademoiselle forget me? To forget her myself? Do you expect me to do this? It is utterly impossible. I could never do it. I shall remain faithful to her, I gave her my word and I repeat that same promise here and now. You must excuse me, Madame, I am losing my head, I must control myself.

There remains one other matter outstanding between us: the letters you are asking me to return. I am indeed sorry to add a further refusal to the offences which you already attribute to me but I beg you to listen to my reasons and, in order to appreciate them, I ask you, with the greatest respect, to remember that my only consolation for my misfortune in losing your friendship is the hope of not forfeiting your esteem.

I have always treasured Mademoiselle de Volanges's letters; now they have become even more precious. They are all that is left me; only they are capable of reviving the memory of a feeling which is the light of my life. Nevertheless, you must believe me when I say that I should still not hesitate for one second to sacrifice them to you, and my regrets at being deprived of them would be swept away by my desire to prove my respect and deference; but I am constrained by powerful considerations whose validity I do not think even you, Madame, will be able to deny.

True, you hold Mademoiselle de Volanges's secret, but allow me to suggest that I have strong reasons for believing that it was acquired by stealth rather than by persuasion. I am not seeking to blame you for your action, perhaps justified by motherly concern. I respect your rights but they do not extend to exempting me from my duties and the most sacred duty of all is never to betray any trust we have been given. To divulge to a third person the secrets of a heart which wished to reveal them to me alone would mean betraying that trust. Should your daughter wish to confide her secrets to you, so be it; you do not need her letters. If on the other hand she prefers to keep them to herself, you will certainly not expect me to inform you of them.

As for your wish that this incident may remain veiled in obscurity, here, Madame, I can set your mind at rest: in any matter which concerns Mademoiselle de Volanges, I can vie even with a mother's heart. In order to remove any misgivings you may have, I have made appropriate arrangements: the precious packet of letters originally marked, 'To be burnt', now bears the inscription: 'Papers belonging to Madame de Volanges.' This decision of mine must also confirm that my refusal to let you have them does not spring from any fear that you might find in these letters a single sentiment that could give you personal cause to complain.

This is an extremely long letter, Madame. It would still not be long enough if it left you in any doubt of the honourable nature of my feelings, of my genuine regret at having incurred your displeasure, and of the deep respect with which I have the honour, etc.

65

The Chevalier Danceny to Cécile Volanges
(*sent unsealed to the Marquise de Merteuil in letter 66*)
9 September 17—

Ah, what's going to become of us, Cécile, my Cécile? What kind God will save us from the calamities which threaten us? May our love at least give us strength to endure them! How can I describe my shock and despair when I saw my letters and read Madame de Volanges's note? Who can have given us away? Do you suspect anyone? Have you inadvertently said or done anything? What are you going to do now? What have they said to you? I'd like to know everything and I know nothing at all. Perhaps you yourself know as little as I do?

I'm sending you your mother's note and a copy of my reply. I hope you approve what I've said to her. And I need your approval, too, for the various steps I've taken since that disastrous event. They're all aimed at providing me with news of you and giving you my news. And who can tell? Perhaps even giving me a chance of seeing you again and more freely than ever before.

Can you imagine, dear Cécile, my Cécile, the bliss of being together again, being once again able to swear to love each other for ever, to read in each other's eyes and feel in our souls that it won't be an empty vow? Surely such a wonderful moment will make us forget all our woes. Well, I have hopes that moment will come as a result of these plans which I am asking you to approve. In fact, it's really because of the kindest of friends and I'd like you to accept him as your friend, too.

Perhaps I should have waited for your permission before telling him our secret? My excuse is my unhappiness and the urgency of our need. Love made me do it and it's in his name that I beg you not to be cross with me and to forgive me for betraying a secret. It was the only possible thing to do because otherwise we might have been parted for ever.* You know the friend I'm referring to, he's the friend of the woman you like best: the Vicomte de Valmont.

In turning to him my plan was at first to ask him to persuade Madame de Merteuil to agree to deliver a letter to you. We didn't think this would be feasible but if she can't help, he vouches for her maid who is under some obligation to him. She will be handing you this letter and you can let her have your reply.

This arrangement will hardly be of much use to us if, as Monsieur de Valmont believes, you're leaving immediately for the country. But then he is ready to help us himself. The woman you're going to stay with is a relative of his. He'll take advantage of this to invite himself at the same time as you and our correspondence will all go through him. He's even promised that if you do as he tells you, he'll find a way for us to meet there without the slightest risk of your being compromised.

And now my darling, if you love me and pity my misery and, I hope, even feel as unhappy as me, you won't refuse to trust a man who will be our guardian angel, will you? Without him I'd be in despair, I'd be helpless to do anything at all to alleviate the troubles I'm causing you. I hope they'll soon be at an end. But dear, loving, Cécile, promise me never to despair yourself, keep hoping always. The thought of how you must be suffering is excruciating for me.

I would sacrifice my life to make you happy. You know that, don't you? So I hope that knowing I adore you will comfort your heart a little! And my own heart needs you to reassure my love that it is forgiven for all the sorrows it's brought you.

Goodbye, my Cécile, my dear, tender, loving Cécile.

66

The Vicomte de Valmont to the Marquise de Merteuil
9 September 17—

When you read the two enclosed letters* you'll see, fairest of the fair, how well I've carried out your plan. Although they both bear today's date, they were written yesterday, in my house and under my own eyes: the little girl's letter says everything we wanted. When one considers the success of your manœuvres, one can only feel humility at the depth of your insight. Danceny's all set to go: at the next opportunity, you'll certainly not find anything to complain about with him. So if our charming little innocent is ready to play, the game will be up for her very soon after she arrives in the country. I've already drawn up dozens of plans. Thanks to your good offices, I'm definitely *Danceny's friend*; it only remains for him to be the *Prince*.*

However, our young hero is still very wet behind the ears. Would you believe, I was quite unable to prevail on him to promise her mother to give up his love? As if giving your word was any problem when you're determined not to keep it! He kept on saying: 'It'd be dishonest.' What an edifying scruple, especially as he wants to seduce her daughter! That's what men are like! Thoroughly dishonourable intentions and when they're too feeble to carry them through, they say it's their sense of decency.

It's up to you to stop Madame de Volanges from becoming scared by these antics in which our young fellow indulged. You must save us from the convent! And try to make her stop insisting on the return of the girl's letters. In the first place he won't give them back if he doesn't want to and I agree with him: love and good sense coincide here. I've read those letters, they're impossibly boring. But they may come in handy. Let me explain.

However careful we are, there may be a fuss and that would put an end to the marriage, wouldn't it? And put paid to our *Gercourt schemes*? But as I myself have a little score to settle with Mama, should that happen I want to retain the possibility of ruining the girl's reputation. Who can say? There may be a lawsuit and with a careful choice and some selective editing those letters could be used to depict the Volanges girl taking the initiative and simply throwing herself at Danceny's head. Some of them might even compromise her mother or at least *smear her* as showing inexcusable neglect of her daughter.* I realize of course that at first our high-minded Danceny would be shocked, but as he'd be personally in the front line, I think we could bring him round. The odds are strongly against things turning out like that but we have to plan for every eventuality.

Farewell, lovely lady. Be an angel and come and have supper at the Maréchale de B——'s tomorrow. I couldn't manage to get out of it.

I fancy I don't need to recommend the utmost discretion with Madame de Volanges concerning my proposed trip into the country: she'd immediately change her mind and stay in town; but once she's down there, she can hardly leave the very next day; and if she gives us just a week, I guarantee the rest.

67

Madame de Tourvel to the Vicomte de Valmont
9 September 17—

I was intending never to write to you again, Monsieur de Valmont, and the embarrassment I feel is proof that I ought not to be doing so. However, I do not wish to leave you with the slightest possible cause for complaint against me. I want to convince you that I have done everything for you that I could.

You tell me that I gave you permission to write to me? I agree; but when you remind me of that permission, do you imagine that I forget the conditions which I set? If I had been as strict in observing them as you have been remiss, would you have received a single letter? Yet here is my third, and while you are doing everything necessary to force me to break off this correspondence, I spend my time finding ways of continuing it! There is a way, but only one; should you reject it, it will be proof enough of how little importance you attach to our correspondence, despite your protestations.

So, you must stop using language to which I cannot and will not listen; refuse to give way to a feeling which both offends and frightens me; and when you consider that it is the obstacle standing in our way, ought you not, perhaps, to be less set on it? Is this really the only feeling you are capable of? And to all the other faults I can see in it, does love add that of excluding friendship? Could it be that you yourself are at fault in not wanting as your friend a woman in whom you had hoped to arouse more tender feelings? That I must refuse to believe: such a humiliating thought would appal me and alienate me from you irrevocably.

In offering you my friendship, I am offering you all that I have, all that is in my power to offer. What more can you want? In order to surrender to this gentle emotion, so dear to my heart, I am waiting for you to utter just one word: friendship; tell me that friendship is enough to make you happy. Then I shall forget everything else I may have been told and put my trust in you to justify my choice.

You see how frank I am and this must prove to you how strong my trust is; it is for you to make it even stronger; but I must warn you that the first word of love will destroy that trust and revive all my fears; more particularly, it will mean that from then on, you will never hear from me again.

If, as you say, you have *repented the error of your ways*, would you not rather enjoy a good woman's friendship than be the cause of a guilty woman's remorse?

Goodbye, Monsieur. You will understand that after speaking to you as I have, there is nothing I can add until you have given me your reply.

68

The Vicomte de Valmont to Madame de Tourvel
10 September 17—

How can I reply, Madame, to your last letter? How can I dare to speak the truth when being sincere can ruin me in your eyes? Never mind; I must and I shall be brave: I say to myself again and again that it is far better to deserve your love than to win it and even were you to deny me a happiness that I shall never cease to desire, I must at least prove to you that my love is worthy of you.

Isn't it a pity that, as you say, I have *repented of the error of my ways*! In what an ecstasy of delight I would have read that same letter which I feel so terrified in answering today! In it, you speak of being *frank*, you have *trust* in me, and finally you offer me your *friendship*! What a cornucopia of good things, Madame; and how much I regret being unable to take advantage of them! Why am I no longer the man I used to be?

If I hadn't in fact changed, if I had merely taken a fancy to you, a light-hearted fancy based on physical attraction and pleasure which these days nevertheless goes by the name of love, I should leap at the chance of enjoying every advantage I could grasp. I shouldn't be too particular about the means as long as they achieved success: I should encourage you to be frank, for I'd be eager to read your mind; I should worm my way into your trust the better to betray it; I'd accept your friendship in the hope of leading it astray. Ah, Madame, doesn't this prospect appal you? Well, it would exactly represent what I should be doing were I to agree to be merely your friend.

Do you really think that I can be persuaded to share with anyone an emotion that has emanated from your soul? If I ever were to tell you so, you must never believe me. From that moment onwards I should be trying to lie to you. I might still desire you but I should assuredly no longer love you.

Not that engaging frankness, gentle trust, heartfelt friendship have no value for me. But love! True love such as you inspire, combining all these feelings and multiplying them a hundred-fold, cannot, unlike them, accept that cool-headedness, that coldness of heart which allows comparisons to be made and even preferences to be shown. No, Madame, I shall not be your friend. I shall love you, with the most tender, the most passionate yet respectful love. You may drive it to despair, you will never destroy it.

And what right have you to determine the fate of a heart whose devotion you refuse to accept? By what subtle, cruel twist do you begrudge me even the happiness of loving you? That happiness is mine alone, it is independent of you: and I can defend it. It may be causing my sufferings but it may cure them.

No, no, and again no! Be as cruel as you like, spurn me, but do not deny me my love. You enjoy making me unhappy! Very well, try to wear down my courage but I shall at least force you to decide my fate; perhaps one day, you will be more fair. Not that I hope ever to soften your heart; but even if I cannot prevail upon you, I shall convince you. You'll say to yourself: I judged him wrongly.

But to speak frankly, it is you who are being unfair to yourself. To know you and not love you, to love you and not love you for ever: both these things are equally impossible; and despite your charming modesty, the feelings which you inspire are surely more likely to cause you to protest than to be surprised. As for me, whose only virtue is to have come to revere you, that is something I have no intention of forfeiting and so far from accepting your insidious suggestion, I fall at your knees and repeat my pledge to love you always.

69

Cécile Volanges to the Chevalier Danceny
(*written in pencil and copied out by Danceny*)
10 September 17—

You ask me what I'm doing: I love you and I'm crying. My mother is refusing to talk to me; she's taken away my paper, pen, and ink.* I'm using a pencil that I fortunately managed to keep and I'm writing on a torn-off corner of your own letter. Of course, I can't do anything but agree to everything you've arranged, I love you too much not to use every possible way of getting news of you and letting you have mine. I didn't like

Monsieur de Valmont and I didn't know he was such a great friend of yours; I'll try to get to know him and like him because of you. I don't know who gave us away; it can only be my maid or my confessor. I'm so miserable. We're leaving for the country tomorrow, I don't know how long for. O Heavens, how dreadful not to be able to see you any more! I've run out of space. Goodbye, hope you can read my writing. These words in pencil may perhaps get rubbed out but the feelings engraved in my heart never will!

70

The Vicomte de Valmont to the Marquise de Merteuil
11 September 17—

I've a serious word of warning for you, dear lady. As you know, I had supper yesterday at the Maréchale de B——'s. Your name came up and as you may imagine, I did not say all the nice things about you which I think are true but all those which aren't. Everybody seemed to share my view and the conversation was flagging, as it always does if people are speaking nothing but well of their neighbour, when a dissenting voice was heard: Prévan's.

'God forbid,' he said, rising to his feet, 'that I should cast doubt on Madame de Merteuil's excellent reputation. But may I hazard the guess that she owes it more to her flightiness than to her principles. Perhaps it's harder to keep up with her than to please her and when you're chasing a woman you can scarcely fail to come across some other women on the way and as, by and large, those others may be just as good or even better, some men get attracted elsewhere, while some give up exhausted. So perhaps she's had less need to defend herself than any other woman in Paris. For my part,' he went on, encouraged by some of the women's smiles, 'I shan't believe in Madame de Merteuil's virtue until I've ridden half a dozen horses to death in her pursuit.'

This bad joke, like all such malicious tittle-tattle, enjoyed a success for just as long as the laughter it aroused. Prévan sat down again and the conversation took another turn. But the two Comtesses de B—— sitting beside our doubting Thomas continued their private conversation on the subject with him and luckily I was close enough to overhear them.

The challenge *to soften your heart* was accepted; a promise to tell everything was given and methinks that of all the promises likely to be made in the course of this episode, this will be the one most religiously observed. But now you are forewarned, and you know the proverb.

It remains for me to tell you that this Prévan, whom you don't know, is infinitely charming and even more clever. If you've sometimes heard me assert the opposite, it's only because I can't stand the man, that I enjoy putting a spoke in his wheel, and because I'm not unaware of the weight which my opinion carries with thirty or so of the smartest of the smart women of our society.

In fact, this is how for some long time I've managed to prevent him from playing any part on centre-stage, as we call it;* so he was performing prodigies without increasing his fame. But his brilliant triple exploit has focused everybody's eyes on him and given him the confidence he's hitherto lacked; it has turned him into a formidable proposition. In a word, he's now possibly the only man whom I'd be afraid to cross swords with; so apart from your own interests, you'd be doing me a real favour by making him look a bit silly on the way. I leave him in good hands and have every hope that by the time I come back he'll have sunk without trace.

In return, I promise to bring the affair with your young neo-phyte to a successful conclusion and to give her as much of my attention as I'm giving my lovely puritan.

She's just submitted a capitulation proposal. Her whole letter is an open invitation to be lied to; it's impossible to find a handier and at the same time more threadbare method: she wants me to be her *friend*. But I'm rather fond of novelty and something more arduous and I've no inclination to let her off so lightly. And I've certainly not taken all this trouble over her to end up with your run-of-the-mill seduction.

My plan is to make her understand the full price she's got to pay, the gravity of each sacrifice she'll be making; never to press on so fast that she can't feel remorse catching up with her; to bring her virtue to a protracted, agonizing death; never to let her lose sight of this prospect and not to grant her the joy of holding me in her arms until I've forced her to realize how much she's panting for it. After all, if I'm not worth the asking, I'm not worth very much. And how could I settle for anything less to pay off my score with an arrogant woman ashamed to admit that she adores me?*

So I turned down the precious offer of friendship and stuck to my guns as a lover. As I'm not unaware that such a status, which at first sight seems a distinction without a difference, is a matter of real importance, I took great care with my letter and endeavoured to scatter freely the signs of turmoil which are the only way to depict this emotion. In a word, since loving equals raving, I raved as much as I could; incidentally, I think this is the reason why women's love-letters are so much better than ours.

I finished mine off with a little flourish of flattery, which again is a result of my deep study of the matter. After women's hearts have been given a good run round, they need a rest, and I've noticed that for all of them, flattery is the softest pillow to provide that.

Goodbye, fair lady. I'm off tomorrow. If you have any instructions to give me for the Comtesse de ——, I'll be stopping off at her place, at least for dinner. I'm sorry to leave without having seen you. Transmit your sublime instructions to me and let me enjoy the benefit of your wise advice at this decisive moment.

Above all, be on your guard against Prévan and may I one day be able to compensate you for this sacrifice! Farewell.

71

The Vicomte de Valmont to the Marquise de Merteuil
From the Château de L——, 13 September 17—

Can you imagine? My idiot of a valet has left the file of all my papers behind in Paris. The letters from my beautiful beloved, Danceny's to the Volanges girl, everything's in it and I need the lot. He's going back to rectify his stupid blunder and while he's saddling his horse, I'll tell you my story of last night's happenings. I want you to see that I'm not wasting my time.

In itself it's a rather trivial adventure; a rehash of my affair with the Vicomtesse de M——. But the details aren't without their interest. I'm glad to be able to demonstrate to you that even if I do have a gift for ruining women, I'm still capable of rescuing them as well, when I put my mind to it. I always go for the hardest solution or the funniest and I never feel guilty at performing a good deed, provided it keeps me amused and on my toes.

So I found the Vicomtesse staying here and when she added her urgings to the other positively bullying invitations being made for me to stay the night, I said to her: 'I agree on condition that I can spend it with you.' 'Impossible,' she replied, 'Vressac's here.' Up till then, I'd merely been trying to be civil; but as always, the word 'impossible' stuck in my gizzard. I felt mortified at being a victim of Vressac and determined not to tolerate it. So I stood my ground.

Circumstances were against me. This man Vressac had been inept enough to get into the Vicomte's bad books so that the Vicomtesse can no longer invite him to her house; hence this trip to the dear Comtesse's, arranged between the two in an endeavour to snatch a few nights away. At first the Vicomte had looked rather put out at seeing him there but since he's even keener on shooting than being jealous, he stayed on none the less; and the Comtesse, the same as you know of old, after giving the wife a room on the main corridor, put the husband on one side and the lover on the other, leaving them to sort things out for themselves. It was their bad luck that I had the room opposite . . .

That very day, that is to say yesterday, Vressac, who as you may well imagine is doing his best to keep in with the Vicomte, had been out shooting with him, even though he's not keen on it, and was looking forward to consoling himself that night in the wife's arms for the boredom the husband was inflicting on him during the day. However, I felt he needed a bit of a rest and I set about devising ways and means of persuading his mistress to give him the chance of getting some.

So at my suggestion she agreed to pick a quarrel with him on the subject of the very same shooting party which he'd quite obviously gone on only for her sake. You could hardly pick on a worse pretext; but though all women are notoriously fonder of nagging than reasoning and never harder to pacify than when they're in the wrong, the Vicomtesse has turned these gifts into a fine art. In any case, it wasn't the right time for arguing and as I only wanted one night, I was prepared to let them make it up next day.

So when he came back, Vressac got the cold shoulder. When he asked the reason: the Vicomtesse jumped down his throat. He tried to justify himself but the husband came up, giving her the opportunity to break off the conversation. In the end Vressac took advantage of a moment when her husband was out of the room to ask if she would agree to give him a hearing that night. Hereupon the Vicomtesse rose to sublime heights: in indignant tones she berated those crude males who, on the grounds that a woman has granted them some favours, assume they have the right to continue to exploit her good nature even when she has legitimate cause for complaint against them. Having thus skilfully changed her ground, she discoursed so eloquently on delicacy and sensitiveness that Vressac was rendered speechless and bewildered and even I was tempted to believe her—you realize, of course, that as a friend of both parties, I was one of the trio during this conversation.

In the end she declared categorically that she had no intention of adding the exertions of love to those of shooting and she would feel downright guilty at interfering with such gentle pastimes. The husband came back and the disconsolate Vressac, now prevented from speaking freely, turned to me and after a lengthy exposition of his reasons, which I knew as well as he, begged me to put in a good word for him with the Vicomtesse. I promised to do so and did in fact have a word with her, but only to thank her and settle the details and time of our encounter.

She explained that as her room was between her husband's and her lover's, she had thought it wiser to go to Vressac's rather than have him in hers and so all I had to do was to leave my door ajar and wait.

Everything went according to plan and about one o'clock in the morning she arrived in my room,

> *dans le simple appareil*
> *D'une beauté qu'on vient d'arracher au sommeil.**

Not being vain, I shan't dwell on the details of that night but you know what I'm like. I wasn't displeased with my performance.*

At dawn, we had to part. This is where the plot thickens. The silly woman thought she'd left the door ajar but we found it shut, with the key inside. You can't imagine the look of utter despair with which the Vicomtesse immediately exclaimed: 'Oh, I'm ruined!' And it can't be denied that it would have been fun to leave her in that predicament. But how could I allow a woman to be ruined through me but not by me? And was I to be at the mercy of events like any ordinary mortal? A way had to be found. What would you have done, fair lady? This is what I did and it worked.

I'd quickly realized that the door in question could be broken down, though with a great deal of noise. So with some difficulty I prevailed on the Vicomtesse to utter terrified screams of Thief! Murder! and so on, while at her first scream I was to break open the door and she would rush in and jump into bed. You can't imagine how long it took to persuade her, even after she'd agreed. However, in the end, it had to be done: she screamed— and with one kick the door came open. It was a good thing the Vicomtesse was quick off the mark for within seconds the Vicomte and Vressac both appeared in the corridor and the maid ran to her mistress's room as well.

I was the only one to keep my head and was thus able to rush over to a nightlight that was still burning and tip it over on to the floor: you'll understand how ludicrous the pretended panic would have seemed in a lighted room. I then rebuked the husband and the lover for sleeping so soundly, assuring them that the screams which had brought me out of bed to knock down the door had been going on for a good five minutes.

Now that she was in bed, the Vicomtesse had recovered her courage and backed me up pretty well, swearing by all the saints that there had been an intruder in her room and declaring, with greater veracity, that she'd never been so scared in her whole life. We searched everywhere without finding anything. Then I pointed out the overturned nightlight and drew the conclusion that no doubt a rat had been the cause of the damage and the scare. My verdict was unanimously accepted and after a few stale jokes about rats, the Vicomte was the first to go back to his room and his bed, requesting his wife in future to keep her rats quiet.

Vressac was left alone with us. He went over to the Vicomtesse and said it was love taking its revenge, to which she replied with a glance towards me: 'Then love must have been very angry because his vengeance was terrible'; adding, 'but I'm worn out and must get some sleep'.

Feeling in charitable mood, before we parted I pleaded Vressac's cause and won it: the two lovers kissed and made friends and both then embraced me. I'd lost interest in the Vicomtesse's kisses but I must confess that I enjoyed being embraced by Vressac. We both left together and after lengthy expressions of gratitude on his part, we each went off to our separate beds.

If you find this story amusing I'm not asking you to keep it to yourself. Now that I've had my fun out of it, it's only fair to give the public its turn. For the moment, I'm only thinking just of the story itself: but maybe we can do the same thing with the heroine some time in the near future.

Goodbye, my man's been waiting for an hour. I've only just time to embrace you and warn you to be particularly on your guard against Prévan.

72

The Chevalier Danceny to Cécile Volanges
(*not delivered until the 14th*)
Paris, 11 September 17—

Dear Cécile, my Cécile, oh, how I envy Valmont! He'll be seeing you tomorrow. It's he who's going to pass this letter on to you while I shall be pining away far from you, brooding in sorrow and misery. Cécile my love, my tender-hearted Cécile, you must commiserate with me for all my troubles but especially for yours, because it is they which are breaking my heart.

How terrible it is for me to realize that I'm the cause of your unhappiness! But for me, you would be happy and at peace. Can you ever forgive me? Oh, tell me that you do, tell me, too, that you love me, that you'll always love me. I need to hear you say those words over and over again, not that I have any doubts but it seems to me that the more certain one is, the more one wants to hear it. You do love me, don't you? Yes, you love me heart and soul. I don't forget that those were the last words I heard you say. And how gladly I gathered them into my heart where they're now engraved so deeply! And how my own heart rejoiced in response!

Alas, at that blissful moment I was far from foreseeing the dreadful fate which was to overtake us! Cécile dear, we must try to find a way to soften its blows. And in order to achieve that, if I can believe my friend, you need only show him the complete trust he deserves.

I must admit that I was hurt by the unfavourable opinion you seem to have of him. I recognized the influence of your Mama's prejudices: it was through deferring to them that for a while I'd been neglecting that truly lovable man who at the moment is doing everything he can for me, who indeed is working to bring us together again now that your mother has come between us. I entreat you, Cécile dear, to look at him in a more favourable light. Remember he is my friend, that he wants to become your friend too, that through him I shall have the joy of seeing you. If these reasons don't convince you, darling Cécile, then you don't love me as much as you used to. O Heavens, if you ever stopped loving me so much, I could never console myself, I'd sooner die. But it's impossible, my Cécile's heart belongs to me for ever and even if I'm suffering the pangs of thwarted love, at least her constancy will spare me the torment of love betrayed.

Goodbye, my enchantress; don't forget how much I am suffering and that only you are able to make me the happiest man in the whole world. Listen to my pledge of love, which comes with love's most tender kisses!

73
The Vicomte de Valmont to Cécile Volanges
(enclosed with letter 72)
At the Château de ———, 14 September 17—

The friend who is helping you learned that you have nothing to write with and he has already attended to the matter: in the antechamber of the room you are occupying, you will find a supply of paper, pens, and ink under the large wardrobe on the left; he will renew these as necessary; he thinks you can leave them there unless you can find any safer hiding-place.

He asks you not to be offended if he appears to pay you no attention in company and to treat you as a child. Such behaviour seems to him appropriate to create the confidence he needs in order to work more effectively towards his friend's and your own happiness. He will try to provide opportunities to speak to you when he has anything to communicate or pass over to you, if you give him your whole-hearted support.

He advises you also to hand back the letters you receive in order to reduce the risk or your being compromised.

Finally, he wishes to assure you that if you let him have your trust, he will do everything in his power to alleviate the persecution being inflicted by an inordinately cruel mother on two people of whom one is already his best friend and the other seems to him to deserve his most devoted attention.

74

The Marquise de Merteuil to the Vicomte de Valmont
Paris, 15 September 17—

Well, well! How long have you been so easy to scare? Is this man Prévan really so formidable? Please note how simple and modest I am! I've met him often, this conquering hero of yours: I hardly spared him a glance! It took your letter to draw him to my attention. I made up for my omission yesterday at the Opéra. He was sitting opposite me and I observed him closely. At least he's pretty, definitely very pretty; such clean-cut, delicate features! He must look even nicer close to. And you tell me he wants to have me? I shall take it as an honour . . . and a pleasure. Seriously though, I do fancy him and I must tell you that I've set the ball rolling. I can't be certain if it'll work but here's what I did.

As we were coming out of the opera he was standing a couple of yards away and in a loud voice I arranged with the Marquise de —— that we should have supper together at the Maréchale's on Friday, that being the only place, I think, where I can meet him. I've no doubt he heard me. And suppose the ungrateful man were to fail to turn up? You know, if he doesn't I shall be really cross for the rest of the evening. As you see, he's not going to find it so terribly hard *to keep up with me*; and here's something you'll find more surprising, he'll find it even less hard *to please me*. 'He wants', he says, 'to ride six horses to death in pursuit of me!' Oh, I can't bear to let those poor little gee-gees die for my sake! You know it's not a principle of mine to let anyone pine away for me once I've made up my mind, which I have about him.

Well now, you must agree that it's a pleasure to give me sensible advice! Your *serious word of warning* has been a great success, hasn't it? But what else can a woman do? I've been vegetating for so long! I haven't had any fun for more than six weeks. And now this chance turns up: how can I turn it down? Isn't the subject worth the trouble? Is there anyone more acceptable in every sense of the word?

Even you yourself feel obliged to give him his due; you don't just praise him: you're actually jealous of him. Well, I'll adjudicate between the two of you but first of all I must investigate and that's what I intend to do. I'm an unbiased judge and shall weigh you both in the same balance. Your own case is already fully documented, so I've no need to investigate you further. Is it not only fair to turn my attention now to your rival? So come along, submit gracefully and for a start tell me all about this threefold adventure of which he was the hero. You talk as if I can't possibly have heard of anything else but I don't know the first thing about it. Apparently it's supposed to have occurred during my trip to Geneva and you were too jealous to write and tell me about it. Please make good this oversight as quickly as possible: don't forget that *nothing which concerns him is indifferent to me*.* I have a vague idea that people were still talking about it when I came back but I had other things on my mind at the time and I very seldom listen to that sort of gossip unless it's something that's actually happened that same day or the day before.

You may be a trifle annoyed at what I'm asking you to do but isn't it a very small return for all the trouble I've been taking over your affairs? Didn't I restore you to your judge's wife when, through your own stupidity, you'd been forced to leave her? And then wasn't it me who placed into your hands ways and means to settle your score with that mischievous old bigot Madame de Volanges? You're always moaning about the time you waste looking round for exciting things to do. Now you have a couple under your very nose. Love or hatred, take your pick, they're both sleeping under the same roof and you can live a double life, fondling with one hand and stabbing in the back with the other . . .

And it's me again you have to thank for your adventure with the Vicomtesse. I'm rather pleased about that but as you say, it mustn't get hushed up because though I can well understand how the situation made you prefer secrecy to stirring up scandal, you must admit that woman didn't deserve such gentlemanly treatment.*

Moreover, I have a grudge against her. Chevalier de Belleroche finds her prettier than I consider proper and I shall be very glad for many reasons of an excuse for breaking off relations with her. And what is more convenient than to have to say to oneself: 'We can't have anything more to do with *that* woman, can we?'

Goodbye, Vicomte. Do remember that, in your situation, time is of the essence! And mine will be spent seeing how I can make Prévan *a happy man*.

75
Cécile Volanges to Sophie Carnay
From the Château de ——, 14 September 17—

Note: *In this letter Cécile gives an extremely detailed account of all the events concerning her which the reader has already seen in letters 49 and later and which there seemed no point in repeating. At the end of her letter she writes about the Vicomte de Valmont in the following terms:*

I assure you he's an extraordinary man. Mummy has hardly a good word to say for him but Danceny thinks highly of him and I think it's he who's right. I've never seen a cleverer man. He managed to slip me Danceny's letter with everybody there and no one saw a thing. It's true I was very frightened because I hadn't been warned at all but now I'll be expecting him. I already know exactly how he wants me to let him have my reply. It's very easy to understand what he means because his eyes tell you precisely what he wants. I don't know how he does it; in the letter I mentioned he told me he wouldn't seem to be paying me any attention in front of Mummy and actually you'd never guess that he's thinking about me at all yet every time I look out for him, I'm sure to catch his eye straight away.

There's a good friend of Mummy's staying here whom I didn't know, who doesn't seem to like Monsieur de Valmont very much, though he's very attentive to her. I'm afraid he'll soon get bored with our life down here and go back to Paris which would be a very great pity. He must be very kind-hearted to come here specially as a favour to his friend and to me! I'd love to show him how grateful I am but I don't know how to arrange to speak to him and even if I got the chance I'd be so bashful that perhaps I mightn't know what to say.

The only person I can speak to freely about my love is Madame de Merteuil. And even though I tell you everything, if I was actually talking to you I expect I'd feel embarrassed. And in spite of myself, I've often felt a bit afraid of saying everything I thought even to Danceny. I blame myself a lot for that now and I'd give anything in the world to tell him for once, just once, how much I love him. Monsieur de Valmont has promised him that if I do as he tells me, he's going to arrange a chance for us to meet. I'll certainly do everything he wants but I still can't see how it's going to be possible.

Goodbye, Sophie dear, I've run out of space.*

76

The Vicomte de Valmont to the Marquise de Merteuil
From the Château de ——, 17 September 17—

Either you're teasing me in a way I can't understand or else when you wrote you were suffering from a particularly dangerous kind of hallucination. If I didn't know you as well as I do, fair lady, I'd really be very scared and that doesn't happen easily, no matter what you may say.

I've read and reread your epistle and still can't make head nor tail of it since there's no way in which I can take it at its face value. So what were you trying to tell me?

Was it merely that there was no point in taking a lot of trouble against such an insignificant foe? In that case, my dear, you might be mistaken: Prévan really is a charmer, more so than you think. In particular he has that most useful gift of involving large numbers of people in his love-life by his clever way of talking about it in public, in everyone's hearing, using every conversational gambit he can think of. There aren't many women who can avoid falling into that trap and responding, because since all women pride themselves on being sophisticated, none of them wants to miss the opportunity of showing it. And as you know full well, a woman who agrees to talk about love quickly ends up feeling it or at least behaving as if she did. This technique, which he's brought to a fine art, has the further advantage of leading women on to provide evidence of their downfall out of their own mouths; and let me say I've seen it happen.

I only knew about this particular case secondhand, because I've never been a close friend of Prévan's. Anyway there were six of us; thinking she was being very subtle and, except for those in the know, apparently talking in quite general terms, the Comtesse de —— revealed in the greatest detail how she'd given herself to Prévan and everything that had taken place between them. She told her story with such aplomb that she wasn't even perturbed by the burst of uncontrollable laughter which came from all six of us simultaneously; and I'll never forget that when one of us tried to apologize by pretending to cast doubt on the veracity of what she was saying or rather seemed to be saying, she solemnly declared that none of us were as well informed as she was and, quite undaunted, asked Prévan outright if she'd got a single detail wrong.

So it seems to me that this man is a danger to everybody. But for you, my dear Marquise, wasn't it enough that he was *pretty*, *definitely very pretty*, as you yourself put it? Or that he would make one of those attacks on you that you occasionally enjoy rewarding because it's so well made? Or that you thought it fun to give yourself to him for some reason or other? Or . . . ? How can I tell? How can I possibly guess the thousand and one whims governing a woman's mind and which are your only feminine attribute? Now you've been warned of the danger, I've no doubt you can easily avoid it but I had to warn you all the same. So I come back to my main question: what on earth were you trying to say?

If you were just poking fun at Prévan, quite apart from the fact that you were very long-winded, what was the point of addressing it to me? He must be made to look publicly ridiculous and I'd like to repeat my request for you to do just that.

Ah, I think I've solved the riddle! Your letter wasn't forecasting what you'll actually do but what he'll think you're ready to do once he's lured into your trap. Well, I fully approve of that plan but you must tread very warily. You know as well as I do that as far as public opinion's concerned, there's absolutely no difference between having a man and accepting his attentions, unless the man is an idiot and Prévan is far from that. If he can achieve just a semblance of victory, he'll brag about it and there'll be nothing more to be said. Idiots will believe him, mischief-makers will pretend to believe him: what defence can you put up then? Listen, Marquise: I'm afraid. Not that I doubt your skills: but it's good swimmers who get drowned.

I don't think I'm more stupid than the next man; I've discovered hundreds, no, a thousand and one ways of ruining a woman's reputation but try as I can I've never been able to think up a single way for her to avoid it. I have even felt, dear lady, that for all your consummate technique, on scores of occasions you've succeeded more by luck than judgement.

But perhaps I'm trying to find a reason for something that hasn't one. I'm amazed at the way I've been spending the last hour taking something seriously which is surely a joke on your part. You're trying to pull my leg! All right, but hurry up and let's talk about something else. Something else? I'm wrong, it's always the same topic, always about women, to be either had or ruined—and often both.

As you very rightly observe, I've enough material on hand here for exercising my talents in both fields—but not equally easily. I foresee that vengeance will move faster than love. The Volanges girl is as good as bedded, take my word for it; it only needs some opportunity and that I can undertake to provide. But it's not the same with Madame de Tourvel: that woman daunts me, I can't make her out. I've got a hundred proofs of her love—and a thousand of her resistance to it. To tell the truth, I'm afraid she's going to slip through my fingers.

The first effects of my return made me hope for better things. You will remember that I wanted to judge for myself and in order to observe her initial reaction, I hadn't announced my arrival in advance and had timed it to take place during a meal. And indeed I arrived out of the blue, like the *deus ex machina* of an opera bringing down the curtain.

I made enough fuss coming in to attract everybody's notice and was able to see at a glance my old aunt's joy, Madame de Volanges's vexation, and her daughter's sheepish delight. My beauty was sitting with her back to the door. She was busy cutting something and didn't even turn her head; but when I spoke to Madame de Rosemonde, at the first word my sensitive little puritan couldn't hold back a cry which I thought contained rather more love than surprise or fright. By now I had moved far enough into the room to see her face: her spiritual turmoil, her conflicting thoughts and feelings were depicted on it in a dozen different ways. I sat down at the table beside her; she hadn't the least idea what she was saying or doing. She tried to go on eating but there was no way she could manage to do so; in the end, after less than a quarter of an hour, her delight or her embarrassment reached such a point that she was reduced to having to ask to leave the table on the pretext of needing a breath of fresh air. She hurried out into the park. Madame de Volanges offered to go with her but our prude with the tender heart declined, no doubt only too glad of the chance of being alone and surrendering unreservedly to her sweet emotions!

I finished my meal as fast as I could. Then hardly had dessert been served than that diabolical old trout Volanges, obviously eager to queer my pitch, got up and went off to find the charming invalid; but I had anticipated her scheme and thwarted it by pretending to take her action as a general signal and got up at the same time, leading her daughter and the parish priest to follow suit. Madame de Rosemonde was thus left sitting alone with old Commandant de T—— and they both decided to rise too. So we all trooped out to join my beauty and discovered her in the shrubbery near the château. As she wanted to be alone rather than take a walk, she was as happy to come back in with us as to have our company out of doors.

As soon as I was sure that Madame de Volanges wouldn't get her chance to speak with her alone, I set about carrying out your instructions to look after the interests of your ward. Immediately after coffee I went up to my room and then into the other rooms as well to reconnoitre the terrain. I made my arrangements for organizing the little girl's correspondence and having accomplished my first good deed of the day, I wrote her a note informing her and asking her to trust me. With this note I enclosed Danceny's letter. I then went down to the drawing-room and discovered my lovely one reclining delightfully relaxed on a *chaise-longue*.

This sight excited me and brought a glint into my eyes which I realized would give them an urgent, loving look. I therefore took up a position to ensure that this would have its full effect. The first result was to make this divine puritan modestly lower her own large eyes. For a while I gazed at her angelic face before letting my eyes wander lingeringly over her whole body, assessing its shapes and curves, regrettably still half concealed under her flimsy dress. After moving from top to toe, I moved up from toe to top . . . Fair lady, her eyes were softly watching me, but only to drop again in a flash. Anxious to encourage them to return, I looked away and we embarked on that tacit convention, the first article in the treaty of coy love, which satisfies a mutual desire to look at each other by allowing glances to alternate until they eventually meet.

Convinced that my lovely lady was completely engrossed in this new pleasure, I looked around to make sure that we were both safe from observation: the others were engaged in fairly animated conversation, paying very little attention to us. I then set out to try and make her eyes give me a plainer message. To that end, I first intercepted some of her glances but so discreetly as not to alarm her modesty; to put the bashful young woman more at her ease, I pretended to be similarly embarrassed. Gradually our eyes grew used to meeting and lingered until in the end we both sat gazing into each other's eyes and I saw in hers that soft yearning look which is the auspicious signal of love and desire. But only for a second: quickly recovering, she rather shamefacedly altered her posture and looked away.

Not wanting to leave her in any doubt that I had been observing her various movements, I sprang to my feet and asked in a concerned voice if she was all right.* Immediately everyone gathered round her. I allowed them to go in front and as the Volanges girl was working at her tapestry near a window and couldn't leave her frame so quickly, I seized the opportunity to hand over Danceny's letter.

I was some distance away and had to toss the envelope on to her lap. She actually didn't know what to do with it. You'd have laughed to see her look of surprise and embarrassment. But it was certainly no laughing matter for me because of the risk that her awkwardness would give us away. However, a glance from me and a pointed gesture finally made her understand that she was to put the envelope into her pocket.

The rest of the day was uneventful. What has happened since may well lead to results which will make you happier, at least as far as your ward is concerned. But it's better to spend our time carrying out our plans than talking about them. Anyway, this is my eighth page and I've had enough. So goodbye.

I hardly need to tell you that the girl has replied to Danceny.* I've also had a reply from my own lovely lady to whom I wrote the day after I arrived. I'm sending you the two letters. You can please yourself whether you read them or not. This everlasting harping on the same theme which I'm already beginning to find rather tedious must be very dull for anyone not directly involved.

Goodbye again. I still love you very much but I do beg of you when you next talk about Prévan to make sure I can understand you.

77

The Vicomte de Valmont to Madame de Tourvel
15 September 17—

What reason can you have, Madame, for continuing to avoid me in so cruel and calculated a manner? How is it possible for you to treat my affectionate attentions in a way that would be hardly justifiable towards a man against whom you harboured the most bitter grudge? How strange! I came back here with a heart full of love and when a lucky chance offered me a seat beside you, you chose to pretend to feel unwell, thereby alarming your friends, rather than continue to sit beside me! How often later that day did you not turn your eyes away and refuse to grant me one single look? And when for a brief second your eyes seemed rather less stern, it was so short that I felt that rather than wanting me to enjoy it, you merely intended to make me realize all that I was missing by being deprived of it.

Dare I suggest that this is no way to treat a man who loves you and surely no way for a friend to act? Yet you well know whether I am such a man and it seems to me that I had the right to assume that you were willing to be the latter. What have I done to forfeit this friendship which you must have considered I deserved since you were good enough to offer me it earlier? Have I harmed my cause by showing too much trust? Are you punishing me for being so frank? But wasn't it to you as my friend that I confided the secret hidden in my heart? Wasn't it to my friend, and only to her, that I felt obliged to refuse conditions which, had I accepted them, would have made it too easy for me to disregard them, perhaps take unfair advantage of them, for my own benefit? And are you trying to make me believe, by your harsh and unfair treatment, that all I had to do to soften your heart was to lie to you?

I don't repent in the least having behaved as I did; I owed it both to you and to myself. But by what unhappy chance does every praiseworthy action of mine seem to lead only to some fresh misfortune?

It was after my conduct had prompted the only praise you had hitherto seen fit to give me that I found myself for the first time in the unfortunate position of incurring your displeasure. It was after I had proved my utter submission to your wishes by forgoing, purely in deference to your scruples, the pleasure of seeing you, that you tried to break off all correspondence with me, robbing me of even that poor compensation for the sacrifice you had demanded of me and snatching out of my hands even the love which alone gave you the right to make that demand. So in fact it is after I had spoken out so frankly in defiance of my best interests as a lover that you are keeping me at a distance as a dissolute seducer whose dishonourable intentions you have succeeded in uncovering!

Won't you ever tire of being so unfair? At least tell me what fresh wrongs of mine have led you to be so stern and do not hesitate to dictate to me your orders for my conduct. I undertake to obey them. Is it too unreasonable to ask what they are?

78

Madame de Tourvel to the Vicomte de Valmont
16 September 17—

You seem to be surprised, Monsieur, at my behaviour and even almost to go so far as to ask for an explanation, as if you have the right to criticize it. I must confess that I should have thought that it was rather I who was more entitled than yourself to be surprised and aggrieved; but after reading your rejection of my request, I have decided to put the matter out of my mind and ignore any further comments or reproaches. However, since you ask me for clarification and as, thank Heaven, I can feel no inner reason not to provide it, I am prepared yet once again to explain myself to you.

Anyone reading your letters would take me to be unfair or even unbalanced. I think that I in no way deserve that description; in particular, it seems to me that you have less right than anybody to think so. Doubtless you felt that by requiring me to justify myself you would be forcing me to go back over all that has happened between us. Apparently you thought that such a review would work only to your advantage; and since, on my part, I do not think I have anything to lose by it, at least in your eyes, I am not afraid of undertaking it. It may perhaps even, indeed, be the only way to discover which of us two has the right to feel aggrieved.

From the very first day you arrived in this château you will admit, I think, that your reputation justified me at the very least in adopting a somewhat wary attitude and that without fear of being accused of excessive prudery, I could reasonably have confined myself to treating you politely but coolly. You yourself would have been indulgent towards me and found it perfectly understandable for a woman as unsophisticated as myself to lack the qualities necessary to appreciate yours. That was surely the path of caution and it would have been all the easier for me to follow since I shall not hide the fact that when Madame de Rosemonde told me you were coming it was only the thought of my friendship for her and of hers for me that prevented me from showing her how vexed I was to hear it.*

I am ready to admit that at first you made a more favourable impression on me than I had expected; but you must admit that this could not last long and that you soon grew tired of the constraints which were apparently an inadequate reward for the good opinion of you which I had been led to form.

Then it was that you took advantage of my good faith and sense of security and had no scruples in speaking to me of a feeling which you must have realized would have offended me; and while you did nothing but aggravate your offence by your continuing misconduct, I tried to find some way of ignoring it by offering you the chance to make amends, at least in part. My request was so fair that you yourself did not feel able to refuse it; but banking on my indulgence, you took advantage of it to ask for my permission to do something to which I should not have agreed but which I granted, with certain conditions, none of which you have observed. Your correspondence took on such a tone that each one of your letters made it my duty not to answer you any more. It was at the very moment that your persistence was forcing me to keep you at arm's length that I humoured you, perhaps wrongly, by trying the only permissible way open to me to reconcile us. But what value do you attach to decent feelings? You despise friendship, pay no heed to the shame and unhappiness you cause by your mad passion, and seek only pleasure and victims for your pleasure.

Your conduct is irresponsible, your accusations absurd; you ignore your promises or rather you wantonly violate them and having agreed to stay away from me, you have come back here without being invited, regardless of my pleas and my arguments, without even being considerate enough to warn me. You had no qualms in subjecting me to a surprise whose effects, though perfectly natural, might well have been interpreted unfavourably by the people there. And far from trying to minimize or divert their attention from this momentary embarrassment which you had provoked, you seemed anxious to aggravate it. You carefully chose a seat next to me; when a slight indisposition compelled me to leave the room before the others, instead of respecting my wish for privacy, you brought everybody along with you to disturb me. After I came back into the drawing-room, whenever I made the slightest move I find you at my elbow; if I say a single word, you're always the one who replies. My most casual remark provides you with an excuse to bring the conversation back to a subject which I don't want to hear about, which could even be compromising for me because after all, Monsieur, however undoubted your skill, I think that something which I notice can equally well be noticed by other people.

So I am prevented from moving or talking freely and still you persist in pursuing me. I cannot raise my eyes without meeting yours. I am continually being forced to look away and then, as a quite incomprehensible consequence, you manage to make everybody turn round to look at me at the very moment when I should have preferred even to have avoided looking at myself.

And then you complain of the way I'm treating you! And you are surprised how anxious I am to avoid you! You would do better to blame me for tolerating you and to be surprised that I didn't leave the moment you arrived! I ought perhaps to have done so and unless you stop persecuting me, you may well force me to take this drastic but necessary step. No, I do not, nor shall I ever, forget the duty I owe to myself, to the bonds which I have and which I respect and hold dear, and I ask you to believe that were I ever to be reduced to the sad choice of sacrificing them or myself, I should never hesitate for a second. Goodbye, Monsieur de Valmont.

79

The Vicomte de Valmont to the Marquise de Merteuil
From the Château de ——, 18 September 17—

I was intending to go shooting this morning but the weather's appalling. My only reading matter is a new novel which would bore even a convent girl. We won't be dining for a couple of hours at the earliest so in spite of my long letter of yesterday, I shall continue our chat. And I'm absolutely certain that I shan't bore you because I'll be telling you about that *definitely very pretty* Prévan. How did you come to miss hearing about his famous escapade, the one which separated the *inseparables*? I bet you'll remember it as soon as I start. Anyway, since you're so anxious to know all about it, here it is.

You'll recall that the whole of Paris was amazed that three women, all three pretty and equally talented, remained on terms of such close friendship from the very first time they went into society. At first people put it down to their extreme shyness but they were soon surrounded by a swarm of eager admirers whose gallant attentions, equally distributed amongst all three, soon proved how popular they were; yet this merely made them all the better friends; the success of one was looked on as the success of all. People were hoping that at least love would introduce a note of rivalry. All our smart young men about town clamoured for the honour of being the apple of discord.* I'd even have joined in the fray myself if the high favour attained at that time by the Comtesse de —— had allowed me to look elsewhere until I'd been fully rewarded . . .

Meanwhile, as if by joint agreement, our three beauties made their choice at the same carnival ball and, far from whipping up the squalls we'd been looking forward to, it only made their friendship all the more interesting by adding the charm of swapping secrets.

The throng of disappointed suitors then joined forces with the jealous females and this positively scandalous constancy became the butt of public disapproval. Some claimed that this *club of inseparables* (as it came to be called) was based on the principle of joint ownership, with love itself falling into this category. Others maintained that while there was no male competition, a certain feminine rivalry wasn't excluded; some even went so far as to claim that the lovers had been let into the club purely as a sop to propriety, honorary members with no executive rights whatsoever.

Be that as it may, this gossip didn't lead to the hoped-for outcome; on the contrary, the three couples realized that if they split up now their reputation would be in tatters. They decided to weather the storm. Public opinion, which tires of everything, soon grew tired of this idle backbiting; with its natural fickleness it turned to other subjects and then, true to form, made a wild swing from disapproval to praise. As in such matters fashion sets the pace, enthusiasm grew and grew until it reached frenzied proportions. It was then that Prévan decided to put these prodigies to the test and settle the question to his own and indeed everyone else's satisfaction.

He started cultivating these paragons and had no difficulty in making their acquaintance. This seemed to him a promising omen, for he was well aware that happy people are not so easily accessible. He quickly discovered that this much vaunted happiness was, as with royalty, more envied than enviable. He noticed that these so-called inseparables were beginning to look for entertainment outside their little circle and were even finding it enjoyable. He reached the conclusion that the bonds of love or friendship were already loosening or severed and that only vanity and force of habit were holding the group together.

However, while the women needed to stick together and maintained a semblance of intimacy, the men, less inhibited in their actions, began to discover other duties and business to attend to; they still grumbled about them but were no longer neglecting them. At evening gatherings, you'd seldom see all six in a group.

This state of affairs was assiduously exploited by Prévan, who naturally used to find himself seated every day beside the unaccompanied lady and was thus able to pay court to each of the three in turn, as circumstances permitted. He soon realized that it would be fatal for him to discriminate in favour of any one of the three: the coy young woman thus singled out would be scared at the thought of being the first to fall, the hurt vanity of the other two would lead them to join forces against the new lover and they would infallibly unleash a barrage of the highest of high principles against him; what is more, jealousy would inevitably bring back the ousted lover who might prove dangerous. He would have faced insuperable odds; his threefold operation made everything easy: women turned a blind eye because each was involved, the men did the same because none of them thought he was.

At that time, Prévan had only one woman to give up and by a stroke of good luck she achieved a certain notoriety: her foreign origin and the attentions of a royal prince, whom she rather astutely turned down, had made her the cynosure of all eyes, at court and in town; some of the honour rubbed off on to him and it stood him in good stead with his new mistresses. His only problem was keeping all three intrigues in step, since they had necessarily to keep pace with the slowest. In fact, one of his close friends told me that he had extreme difficulty in holding one of them back when she came to the boil a fortnight before the other two.

Finally the great day arrived. Having obtained the three women's consent, Prévan was now in complete control of the operation which he now finished off as you'll see. Of the three husbands, one was away, another was due to leave early next day, and the third was in town. The three girls were intending to have supper with the prospective grass-widow but their new master had refused permission for their former attendants to be invited. That morning he made up three packets of his mistress's letters. In one of them he put a portrait of herself which she'd given him; in the second, the lady's monogram lovingly painted by herself; in the third, a lock of her hair. Each of the three received this third part of his sacrifice in full settlement and in return agreed to send a resounding letter of dismissal to her disgraced lover.

So far, so good; but more was in store. As the one with the husband in town was free only during the day, a diplomatic illness was invented to excuse her from going to supper with her friends; Prévan could spend the whole evening in her company. The woman whose husband was away offered him that night, while the third one, whose man was due to leave at daybreak, reserved that time as her hour for love.

Prévan, as ever the perfect organizer, now dashes round to his foreign lovely armed with the appropriate foul temper which he passes on to his beloved and departs only after he has sparked off a row guaranteed to provide him with twenty-four hours' leave. These arrangements completed, he went home hoping for some rest; but here further business awaited him.

Their letters of dismissal had suddenly opened the disgraced lovers' eyes; none of them could possibly doubt that Prévan was

the culprit and in their resentment at having been tricked, along
with the annoyance almost always associated with the minor
humiliation of having been given their marching orders, all three
had, independently but as it were by common agreement, decided to demand satisfaction from their fortunate rival.

So on arriving home Prévan found three challenges waiting
for him. He accepted these without demur but not wanting to
forfeit any of the pleasures or the glory of his escapade, he
arranged all three encounters for the following morning, at
the same time and place—at one of the gates of the Bois
de Boulogne.

That night he completed his triple run, all with equal success—at least he later bragged that each of his new lady-loves
received three pledges and proofs of his love. As you no doubt
realize, any historical evidence for this is lacking. All that an
objective historian can do is to point out to any cynical reader
that an inflated vanity and a heated imagination are capable of
working miracles; and moreover, that his brilliant performance
that night was going to be followed by a morning that seemed
bound to excuse him from having any concern for the future. Be
that as it may, the following facts are better authenticated.

Prévan arrived punctually at the spot he'd indicated and
found his three rivals waiting, rather taken aback at meeting each
other and maybe already somewhat mollified by seeing they were
brothers in misfortune. He approached them in his affable,
casual manner and made the following speech, which has been
accurately reported to me:

'Gentlemen, seeing yourselves gathered together here, you
have no doubt guessed that you all have the same grievance
against me. I am ready to give you satisfaction. I suggest you
draw lots to decide who will be the first to try to settle his account
with me, as you are all entitled to do. I haven't brought along any
witnesses or any seconds. I didn't have any whilst perpetrating
the offence and I shan't ask for any in answering for it.'

At this point the gambler in him led him to add: 'I know
that one hardly ever wins when one *goes for seven** but whatever
the fate awaiting me this morning, if we've had time to win the
love of the ladies and the esteem of men, we've lived long
enough.'

While his opponents looked at each other in surprise, perhaps already having scruples as to the fairness of this triple contest, Prévan went on:

'I shan't deny that last night's exertions have left me in pretty poor shape. If you could give me a chance to recover, I should appreciate your generosity. I've ordered breakfast to be prepared. Won't you do me the honour of being my guests? We can have breakfast together and we must try to make it a cheerful affair. We can fight over such trifles but above all, don't let us allow them to spoil our good humour.'

The invitation was accepted. It's said that Prévan had never been more charming. He skilfully avoided humiliating any of his rivals and persuaded them that they would all have succeeded just as easily; in particular, he got them to agree that they wouldn't have let the opportunity slip either. This having been established, the whole affair collapsed of its own accord. Before breakfast was over, they had already repeated a dozen times that gentlemen had better things to do than fight over such worthless women. This thought produced a feeling of good fellowship, further stimulated by the wine, and it wasn't long before they'd not only forgotten all their grievances but were swearing eternal friendship.

While no doubt preferring this outcome to its alternative, Prévan didn't want to forgo any of the fame. Cleverly adapting his plan to the circumstances, he said to the three men he'd offended: 'In fact, it's your three mistresses whom you ought to be settling your score with, not me. I'll give you the chance. I can already see that it won't be long before I'm likely to suffer the same humiliating fate as you; if each of you wasn't able to keep one woman faithful, what hope have I got of doing it with three of them? I'll have the same grudge as you. So, please accept an invitation to supper tonight in my little house and I hope your revenge won't be long delayed.' They all accepted and having embraced their new-found friend, parted until the evening, looking forward to seeing the result of his promises.

Prévan returned to Paris without delay and in accordance with the prescribed custom called on his three new conquests. He persuaded all three to come to supper with him that evening, tête-à-tête in his little house. Two of them did, in fact, raise some objections but what can you refuse on the morning after? He arranged for them to come at hourly intervals, long enough for him to carry out his plan. Having settled this, he went off to warn his fellow-conspirators and all four left together in high spirits to wait for their victims.

In comes the first one: Prévan appears alone, welcomes her with a great play of eagerness and takes her into his sanctuary of which she thought she was the tutelary goddess. Then, on some slight excuse, he slips away to be immediately replaced by the outraged lover.

You can imagine how at such a moment, a bewildered woman still not used to having affairs was a very easy prey: any accusation not made was taken as a pardon and the runaway slave was once more at the mercy of her former master and only too glad to be forgiven by accepting her former chains. The peace treaty was then ratified in a more private place and the empty stage was now filled by the other actors in their turn, more or less in the same roles and above all with the same ending.

Till now each woman had thought she was the only one involved. It was an even greater shock and embarrassment when all three couples came together again at supper-time. But their confusion reached its peak when Prévan appeared in their midst too and apologized to the three faithless women, thereby mercilessly exposing their secret and bringing home to them without any shadow of doubt how badly they'd been tricked.

However, they all sat down to supper and it wasn't long before all their embarrassment evaporated: the men let themselves go and the women took it . . . lying down. Every heart was full of hatred but tender words were exchanged; the high spirits aroused desire which lent added charm. This amazing orgy lasted till dawn and when they parted, the women must have felt that they were forgiven; but the very next day, the men, still resentful, sent all three packing. And not content with leaving their fickle mistresses, they completed their revenge by making their escapade public. Since then, one of them has gone into a convent, the two others are moping around in exile on their country estates.*

So that's Prévan's story. It's up to you to see if you want to add to his fame and be harnessed to his triumphal chariot. Your letter made me really worried and I can't wait to get a clear and more sensible reply from you.

Farewell, dear lady. Beware of those amusing or eccentric ideas of yours which you find it so hard to resist. Don't forget that with the sort of life you are leading, sheer intelligence isn't enough; one false step and you're condemned without reprieve. And please, please allow a cautious friend to guide your pleasures, just occasionally.

Farewell. I still love you as much as if you were sensible.

80

The Chevalier Danceny to Cécile Volanges
Paris, 18 September 17—

Cécile, my Cécile, whenever shall we meet again? How can I possibly get used to living so far away from you? Where can I find the strength and the courage? No, no, I shall never, never be able to bear this dreadful exile! As each day goes by, my misery grows worse; and never an end in sight! Valmont had promised to help and comfort me and now he is ignoring me, perhaps even forgetting me! He is close to the woman he loves and he no longer thinks how greatly one can suffer when one is far away from one's beloved. When he arranged for your letter to be delivered to me, he didn't put in any letter of his own. But it's he who is going to let me know when I shall be able to see you and how. Hasn't he got anything to tell me? And you don't mention it either. Don't you still feel the same longing for us to meet? Oh, Cécile, Cécile, I'm so miserable. I love you more than ever and though that love is the light of my life, it is turning into an agony. I can't go on like this, I must see you, I must, I must, if only for a second. Every day when I get up, I say to myself: 'I shan't be seeing her'; and when I go to bed, I say: 'I haven't seen her.' My days drag on and on with never one single moment of happiness; I'm just sunk in misery and despair; and all this comes from something that I was expecting to bring me every imaginable joy! And if you add my anxiety over your problems to my own dreadful worries then you have some idea of my state of mind. I think of you every minute of the day but never without foreboding. If I imagine you unhappy and suffering, I suffer with you; if I imagine you calm and collected, my own sufferings become far greater. All around I can see only misery.

Oh, how different it was when we were both living in Paris! Then everything was pure joy. Even the times when you weren't there were made brighter by the certainty of seeing you; every minute of the hours I spent away from you brought me nearer to you. And what I did during those hours was always in some way related to you. If I was working at some task, I felt I was making myself more worthy of you; if I was pursuing some artistic interest, it was in the hope of giving you greater pleasure. Even when the social whirl took me away from your company, I was still with you in spirit. In the theatre, I tried to guess which things would have interested you; at the concert, I remembered how well you played and the lovely times we'd spent together. In a drawing-room or driving out in a carriage, I'd seize on the slightest sign of similarity to you, I compared you with every-body and you were always the loveliest. For every moment of my day I paid tribute to you and every evening I placed my tributes at your feet.

And now what's left? Pain, regret, endless frustration, and the slight hope that Valmont will break his silence—a hope that your own silence turns into anxiety. You're only a bare twenty-five miles away, no distance at all, yet for me—for me alone—those few miles are an insurmountable obstacle! And when I plead with my friend and my love to help me overcome this obstacle, they both remain calm and aloof. And not only do they not help me, they don't even bother to reply!

Whatever happened to Valmont's promise to help? And above all, what has happened to your tender affection which gave you all those ingenious ideas for ways and means to see each other every day? Sometimes I remember how, very unwillingly, I was obliged to sacrifice my longing to see you because of other com-mitments or considerations: what didn't you have to say to me then! What arguments didn't you find to stop me! And you will remember, Cécile, how my arguments always gave way before yours. I'm not claiming any credit for that; I didn't even see it as a sacrifice at all, I was so anxious to let you have everything you wanted. But now it's my turn to ask for something. What is it?

To see you just for a second, to be able to renew my pledge to love you for ever and ever and to hear you say those very same words . . . Isn't your happiness still inextricably bound up with mine? Ah, if not, that is a hateful thought that I utterly reject; it would be the death-blow to all my hopes. You love me and you always will: that's what I believe, that's something I'm certain of, something I can never doubt . . . But my situation is frightful and I can't bear it any longer. Goodbye, Cécile.*

A feminist perspective

81

The Marquise de Merteuil to the Vicomte de Valmont
Paris, 20 September 17—

Oh, my dear Vicomte, how my heart bleeds for you! And how your fears do indeed prove my superiority! And you want to be my guide and tutor? Oh, you poor dear, what a gap still exists between us! And not even all your male pride would ever succeed in bridging it! Just because you couldn't carry through my schemes, you think they're impossible. And this weak, vain character actually has the effrontery to assess my capabilities and my resources! Truly, Vicomte, I can't conceal the fact that your advice had made me very cross indeed.

If, to disguise your incredibly inept handling of your judge's wife, you try to parade triumphantly your success in having, for one short second, disconcerted that shy young woman who loves you, all right, I'll agree. If you manage to extract a glance, one single glance, from her, well, I shall merely smile and let you enjoy your glance. If, realizing, in spite of yourself, the pettiness of your conduct, you hope to distract my attention by humouring me with an account of your sublime effort to bring together two young people, both positively yearning to meet and who, by the way, owe that yearning entirely to my efforts, all right again, I'm prepared to grant you that, too. If, finally, basing yourself on these glorious actions, you claim the right to inform me pompously that *it's better to spend your time carrying out your plans than talking about them*, well, that's merely a bit of harmless vanity that doesn't affect me and I forgive you. But if you imagine that I need your prudential wisdom, that I'd be lost if I didn't defer to your advice and that I should in consequence refuse myself a pleasure, something that tickles my fancy, well there, Vicomte, you really are taking the trust I'm prepared to have in you too much for granted.

In point of fact, what have you ever done that I haven't done a thousand times better? You've seduced and even ruined large numbers of women but what difficulties did you ever encounter in making all your conquests? What obstacles did you have to overcome? What credit can you actually claim for yourself in all that? Good looks? Pure chance. Social graces? How could anybody avoid picking those up if he spends a lot of time in society. Wit? Certainly; but at a pinch fashionable jargon will work just as well. Highly commendable impudence? Yes, but perhaps entirely attributable to your first easy conquests. Unless I'm much mistaken, that's your entire equipment. After all, with regard to any fame you may have acquired, I imagine you won't mind if I don't attach much importance to your skill in creating or taking advantage of scandal?

As for prudential wisdom or subtlety, I won't speak for myself, but is there a single woman who hasn't got more than you? Take your own case: that judge's wife is leading you by the nose.

Believe me, Vicomte, people rarely acquire qualities they can do without.* When there's no danger, why give a damn? In fact, for you males, defeats merely mean fewer successes. In this highly unfair contest, if we don't lose, it's our good luck and if you don't win, it's just bad luck for you. Even if I were to grant that you have as many gifts as we have, we'd still be that much better than you because we need to make use of them all the time.

Very well, let's assume that you require as much skill to conquer us as we do to defend—or not to defend—ourselves; but you must at least agree that once you've succeeded, your skill has lost its point. You'll be completely absorbed in your new enjoyment and abandon yourselves to it unconditionally, without any qualms: for you, it's quite unimportant how long it lasts.

In fact, in this mutual exchange of the bonds of love, to use the current jargon, only you men are able to decide whether to strengthen them or break them. We can consider ourselves lucky indeed if, in your flighty way, you prefer to lie low rather than show off and are content merely to humiliate us by deserting us and not turn the woman you worshipped yesterday into today's victim!

But should some unfortunate woman find her shackles irksome before the man does, what risks she has to run if she attempts to slip out of them or even dares to shake them! What fear and trembling, should she try to escape from a man whom in her heart she finds repugnant! And if he stubbornly clings on, then fear will force her to grant him what she used to grant out of love: her arms still open though her heart is closed; and to undo those bonds which you men would merely have snapped she will need great care and cunning. She's at her enemy's mercy; if he acts shabbily, she's helpless. And how can he be expected to behave otherwise when, though he may sometimes be praised for being generous, he's never blamed for being the opposite?

You'll surely not deny such self-evident truths which have now become commonplaces. If, however, you have noticed me, regardless of the circumstances and of public opinion, making these males jump like puppets to my fads and fancies, imposing my will on some and rendering the others powerless to harm me; if, following the vagaries of my likes and dislikes, I've either enrolled into my following of admirers or else sent packing those throneless tyrants who have become our slaves;* if, in the course of all these frequent and violent changes, my reputation has remained unscathed, mustn't you have been forced to conclude that, having been born to avenge my sex and subjugate yours, I must have succeeded in elaborating certain methods hitherto unknown?

Oh, Vicomte, you must save your advice and your misgivings for those frenzied women, self-styled *women of feeling*, whose heated imagination would lead one to think that nature had put their senses in their heads, who have never given the matter proper thought and continually confuse love with the lover, who suffer from the wild delusion that the man whom they have chosen for their pleasure is the only one capable of providing them with it and are so truly superstitious that they offer the priest the respect and belief which properly belongs only to Eros himself.

And please reserve your fears also for those women whose vanity outruns their caution and, when it comes to the point, can't face the prospect of getting their lover to leave them.

But above all, reserve your greatest fears for those restless, idle females whom you call sensitive and who fall so easily and so helplessly into the grip of love, who feel the need to think about it even when they're not experiencing it and hurl themselves headlong into the turmoil of their ideas, producing those letters so full of tenderness and so dangerous to write and who aren't afraid of entrusting this evidence of weakness to the object of their affection: foolhardy women who are incapable of recognizing in their current lover their future enemy.

But what have I got in common with these feckless women? When did you last see me depart from the rules which I've laid down for myself and be untrue to my principles? I say my principles deliberately since I don't mean other women's haphazard principles, accepted uncritically and followed out of sheer habit; mine are the fruit of deep cogitation, created by myself. I can truly say that I am a self-made woman.

When I went into society I was still a child, required to be seen and not heard; but I made use of my inactivity to observe and reflect. While people thought me scatterbrained or dreamy, paying little attention to the words of wisdom they were so keen to impart, I was carefully noting everything they were trying to conceal.

This curiosity helped my education by teaching me how to dissemble; being frequently obliged to hide what I was observing from the eyes of those around me, I tried to control my own and ever since I've been able to put on that dreamy look which you've so often admired. Encouraged by this early success, I tried similarly to control my facial expressions.

If I felt distressed I made a great effort to look composed or even delighted; I even went so far as to deliberately cause myself pain and practise looking pleased at the same time. I made a similar effort, though this was harder, to repress the outward signs of any unexpected joy. This is how I've managed to achieve that mastery over my features that I've noticed sometimes so surprises you.

I was still young and not very interesting; but my thoughts were the only things that belonged to me and I felt indignant that someone might snatch them from me or detect them against my will. Thus armed, I was keen to try my hand: not content with preventing people from reading my thoughts, I delighted in showing off different aspects of myself: having mastered my gestures, I directed my attention to my words and controlled both of them according to the situation or even as my whims dictated. From that time onward, I was in complete command of my thoughts and I revealed only the ones it was useful for me to show.

Analysing myself had made me interested in faces and the way they reveal character; it gave me that insight which experience has taught me not to trust completely but which, all things considered, has rarely let me down.

I still wasn't fifteen and I already possessed the skills to which the majority of our politicians owe their success; yet I was still a novice in the science which I wished to master.

You can imagine that like all young girls, I was curious to learn about love and pleasure; but not having been brought up in a convent, without any close friend of my own sex and under the ever-watchful eye of my mother, I had only the vaguest of notions which I couldn't exactly define. Even nature, which has certainly been very kind to me since, didn't as yet give me any hint; it seemed almost as if she was working silently to bring her work to perfection. But my head was seething: I didn't want the delights of love, I wanted to know about it. This desire for information suggested to me how I might approach the matter.

I had the feeling that the only man whom I could talk to about it without compromising myself was my confessor. I made up my mind on the spot; swallowing my slight embarrassment, I boldly laid claim to a sin which I hadn't committed, accusing myself of *doing everything that women do*. That was how I put it but I honestly didn't know what I was talking about. My hopes were neither completely dashed nor entirely satisfied: I was prevented from finding out what I wanted to know by fear of giving myself away; but the good reverend father made my trespass sound so cataclysmic that I concluded it must be extremely pleasurable and my desire for knowledge was replaced by the desire to enjoy it.

I've no idea where that particular desire might have led me; being completely innocent, I might perhaps have been ruined by just one experience. Luckily for me, a few days later my mother announced that I was going to be married, so being now certain of learning all about it, my curiosity immediately evaporated and I landed up in Monsieur de Merteuil's arms *virgo intacta*.

When the moment of truth eventually came, I felt so calm and collected that I had to keep my wits about me to put on the proper embarrassment and reluctance. That first night which girls normally look forward to as something very nice or expect to be rather horrid, I believed purely as an experience: I took accurate note of the pain and the pleasure and saw my various sensations merely as a means of gathering information for later evaluation.

I soon developed a taste for this sort of study but true to my principles and perhaps instinctively sensing that my husband must be the last person to be taken into my confidence, I resolved, just because I was attracted by love, to show myself as completely unfeeling with him. This apparent frigidity was later to provide the basis for his blind and unhesitating trust in me. After careful thought, I added to this an image of a scatterbrain, justified by my tender years. He never thought me more of a child than when I was giving my most barefaced impersonation of one.

However, I admit that at first I allowed myself to be carried away in the whirl of society and gave myself up entirely to its futile distractions. But a few months later, after Monsieur de Merteuil had carried me off into his gloomy country estate, dread of being bored revived my interest in my studies and as the people surrounding me down there were so inferior in rank as to preclude any suspicion, I was able to extend my field of operations. In particular, it was now that I was able to satisfy myself that love, so highly commended as the cause of our pleasures, is at most nothing but the pretext for them.*

These agreeable pastimes were cut short by Monsieur de Merteuil's illness; I was obliged to follow him back to Paris where he went for treatment. As you know, he died a short time later and though, by and large, I had no grudge against him, nevertheless I keenly appreciated the freedom I'd be enjoying as a widow and I made myself a solemn promise not to waste it.

My mother was expecting me either to go into a convent or to go back and live with her. I refused both these courses and my only concession to the proprieties was to return to the same country estate where I still had some investigations to complete.

I complemented them from books but you mustn't assume that they were purely the ones you think.* I studied our manners and customs in novels, our views on life in the philosophers, I even tried to discover how our most high-minded moralists want us to behave, thereby ascertaining what you could do, what you ought to think, and the appearances you must keep up. Once I knew these three things, the only one that presented any problems was the last: I hoped to solve them and I set my mind to it.

I was beginning to become bored with countrified pastimes which didn't provide the necessary variety for my lively mind. I was feeling the need to be flirtatious and this reconciled me to love, not of course to feeling it but to inspiring it and shamming it. In spite of reading and being told that it was impossible to fake love, I could see that all I needed was a writer's wit and the gifts of an actor. I practised both of these skills, perhaps not unsuccessfully; but instead of courting the empty applause of theatre audiences, I resolved that whereas so many people squander their talents to satisfy their vanity, I would use mine for pleasure.

A year passed in these different pursuits. As my mourning was now over, I could again go back into society and I returned to Paris, full of my grand design. I immediately struck an entirely unexpected obstacle.

My solitary existence and my long retreat had given me a gloss of prudery which scared off the smartest of the young men about town. They held off and left me at the mercy of a host of bores who all wanted to marry me. Turning them down was no trouble but some of the rejects were approved of by my family and in the course of these domestic squabbles I wasted a lot of time that I had been promising myself to spend so agreeably. So in order to attract the smart young men back and scare off the others, I was compelled to commit some public indiscretions and put as much effort into spoiling my reputation as I had hoped to put into keeping it. As you may imagine, I had no difficulty at all. But as I steered clear of passion, I did only as much as I felt necessary and dispensed my peccadilloes in discreet doses.

As soon as I'd achieved my objective, I did an about-turn, giving the credit for my conversion to a few of those women who, since they have no possible claim to being attractive, take refuge in integrity and high principles. It was a master-stroke which succeeded beyond all my expectations. In their gratitude these superannuated matrons became my staunchest supporters and their blind devotion to my cause—they described my reform as their work—reached such heights that at the slightest comment anyone dared to make, the whole tribe of puritans cried 'shame!' and 'scandal!' Similarly I also won the support of our aspiring sirens who, being convinced that I was giving up competing against them, insisted on covering me with praise every time they were anxious to demonstrate that they didn't slander everybody all the time.

Meanwhile my earlier conduct had brought back the lovers and in order to propitiate them as well as my injudicious champions, I put myself forward as impressionable but difficult to please, a woman whose extreme fastidiousness made her proof against love.

I now started to deploy the skills I'd developed on the big stage. My first concern was to gain a reputation for being invincible. To acquire this, the only men whose attentions I seemed to be accepting were the ones I couldn't in fact stand. I used these to establish myself as a woman who said no; meanwhile I could say yes to the man of my choice without risk. However, my pretence of demureness prevented him from ever being able to join me in society. In this way, the eyes of the company were always directed on the *hapless* lover.

You know how quickly I make up my mind. I do this because I've noticed that it's almost always the preliminary manœuvres which give a woman away; however hard one tries, the tone before and after succeeding is never the same. This difference never escapes the eye of any close observer. So I've found making the wrong choice less dangerous than letting it be found out. My method has the added advantage of eliminating the presumptions which are all that people have to go on.

Such precautions and the care I take never to write, never to provide evidence of my surrender, may seem excessive; for me, they never seemed really adequate. By looking deep into my own heart, I have been able to explore other people's and I've discovered that there is nobody who doesn't conceal a secret which it is essential never to let anyone find out. This is a truth which was better understood in the olden days than now, a truth perhaps subtly symbolized by the story of Samson. I'm a modern Dalila and like her, I've always been able to worm out that important secret. Ah, the number of Samsons whose hair I've got between the blades of my scissors! And as I'm not afraid of those any more, they're the only ones I've sometimes risked humiliating.* With the others, I've been more crafty. I've guaranteed their discretion by getting them to deceive me to avoid appearing fickle myself, pretending to be friendly, seeming to trust them, treating them generously, leaving each of them with the flattering thought of having been my only lover. And failing all that, I anticipate the end of the affair and make them look ridiculous or spread malicious gossip to destroy any credibility such dangerous men might have.

You have seen me using such tactics time and time again: how can you still have doubts as to my cautiousness? Just cast your mind back to the time when you first started paying me your attentions. I'd never felt more flattered; I wanted you even before I met you. I was fascinated by your prestige; I could see you as the finest feather in my cap and I couldn't wait to come to grips with you. You are the only one of my flames that ever for a second made me lose my self-control. Yet if ever you had wanted to ruin me, how could you possibly have done so? Empty words that leave no echo, that your reputation itself would have rendered suspect, a series of implausible acts which in any honest account would have looked like a badly constructed novel. True, since that time I have revealed all my secrets to you but you know the concerns we have in common and who is the reckless one of us two.*

Since I'm in the process of explaining myself to you, I want to do so thoroughly and accurately. I can hear you saying that my maid has the whiphand over me; indeed, even though she doesn't know my secret feelings, she does know my secret actions. When you raised this point earlier, I merely told you that I was sure of her and my reply obviously put your mind at rest because since then you have yourself confided quite risky secrets of your own to her. But now that Prévan seems to be getting under your skin and causing you some confusion, I suspect you're no longer prepared to take my word for it. So let me enlighten you further.

In the first place, that woman is my foster-sister, a relationship which is hardly considered one by us but carries a good deal of weight with people of her class. Moreover, I know her secret and even more: she was once madly in love and paid the price; if I hadn't come to her rescue, she'd have been ruined. Her parents, bristling with honour, wanted nothing less than to shut her away in a convent. They came to see me. I saw at a glance that their wrath might be useful to me. I endorsed their plan and applied for and obtained the necessary order. Then I suddenly switched to a more lenient view, persuaded her parents, pulled strings with the old Minister and got them all to agree to leave the authority in my hands, with the power either to suspend or execute its provisions as I think fit, in the light of the girl's future behaviour. So she knows that her fate is in my hands and if, by some remote chance, these powerful inducements weren't enough to keep her quiet, isn't it quite obvious that revealing her past conduct and its legitimate punishment would quickly destroy her credibility?

These are what I describe as basic precautions but I use hundreds of others too, as the occasion or situation demands, relying on my brains and long experience, when the need arises. I won't bore you with the minutiae but I adhere to them most scrupulously and if you want to understand them properly you must take the trouble to look at them in the context of my conduct as a whole.

But to imagine that I've taken such care only to fail to reap the fruits of my labours; that having raised myself with such arduous efforts above the ordinary run of women, I could ever consent to cringe like them, wavering between cowardice and recklessness, and above all that I could be so scared of any man as to flee for my life, no, Vicomte, never, never! I must conquer or die in the attempt.* As for Prévan, I want to have him and have him I shall; he wants to tell and he won't: that's our romance in a nutshell. Goodbye.*

82

Cécile Volanges to the Chevalier Danceny
From the Château de ———, 21 September 17—

Oh, your letter's made me so sad! And to think I was looking forward to it so much and hoping it would help console me and now I'm more miserable than ever! How I cried as I was reading it, though I'm not blaming you for that, I've cried such a lot because of you before without being so sad but this time it was different.

What do you mean when you say that your love is turning into agony? That you can't go on living like this or put up with our situation any longer? Are you going to stop loving me just because it's not so pleasant as it used to be? It seems to me that I'm just as badly off as you, in fact more so, yet I just love you more and more. It's not my fault if Monsieur de Valmont hasn't written to you. I haven't been able to ask him to because I've not been alone with him and we'd agreed that we wouldn't ever talk to each other in public; and that's for your sake, too, so he can do what you want him to more quickly. I'm not saying that I don't want it too, but what can I do about it? If you think it's so simple, please let me know how, there's nothing I'd like better.

Do you think it's very pleasant to be told off all the time by Mama, who never even used to speak to me at all before? Well, I can tell you it's not. It's worse now than if I was in the convent. My only consolation was the thought that it was for your sake; there were even times when I thought I was quite happy; then when I think that you're annoyed too and when it's not my fault at all, I get even more depressed than by all the things that have happened to me up till now.

Just getting your letters is difficult and if Monsieur de Valmont wasn't so obliging and so clever I don't know how I'd manage; and writing to you is even harder. I don't dare do it at all during the morning because Mama is never far away and keeps coming into my room all the time. Sometimes I can do it during the afternoon by saying I'm going to practise my harp or singing and even then I have to break off all the time so that I can be heard practising. Luckily my maid sometimes gets drowsy in the evening and I tell her I can easily put myself to bed so that she can go away and leave me with a light. And then I have to hide behind my bed-curtains so they can't see the light and I have to keep an ear open for the slightest sound so as to hide everything under my bedclothes if anyone comes in. I'd like you to be here so that you could see! You'd certainly see how very much I must love you to do all that! Anyway it's certainly true that I'm doing everything I can and I'd like to do still more.

Of course I'm not refusing to tell you I love you and I always shall. I've never meant it more than now and yet you're annoyed! Yet you certainly told me before I said it to you that it was enough to make you happy. You can't deny that, it's in your letters. Although I haven't got them now, I can remember them as well as when I used to read them every day. And because we're separated, you no longer think the same way! But we're not going to be separated for ever, I assume? O Heavens, how miserable I am! And it's certainly you who's making me like that!

Talking of your letters, I do hope you've kept the ones Mama took away from me and sent to you. The day will certainly come when I shan't have all the problems I've got now and you'll be able to let me have them all back. How happy I'll be when I can keep them for ever without anybody having the right to interfere! For the present I'm sending them back to Monsieur de Valmont because otherwise it'd be too risky. All the same, I can never give any of them back without feeling a pang in my heart.

Goodbye, dear, dear friend. I love you with all my heart and I shall love you for ever. I do hope that now you've stopped feeling cross and if I was sure of that, I shouldn't be either any more. Write to me as soon as you can, because I feel that until then I'll always be miserable.

83

Vicomte de Valmont to Madame de Tourvel
From the Château de ——, 23 September 17—

For pity's sake, Madame, can we not meet and talk together once more, since our last meeting was so unfortunately cut short? Let me finally prove to you how different I am from the man whom you depicted in such hateful colours. Above all, let me once again enjoy that friendly trust which you were beginning to show me. You make virtue seem so charming, just as you make every decent feeling lovelier, more precious! Ah, therein lies your charm, your irresistible charm, a unique combination of strength and respectability!

No doubt seeing you is enough to make anyone desire to please you and hearing you talk in company only adds to that desire. But anyone who has the good fortune to know you more closely, who can sometimes read into your soul, is soon swept away by a nobler emotion, in which devotion turns to veneration; he comes to worship you as the incarnation of all the virtues. And I, who perhaps was more ready than others to love and follow the paths of righteousness even though I had been led astray by certain youthful errors, have been brought back to them by you, for you have made me more susceptible to all their charms. Will you brand this new-found love of mine as a crime? Will you condemn your own handiwork? Would you even blame yourself for the interest you might feel for it? What danger can you fear from so pure a feeling? And what sweet pleasures might you not enjoy through it?

So you feel threatened by my love, you find it violent, frenzied? Then tame it by the greater gentleness of your love. Don't reject the power I am begging you to wield over me, a power from which I swear never to escape and which, it seems to me, would not be utterly devoid of virtue. What sacrifice could I ever find too painful when I am certain that your heart would understand how much it cost me? What man could be such a wretch as to be unable to enjoy the deprivations which he is freely accepting, not to prefer a glance freely granted to any of the more material delights he might be able to snatch or take by surprise? And you took me for that sort of man! And you were afraid of me! Oh, why is your happiness not completely in my hands! How I would avenge myself—by making you happy! But such sweet power can never grow out of a barren friendship: it can come only from love ...

That word intimidates you! Why? A fonder affection, a stronger union, two minds that think as one, happiness and sorrow equally shared, what is there in all this that your soul finds repugnant? We are talking of love! That at least is what you have inspired and what I feel! Above all, it is love which by its unselfishness can judge actions according to their real and not their superficial worth. It is an inexhaustible treasure-house for sensitive hearts, where everything done for it or by it becomes infinitely precious.

How can these truths, so self-evident, so pleasing to put into practice, possibly be frightening? And what can you have to fear from a man of feeling whose love forbids him to look for any happiness beyond your own? For this is now my sole desire: I shall sacrifice everything to fulfil it—except the feeling which inspires it; and if you agree to share that feeling, you will even be able to control it at will. But we must not allow it to come between us any longer, when it ought instead to be bringing us closer together . . . If the friendship you have offered me isn't just an empty word, if, as you were telling me yesterday, it is the tenderest emotion known to your soul, let it be the arbiter between us, I shall not raise any objection; but since it will be passing judgement on love, it must agree to listen to what love has to say; any refusal to listen would be an injustice and friendship cannot countenance injustice.

Our second meeting will present no more drawbacks than our first; chance may again provide us with the occasion; you yourself could fix a time. I'm ready to believe that I'm mistaken; won't you try to win me round to your view rather than fight me? Do you have any doubts as to my meekness? If that tiresome interruption hadn't occurred, I might perhaps have been completely converted to your view. Who can estimate the full extent of your power?

May I make a confession? At times I even find myself scared by your absolute domination, which I submit to without daring to struggle against it, your irresistible charm which makes you able to dictate my thoughts as well as my actions. Alas, it may even be I who ought to be afraid of this interview for which I'm asking. Afterwards, I shall perhaps find myself bound by my promises and reduced to suffering from a burning passion, knowing that I can do nothing to assuage it—and not even daring to plead for your help! Oh, for pity's sake, Madame, I beg you again not to abuse your power. Yet so be it! If it will make you happier, if, as a result, I may appear worthier in your eyes, then indeed won't that be a great comfort for my suffering? Yes, I feel that talking with you once again will be supplying you with even more ammunition against me; it will mean bowing even more completely to your will. It's easier to defend yourself against letters; they may contain the same arguments but you are not there in person to add your charm to them. Nevertheless, the pleasure of hearing your voice makes me ready to face that danger; at least I shall be glad to have done everything for your sake, even if to my own disadvantage; my sacrifices will be my tribute to you. And I shall be only too happy to prove in a thousand and one ways something which in a thousand and one ways I also feel: that without the exception even of myself, you are the one dearest to my heart.

84

The Vicomte de Valmont to Cécile Volanges
24 September 17—

You saw all the difficulties we had yesterday. Not once during the whole day was it possible to deliver the letter I have for you; and I have no idea if it will be any easier today. If I'm over-eager, I can bungle it and you're compromised, your happiness is destroyed for ever and your friend will be reduced to despair by a disaster brought about by my rashness. That's what I'm afraid of and I should never forgive myself. But I know how impatient lovers are and I can feel how terrible your situation must be through these enforced delays in receiving the only comfort you can enjoy for the present. I've been giving a great deal of thought to possible ways of overcoming these obstacles and I've found one which will be easy, if I can rely on your co-operation.

I think I've noticed that the key to the door of your room which opens on to the corridor is always lying on your Mama's mantelshelf. You realize that if we had that key everything would be simple; however, failing that, I can provide you with a copy of it which will serve the same purpose. To do this I shall need to have the key itself for a couple of hours. It must be easy for you to find an opportunity to get hold of it without anyone noticing that it's missing: here is a key of mine similar enough for the change not to be detected unless someone tries it in the door, which no one will think of doing. You'll only need to make sure to attach a faded blue ribbon to it similar to the one attached to yours.

You must try to get that key by breakfast-time tomorrow or the day after because it will be simpler for you to give it to me then and it can be put back by evening, when your Mama might be more likely to keep her eye on it. I shall be able to let you have it back at dinner, if we can work out a plan together.

You know that when we leave the drawing-room to go into the dining-room, Madame de Rosemonde always comes last. I'll give her my hand. You'll only need to leave your tapestry work slowly or else drop something so as to bring up the rear. That will enable you to take the key from me. I shall be careful to be holding it behind my back. Immediately after taking it, you must be sure to catch up with my old aunt and be particularly affectionate towards her. If you happen to drop the key, don't lose your head, I'll pretend I've done it. You can rely on me absolutely.

In any case, your mother's lack of trust and her harsh treatment of you fully justify this little subterfuge. What is more, it is the only way of continuing to receive Danceny's letters and delivering yours to him. Any other method is far too risky and might completely wreck the hopes of both of you for ever. As your friend, I feel it not only unwise but irresponsible to go on using it.

Once we have got the key, there are still one or two precautions to be taken against the noise made by the door and the lock but they aren't particularly difficult. Under the wardrobe where I put your paper, you will see some oil and a feather. As you sometimes go to your room alone, you must use the opportunity to oil the lock and the hinges. The main thing is to be careful not to leave any telltale stains. You must also wait until night, because if you do it as cleverly as I know you can, there won't be any trace next day.

However, if it is noticed, don't be afraid to say it's the mainte-nance man. In that case, you must mention the exact time and even his exact words, for instance that he was doing it to stop the little-used locks from rusting. It's obvious you wouldn't have been likely to be put to that inconvenience without asking the reason. It's the little details that make for plausibility and plausibility makes fibs immaterial because nobody feels the need to check them.

Once you've read this letter, please read it again and even think it over, first, because to do something properly you have to know it properly, and secondly, to make sure in your own mind that I haven't omitted anything; I'm not in the habit of using such tricks for myself and I'm not very experienced; but for my close friendship with Danceny and the sympathy you have yourself aroused in me, I couldn't have brought myself to do it. I hate anything that has the slightest hint of deceit, I'm like that. But my heart has been so touched by your misfortunes that I'm prepared to make every effort to alleviate them.

You will, of course, realize that once this line of communication has been opened between us, it will be far easier for me to arrange the meeting which Danceny wants with you. But don't say anything to him about this for the moment. You would only be making him more impatient and the time is not yet quite right to satisfy him. I think you have to calm him down rather than make him disgruntled. I'll leave it to your own tact. Goodbye, my lovely ward, because I do look on you as my ward and I hope you may feel a little fond of your guardian and, above all, do what he tells you. It's for your own good. I am making every effort to ensure your happiness and you can be certain that when you're happy, so shall I be.

85

The Marquise de Merteuil to the Vicomte de Valmont
Paris, 25 September 17—, 7 p.m.

Now you can at last relax and, above all, give me my due. Listen to what I have to tell you and stop mistaking me for all those other females: I've just polished off my adventure with Prévan— *polished off*: I do hope you get my exact meaning. And now you'll be able to judge which of us has something to brag about. Telling it won't be quite as much fun as doing it and anyway, it wouldn't be fair for you, who've done nothing more than produce arguments, good or bad, on this whole business, to enjoy it as much as I did, seeing that I've been giving it such a lot of my time and attention.

However, if you have some major coup of your own in mind, if you're contemplating some exploit where he might have been of concern as a potentially dangerous rival, now's your chance, he's left the coast clear for you, at least for a while; he may even never recover from the blow I've dealt him.

Aren't you lucky to have me as a friend! I'm your good fairy. There you were pining away far from the beauty who has you in her thrall and with one word from me, abracadabra—you're back with her. You want to get even with a woman who has done you wrong—I point out the exact spot to strike and hand her over to you on a plate. And finally, you turn to me to remove a formidable competitor from the lists and, hey presto!—I fulfil your desire. Truly, Vicomte, if you don't spend the rest of your life offering up thanks to me, you're an ungrateful beast. But let's come back to my adventure and start from the beginning.

You remember my letter of 15 September? My loud announcement* as I left the Opéra did *not* fall on deaf ears. Prévan duly turned up and when the Maréchale remarked in her friendly way how flattered she felt at seeing him at one of her gatherings twice in a row, he took great pains to explain how he had called off absolutely hundreds of engagements that Tuesday evening so as to be free. Forewarned is forearmed! However, since I wished to establish more definitely if I really was the object of this flattering enthusiasm, I tried to force this most recent of my admirers to choose between me and his real passion: I stated that I would not be playing cards and, lo and behold, he too found absolutely hundreds of excuses not to play either. My first victory was achieved over lansquenet.*

As my partner in conversation I enlisted the Bishop of ——;* I chose him because he has connections with this hero of the hour and I wanted to offer him every chance of approaching me. I was also very glad to provide myself with a respectable witness who could, if need arose, give evidence of my behaviour and speech. This arrangement worked like a charm.

After the usual small talk, Prévan quickly took over the conversation and struck various notes one after the other to see which one I might respond to. Sentiment I firmly rejected, as a sceptic; I put a stop to any banter by looking serious: that was too frivolous a gambit; he had to fall back on a gently friendly tone and it was under this undistinguished banner that we launched out on our joint campaign.

At supper-time, the Bishop didn't go down so Prévan handed me in and naturally sat down beside me. Let's give honour where honour's due: he kept our private discourse moving very adroitly while appearing concerned only with the general conversation, where he seemed to be doing all the talking. Over dessert, a new play was mentioned as being given at the Comédie-Française the following Monday. I remarked that I was sorry not to have my box available then; he offered his; I refused, of course, as expected; hereupon he replied rather amusingly that I had misinterpreted him: he would certainly never give up his box to someone he didn't know, he was merely letting me know that his box would be at Madame la Maréchale's disposal. She joined in the joke and I accepted.

After we'd gone back up to the drawing-room, as you can imagine he asked if he might have a seat in that box and when the Maréchale, who treats him in a very friendly way, promised him he might, *if he behaved himself*, he seized the opportunity to embark on one of those ambiguous conversations which you told me he was so good at. Falling down on his knees like a good little boy, so he said, as an excuse to ask her advice and appeal to her judgement, he paid a large number of compliments of a rather affectionate nature which it was easy for me to take for myself. Since a good few people hadn't gone back to cards after supper, the conversation became more general and less interesting; but our eyes spoke volumes. I said our eyes but I ought to say his, for mine spoke only one language: surprise. He must have thought I was amazed and extremely preoccupied by the prodigious effect he was having on me. I think I left him greatly satisfied; and I wasn't at all dissatisfied myself.

The following Monday I went to the Comédie-Française as we'd arranged. In spite of your great literary curiosity, I can't tell you a single thing about the performance except that Prévan has an outstanding gift for flattery and that the play was a flop: that was all I managed to gather. I was sorry to see the evening coming to an end for I was really enjoying myself, so in order to prolong my pleasure, I invited the Maréchale to come back to supper at my place; this provided me with an excuse to ask the charming flatterer too; he merely asked for a few moments to dash round to the Comtesses de P—— to make his apologies. Their names* refuelled my wrath; it was obvious he was starting his tale-telling. I recalled your wise counsels and made a promise . . . to pursue my adventure, certain that I would be able to cure him of this dangerous habit of indiscretion.

Not being part of my circle of friends, of whom there weren't very many that evening, he had to show me the customary civilities, so when supper was announced, he offered me his hand. As I accepted I mischievously imparted a slight tremor to mine and as we walked in, I kept my eyes lowered and breathed heavily, seeming as though I was foreshadowing my downfall and apprehensive of my conqueror. He took note of all this wonderfully well and the gay deceiver now changed his tone and his demeanour on the spot. Till then he'd been urbane; he now grew loving. Not that his words were different, for our circumstances prevented him from speaking in any other way, but his glances became less spirited and more tender, his voice more softly inflected, his smile less sly and more smug. And then as he spoke, his wit gradually lost its sparkle, he became gentle. I ask you, Vicomte, could you have done any better yourself?

For my part, I took on such a dreamy look that people were forced to take notice of it; and when they took me to task, I carefully launched into clumsy protestations, looked flustered and cast a quick sly glance at Prévan, encouraging him to believe that my only fear was in fact that he might guess why I was upset.

After supper, I took advantage of one of those stories that our good Maréchale never fails to tell and stretched out voluptuously on my ottoman in a dreamily rapt attitude. I was not sorry for Prévan to see me so preoccupied and in fact he honoured me with his very special attention. You'll understand how reluctant I was for my shy glances to cross the eyes of my conqueror but when in all humility I did turn them towards him, they quickly informed me that I was achieving the desired effect. I still had to persuade him that I shared his feelings, so when the Maréchale announced that she would have to go, I exclaimed in a melting voice: 'Oh dear, it was so lovely lying there!' However, I stood up but before we parted I asked her what plans she had, so as to have an excuse for telling her mine and I let her know that I should be 'At home' two days later. After which, we all went our separate ways.

I now put on my thinking cap. I had no doubt Prévan would take advantage of the quasi-rendezvous that I had just suggested, that he would turn up early so as to find me alone, and that he'd make a spirited attack; but I felt absolutely sure, too, that in the light of my reputation, he would not treat me with the lack of ceremony which anyone with the smallest claim to being a gentleman would show only towards disreputable or inexperienced women; and that once he'd uttered the word love and above all if he supposed he could get me to say it, I could see no prospect of failure.*

It's such a convenience having dealings with you *men of strict principles*! Occasionally, some muddle-headed lover disconcerts you through his shyness or embarrasses you by his passionate raptures; it's a sort of fever like any other: it brings shivers and hot sweats and sometimes various other symptons. But your clockwork routine is so easy to see through! Your arrival, your stance, your tone, your very words, I knew the lot before he arrived! So I won't bother you with the details of our conversation which you can easily fill in yourself. Note merely that while pretending to defend myself, I did all I could to help him along: embarrassment, to give him time to speak; weak arguments, for him to refute; fear and mistrust, to encourage his protests and this everlasting refrain of his: 'I'm only asking for one word'; and this silence of mine which seemed to be keeping him in suspense merely to make him more anxious to hear that magic word; and throughout all this palaver, a hand frequently grasped, as frequently withdrawn but never completely refused . . . You could spend a whole day like that; we spent one solid hour; and perhaps we should still be at it if we hadn't heard a coach driving into my courtyard. As you would expect, this fortunate setback made him all the more pressing and seeing that I was now free from attack, I vouchsafed the magic word. People were announced and I was soon surrounded by quite a large number of callers.

Prévan asked if he could call on me the following morning and I agreed; but to guard against any surprises which I was anxious to avoid, I instructed my maid not to leave the bedroom all the time he was with me; as you know, you can see from there everything that happens in my dressing-room, where I received him. As we were able to talk freely and we both wanted the same thing, it didn't take long to come to an agreement: but we couldn't accept any unwelcome onlooker and this gave me the chance I was looking for.

So I now outlined my domestic arrangements to fit in with my plans and had no trouble in persuading him that we would never get a moment to ourselves and we must regard the golden opportunity we enjoyed yesterday as a sort of miracle which even then was fraught with dangers too great to risk again since someone might come into the drawing-room at any moment. I was careful to point out that this situation had arisen because up till now these habits had never caused me any inconvenience; at the same time, I emphasized how impossible it would be for me to change them without compromising myself in the eyes of my domestic staff. He tried to look disconsolate and upset and told me I didn't really love him; and you can guess how greatly affected I was by all this! However, being keen to strike a decisive blow, I took refuge in tears. It was a case of: *Zaïre, you are weeping!;** and all Orosmane's love was replaced by the thought of the power he had over me and the hope this gave him of ruining me at his own good pleasure.

Once this dramatic moment had been played out, we came back to settling our arrangements. Since daytime was impossible, we turned to the alternative of night; but there was an insurmountable obstacle—my doorkeeper—and I refused to allow any attempt to bribe him. He suggested the sidegate to my garden but I'd anticipated that and invented a watchdog who, meek as a lamb during the day, turned into a ravaging hellhound at night. My willingness to go into all these details was exactly designed to encourage him and he now came up with the most ridiculous stratagem of all, which I promptly accepted.

In the first place, it appeared that his servant was as trustworthy as himself—which I was quite prepared to believe: there's nothing to choose between the pair of them. I was to give a big supper-party in my house; he'd be invited and would choose his own time to leave, alone. His wily accomplice would call for his carriage, open the door and he, Prévan, would surreptitiously slip away. His coachman couldn't possibly notice anything and so, being now still in my house although everybody would have seen him depart, the question was how to get up to my rooms. I confess that at first I had some trouble in finding enough poor arguments against his plan for him to seem to brush aside; he replied by quoting examples. Listening to him, you would have thought that it was the most normal thing in the world; he himself had used it a dozen times, in fact, it was his favourite method, since it was the least risky.

Bowing to these incontrovertible precedents, I frankly admitted the existence of a secret staircase leading up to the vicinity of my boudoir; I could leave the key in the door and he'd be able to shut himself in there and wait for my women to go to bed, without much risk. Then, to make my agreement sound more plausible, I changed my mind: I could only agree to our plan on condition that he promised to obey me unreservedly and behave himself properly . . . Ah, behave properly! In a word, I was quite willing to prove my love for him but not to satisfy his.

I was forgetting to mention how he was finally intending to leave: he was to make his exit through the garden gate; he would need only to wait until daybreak, when my Cerberus* would be as silent as the grave. At that time, there's not a soul about and everyone's most soundly asleep. If you're surprised at such drivel it's because you're forgetting the situation existing between us: why should we need better arguments? He asked nothing better than for everything to be discovered, I was absolutely sure it wouldn't be . . . We fixed the date for two days later.

Note that this whole thing had been arranged without Prévan's once being seen in my company. I'd met him at supper in the house of one of my friends; he'd offered her his box for a new play and I'd accepted a seat in it. I then invited that woman to supper, in Prévan's presence; I can hardly avoid inviting him to join us. He accepts and two days later pays the obligatory call on me. True, he does come to see me the following morning; but apart from the fact that morning visits don't count, all I need to do is to say that I looked on it as something of an impertinence on his part and in fact I then place him fairly and squarely into the category of less intimate acquaintances by sending him a written invitation to a formal supper party. I can certainly say, with Annette: *And that was all there was to it!**

The fateful day arrived, that day when I was to lose my honour and my reputation; I gave my trusty Victoire her instructions which she carried out in the way you're about to see.

Meanwhile, evening came; when Prévan was announced, a lot of my guests had already arrived. I greeted him with pointed politeness to stress how slightly I knew him and sat him at the Maréchale's table, as it was through her that I had made his acquaintance. The evening brought forth nothing except a very short note that my discreet admirer managed to slip me and which I burned, in accordance with my usual practice. In it he assured me that I could rely on him and he wrapped this simple message up in the usual sycophantic words—love, happiness, and so forth—which never fail to crop up when such romps are concerned.

At midnight, as all the games had finished, I suggested a brief spell of gallimaufry.* This had the dual purpose of facilitating Prévan's exit and at the same time making it obvious to everybody, as it was bound to be, in view of his reputation as a gambler. I was also glad that people would be able to recall, if need be, that I'd been in no hurry to be left on my own.

The game lasted longer than I'd anticipated. The Devil was tempting me and I succumbed to my longing to go and comfort my impatient captive. So there I was, heading for disaster when the thought struck me that once I'd given myself completely, I'd no longer have the power to force him to remain decently dressed, as my plan required. I had the strength to resist. I retraced my steps and came back, rather crossly, to take part in the interminable game. However, end it finally did and everyone took themselves off. As for me, I rang for my maids, undressed in a flash, and sent them off too.

And now, Vicomte, behold me in my night attire, walking shyly and demurely to my doom, with hesitant hand opening the door to my future lord and master. He catches sight of me: it was like greased lightning. What can I say? Before I could utter a word to stop him or to defend myself, I was overrun, but completely overrun! So far, so good: but now he becomes disgruntled, he felt uncomfortable all dressed up, it was preventing him from making closer contact, he wanted to be in a state more appropriate to our situation, to come to grips with me on equal terms. But my extreme modesty thwarted his plans and my fondling hands left him no respite to put them into operation. He turned his attention to other things . . .

Having now doubled his stakes, he again started insisting. But this time it was my turn. 'Listen to me,' I said. 'Up till now the tale you'll have to tell the two Comtesses de P—— and hundreds of others will be rather droll; but I'll be interested to know how you'll be telling the sequel and end of your little adventure.' As I spoke, I tugged my bell-pull with all my might; this time, my action was quicker than his words. He was just beginning to stammer something when I heard Victoire come running in, calling out to the other servants she'd been keeping in her room, as I had instructed. Then, raising my voice and in my most regal tones, I proclaimed: 'Leave this room, Monsieur, and never have the audacity to appear in my sight again!' Thereupon, all my servants swarmed in.

Poor Prévan lost his head and mistaking what was just a bit of fun for an ambush, drew his sword but immediately regretted it, for my footman, a tough and plucky young man, seized him round the body and flung him down on the floor. I confess I was petrified. I called to my servants to stop and ordered them to let him go, making sure he left the premises at once. They obeyed but not without a great deal of loud and angry muttering: they were furious that their virtuous mistress had been subjected to such disrespect. They all escorted the hapless chevalier to the door with a great deal of noise and commotion, as I'd hoped. Only Victoire stayed behind to help me tidy up my bed.

My servants now came back, extremely agitated, and still in a state of shock I asked them how it was that, most luckily for me, they were still up; Victoire explained that she had had two of her women friends to supper and they had all gone on to continue the evening in her room; in fact, she told me precisely what we'd both arranged together. I thanked them all and told them they could go but sent one of them to fetch my doctor straight away. It seemed to me that I was justified in feeling apprehensive over the effect of my appalling experience and this was guaranteed to spread the news and ensure complete notoriety for the incident.

The doctor came, commiserated with me, and merely prescribed rest. I also told Victoire to go out early that morning and gossip with all the neighbours.

All this was so successful that before noon, as soon as my door was open to receive visitors, my pious neighbour was already at my bedside to discover the truth and the lurid details of this adventure. I found myself obliged to join with her for a solid hour in expressing horror at the depravity of our times. A moment later I received a note from the Maréchale which I'm enclosing. And finally, before five o'clock, to my amazement, who should call but Monsieur ——, Prévan's commanding officer, who came, he said, to apologize for such extreme disrespect on the part of his officers. He'd only heard about it at dinner at the Maréchale's and on the spot had issued an order for Prévan to place himself under arrest, in gaol. I pleaded for him but in vain. So I thought that as an accomplice it was up to me to do my bit as well and at least observe house arrest: I gave out that I was indisposed and not at home to anyone.

And my solitary state is the explanation of this long letter. I'll be writing to Madame de Volanges as well, she'll certainly read it out to all and sundry and you'll be able to hear the official version which you have to pass on.

I forgot to tell you that Belleroche is livid and mad keen to call Prévan out. Poor boy! Fortunately I'll have time to set his mind at rest. Meantime I'm going to give mine some rest, too, it's tired of writing. Goodbye, Vicomte.

86

The Maréchale de —— to the Marquise de Merteuil
(*note enclosed with letter 85*)
Paris, 25 September 17—

Gracious Heavens, what is this extraordinary thing I've just heard, my dear? Is it possible for young Prévan to have behaved so disgustingly! and towards you, too! Oh, the trials we woman have to bear! But something I shall never forgive myself for is that I feel partly to blame for your inviting such a monster into your house. I can promise you that if what they've been telling me about him is true, he'll never set foot in *my* house again! And that's the way every decent woman will treat him if they do what is right.

I'm told that you're not at all well and I'm greatly concerned about your health. My dear Marquise, please let me know how you are or if you don't feel well enough to do it yourself, get one of your maids to let me have news of you. Just a brief word to reassure me. I would have come round to see you this morning myself but my doctor absolutely forbids me to interrupt my bath cure and I have to go out to Versailles this afternoon, still on my nephew's business.

Goodbye, dear Madame. I don't need to remind you of my deep and everlasting friendship.

87

The Marquise de Merteuil to Madame de Volanges
Paris, 26 September 17—

Dear kind friend, I'm writing this letter from my bed: a most disagreeable and quite unforeseeable incident has laid me low with shock and horror. Not that there was anything that I could do about it but it is always so distressing for any respectable woman who tries to preserve the modesty of her sex to become the focus of public attention that I would have done anything to prevent this unfortunate incident. Indeed, I am not yet certain whether I shan't decide to go down into the country until everything has blown over. Let me tell you what happened.

At the Maréchale de ——'s house I met a Monsieur de Prévan whom you will certainly know by name but with whom I was not otherwise acquainted. But meeting him there, I was, it seems to me, surely entitled to think that he was a man of breeding. He's quite personable and he seemed to me not without wit. By chance and the boredom of playing lansquenet, I found myself left alone as the only woman with him and the Bishop of ——, as everybody else was playing cards. All three of us talked together until supper was served. At table, a new play was mentioned and he offered the Maréchale his box for the evening; she accepted and it was agreed that I might have a seat in it. That was for last Monday's performance at the Comédie-Française. Afterwards the Maréchale came to supper with me so I suggested to Monsieur de Prévan that he might care to accompany her and he came too. Two days later he called on me and we exchanged the usual civilities without anything unusual happening. Next day he called on me in the morning, which did strike me as somewhat impertinent but I thought that instead of showing him how tasteless I found such behaviour by my manner, it might be more appropriate to warn him, politely, that we weren't on such close terms as he seemed to be assuming. For this purpose, I sent him that same day a very bald and extremely formal invitation to a supper party I gave a couple of days ago. I hardly exchanged more than two or three words with him in the course of the whole evening and on his part he left as soon as the cards were over. You will agree that till then there was nothing less likely to lead to an affair! After the cards, someone suggested a gallimaufry and this took us up to nearly two o'clock. Finally I got to bed.

My maids had been gone a good half an hour at least when I heard a noise in my apartment. Feeling very scared, I peeped through my bed-curtains and saw a man coming through the door leading from my boudoir. I screamed and my nightlight enabled me to recognize this Monsieur de Prévan who with incredible impudence told me not to be alarmed: he was going to explain his strange behaviour and begged me not to make any sound. As he was talking he lit a candle. I was too shocked to utter a word and I think his calm and brazen manner petrified me even more. But before he had said more than two more words, I realized what his strange behaviour meant and as you can imagine my only reply was to tug my bell as hard as I could.

By a most extraordinary piece of good luck, all my household staff had been spending the evening with one of my maids and were still up. As she was making towards my room, my maid heard me speaking in a very agitated voice and immediately called out to the others. You can imagine the commotion and scandal! My servants were quite enraged and for a moment I could see my footman killing Prévan. Though I confess that, at the time, I was very glad to see that I had the upper hand, thinking about it later I should have preferred it had only my maid come to my rescue, as I might have avoided all this dreadful fuss and bother.

But instead, this hullabaloo woke the whole neighbourhood, my servants have been gossiping, and since yesterday it's been the talk of the town. Monsieur de Prévan is in prison on the orders of his commanding officer, who was civil enough to call on me to offer his apologies, so he said. This prison sentence will only increase the scandal but I could do nothing to make them change their minds. The Town and Court have been signing my visitors' book and I've given orders that I'm not at home to anyone. The few people I've seen have told me that everybody thought I was justified and that public feeling against Prévan was running very high. This he most certainly deserves but that doesn't prevent the whole business from being excessively disagreeable.

What's worse is that this man certainly has friends and those friends are bound to be malicious: who knows, who can even guess, what terrible things they will try to fabricate to damage my reputation? O Heavens, how dreadful it is to be a young woman! It is not enough for her to guard against gossip, she has even to protect herself against actual slander!

Please write and tell me what you would have done and what you would do now, in my place; in fact, tell me what you think about the whole affair. It's always been you who've given me the most valuable and comforting advice and it's from you that I'm always most glad to have it. Goodbye, dear, good friend; I don't need to tell you the deep affection I have for you at all times. My kindest greetings to your delightful daughter.

PART III

88

Cécile Volanges to the Vicomte de Valmont
26 September 17—

I do very much enjoy getting letters from Monsieur the Chevalier Danceny and, like him, I certainly hope for us to be able to meet again without anyone being in a position to stop us, but I'm afraid, Monsieur, that I still don't dare do what you suggest. In the first place, it's too risky: it's true that the key you want me to put on the mantelshelf in place of the other one certainly is quite like it, but they're still not identical and my Mama really does look very closely and notices everything. In addition, although no one has yet used it since we've been here, it would only need for something unexpected to happen and if it comes out, then I'll be ruined for ever. And then it seems to me too that it would be very wrong; surely making an extra key like that is going rather too far? It's true that you've kindly offered to see to it but in spite of that, if it ever came out I would still be as much to blame and in the wrong because you would have done it for me. Anyway I've tried twice to see if I could take it and if it was something else it would be very simple but I don't quite know why, I started to tremble and I've never managed to pluck up courage to do it. So I think we'd better go on the same way as before.

If you are still kind enough to help us as you have been doing up to now you will certainly always manage to find a way to let me have a letter. Even the last one would have been quite all right if you hadn't unfortunately turned round at that particular moment. I certainly realize that you can't spend your whole time thinking about it like me but I'd rather be patient and not take so many risks. I'm sure Monsieur Danceny would say the same because every time he wanted to do something that would have worried me he always agreed that we shouldn't do it.

Together with this letter for you, Monsieur, I'm letting you have one for Monsieur Danceny and your key as well. I am still terribly grateful to you for all your kindness towards me and I do hope you can go on helping me. It's certainly true that I'm very unhappy and without you I'd be even unhappier but after all, she is my mother and I shall have to go on being patient. And as long as Monsieur Danceny goes on loving me and you don't abandon me, maybe better times will come.

With my sincerest thanks again, Monsieur, yours very truly and obediently, etc.

89

The Vicomte de Valmont to the Chevalier Danceny
From the Château de ——, 26 September 17—

My dear friend, if your affairs are still not progressing as fast as you'd like, please don't think that I'm entirely to blame. I've more than one obstacle to overcome and Madame de Volanges's watchfulness and strictness are not my only difficulties: your young friend is also providing me with some. Either because she's scared or ill-disposed, she doesn't always follow my advice, although I think I know better than she what is required.

I'd hit on a safe, simple, and convenient method to pass on your letters and even, later, to provide you both with better opportunities for meeting, as I know you want to; but I couldn't succeed in persuading her to adopt it. I'm all the more upset since I can see no other way possible of bringing you both together again; and even for your correspondence, I'm continually apprehensive of compromising all three of us. And as you know, that is a risk which I don't want to run myself or expose either of you to.

All the same, I would be very sorry if your little girl's lack of trust were to prevent me from being of help to you; it might perhaps not be a bad idea to write to her about it. You'll have to see what you wish to do, because it is not enough merely to help one's friends, one must help them in the way they want. It might also be a way of ascertaining her own feelings towards you because a woman with a will of her own is not as much in love as she proclaims.

It's not that I suspect your young woman of being flighty; but she is very young; she's terrified of her mama who, as you're aware, wants nothing better than to harm you; and it might perhaps be dangerous to leave the girl too long without reminding her of your existence. But please don't worry unduly about what I'm saying. Basically, I've no reason to mistrust her, it's purely that, as you well know, I'm concerned about you.

I shan't write at greater length because I've a number of affairs on hand for myself. I haven't made as much progress as you but I am as much in love and that is one consolation; and even if I don't succeed myself, I shall consider that I haven't wasted my time if I can manage to be of some assistance to you.

Goodbye, dear boy.

90

Madame de Tourvel to the Vicomte de Valmont
27 September 17—

I am most anxious, Monsieur, that this letter should not make you unhappy or, if it does, at least you may be comforted by the thought of how unhappy I feel writing it. You must by now know me well enough to be quite certain that I have no desire to distress you but you yourself would surely not wish to cast me for ever into despair. So I appeal to you, in the name of the affection and friendship which I promised you and even for the sake of the perhaps stronger but assuredly no more sincere feelings which you have for me, let us stop seeing each other. You must go away, and until that time let us above all avoid those private, all too dangerous, conversations between us in the course of which, by some magical influence, I spend my time hearing things which I shouldn't be listening to and never succeeding in saying to you the things I wish to say.

Once again, only yesterday when you came up to me in the park, I had certainly no thought in mind but that of telling you what I am now putting in writing. Yet what did I do? Nothing but talk about your love . . . that love to which I can never respond! Oh, for pity's sake, please go away!

You need never fear that by not seeing you, my feelings towards you will ever change. How could I succeed in overcoming them when I've even lost heart to fight against them? As you see, I am not hiding anything from you; I am more afraid of giving way to my weakness than confessing it. But if my emotions are beyond my control, I can still control my actions and shall continue to do so, even if it cost me my life.

It is not so very long ago, alas, that I felt quite confident of never having to face such a struggle. I delighted in the thought and took great pride in it—excessive pride perhaps and for that, God has punished me, cruelly punished me. But in His infinite mercy, even while striking us down, He warns me before I fall, and I should be doubly guilty if I were to continue to act imprudently now that I have been given notice of my weakness.

You have told me time and again that you would never wish for a happiness that would cause me distress. Alas, it is too late now to talk of happiness! But at least give me back my peace of mind!

If you agree to my request, think of the fresh claims you will have upon my heart! And those claims will be grounded on virtue and I shall not have to defend myself against them. And in my gratitude, how happy I shall be! You will have given me the sweet pleasure of indulging in a delightful emotion without fear of remorse. Now, on the contrary, I am pursued by fear, fear of my feelings and my thoughts, as terrified of thinking about you as about myself. The very thought of you fills me with dread; when I can't prevent myself, I struggle against it but I can never put it out of my mind, I merely push it to one side.

Isn't it better for both of us to put an end to this agitation and anxiety? Oh, you still have a feeling heart which, even in the midst of its errors, has remained attached to virtue: you will not reject my plea! This wild turmoil will be replaced by a more gentle but no less affectionate interest; with your kind help my life will take on a new value and with joy in my heart I shall be able to declare: I owe this peace of mind to my friend.

By submitting to some slight hardship which I shall not impose on you but merely ask you to accept, do you feel that the price you will be paying to put an end to my torment is too high? Ah, if all that was needed to make you happy was to agree to be unhappy myself, you may believe me that I should not hesitate one second . . . But to become a guilty woman! . . . No, my dear Vicomte, I would sooner die a thousand times.

And even now I feel harassed by shame, dogged by remorse, when I'm in company I blush all the time and when I'm alone I start trembling. My life is one long calvary; unless you agree, I can never know any kind of peace. Even my good resolutions can't ease my mind; I made up my mind to write this letter yesterday, and I spent the night in tears.

So now you see your friend, the friend whom you love, bewildered and appealing to you for help, begging you to give her back her peace and innocence. O Heavens, but for you would she ever have been reduced to making such a humiliating request? I am not blaming you, I can feel within myself all too well how hard it is to resist so tyrannical an emotion; a call for help is not a complaint. So if you can do out of the goodness of your heart what I am doing out of a sense of duty, then I shall be able to add, to all the other feelings you have aroused in me, a feeling of eternal gratitude.

Farewell, farewell, Monsieur de Valmont.

91

The Vicomte de Valmont to Madame de Tourvel
27 September 17—, in the evening

So taken aback was I by your letter that I still hardly know how to answer it. Certainly, if a choice has to be made between your happiness and mine, I must sacrifice myself and I shall do so without hesitation. But before taking any action, it seems to me that questions of such importance are surely worth being discussed and clarified; and how can that be done if we are not to see nor speak to each other any more?

So now that we are bound together by such deeply precious emotions, blind panic is enough to separate us, perhaps for ever! Devoted friendship and ardent devotion have lost their rights; their voice can no longer be heard! And why? What is this pressing danger which is threatening you? Ah, believe me, Madame, fears such as these, perhaps lacking any substance, seem to me very substantial proof that no danger exists.

You must not feel offended if I say that I can detect in your attitude traces of the unfavourable reports about me that you have been given. With a man of good reputation there are no such misgivings; above all, no one will banish a man who has been deemed worthy to be a friend: it is the dangerous man who is to be feared and shunned.

Yet was there ever anybody more respectful, more obedient than I? As you may observe, I'm already choosing my words carefully; I no longer feel free to use those names, so dear and pleasing to my heart and which my heart still continues to utter secretly. I'm no longer the faithful and hapless lover receiving advice from an affectionately devoted friend but the accused facing his judge, the slave facing his master. These new roles no doubt impose new rules: I undertake to observe them all. Listen to my plea and if you condemn me, I shall bow to your judgement and leave. I shall promise you even more; do you prefer to be this dictator who pronounces sentence without granting a hearing, do you have the heart to be unjust? Command and I shall still obey.

But I need to hear this sentence, this command, from your own lips. Why so, I hear you say. Ah, if you ask that question, how little you know of love and of my heart. Is seeing you just once more so trivial? And as you plunge my soul into the depths of despair, perhaps one last glance from you may comfort me and give me the strength to survive. If I am to give up my love and the friendship which alone makes my life worth living, at least you will see your handiwork and I shall be able to recall your pity. And even if I should not deserve that last small favour, it seems to me that by submitting to your will, the price I am paying is high enough to warrant it.

And so, Madame, you are going to send me away! You are ready for us to become strangers for each other. I say 'ready'; you actively want it to be so! And all the time, while you keep assuring me that your feelings towards me will never change when I have gone, you are speeding my departure merely to ensure that those feelings may be the more easily destroyed!

You're already talking of replacing them by gratitude . . . So what you're offering me is the same sort of feeling which you would have for any stranger who has done you some trifling service or even for an enemy who has stopped attacking you! And you expect my heart to be content with that! But look into your own heart, Madame. If your friend, if your lover, came to you one day talking of their gratitude, wouldn't you say to them indignantly: 'Go away, you ungrateful creatures'?

I must stop and ask you to bear with me. Forgive me for dwelling on my distress, a distress which is of your making. What I have said will not in any way prevent my complete submission. But in my turn, I appeal to you, on behalf of those gentle emotions which you yourself claim to feel, not to refuse me a fair hearing and out of pity for the dreadful turmoil into which you have thrown me, at least not to keep me too long in suspense. Goodbye, Madame.

92

The Chevalier Danceny to the Vicomte de Valmont
Paris, 27 September 17—

O dear friend, your letter has made my blood run cold! Cécile . . . O God, can it be possible? Cécile doesn't love me any longer! Yes, through the kindly veil under which you hid the truth, I saw that you were trying to prepare me for the fatal blow. I am grateful to you for your tact; however, love is not so easily deceived. It can anticipate anything which affects it, it doesn't need to be told its fate, it can predict it. I'm left in no doubt as to mine, so you can speak out plainly and I hope you will. You must tell me all; tell me what first aroused your suspicions and how they were confirmed. The smallest details are valuable. Try particularly to recall her words. One ill-chosen word can change the whole meaning of a sentence and the same word sometimes has more than one meaning.* You may have been mistaken . . . Poor me, I'm still trying to delude myself. What did she say? Did she blame me for something? Doesn't she at least deny doing anything wrong? I ought to have been fore-warned by the difficulty she's been finding recently in doing anything at all. Love doesn't recognize so many obstacles, it laughs at locksmiths.

What can I do? What's your advice? Supposing I tried to see her? Is that really impossible? Absence is such a cruel thing; it can lead to disaster! And so she turned down a way of seeing me? You don't say what it was and if it actually was too dangerous, she knows I don't want her to take too many risks. But I know how cautious you are and I can't possibly not do what you advise, even if I would sometimes prefer not to.

What shall I do now? How can I write to her? If I let her know my suspicions, they may upset her and if they're unjustified, would she forgive me for having upset her? If I conceal them, then I'm deceiving her and I'm incapable of hiding anything from her.

Ah, if she could only know how I'm suffering, her heart would be touched; I know how tender-hearted she is and I've had a thousand and one proofs of her love. Perhaps she was scared or embarrassed. She's so young! And her mother's so strict! I'll write to her, I'll be very discreet, I'll merely ask her to place herself entirely in your hands. Even if she still won't agree, she can't possibly be offended by that request and perhaps she will agree after all.

Dear friend, I must apologize to you on her behalf and on mine as well. I promise you she does appreciate all your trouble and is grateful to you. It's not distrust, it's diffidence. You must be tolerant, it's the most precious quality of a friend and your friendship is so precious, I can never thank you enough for all that you're doing for us . . . Goodbye, I'll write to her straight away.

I feel all my old misgivings creeping back . . . Who would ever have thought it would be so hard for me to write to her? And only yesterday, dear God, it was my only pleasure.

Farewell, dear friend. Please continue to help and feel pity for your, etc.

93

The Chevalier Danceny to Cécile Volanges
(enclosed with letter 92)
Paris, 27 September 17—

I can't pretend that I wasn't terribly upset to hear from Valmont that you still don't trust him. You know very well that he's my friend and the only person able to bring us together again. I thought that these two facts would have been enough and I'm sorry to see I was mistaken. I hope at least that you'll let me know your reasons. Or will you find even more difficulties standing in your way? Yet otherwise there's no way in which I can solve the mystery of your behaviour. I don't dare to suspect your love, any more than you doubtless would never dare to betray mine. Ah, Cécile! . . .

Is it true then that you wouldn't agree to use a method to enable us to meet that was *safe, simple, and convenient*?* And that's the way you show your love! We've been separated for such a short time but your feelings have changed so much! But why won't you tell me the truth? Why say you still love me, that you love me more than ever? Has your mother destroyed your honesty as well as your love? If she has at least left you with a certain compassion in your heart, you can't fail to realize what a dreadful ordeal you're subjecting me to! Ah, Cécile, it would be less painful for me to die!

So tell me, have you shut me out of your heart for ever? Have you completely forgotten me? Thanks to your rejection of my friend's offer, I've no way of knowing if you will be able to read my appeals nor when you will be ready to respond to them. He had given us the possibility of corresponding but you didn't want that, you raised difficulties, you preferred to make it harder for us. No, I shall stop believing in love or honesty. If Cécile has deceived me, who else can be trusted?

Oh, please, please, do answer me! Is it true that you've stopped loving me? No, it can't be possible; you're deceiving yourself, you're belying your own feelings. You had a moment of fear, of discouragement, and now love has quickly made them disappear! That's what happened, wasn't it, Cécile? Oh, I'm surely wrong to accuse you. And how glad I'd be if I was! How I would love to offer you my tender apologies and make amends for my moment of unfairness by offering you my eternal devotion!

O Cécile, my Cécile, you must take pity on me! Agree to see me, no matter how! See what happens when we don't meet— fear, suspicion, perhaps even indifference! Just one single word, a single glance, will make us happy. But can I really still use the word love? For me, perhaps, love is lost, it's vanished for ever! I'm tortured by fear, cruelly torn between unfair suspicions and an even crueller truth, I can't think where to turn! My whole life is being consumed by love and by suffering . . . Ah, Cécile, you have the power to give me back a desire to live and I'm waiting for you to utter a word to tell me straight away if I can ever be happy again or am finally doomed to despair for ever!

94

Cécile Volanges to the Chevalier Danceny
From the Château de ———, 28 September 17—

I can't make anything out of your letter except that it made me absolutely wretched. What did Monsieur de Valmont say to make you think that I don't love you any more?—which might, incidentally, perhaps be a very good thing for me; because I'd certainly be much less tormented, and it's very hard when I love you as much as I do to see that you always think I'm wrong and instead of trying to comfort me, all the nasty things that make me most miserable always seem to come from you. You think I'm deceiving you and saying things that aren't true! That's a nice idea to have of me! But what would be the point of not telling the truth like you accuse me of doing? If I didn't love you any more, all I'd need do would be to tell you straight out and everybody would approve. Unfortunately, I can't help myself . . . And I have to be in love with someone who gives me no credit for it whatsoever!

What can I have done to make you so angry? I didn't dare take the key because I was frightened Mama would notice and that would have landed me in even bigger trouble, and you too, because of me; and also because it seems to me not the right thing to do. But it was only Monsieur de Valmont's suggestion, so I couldn't tell if you wanted it or not, because you didn't know anything about it. Now I do know you want it, can you possibly think I'll still refuse to take it? I'll get the key tomorrow and we'll see what you have to say then.

I know Monsieur de Valmont is your friend but I reckon I certainly love you at least as much as he possibly can, yet he's always right and I'm always wrong. I can tell you, I feel really fed up . . . You don't mind, of course, because you know I always calm down straight away and now I shall have the key, I'll be able to see you whenever I want, but I can tell you that I certainly shan't want to if you behave like that. If I've got to be unhappy, I'd still prefer it to come from me rather than you: think about what you want to do.

If you wished, we could love each other so much! And then at least all our troubles would come from outside! I can tell you that if I was in charge you'd certainly never have any reason to find fault with me! But if you don't believe me, we shall always be wretched and it won't be my fault. I hope we'll soon be able to meet and then we'll have no more chances of upsetting each other.

If I'd been able to foresee what would happen, I'd have taken the key straight away, but I really and truly thought I was doing the right thing. So please don't be cross with me any more. And stop being sad and love me always as much as I love you, then I'll be very, very happy. Goodbye, dear, dear friend.

95

Cécile Volanges to the Vicomte de Valmont
28 September 17—

May I ask you, Monsieur, to be kind enough to let me have back the key you gave me to put in place of the other one? Since that's what everybody wants, I shall have to agree, too.

I'm afraid I can't understand why you told Monsieur Danceny that I did not love him any more; I don't think I ever gave you any cause to think that and it upset him very much, and me as well. Certainly, I know that you're his friend but I don't think that is any reason to make him worried nor me either. The next time you write to him, I should be very pleased if you could tell him the reverse and say you are quite certain of it, because it is you he trusts most and when I say something and people don't believe it, I don't quite know what to do.

As for the key, you can rest assured that I have remembered perfectly all you recommended me to do in your letter. However, if you still have it and would care to let me have it back at the same time, I promise you I shall pay great attention to it. If you could do it tomorrow as we go into dinner, I can give you the other key next day at breakfast and you could give it back to me, like you did the first time. I would very much prefer it not to take any longer because there would be less time for Mama to have a chance of noticing it.

And once you've got the key, may I please ask you to use it for picking up my letters as well and in that way Monsieur Danceny will have news of me more often. It's true that it will be much more convenient than it is now but the fact is that I was too scared. Please forgive me and I hope that this will not prevent you from still being as kind and helpful as you have been in the past. I shall always be very grateful to you as well.

Please believe me, Monsieur de Valmont, yours very truly and humbly, etc.

96

The Vicomte de Valmont to the Marquise de Merteuil
From the Château de ———, 1 October 17—

I bet that ever since your little escapade you've been living in daily expectation of receiving my congratulations and praise. And indeed I fancy that my long silence must have rather peeved you; but what can I say? I've always felt that when the only thing we have to offer a woman is praise, we could leave that to her and get on with something else. However, I must thank you on my own behalf and congratulate you on yours. And if it's going to make you completely happy, I'm even prepared to agree that, on this occasion, you've actually exceeded my expectations. Having said which, let's see if, in my poor way, I have, at least to some extent, come up to yours.

I don't want to tell you about Madame de Tourvel; you dislike her slow progress. You're only attracted by affairs that are sewn up. Long-drawn-out scenes bore you whereas for my part, I'd never enjoyed anything quite as much as these so-called long-winded passages.

Yes, I love watching, contemplating that prudent woman launched unwittingly and inexorably on a steep and slippery slope which is carrying her down despite herself and forcing her to follow me. She is terrified of the risks she is running and would like to stop but can't hold back. With skill and care she may perhaps slow her progress down but her legs keep propelling her on. Now and again, afraid of the danger facing her, she closes her eyes and lets herself go, placing herself in my hands. More often, she is spurred on to greater efforts by some new terror, and with death in her heart, struggles to retreat; exerting all her strength she manages to climb laboriously a few steps backwards; but soon, by some magical power, she finds herself once more closer than ever to the danger she's been vainly trying to escape. Then, having no other guide or support but me, she abandons any idea of blaming me for her inevitable downfall but appeals to me to postpone it. And now she offers up to *me* the fervid prayers and humble entreaties that poor fearful mortals offer to the Divinity. And you expect me to be deaf to these appeals, to destroy her worship of me by my own actions, and use the power in which she is hoping to find salvation to seal her doom! Oh, at least let me have time to contemplate this touching struggle between love and virtue.

Do you really think that such a performance, which you flock into the theatre to watch and applaud with wild enthusiasm, is less fascinating in real life? You listen eagerly to the outpourings of a pure and tender soul filled with dread at the prospect of the happiness she is longing for and who still continues to defend her virtue even when she has stopped resisting: then is the man who inspires such emotions to be the only one not to enjoy them? Yet these are the marvellous delights which this heavenly woman is offering to me every day. And you blame me for savouring such joys! Ah, the time will come soon enough when she will have been degraded by her downfall and have become in my eyes a woman like all the rest.

But I'm talking about her and forgetting that I promised myself not to talk about her: I feel linked to her by some mysterious force which draws me back to her, even while I'm treating her abominably. Such ways are dangerous! Let's change the subject. I'll become my old self and talk about something more cheerful: your ward—who's now become my ward. I hope you'll appreciate that I haven't lost my touch.

As my tender-hearted puritan has been treating me rather more nicely the past few days, I've been paying her less attention and I realized that the Volanges girl is, in fact, extremely pretty and while it was stupid to be in love with her like young Danceny, perhaps it was no less stupid not to use her for a little distraction, something which I sorely need in my current solitary state. And it seemed to me only fair to get some return for all my efforts on her behalf; I also remembered that you'd offered her to me before Danceny had any lien on her and I felt it reasonable to claim some rights on a property he owned by default purely because I'd turned it down. The little miss's prettiness, her fresh lips, her childish looks, and even her gawkiness reinforced these judicious observations and I resolved to take appropriate action, which has been crowned by success.

You're already agog to learn how I managed to supplant her beloved suitor so speedily and how one sets about seducing such a young and untried filly. You needn't worry; I didn't need any charm at all. Whereas to achieve your goal you artfully deploy the dainty wiles of your sex, I claimed the inalienable prerogative of the male and asserted my authority. Since I was confident of subduing my prey once I could lay hands on it, the only wiles I needed were to make contact and those I employed hardly deserved the name.

I took advantage of the first letter I got from Danceny for his beloved and having informed her by means of a pre-arranged signal, instead of cleverly handing it over, I cleverly avoided doing so, feigning to share her anxiety at the delay which I was myself engineering. Having created the problem, I then indicated the solution.

The young lady's bedroom has a door opening on to the corridor but as might be expected, her *Mummy* had charge of the key. All that was needed was to get my hands on it. Child's play: if I had it in my possession for a couple of hours, I could guarantee to get a copy of it. Then everything—correspondence, private conversations, secret nocturnal rendezvous—would be safe and simple. But would you believe it, the timid child took fright and refused. Anyone else would have desponded: I merely saw the chance of indulging in an even more titillating pleasure. I wrote off to Danceny complaining of her refusal, with such success that our stupid young man couldn't wait to persuade his timorous sweetheart, indeed even insist, that she must grant my request and do everything I asked.

I must confess that I was delighted to have swapped roles with the youngster and got him to do for me what he was relying on me to do for him. This seemed to me to double the fun; so, as soon as I'd got this precious key, I lost no time in making use of it straight away. That was last night.

Having ascertained that everything was quiet in the château, armed with my dark lantern and dressed in a manner appropriate to the late hour and required by the circumstances, I paid my first visit to your ward. I'd ensured that everything was in order—in fact, she'd done so on my instructions—to get in without making a sound. She was in her first sleep, the sound sleep of youth, and so I was able to approach her bed without waking her. At first I was tempted to go straight into action and try to pass myself off as a maiden's dream, but I was frightened by the possible consequences of her surprise and the ensuing noise, so I chose to waken the charming sleeper gently and in fact managed to prevent her from crying out as I feared.

After calming her first fears, since I hadn't come to see her just for a chat I risked taking a few liberties. No doubt she hasn't been properly taught in her convent about all the dangers to which a shy, innocent girl is exposed and what parts of her person she has to defend in order not to be overrun in a surprise attack, for she concentrated her whole attention and efforts on protecting herself from being kissed. But as the kiss was a feint, all the rest was left undefended. How could I possibly resist such an opportunity? So I changed my tactics and immediately occupied another outpost. Here we both nearly came to grief: terribly scared, the little girl genuinely attempted to scream but fortunately her voice faded into tears. She also flung herself towards her bell-pull but I cleverly stopped her in time.

'What do you think you're doing?' I said. 'Do you want to destroy your reputation completely? What do I care if somebody comes? How will you be able to persuade them that I'm not here with your full consent? Is there anybody but you who could have provided me with the means to get in here? And how will you set about explaining what this key is being used for—a key you've given me and which couldn't have possibly been obtained without your help?' This short lecture didn't calm either her anger or her distress but it did make her sue for peace. I don't know if my tone lent wings to my eloquence and it's true that my gesture was strictly earthy. But what sort of elegance of expression can you expect in my situation with one hand holding her down and the other amorously engaged? But if you have a clear picture of my position, you'll at least have to agree that it favoured launching an attack. However, as you once said, I don't know anything about anything and the simplest of women, a convent girl, can twist me round her little finger . . .

This particular convent girl, while still creating a lot of fuss, realized that she had to make up her mind and parley. Since her pleas left me unmoved, she had to proceed to make a bargain. You perhaps imagine I set a high price for abandoning my tactical advantage? Dear me no; I promised her everything she asked for in exchange for a kiss. True, I didn't keep my promise but I did give good reasons for failing to do so: had we properly agreed whether it was to be a kiss given or received? After a lot of haggling, we agreed on a second kiss which, this time, was to be received.

So, guiding her timid arms round my body and clasping her more ardently with one of mine, this delectable kiss was received very nicely indeed, in fact so perfectly received that a lover couldn't have done it better . . .

Such honesty deserved some reward and I at once granted her request: my hand relinquished its post but by some odd chance, I'd slipped into the place it'd been occupying. And now you'll assume that I would eagerly move into action on the spot, won't you? Well, you're quite wrong. As I've explained before, I've developed a taste for dawdling. Once your destination's in sight, why rush?

But quite seriously, I was really glad to observe an instance of the irresistible force of opportunity which was operating here without any extraneous influences. In fact, she was having to struggle against the force of love, supported by maidenly modesty or purity, further strengthened by the foul temper I'd managed to put her into, which was very foul indeed. It was nothing but opportunity, but it was there, on offer and present on the spot, and love was not.

To verify my observations, I mischievously applied just sufficient force for her to be able to resist. But when my charming foe, taking advantage of my leniency, was on the point of escaping, I held her back by the same fear which had previously proved so successful and without any further effort, the little love-bird, forgetting all her vows, first of all capitulated and finally acquiesced. Not that after this first moment, reproaches and tears didn't start up again more violently than ever. I'm not certain whether they were true or false but as is always the case, both ceased abruptly as soon as I set about giving further grounds for them. Finally, after shifting from weakness to reproaches and back, we did not part until mutual satisfaction had been achieved and we were both looking forward to a repeat performance tonight.

I didn't get to bed till dawn, dog-tired and ready to drop from lack of sleep but I decided to forgo bed so as to be able to go down to breakfast: I'm passionately fond of seeing how people look the morning after . . . You can't imagine how this little girl looked! How embarrassed she was! And the trouble she had walking! Never daring to raise her eyes, so terribly swollen, with big blue circles under them! And that little round face had become so long! You can't imagine anything funnier. And for the first time her mother showed concern at this extraordinary change and seemed to show her some affection! And Madame de Tourvel was fussing over her too. Well, that solicitude is only out on loan; the time will come for it to be called in and that time is not too distant. Farewell, fair lady.

97

Cécile Volanges to the Marquise de Merteuil
From the Château de ——, 1 October 17—

O Heavens, dear Madame de Merteuil, I can't tell you how dreadfully upset and miserable I am! Where can I find someone to console me and advise me? I'm in such a horrible fix! That Monsieur de Valmont! . . . And Danceny! Oh no, whenever I think of him I feel so awful! . . . How can I begin to tell you about it? What can I say? I just don't know what to do! But my heart is so full, I must talk to someone and you're the only person whom I can possibly dare confide in. You've always been so kind to me!

But this time you mustn't be kind, I don't deserve it! How can I put it? I don't want it! Everybody here has been concerned about me today and they've all just made me more upset. I knew perfectly well that I didn't deserve it! But you must do the opposite, you must tell me off really badly because I've been a very naughty girl. But after that you must help me because if you won't be kind and help me I shall die of grief.

So let me explain . . . oh, my hand's trembling, as you can see I can hardly hold my pen, I can feel myself blushing all over, that's because I'm red with shame. Ah well, I shall have to bear it, it will be the first part of my punishment for doing such a terrible, terrible thing. I'm going to tell you everything.

Well, up to now Monsieur de Valmont has been passing on Monsieur Danceny's letters to me and then he suddenly decided it was too difficult and asked for a key to my room. I can assure you that I wasn't at all keen but he went and wrote to Danceny about it and Danceny wanted it as well and as I feel so unhappy whenever I have to refuse him something, particularly since me going away has made him so miserable, in the end I agreed. I had no idea what a dreadful thing it was going to lead to.

Last night Monsieur de Valmont used the key to come into my bedroom when I was asleep. It was so completely unexpected that I was very frightened when he woke me up but as he spoke to me straight away I recognized him and didn't cry out. And then my first thought was that perhaps he was bringing me a letter from Danceny. But it wasn't that at all, for a second or two later he tried to kiss me and while I was naturally trying to stop him he managed to do something that I wouldn't want anyone in the whole world to do . . . but first he wanted a kiss. So I had to give him one because what else could I do? After all, I'd tried to call out but apart from the fact that I couldn't, he carefully pointed out that if anyone came, he'd throw all the blame on to me and of course it was very easy to do that because of the key. Afterwards he still wouldn't budge, he wanted another kiss and this time, I don't quite know exactly how it happened, but he got me all flustered and after that it was worse than ever . . . Oh dear, it was really very wrong . . . Anyway, in the end! . . . you won't mind if I don't tell you the rest, will you, but I'm as miserable as anyone can possibly be.

The thing I blame myself for most, I'm afraid I've got to tell you, is that I've got a dreadful feeling I didn't resist him as much as I could have done. I don't know how that happened, I certainly don't love Monsieur de Valmont, quite the opposite, yet there were moments when I felt as if I did. Don't imagine that prevented me from saying no all the time but I could feel that I wasn't doing quite the same thing that I was saying, it was as if I couldn't help myself and I was dreadfully confused as well! If it's always so hard as that to defend yourself, you must have to get very used to doing it! It's true Monsieur de Valmont has a way of talking so that you don't quite know how to answer. Anyway, when he left I felt almost sorry and I was weak-minded enough to agree for him to come back tonight. That is what upsets me more than anything else.*

But I can certainly guarantee that I shan't let him in. And the moment he'd gone I certainly realized that I was quite wrong to have promised him. And I've been crying all the time since then. It's Danceny who makes me particularly sad! Every time I thought of him, I cried more than ever till I nearly choked and I still couldn't get him out of my mind and I'm still not able to now—as you can see my paper's all wet. No, I'll never be able to get over it, if only because of him. Anyway, I was quite exhausted but I still couldn't get a minute's sleep all night. And when I got up this morning and saw myself in the mirror, it was frightful how changed I looked.

Mummy noticed it as soon as she saw me and asked me what was the matter. I burst into tears. I thought she was going to tell me off and then perhaps I might not have felt so miserable. But just the opposite, she spoke to me so nicely! I really didn't deserve it! She told me not to be so upset! She didn't know why I was! She said I'd be making myself ill! Oh, sometimes I wish I was dead. I couldn't bear it any longer, I flung myself into her arms and said: 'Oh, Mummy, your daughter's so unhappy!' Then Mummy couldn't help shedding a tear too and all that only made me feel worse. Luckily she didn't ask why I was so unhappy, because I wouldn't have known what to say.

Oh, dear Madame de Merteuil, do please write to me as soon as you can and tell me what I must do because I haven't the heart to think of anything and I just keep on feeling upset. Please send your letter via Monsieur de Valmont but if you're writing to him at the same time, don't tell him I've said anything to you.

With kindest regards, Madame, yours faithfully and respectfully... but I don't dare sign my name.

98

Madame de Volanges to the Marquise de Merteuil
From the Château de ——, 2 October 17—

Dear, dear friend, only a few days ago you were asking me for comfort and advice and now it's my turn to make the same request. I really am most upset and afraid lest I haven't done all I ought to avoid this situation which is causing me such distress.

My anxiety concerns my daughter. Ever since we left Paris I had not failed to observe that she was sad and depressed. However, I was expecting this and had steeled my heart to act with all the strictness I deemed necessary. I hoped that absence and other interests would quickly destroy her love, which I saw more as a childish infatuation than a truly passionate feeling. However, far from achieving anything during our stay here, I have become aware that my child is falling more and more deeply into a dangerous decline and I have serious fears for her health. During the last few days particularly there has been a marked change for the worse; this struck me especially yesterday and we were all very much alarmed here.

Further evidence that she is greatly affected is her readiness to overcome the shyness she has always shown me. Yesterday morning when I simply asked her if she was unwell, she flung herself into my arms sobbing and saying that she was terribly unhappy! I cannot tell you how upset she made me feel: tears suddenly came into my own eyes and I barely had time to turn my head away to prevent her from seeing them. Luckily I had the tact not to ask any more questions but none the less it is clear that she is tormented by this unhappy passion.

So what ought I to do if this situation persists? Shall I bring about my own daughter's unhappiness? Constancy and sensitivity are the most precious qualities* of the human heart: am I to turn them against her? Is this a mother's role? And even if I were to stifle that most natural of feelings which bids us to seek our child's happiness; were I to regard it as a weakness to do what on the contrary I regard as the first and most sacred of our duties; if I force my choice on her, shall I not bear the responsibility for the disastrous consequences that may ensue? A strange use of a mother's authority to force her daughter to choose between unhappiness and crime!

No, my dear friend, I do not intend to set an example that I have so often criticized. No doubt I have been attempting to make a choice on my daughter's behalf; in so doing I was merely giving her the benefit of my experience; I wasn't exercising any right, I was fulfilling a duty. But were I to make the decision for her and ignore this attachment which I had no means of preventing, when neither she nor I can predict how strong it will be or how long it may last, then I should be betraying that duty. No, I shall not agree to her marrying one man because of her love for another. I'd rather put my authority at risk than her virtue.

So I think the most sensible decision is for me to withdraw my acceptance of Monsieur de Gercourt's proposal. I've explained my reasons to you and I think that they outweigh the promise I made. I'll go further: in the present circumstances, keeping my word would really amount to breaking it. After all, if I owe it to my daughter not to reveal her secret to Monsieur de Gercourt, I owe it to him at least not to take advantage of my failure to inform him and to do for him everything that I think he would do himself if he were so informed. On the contrary, shall I be so dishonest as to mislead him when he is relying on my good faith and, at a time when he is honouring me by choosing me as his second mother, deceive him in his choice of the mother of his children?* Such considerations, whose validity I cannot deny, I find more alarming than I can say.

I compare these disastrous premonitions with the picture of my daughter happily married to the man whom her heart has chosen, her wifely duties a pleasure, my son-in-law equally content, congratulating himself every day on his own choice and the pair of them happy purely by making each other happy; and their mutual happiness combining to make me happy too. Am I to sacrifice such a golden prospect for futile considerations which in fact are purely financial? What is the point of my daughter having been born rich if she becomes nothing but a slave to her wealth?

I agree that perhaps Monsieur de Gercourt is a better match than I could have hoped for my daughter and I even admit to having been extremely flattered when his choice fell on her. But after all, Danceny is from an equally good family and his personal qualities are in no way inferior to Gercourt's; and he has the benefit of loving and being loved by my daughter. True, he's not well off but isn't my daughter wealthy enough for two? Ah, why deprive her of the enjoyment of making the one she loves a rich man?

Aren't those marriages based on calculation rather than on compatibility, so-called arranged marriages where everything is accommodated except personal tastes and temperament, the most fertile cause of these scandals which are becoming commoner every day? I prefer to wait and see; at least I'll have time to get to know my daughter who is almost a stranger. I feel I have the strength of mind to make her temporarily unhappy if, in the end, it results in a happiness based on a firmer foundation; but I have no heart to condemn her to endless despair.

Well, dear friend, these are the thoughts which are plaguing me and on which I wish to ask your advice. Such serious matters are far removed from your own charming, lively nature and they seem inappropriate to your young age but you are a tower of strength far beyond your years! In any case, your friendship will be at hand to reinforce your caution and I have no fear that either of them will fail to come to the aid of a worried mother who is anxiously appealing to you for help.

Goodbye, dear, kind friend from, as always, sincerely your, etc.

99

The Vicomte de Valmont to the Marquise de Merteuil
From the Château de ——, 2 October 17—, in the
evening

A couple of minor incidents, fair lady; no real activity, merely scenes. So possess your soul in patience, indeed quite a lot of patience, for while my judge's wife is advancing very gingerly, your ward is retreating and that is far worse. Well, I have the good sense to laugh at such trifles. I'm really warming to my stay here and I can honestly say that in my old aunt's gloomy château I've never felt a single moment of boredom. In fact, aren't I experiencing delights, frustrations, hope, suspense? What more can you expect on a larger stage? An audience? Ah well, let's just wait and see, one will turn up. Even if they won't be seeing me on the job, I'll be able to show them the finished product and they'll only need to admire and applaud. Oh yes, they'll be applauding all right, for I can now at last foresee with complete confidence the moment of my pious prude's downfall. This evening I witnessed the death-throes of her virtue and in its place tenderness and frailty will prevail. I can set the date as not later than our first private conversation. But I can already hear your protests: 'What arrogance! Predicting victory and bragging about it in advance!' Now, now, dear lady, not so fast! So to prove how actually modest I am, let me begin by telling you the story of one of my defeats.

Your little ward really is quite ludicrous! She's certainly a child who deserves to be treated as such. She should be glad to get away with no worse punishment than being stood in the corner! Would you believe it, after what took place between us two nights ago and the friendly terms on which we parted yesterday morning, when I tried to go back last night, as we'd agreed, I found her door locked on the inside! What do you say to that? Occasionally one does come across this sort of childishness the day before . . . but the day after? Isn't that droll?

However, at first I didn't find it a laughing matter, in fact I've never felt my explosive nature react more strongly. True, I wasn't actually looking forward to this further meeting, it was merely a matter of routine; I badly needed my own bed which for the moment seemed preferable to anyone else's and I'd been sorry to have to vacate it. Yet no sooner had I met an obstacle than I felt myself champing at the bit; above all, I felt humiliated at having been made a fool of by a slip of a girl. So I retreated in a foul temper determined not to have anything further to do with the stupid child or her affairs. I sat down and immediately wrote her a note telling her exactly what I thought of her, intending to hand it to her today. But after having, as they say, slept on it, next morning I bethought myself that, since there's not much choice of fun here, I might as well hang on to this bit, so I tore up my rude letter. Thinking it over since, I still feel some surprise that the thought even crossed my mind of putting an end to an adventure before collecting enough evidence to ruin its heroine. Amazing how impulse can lead us astray! Happy, fair lady, the person who, like yourself, has managed early in life to acquire the habit of never giving way to it! Anyway, I've put off my revenge, a sacrifice I make in furtherance of your plans for Gercourt.

Now I'm no longer angry, your ward's behaviour seems to me merely ludicrous. I should very much like to know what she hopes to gain by it! I confess I'm completely at a loss; if it's just to defend herself, it must be said that she's left it a trifle late. One day she really must give me the key to this riddle, I'm highly intrigued. Perhaps she was just tired? Frankly, that might well be the answer, since she doubtless isn't aware that love's arrows, like Achilles' spear,* carry with them the antidote for the wounds they cause. But on second thoughts, I hardly think so: to judge by the long face she's been putting on all day, I'd be inclined to think that there's a spot of remorse involved . . . a whiff of virtue. Virtue indeed! She's a fine one to feel virtuous . . . Ah, she should leave such matters to a woman really born to be virtuous, the only one who can make it something wonderful and lovable . . . Forgive me, fair lady, but it was only this evening that a scene took place between Madame de Tourvel and me that I must tell you about and I'm still somewhat overwhelmed and trying to get rid of the impression it made on me. In fact, it's to help me to do this that I began this letter to you in the first place. You must let me describe it to you. Allowances have to be made for these first reactions . . .

For some days now, Madame de Tourvel and I have been agreed as to our mutual feelings; any disagreement now is purely verbal. It was indeed *her friendship* always corresponding to *my love*; but this conventional language made no difference to the fundamental fact and had we remained within this convention, I should have perhaps moved more slowly, if not less surely. There was already no question of my having to leave, as she'd at first insisted; and as for our conversations, which are now a daily occurrence, I make a point of offering her the opportunity which she is no less eager to grasp.

As our little lovers' meetings usually take place during a walk, the appalling weather which we've had all day offered me little prospect. I was really put out; but I failed to foresee what I would gain through this hitch.

As we couldn't go for a walk, on leaving table a game of cards was proposed and as I'm not a keen card-player and was no longer needed, I seized the opportunity to go up to my rooms, planning to stay there until the game was likely to be ending. As I was going downstairs to join them again I passed my charmer about to go into her apartment and either through lack of caution or through weakness she asked me in that soft voice of hers: 'Where are you going? There's no one left in the drawing-room.' As you may imagine, I needed no further invitation to try to go into her room with her; I found less resistance than I'd expected. It's true that I took the precaution of starting our conversation outside the door with a few casual remarks; but scarcely had we settled down than I turned to the real agenda, namely *my love for my friend*. Her first reaction, although straightforward, seemed to me rather promising. 'Oh, please let us not talk about that here,' she said; and she was trembling. Poor woman! She can see the writing on the wall.

Yet she was wrong to be afraid. Since I'm confident of success one of these days and I can see her using up so many of her reserves of energy in her hopeless struggle, I have for some time past decided to husband my own and wait passively until she gives in exhausted. You surely appreciate that in this case unconditional surrender is required and I don't want to be helped by favourable circumstances. It was indeed after planning this campaign and so as to be able to press her without committing myself too deeply that I had insisted on the word love which she so stubbornly rejected. Knowing that my love was thought to be ardent enough, I tried a more tender note: I'd stopped being angry at her refusal, merely distressed; so didn't my friend, sensitive as she was, owe me some consolation?

In the course of this consolation, her hand remained clasping mine, her shapely body pressed against my arm and we were extremely close to each other. You have certainly noticed how, in such situations, as the defence crumbles, the exchange of requests and refusals grows more intense, then the head turns away, eyes are lowered, and speech is reduced to a few broken, whispered words. These precious symptoms show quite un-equivocally that the heart has given its consent; but this consent has rarely communicated itself as yet to the senses. I even hold the view that it is always risky to make too overt a gesture because this stage of surrender is always accompanied by a delicious feeling of well-being and any attempt to jerk the person out of this state would create a mood which would infallibly work in favour of the defence.

In the present instance caution was all the more indicated since my romantic dreamer would undoubtedly be terrified at having lost control of herself. So I warily didn't even ask her to utter the word I'd been begging her for; no, a glance would be sufficient, one single glance would make me a happy man.

And fair lady, those lovely eyes did indeed look into mine and those heavenly lips even said, 'Well, yes, I . . .' But all of a sudden her eyes went blank, her voice died away and the adorable woman fell into my arms. I'd hardly had time to catch her before she shook herself free and wild-eyed, with her hands held heaven-wards, she cried out, 'O God, dear God, oh save me!', and immediately, quicker than lightning, fell on her knees ten steps away from me. I heard her almost choking and rushed forward to help her but she caught hold of my hands, bathing them in her tears and sometimes even clasping my knees, exclaiming: 'Yes, you will do it, you will be my saviour! You cannot want me to die. Leave me! Save me! Leave me! Oh, in God's name, leave me!' These disjointed words could barely be heard through wild bursts of sobbing. Meanwhile she was holding on to me with such force that I would have been quite unable to leave. So gathering all my strength, I raised her up into my arms. At the same moment her sobs ceased, she stopped talking, her limbs became rigid, and her frenzied outburst turned into violent convulsions.

I confess that I too was violently moved and I believe I would have done as she asked even if the situation hadn't forced me. The fact remains that after giving her assistance, I left as she had requested. I'm delighted to have done so: I've already received most of my reward for it.

I had been expecting that, as on the day of my first declaration, she would fail to appear that evening. However, at about eight o'clock she came down to the drawing-room and merely announced to the assembled company that she had felt very unwell. Her face was extremely drawn and her voice weak, though she looked quite composed; but there was a gentle look in her eyes which frequently rested on me. When she declined to play cards and I was obliged to take her place, she sat down beside me. During supper she remained alone in the drawing-room. When I went back there I thought I detected that she had been crying; to discover if I was right I said that it seemed to me as if she had been feeling unwell again, to which she replied, in a friendly voice: 'That sort of illness takes longer to cure than to catch!' Then when we all retired for the night, I offered her my hand and at the door of her room she gripped mine firmly. It's true that her action seemed somehow involuntary: so much the better, it's further proof of my power over her.

I wouldn't mind betting that at the moment she's delighted at her situation: she's paid her dues in full, and all that remains for her is to cash in on all the benefits! Perhaps she's pondering over this pleasant thought even while I'm writing this letter! And even if she's doing the opposite and thinking up some new method of defence, don't we well know how all such plans turn out? I ask you, can it possibly extend beyond our next meeting? Of course I expect that, naturally enough, it won't be granted without a little fuss: that's fair enough; but once these earnest, prudish females have started kicking over the traces, what's to hold them back? Their love is literally like an explosion: any resistance only makes it more violent. If I were to stop pursuing her, my coy puritan would set off after me.

And so, fairest lady, at any moment you may expect to see me on your doorstep claiming my reward. You won't have forgotten what you promised me once I had succeeded, will you? A small matter of cuckolding your Chevalier? Are you ready? For my part I'm looking forward to it as much as if we'd never known each other. Besides, knowing you is perhaps a good reason for wanting it all the more . . .

Je suis juste et ne suis pas galant.*

It will also be the first time I've been unfaithful to this earnest woman whom I've finally subdued and I promise to use the first possible excuse to slip away from her for twenty-four hours. It will be her punishment for having kept me away from you for so long. Do you realize I've been busy on this affair for more than two months? Yes, it's two months and three days; it's true that includes tomorrow because the consummation won't take place till then. I'm reminded that Madame de B—— resisted for three whole months. I'm delighted to see that downright flirts have better defences than strict puritans . . .

Goodbye, fair lady, I must leave you, for it's very late. This letter has taken longer than I'd intended but as I'm sending some things to Paris early tomorrow I was anxious to seize the opportunity of letting you know as quickly as possible of your friend's good fortune.

100

The Vicomte de Valmont to the Marquise de Merteuil
From the Château de ——, 3 October 17—

Dear lady, I've been fooled, betrayed, ruined.* I'm in despair: Madame de Tourvel has left—and left without informing me. And I wasn't there to stop her, to reproach her for her shameful betrayal! Oh, don't imagine that I'd have let her leave! She would have stayed, yes, she'd have stayed even if I'd had to use brute force. But I was lulled into a false sense of security, I never suspected anything; yes, I was asleep and the lightning struck. No, I just can't think what possessed her, I shall have to give up trying to understand women.

When I recall what happened yesterday! No, that very evening! Those gentle glances! That loving voice! And her pressure on my hand! And all the time she was plotting to run away from me! Oh, women, women! And you complain if you are deceived! Yet all our betrayals are copied straight from you.

Ah, the pleasure of vengeance! I'll seek that faithless woman out and impose my will on her again. Love enabled me to do it before, just think what can be achieved by love spurred on by revenge! Once more she'll be weeping at my feet, trembling, bathed in tears, begging for mercy in her deceitful voice. And I shall be merciless.

What will she be doing at this moment? What will she be thinking? Perhaps she's rubbing her hands with glee at having deceived me and, like all her sex, that's what she most enjoys . . . What her much-vaunted virtue failed to achieve, her guile has succeeded in doing, effortlessly . . . I must have been out of my mind! I was daunted by her high principles; my real danger was her dishonesty.

And I've got to swallow my resentment, not dare show anything but affectionate concern when my heart is boiling with fury! To see myself once again reduced to pleading with a defiant woman who has broken away from my authority! Did I have to be humiliated in this way? And who's done it? A timid little woman who's never been trained to fight. What benefit have I gained from winning a place in her heart, firing her with love, exciting in her a frenzy of desire when she's now sitting calmly in her safe retreat feeling prouder at having run away than I am of all my victories? And am I supposed to take this lying down? Dear lady, you can't possibly think that; such a low opinion of me would be too humiliating!

But what dreadful fate forced me to become so attached to that woman? Aren't there a hundred others longing to receive my attentions? Wouldn't they rush to respond to them? Even if none of them is as good, isn't the charm of variety, the lure of fresh conquests, the prestige of having so many women a sufficiently pleasant prospect? Why chase after someone and ignore all those lined up waiting? Why, oh why? I have no idea, yet I cannot deny the strength of my feelings.

My happiness and peace of mind are utterly dependent on getting that woman whom I love and hate with equal intensity. I cannot come to terms with my fate until I control hers. Not until then shall I be able to watch, calm and relaxed, as she is buffeted in her turn by the storms which I'm enduring at present. And I shall whip up hundreds more: I shall fill her heart with hope and fear, suspicion and trust, every calamity that can be thought up by hatred, every benefit offered by love, in an orderly succession orchestrated by me. That time will come . . . But what efforts I still have to make! Yet how close I was to my goal yesterday! And how far I am from it today! How can I get at her? I daren't risk doing anything at the moment; before deciding on anything, I need to be calm and I'm seething . . .

What upsets me even more is how calmly everyone is responding to my questions on what's happened, what's caused it, on all its extraordinary aspects. Nobody knows anything or even wants to know: people would hardly have mentioned it if I'd been content to talk of something else. When I rushed round to see Madame de Rosemonde as soon as I heard the news, she replied with the indifference of old age that it was the natural result of Madame de Tourvel's indisposition yesterday: she was afraid she was sickening for something and preferred to be in her own home; she considered it perfectly normal, she'd have done the same. As if there was any possible comparison between them: my aunt tottering on the brink of the grave and that other woman, the torment and the charm of my life!

Madame de Volanges whom I'd suspected of being a party to the matter seemed concerned only because she hadn't been consulted. I confess that I'm delighted that she wasn't given the chance of hurting me; she'd have really enjoyed that! It also proves that she's not in that woman's confidence as much as I'd feared: that's one enemy the fewer. How delighted she'd be to know that I was the person Madame de Tourvel was escaping from! And how positively bloated with pride if she knew it was on her advice! What a boost that would have been to her self-esteem! God, how I loathe that woman! Oh, I must pick up the threads of my affair with her daughter again; I want to mould her to my will. So I think I'll stay on here for a while; at least the few thoughts I've been able to collect up till now lead me to that view.

Don't you think, in fact, that after such a flagrant act, that ungrateful woman of mine will be dreading to see me appear on her doorstep. But if she thinks I'm likely to pursue her, she'll not have failed to give instructions not to admit me; and I'm as anxious to stop her from getting into the habit of using such tactics as I am to avoid being humiliated by them. So instead, I think it's better to let her know that I'm staying on here; I'll even try to persuade her to return and when she's really convinced that I'm keeping away, I'll turn up at her house and we'll see how she reacts to that sort of meeting. But to increase the impact, I shall have to delay it, and I'm not sure that I have the patience; a dozen times today I've had to bite back my order to hitch up my horses. But I intend to control myself; I promise to wait here for your reply; my only request, fair lady, is that you don't keep me waiting too long.

The most tiresome thing would be to remain in ignorance of what's happening; but my man who's in Paris has certain rights of access to her maid and he may be able to help me. I've sent him instructions and some money. Will you please let me enclose them in this letter and make sure that they are delivered to him personally by one of your servants? I'm taking this precaution because the rogue has the habit of never receiving my letters when they require him to do something which he finds inconvenient and because he doesn't seem quite so attached to his lady-love at the moment as I'd like him to be.

Farewell, lovely lady. If some bright idea occurs to you, some way of speeding my cause, do let me know. I've seen more than once how great a help your friendship can be for me and I can feel it again now, for since starting this letter I've grown progressively calmer. At least I'm talking to someone who understands me and not to the automata I've been vegetating amongst since this morning. Truth to tell, the longer I live, the more I'm tempted to think that the only moderately worthwhile people in the world are you and I.

101

The Vicomte de Valmont to his valet Azolan
(*enclosed with letter 100*)
From the Château de ——, 3 October 17—

What a complete idiot you are to have left here this morning without realizing that Madame de Tourvel was leaving too or, assuming you did know, not to have come and warned me. What's the use of wasting my money boozing with the servants and making eyes at other people's maids instead of attending to me, if you can't keep me better informed of what's going on? It's one of your typical cock-ups! But I warn you that if you make just one more in this business, it'll be the last one you make in my service.

You're to report back everything about Madame de Tourvel's household: the state of her health; how she's sleeping; if she's sad or cheerful; how often she goes out and whose houses she goes to; if she has callers and who they are; how she spends her time; if she treats her maids well or badly, particularly the one she had with her here; what she does when she's alone; if when she's reading she does so uninterruptedly or whether she breaks off to dream; similarly when she's writing. Also arrange to make friends with the man who takes her letters to the post. Keep offering to do this job for him and when he accepts, post only those letters that appear unimportant, letting me have the others, particularly those addressed to Madame de Volanges, if there are any.*

So arrange to remain in your Julie's good books for a little while longer. If, as you thought, she's got another lover, get her to agree to share her favours and don't make too much of a fuss: you'll only be joining many of your betters in similar circumstances. And if this second string gets in the way, if, for instance, you see him taking up too much of Julie's time during the day and she's spending less with her mistress, try to find some way of ousting him or else pick a quarrel with him. Don't be scared of the consequences, I'll back you up. Above all, hang around the house. It's by being constantly on the spot that you'll see everything and see it thoroughly. If one of the servants even happens to get the sack, apply for the job yourself, saying you're no longer in my employ. In such a case, mention that you left me in order to find a quieter and better-run household. Anyway, try and get the job. I'll still keep you on during that time: it'll be the same as your stay at the Duchesse de ———'s and in the end you'll be similarly rewarded by Madame de Tourvel.

If you were bright enough and keen enough, these instructions should be sufficient, but in order to improve your performance in both these areas I'm sending you some money. As you see, the enclosed note authorizes my agent to pay you twenty-five louis:* I've no doubt you're broke. Out of this sum, give

Julie enough to persuade her to enter into correspondence with me. Anything left over will pay for your drinking sessions with Madame de Tourvel's servants. Try as far as possible to include the butler so that he looks forward to seeing you come to the house. But don't forget that I'm subsidizing your services, not your pleasures.

Get Julie into the habit of observing and reporting everything, even things that might seem utterly trivial. It's better for her to include a dozen useless details than to leave out one interesting one and often something that looks quite unimportant isn't so. As I need to be kept informed immediately if something happens which seems to you worth notifying, as soon as you get this letter, send Philippe off with the spare horse to install himself at M———* where he's to stay until further notice; he will provide a relay if needed. For ordinary communications the normal post will be adequate.

Be careful not to lose this letter. Reread it every day, both to make sure you haven't forgotten anything and that you've still got it. In fact, do everything that needs to be done now that I've done you the honour of entrusting you with this task. You know that if I'm pleased with you, you can expect to be pleased with me.

102

Madame de Tourvel to Madame de Rosemonde
3 October, 1 a.m.

You will be greatly surprised, dear Madame de Rosemonde, to hear that I am leaving so hurriedly. My action must seem most extraordinary to you but your surprise will undoubtedly be far greater when you learn the reasons for it! You may possibly think that in confiding them to you I am showing a lack of consideration for the peace of mind so necessary at your age, or even wanting in the respect due to you on so many counts. So I ask your forgiveness but my heart is oppressed and needs to pour out its burden into the bosom of a friend who is as kind as she is wise. Whom could it choose but you? Look upon me as your daughter; I beg you to show me a mother's kindness. I hope that my feelings for you may perhaps give me some claim on yours.

Ah, where are those days when those feelings were all honourable, when I was untroubled by those now causing me such dreadful turmoil and rendering me powerless to control them while at the same time making it my duty to do so? Ah, that fatal trip has proved my ruin!

So what can I say? I am in love, yes, desperately in love. Alas, this is the first time I have ever written this word which has been so frequently requested and never granted, yet I would give my life for the pleasure of letting the man who has inspired it hear it just once from my lips; yet I must continually refuse to utter it. So yet again he will be doubting my feelings and thinking he has the right to reproach me for my behaviour. Ah, how wretched I am! Why can't he read in my heart as easily as he dominates it? Yes, if he knew all that I am suffering, I should suffer less; yet even you whom I'm telling about it will still have only the smallest conception of my sufferings!

In a moment, I shall be fleeing from him and causing him distress. While he will still be thinking he is close to me, I shall be far away. At a time when I have become accustomed to seeing him every day, I shall be in places where he has never been and where I must never allow him to come. I have already made my preparations; it's all there under my very eyes; there's nothing in sight that doesn't proclaim the cruel fact of my departure. Everything's ready, except me. And the more my heart resists, the more it proves how necessary it is for me to submit.

I shall no doubt submit; better to die than live in guilt. And I can already feel that I'm all too guilty; the only thing I've salvaged is decorum; my virtue is in ruins and I must confess to you that what little is left I owe to his generosity. I was intoxicated with the pleasure of hearing him and seeing him, with the bliss of feeling him close beside me, with the even greater happiness of being able to make him happy; I was powerless and helpless; I barely had strength enough to continue to struggle, let alone to resist. I was trembling on the brink of the abyss but incapable of avoiding it. Well, he saw my anguish and took pity on me. How could I fail to adore him? I owe him more than my life.

Ah, if it were only my life that was in danger by staying here, believe me, I should never agree to leave. What is my life worth without him? Wouldn't I be only too glad to sacrifice it? Since I'm doomed for ever to make both him and myself unhappy, forced to defend myself not only against him but against myself, never venturing either to console him or to complain myself, spending my whole time causing him distress when all I want is to devote it to making him happy: isn't such a life like dying a thousand deaths? Yet that will be my fate. But I'll not give way, I have courage enough; I swear it and I want you, my adoptive mother, to bear witness to that promise.

And I swear to you as well never to conceal from you any of my actions; I appeal to you to accept that promise too, for I need your help: if I am committed to telling you everything, I shall grow used to thinking of you as always being at my side. Your virtue will double for mine. I shall surely never be prepared to blush in front of you; you will have the power to restrain me and I shall cherish you as an indulgent friend to whom I can confide my shortcomings as well as worshipping you as my guardian angel who can protect me from bringing shame on myself.

It is surely shameful enough to have to make such a request. A fatal consequence of overweening confidence! Why didn't I beware sooner of the sympathy I felt growing inside me? Why did I delude myself that I could control it or rise above it at will? Sheer madness! How little I knew of love! Ah, if I had given more care to my struggle against it, perhaps it might never have become so all-powerful! Then I should perhaps not have needed to leave or even, while still bowing to this painful necessity, I should have been able to avoid having to break off our relationship completely and merely try to ensure that it was less close! But having to give up everything at one blow! And for ever! Ah, my dear, dear friend . . . But what has come over me? Even while I'm writing my mind is straying towards guilty hopes and desires . . . Ah, let us go away, far away from here and may these sins which I cannot control be washed away by my sacrifice . . .

Farewell, my dear respected friend, adopt me, love me as a daughter. You can rest assured that with all my weakness, I would rather die than prove unworthy of your choice.

103

Madame de Rosemonde to Madame de Tourvel
From the Château de ——, 3 October 17—

I was more distressed by your leaving, dear young friend, than surprised by its cause: long experience and my great interest in you made the state of your heart clear enough and, to tell the truth, your letter told me little or nothing new.* If you were the only source of my information I should still not be aware of the name of the man you love, for by speaking throughout of *him* you did not once disclose who he is. I did not need you to do so; I know his identity perfectly well. But I remark on it because I am reminded that such has always been the case in matters of love; I see that things haven't changed since my day.

I scarcely imagined I should ever find myself delving into memories so remote from my present concerns and so alien to my age. Nevertheless since yesterday, in my desire to find some sort of help for you, I really have been thinking very deeply on the subject. But what can I do except feel admiration and pity? I applaud your wise decision but it frightens me since it tells me that you considered it necessary, and once someone has reached that stage, it is always difficult to remain at a distance from the man when our heart continually draws us towards him.

But you must remain staunch and steadfast. For noble souls like yourself nothing is impossible and even if you should have the misfortune to succumb (which God forbid), believe me, dear young friend, you will at least still have the consolation of having fought with all your might. And things which human wisdom cannot achieve may be accomplished by God's grace whenever He so pleases. His help may be about to descend and your virtue, tried and tested in your painful struggle, will emerge purified and shining more brightly than ever. You must hope that tomorrow you will be granted the strength which you lack today.

Do not put your trust in Him alone; but He will urge you on to make every effort yourself.

So I must leave you in the hands of divine Providence to help you in a peril against which I can do nothing; but I shall watch and wait, supporting and comforting you as far as lies in my power. I cannot relieve you of your weight of suffering but I will share it. So I shall gladly listen to your confidences; I can understand that you must feel the need to unburden your heart and I shall open mine to you. Age has not yet chilled it so much that it is dead to friendship. You will always find it ready to welcome you; never hesitate to come and confide in me and let your troubled heart find rest in mine. It will not provide great comfort for your distress but at least you will not be crying alone. And whenever this unhappy love threatens to overpower you and you feel obliged to talk about it with someone, it is better that you do so with me rather than with *him*. And now I'm talking like you and I think that the pair of us together will never manage to spell out his name . . . But in any case, we know what we mean.

I do not know if I am doing right to tell you that he seemed greatly affected by your leaving. It would perhaps be wiser not to mention this to you; but I don't like the sort of wisdom which distresses our friends. However, I find myself forced not to say anything further on that subject: my poor sight and my shaking hand prevent me from writing long letters when I have to pen them myself.

So farewell, my dear young friend; goodbye, dear, lovely child: yes, I'm delighted to adopt you as my daughter and you have every good quality to make a mother proud and happy.

104

The Marquise de Merteuil to Madame de Volanges
Paris, 4 October 17—

Reading your letter, dear, kind friend, I must confess that I was barely able to repress a movement of pride. You are actually doing me the honour of confiding in me! And confiding to the point of asking my advice! Oh, how happy I shall be if I really can deserve your good opinion of me and it does not come merely from friendly prejudice in my favour! Whatever the grounds, your trust is none the less heart-warming for me and to have acquired it is in my view a further reason to make a greater effort to be worthy of it. So, while making no claim to be offering you advice, I shall give you my frank opinion. I am full of misgivings, because it differs from yours but when I have explained my reasons, you must judge for yourself and if you reject them, I am ready to endorse your objections in advance. I shall at least be wise enough not to think myself wiser than you.

However, if, on this one occasion, my opinion happened to be preferable, the explanation would have to be found in the illusions of motherly love. Since this is an entirely admirable feeling it is certain to be found within your heart. Indeed, it is that feeling that must have dictated the decision which you are being tempted to take. That is why, if you sometimes happen to err, it is only ever in your choice between paths of virtue.

To my mind, when someone else's fate is at stake, the cautious path is the better one to take, above all when the decision involves the indissoluble union of holy wedlock. It is in such cases that a mother as loving as she is wise must, as you so aptly say, *give her daughter the benefit of her own experience*. Now I must ask you: what is she to do in order to achieve this? Surely it is merely to make the distinction, on her behalf, between what is agreeable and what is right and proper to do.

Would it not be debasing maternal authority, indeed utterly destroying it, to make it bow to a frivolous fancy, to a whim, which can however grow into a frenzy, with a power of illusion which threatens only those who fear to face up to it and must vanish as soon as they have learned to despise it? For my part I confess I have never believed in those heart-stirring, irresistible passions which we seem generally agreed to offer as an excuse for our profligate behaviour. I cannot conceive how a fancy, here today and gone tomorrow, can outweigh the rock-solid principles of decency, honesty, and modesty nor can I understand why a woman who offends against them should find justification in her alleged passion, any more than a murderer should in a desire for vengeance.

And who has never had to struggle? But I have always tried to convince myself that in order to resist, you need only have the will-power and, till now at least, my experience has confirmed that view. What would be the value of virtue if it did not involve duties? We worship it by sacrificing to it and its rewards are in our hearts. These truths can be denied only by those who have an interest in repudiating them and who, being already depraved, hope to hoodwink others, if only momentarily, by using bad reasons to try and justify their bad conduct.

But how could a shy, simple girl, your own flesh and blood, ever give cause for such fears when her modest, chaste upbringing can only have reinforced her natural advantages? Yet you wish to sacrifice the favourable match which you, in your wisdom, had arranged for her, to just such fears, which I venture to describe as humiliating for your daughter! I am very fond of Danceny and as you know, for some time now have seen little of Monsieur de Gercourt; but my liking for the former and my indifference towards the latter in no way blind me to the enormous difference between the two suitors.

I agree that they are equally well-born; but one of them is penniless and the other one is so wealthy that he could have risen to any position even without his birth. Of course, money doesn't equal happiness but it must be admitted that it does facilitate it. As you say, Mademoiselle Volanges is rich enough for two; nevertheless, an income of sixty thousand francs a year is not over-much when your name is Danceny and you have to set up and maintain a style of living to match that name. We're no longer living in the days of Madame de Sévigné.* Luxury is all-consuming: we deprecate it but we have to adopt it and inessentials end by depriving us of essentials.

As for the personal qualities to which you most rightly attach such great importance, in this respect Monsieur de Gercourt is certainly beyond reproach; he has been tried and not found wanting.* I like to believe, indeed I do believe, that Danceny is in no way inferior on this point; but can we be quite so sure? It's true that till now he has seemed free from the faults of his age and, in contrast to the contemporary trend, he shows a liking for decent society which bodes well for his future conduct; but who can say whether this apparently seemly behaviour is a result of his limited means? However unaverse you might be to lead a drunken or disorderly life, in order to be a gambler or a rake you do need money and you can still have a hankering for a sinful life while being afraid of its excesses. After all, he wouldn't be the first or the last person to frequent good society purely because he couldn't do any better.

I am not saying, Heaven forbid, that I do think he is at all like that: but you would always run that risk and how bitterly you would blame yourself if the marriage were to turn out unhappily! What reply would you give your daughter were she to say: 'Mother, I was young and had no experience of life; I had even been misled by an error excusable at my age; but Heaven had anticipated my weakness and provided me with a wise mother to correct and defend me from it. Then why did you throw away your caution and allow such a misfortune to occur? Was it for me to choose a husband when I knew nothing about marriage? Even if I wanted to, shouldn't you have opposed it? But in fact I was never so mad as to want to, I had made up my mind to respect your choice, to obey and resign myself; I have always been a dutiful daughter and bowed to your decisions yet now I'm being punished as if I'd been rebellious. Ah, Mama, your weakness has led to my ruin!' Her respect for you might cause her to stifle her protests but a mother's love would recognize them and even if your daughter's tears were shed secretly, they would still flow into your heart and conscience. What consolation will you have then? Will you find any comfort in this mad love that you should have warned her against and which on the contrary you allowed to lead you astray?

I don't know, dear lady, if I have too strong a prejudice against passion but I think that it is something to be feared even in marriage. Not that I think it wrong for warm, decent feelings to exist between married couples; such feelings enhance the bond and, as it were, alleviate the duties it demands, but they can have no part to play in the tying of this bond. A passing infatuation is no basis for a choice affecting the whole of our life. To choose you have to compare and how can you do that when you have eyes for one person only; and when even that person is impossible to know since you are blinded and drunk with passion?

As you may believe, I have met a number of women afflicted by this dangerous disorder; some of them have confided in me. To listen to them there's not one who isn't loved by the Perfect Man; but these extravagant perfections exist only in their imagination. In their wild dreams they see nothing but charms and virtues and gleefully deck out the men of their choice in all these qualities; but these glittering robes fit for a God often drape an abject model; but whatever he is, no sooner have they dressed him up than, dazzled by their own handiwork, they prostrate themselves to adore him.

Either your daughter doesn't love Danceny or else she is suffering from a similar delusion; and if their love is shared, so too is their delusion. So your reason for joining them in marriage for ever comes down to the certainty that they don't know each other and indeed cannot possibly know each other. But you will say to me: do Gercourt and my daughter know one another any better? No, indeed they do not but at least they are not suffering from any delusions about themselves, they merely don't know each other. What happens in such cases between a couple, assuming they are both decent, honourable people? They study each other, they inwardly examine themselves and their relationship to the other, try to discover and soon realize which of their likes and wishes they have to give up for the sake of domestic harmony. Such slight sacrifices offer no difficulty because they are mutual and they have been anticipated; soon they create a mood of mutual goodwill; and habit, which strengthens all our natural inclinations that it doesn't destroy, gradually creates this gentle atmosphere of friendship, trust, and affection which, together with respect, combines to form what seems to me a true and lasting happiness.

Love's illusions may be sweeter but who doesn't also know that they are less durable? And what dangers there are lurking when they are demolished! The smallest shortcomings seem unbearably shocking in contrast to the ideal which had misled us. However, each of the couple thinks that it is only the other who has changed and that they still have all the splendid qualities with which they were mistakenly and fleetingly invested. They are surprised to find they no longer exert the charm which they no longer feel themselves. They feel humiliated; wounded vanity embitters their minds and increases their sense of wrong, producing resentment and creating hatred; frivolous pleasures have to be paid for by endless misfortune.

So there, dear, dear friend, are my thoughts on the matter we are considering; I am not necessarily defending them, I'm merely putting them forward: it is for you to make your decision. But if you persist in your own view, I merely ask you to let me know the reasons which you consider outweigh mine: I shall be only too glad to be enlightened by you and particularly to be reassured as to the fate of your dear daughter whom I am so passionately anxious to see happy, both because of the very deep friendship I feel for her and my undying friendship for you.*

105

The Marquise de Merteuil to Cécile Volanges
Paris, 4 October 17—

Well, what a cross little girl we are, aren't we? And feeling so ashamed, too! And what a naughty man Monsieur de Valmont is, isn't he? Goodness me! He's had the audacity to treat you like the woman he's most fond of! He's been teaching you something that you were dying to learn! What unforgiveable behaviour, indeed . . . And as for you, you want to remain chaste for your sweetheart, who's making no great demands on you; so what you really want are love's sorrows and none of its pleasures!* Splendid! Keep following that line and you'll end up as a perfect heroine for a novel. Passion, adversity and, above all, virtue: how superb it all sounds! And in the course of this magnificent parade, you'll certainly be bored at times but you'll surely be giving as good as you get!

Yes, we really have to feel sorry for the poor little girl! The morning after, she had dark rings round her eyes! And what will you have to say when it's your lover's eyes with dark rings? Never mind, you dear angel, they'll not always be like that: not all men are Valmonts. And not daring to raise those eyes, either! Now that was really bright of you, wasn't it? So everybody would have been able to read the story of your little adventure in them, would they? But if that were the case, believe me there would be many more downcast eyes amongst married women and even amongst young ladies . . .

Despite all the praise which, as you see, I feel impelled to give you, it must none the less be admitted that you failed to pull off your master-stroke: telling your Mama everything. Yet you'd already made such a good start, flinging yourself into her arms . . . sobbing . . . and she was shedding a tear, too . . . What a scene! Real pathos! What a pity you didn't play it through to the end. In an ecstasy of delight and to add weight to your virtue, she would have packed you off to spend the rest of your life in a convent where you'd have been able to love your Danceny to your heart's content, with no rivals—and in absolute chastity. You would have eaten your heart out as much as you wanted and Valmont would certainly not have come between you and your woes with any tiresome offers of pleasure.

But seriously, how can a girl who's past her fifteenth birthday be so positively childish? You're absolutely right: you don't deserve my kindness. Yet I did want to be your friend and with the mother you've got and the husband she wants you to have, you certainly may need one! But if you can't pull yourself together, what on earth can you expect other people to do for you? What hope is there if something which opens other girls' eyes merely blinds yours?

If you could make the effort to think for a moment you'd soon realize that instead of moaning you ought to be celebrating. But you're feeling ashamed and thus embarrassed. Well, stop worrying: the shame produced by love is like the pain: you only feel it the first time. You may pretend to have it on later occasions; you don't really feel it. But pleasure doesn't go away and that's surely something. I even seemed to gain the impression, in your muddled little rigmarole, that you might be quite attracted by it. So, how about being honest? That *confusion* which prevented you from *doing quite the same thing as you were saying*, which made you feel *almost sorry* when Valmont left, was that caused just by shame or was it pleasure? And the way he talked *so that you didn't know how to answer*, didn't that come from the way he acted? Now now, little girl, you're fibbing and you're fibbing to your good friend. That's naughty. But let's leave it there.

Something that everybody would consider a pleasure, and perhaps nothing more, for someone in your position is a real godsend. Don't you realize in fact that situated between a mother whose love you value and a lover whose love you want to keep for ever, the only way to combine these conflicting interests successfully is to turn your attention to a third party? In the diversion offered by this new affair you'll be seen to be deferring to your mother, sacrificing a lover she disapproves of and at the same time gaining a reputation by your strong resistance in your lover's eyes. You can continue to reassure him of your love while never going all the way to prove it. This steadfast refusal, completely painless in the situation in which you'll be, won't fail to be attributed to your high moral principles; he may grumble but he'll love you all the more. For your mother, you'll be seen to be sacrificing your love; for your lover, resisting it: and the cost of this double bonus will be . . . to enjoy its pleasures. Oh, how many women who've lost their reputations would have discreetly kept them if they had been able to rely on that kind of support . . .

Doesn't the course I'm suggesting seem the most sensible and the pleasantest? Do you know what you've achieved by behaving as you did? Your mother has got it into her head that you've been sadder recently because you're more in love than ever; she's outraged and she's waiting to confirm her belief in order to punish you for it. She's just written to me to that effect; she'll do everything possible to extract a confession from you. She is even thinking, she told me, of suggesting that you marry Danceny, so as to get you to betray yourself. And if you let yourself be taken in by her pretended affection and speak from the heart, you'll quickly find yourself shut away for many years, perhaps for ever, with ample time to mourn your blindness and gullibility.

You must counter this trick which she's intending to play on you with one of your own. So start by not looking so sad and make her believe that you're thinking less about Danceny. She'll allow herself to be persuaded all the more easily as this is the normal effect of absence and she'll be extra grateful to you because it'll give her the chance of thinking how clever she is in listening to the voice of caution. But if she still harbours certain doubts and were to go so far as to talk of marriage, behave like a

well brought up little girl and retreat into a completely submissive attitude. And when it comes to the point, what are you
risking? For what wives do to their husbands, any husband's as
good as any other and even the most tiresome is less troublesome
than a mother.

Once she's more satisfied with your conduct, your mother will
finally marry you off and then, with your greater freedom, you'll
have your choice, to leave Valmont, to take Danceny, or even
to keep both of them. Because, make no mistake about it,
Danceny's a nice boy; but he's one of those men you can get
whenever you like and as often as you like, so there's no need to
bother about him. It's not the same with Valmont: he's hard
to keep and dangerous to drop. To handle him you need to be
very cunning or, failing that, very amenable. But supposing you
succeeded in winning his friendship? What a prize that would
be! He'd immediately set you up amongst the smartest of smart
women. That's the way to achieve a solid reputation in society
and not by blushing and snivelling, as when your nuns used to
make you go down on your knees to eat.

So if you're wise, you'll try and make it up with Valmont, who
must be very cross with you, and as it's necessary to know how to
make amends for silly conduct, don't be afraid to make advances
to him, for you'll soon learn that if the first approaches are made
by men, the second almost always have to come from us. You've
got a pretext, because you mustn't keep this letter; I ask you, in
fact demand you, to hand it back to Valmont as soon as you have
read it. And don't forget to seal it up again first. For one thing,
your conduct towards him must appear to be spontaneous and
you mustn't seem to be following anyone else's advice: and for
another, you're the only person in the world who is a close
enough friend for me to talk to as I have been talking to you.

Goodbye, you angel. Follow my advice and you'll let me know
if you feel better for having done so . . .*

By the way, I was forgetting . . . One last word: do try and do
something about the style of your letters. You're still writing like
a child. That's all right between you and me, we aren't supposed
to have any secrets from each other: but doing it with everybody!
And particularly your lover! You'd always look like a silly little
girl. You can surely see that when you're writing to someone, it's

meant for him and not for you. So you must try to say not what you really think but what you think he'll most enjoy hearing.

Goodbye, my pet. I'm not going to tell you off, I'm going to give you a kiss and hope you'll be a sensible girl.

106

The Marquise de Merteuil to the Vicomte de Valmont
Paris, 4 October 17—

Well done, Vicomte! And this time my love for you knows no bounds! In any case, after the first of your two letters, the second one was only to be expected, so I wasn't in the least surprised and while you were boasting of your imminent success and already applying for your reward by asking *if I was ready*, I could see quite plainly that there was no need for me to be in any hurry. Yes, honour bright! Reading your enthralling account of that tender little scene which had moved you so *violently* and noting your masterly restraint, reminiscent of the finest traditions of French chivalry, I kept saying to myself: 'I scent disaster!'

But there could really have been no other outcome possible. Here's a poor woman who's surrendered and not been taken: what else can you expect her to do? Yes indeed, in such cases honour must at least be saved and that's what your judge's wife has done. I certainly know that for my own part, having gained the impression that the course she's been following has worked quite well, I'm proposing to do the same thing myself at the first decent opportunity but I can promise you that if the man for whom I've been taking so much trouble doesn't take better advantage of it than you have, he can say goodbye for ever to any hope of having me . . .

So now you're left completely empty-handed! And that in spite of having two women on hand, one of them already in the 'morning after' stage and the other one asking nothing better than to be there, too! Well, you're going to think I'm boasting and say it's easy to be wise after the event, but I swear to you that I was expecting it. The fact is that you haven't any real natural gift for your profession; you know only what you've learned and you lack any spark of imagination. So as soon as circumstances don't fit into your fixed formulas and you have to leave the beaten track, you're caught out like a schoolboy. Thus a touch of child-ishness on the one hand, a relapse into prudery on the other, are enough to throw you into disarray because you don't meet them every day and you're incapable of either predicting them or handling them. Oh, Vicomte, Vicomte, you're teaching me never to judge men by their successful reputations; we'll soon be saying of you: Well, he did show a lot of dash, once . . . And when you've committed one stupidity after another, you turn to me for help. It would seem that I've nothing else to do but bail you out. It's true that that would be quite a big job . . .

However that may be, one of those two adventures you under-took against my wishes and it doesn't concern me; as for the other, since you did it partly to oblige me, I'll take it in hand. I enclose a letter; after reading it, pass it to the Volanges girl; it will be more than adequate to send her back to you. But please do give the child a little attention and between us let's turn her into a real disaster for her mother and Gercourt. Don't be afraid of stepping up the dose: it's quite obvious to me that she won't be scared; and once our plans have borne fruit, she can turn into whatever she likes.

Personally, I've no further interest in her. I'd toyed with the idea of, at least, enlisting her help in my intrigues and taking her on as my second fiddle but I don't think she's got it in her; she suffers from a silly sort of ingenuousness that didn't even respond to your specific treatment, though that rarely fails; to my mind, that's the most dangerous woman's disease there is. In particular, it points to a character weakness well-nigh incurable and gets in everybody's way. We'd be spending our time trying to turn the little girl into a charmer and merely teaching her how to become a trollop. I can't think of anything more dull than that stupid sort of acquiescence, a girl who goes to bed without knowing how or why but merely because she's been attacked and can't say no. Women like that are nothing but pleasure machines.*

You'll say that that's all we want her to be and quite enough for our plans. Fine! But let's not forget that everyone soon learns how such machines work, so that in order to make safe use of it, you need to move quickly, not go on too long, and then dismantle it. True, we shan't be short of ways and means of dumping her and Gercourt will certainly always be ready to have her put away in a convent whenever we want. And in any case, once he can no longer have any doubts as to his mishap, once it's public and known to all, what does it matter if he takes his revenge, as long as he's left without any consolation? And, no doubt, your thoughts on the mother are on the same lines as my remarks on the husband, so the whole thing's as good as done.

As I think this is the best course and intend to pursue it, I have made up my mind, as you'll see in my letter, to push her along rather smartly; this makes it most important to leave nothing in her hands which might compromise me and I ask you to make sure that this happens. Once this precaution has been taken, I can answer for her mental attitude; the rest is up to you. All the same, if we see later on that this ingenuousness of hers shows signs of improvement, we'll still have time to change our plans whenever we want. In any case, sooner or later we should always have had to do what we're about to do, so whatever happens we'll not be wasting our time and trouble.

Do you know, mine nearly were wasted and Gercourt's lucky star very nearly prevailed over my cautious approach. Didn't Madame de Volanges suffer a moment of motherly weakness? Didn't she think of giving her daughter to Danceny? That was the meaning of her more affectionate attitude which you noticed *the morning after.* That would have been another of your marvellous master-strokes! Luckily the tender-hearted mama wrote to me on the subject and I hope that my reply will have put her off it. I spoke at such lengths about virtue and above all flattered her so much that she's bound to think I'm right.

I'm only sorry I haven't the time to make a copy of this edifying epistle to demonstrate to you the strictness of my morality. You'd appreciate the contempt I bestow on women who are depraved enough to take lovers! It's so cosy being strict in writing! It never does any harm except to other people and doesn't have the slightest effect on us. And I'm not unaware either that in her younger days the good lady had her lapses like anyone else and I wasn't sorry to be able to have a little dig at her to mortify her conscience; it consoled me somewhat for having to violate my own by praising her so highly. Similarly, in the same letter, it was the thought of hurting Gercourt which encouraged me to say nice things about him.

Farewell, Vicomte. I strongly approve of your decision to stay on where you are for a while. I've no means at all of furthering your progress in one direction; however, I do invite you to relieve your boredom with our joint ward. As for myself, despite your polite writ of summons, you will certainly appreciate that you still have to wait; and you will doubtless have to agree that it's not my fault . . .

107

Azolan to the Vicomte de Valmont
Paris, 5 October 17—, 11 p.m.

Your lordship,

In accordance with instructions, on receipt of your letter I promptly called on Monsieur Bertrand who gave me the twenty-five louis as your lordship had ordered him. I asked him for two more for Philippe who I'd told to leave immediately as your lordship said but he hadn't got any money. But as Monsieur Bertrand didn't want to do this, seeing as your lordship hadn't given him any instructions, I had to give Philippe them out of my own pocket which I hope your lordship will be pleased to take into account, if your lordship so pleases.

Philippe left yesterday evening. I told him not to leave the inn under any circumstances so we can be sure of getting hold of him if need be.

I then proceeded at once to Madame de Tourvel's residence to see Mademoiselle Julie but she was out and I was only able to speak to La Fleur but he couldn't tell me anything as he's only been in the house at mealtimes since his arrival. It's the second footman who has been on duty and as your lordship will know, I have never met him. But I started to get to know him today.

This morning I called back to see Mademoiselle Julie and she seemed very glad to see me. I questioned her as to why her mistress had come back but she told me she didn't know anything about it and I believe she's telling the truth. I made a fuss because she hadn't warned me she was leaving and she gave me her word that she only knew herself that evening when her mistress was going to bed, so much so that she had to spend the whole night packing and tidying up and the poor girl didn't get more than two hours' sleep. She didn't get away from her mistress's bedroom until after one o'clock and as she left her mistress had just started writing.

When she went off that morning Madame de Tourvel left a letter with the porter of the château. Mademoiselle Julie doesn't know who it was for, she says perhaps your lordship but your lordship didn't mention it.

During the whole drive Madam wore a big hood over her face which meant it couldn't be seen but Mademoiselle Julie feels pretty sure she was crying a lot. She didn't say a word during the journey and didn't want to stop at ———* as she had on the way down which didn't please Mademoiselle Julie very much because she hadn't had any breakfast. But as I told her, mistresses will be mistresses. Madam went to bed as soon as she arrived but only for a couple of hours. When she got up she sent for her major-domo and instructed him not to let anyone in. She didn't get properly dressed at all. She sat down at table for dinner but only took a little soup and then immediately left and had her coffee sent up to her room and Mademoiselle Julie went in at the same time. She found her mistress tidying papers away in her secretaire and saw that they were letters. I'd bet they were your lordship's and one of the three letters which came for her that afternoon was still lying on her desk that whole evening. I feel positive that was one of your lordship's too. But why did she go away like that? It seems very surprising to me. But your lordship knows all about it and it's none of my business anyway.

During the afternoon Madame de Tourvel went into her library and took two books up to her boudoir but Mademoiselle Julie swears she didn't spend even a quarter of an hour reading them the whole day long and all she did was to read that letter and day-dream, resting her head on her hand. I thought your lordship would be very glad to know what the books were and as Mademoiselle Julie didn't know, today I got her to take me into the library on the excuse of wanting to see what it's like and there's a gap for only two books, one is the second volume of

Christian Thoughts and the other the first volume of a book called *Clarisse*.* I'm spelling it as it was printed, maybe your lordship will know all about it.

Yesterday evening Madam didn't have any supper, just a cup of tea. This morning she rang for her maid early, asked for her carriage at once and went to the Cistercians before nine o'clock and heard Mass. She wanted to confess but her confessor is away and won't be back for a week or ten days. I thought your lordship would be interested in knowing this.

Next she came back and had breakfast, then she started writing and wrote for nearly an hour. I soon had the chance to do what your lordship specially wanted, because I took the letters to the post. There wasn't one for Madame de Volanges but I'm sending your lordship one addressed to Monsieur de Tourvel. I thought that would be the one likely to be the most interesting. There was also one for Madame de Rosemonde but I imagined your lordship would certainly be seeing that one any time he wanted and I sent it off. Anyway, your lordship will certainly learn everything since Madame de Tourvel has written to him as well. In future, I'll get all the letters I want because it's almost always Mademoiselle Julie who gives them to the servants and she's promised that because she's fond of me and of your lordship too, she'll be happy to do whatever I like.

She didn't even want the money I offered her but I think your lordship will certainly want to give her a little present and if that is your lordship's wish and he would like me to see to it, I can easily find out what she'd like.

I do hope your lordship won't think I've been slack in serving him and I'm very anxious to prove that your lordship's accusations are unjustified. If I didn't know that Madame de Tourvel was leaving, it was in fact because I was so keen to serve your lordship that I left the château at three a.m. and this prevented me from meeting Mademoiselle Julie the previous evening as usual, as I slept the night at the servants' lodge* so as not to wake anyone up in the château.

As for what your lordship told me off for about never having any money, for a start, it's because I always like to be properly turned out as your lordship can judge and then you have to keep up the dignity of your position. I know I ought perhaps to put something by for the future but I hope I can rely on your lord-ship's generosity, as your lordship is such a good master.

As for going into Madame de Tourvel's service while staying on with your lordship, I hope your lordship won't insist. It was very different with the Duchesse de ——; but I certainly don't want to be a liveryman and a judge's liveryman* at that, after having the honour of being your lordship's personal valet. As for the rest, your lordship has only to command someone who has the honour to be with respect and devotion, your lordship's most humble obedient servant,

Roux Azolan

108

Madame de Tourvel to Madame de Rosemonde
Paris, 5 October 17—

Oh, what a kind, indulgent mother you are! And how badly I needed your letter! I thank you from the bottom of my heart; I've been reading it over and over again; I couldn't put it down. It's provided me with the few less unhappy moments I have had since I left you. How good you are! So being wise and virtuous doesn't exclude sympathy for a weak woman! You take pity on my sufferings. Ah, if you only knew what they are like: they are appalling. I thought I had suffered all the pangs of love—alas, I've experienced little else but its pangs! But parting from the man you love, perhaps for ever, is an indescribable torment which you have to experience in order to have the slightest idea of its pain. And that pain torturing me today will still be there tomorrow and the next day and the next, for the rest of my life! Dear God, I am still so young and so many years of sorrow still lie in front of me!

Creating your own misfortune; rending your heart with your own hands; and while you suffer such unendurable agony, feeling all the time that you could put an end to it with one single word . . . but this word would constitute a crime! Ah, dear, dear friend! . . .

When I took this painful decision to go away and leave him, I hoped that absence would give me courage and strength: how mistaken I was! On the contrary it has shattered them both. True, I no longer have to struggle; but even while I was resisting, I was not utterly forlorn; at least I was able to see him sometimes; indeed often, although I didn't even dare look in his direction, I could sense his eyes on me, yes, dear friend, I could sense them, they seemed to set my soul on fire and though they didn't pass through my own eyes, they could still reach into my heart. And now I'm lonely and unhappy, isolated from everything that is dear to me, every moment of my miserable existence is punctuated by my tears, there is nothing to sweeten its bitterness, nothing to console me for the sacrifices I have made; and till now, these have succeeded only in making those yet to come even more agonizing . . .

Even yesterday I again sensed his presence. Amongst my letters, there was one from him; the servant bringing them was still some yards away from me when I recognized it amongst the others. In spite of myself I sprang to my feet; I was trembling, I could scarcely hide the state I was in; it was an emotion not without pleasure . . . A few seconds later, left on my own, this illusory glow quickly died away and I was left with yet one more sacrifice to make. Indeed, how could I open this letter that I was dying to read? I cannot escape my fate: even the consolations which seem to be open to me lead only to fresh frustrations and the thought that they are shared by Monsieur de Valmont only makes them more cruel . . .

And there at last you have the name which is haunting me all the time and which has been so hard for me to write. I was truly alarmed by the half-reproachful way in which you spoke to me on this point and I do beg you to believe that my reticence did not mean lack of trust in you; indeed, why should I be afraid of mentioning him by name? It's my feelings that make me ashamed, not the object of them. Is there any other man more worthy of inspiring them? Yet somehow his name did not come at all naturally to my pen and even this time I needed to think hard before writing it.

I come back to him: you tell me he seemed *greatly affected by my leaving?* What did he do? What did he say? Did he mention returning to Paris? I beg you to try to dissuade him from doing that as vigorously as you can. If he has judged me rightly, he won't bear me any grudge for my action; but he must also feel that it is an irrevocable decision. One of the things which most torments me is not knowing what he is thinking. Of course, his letter is still lying there . . . but you surely agree with me that I mustn't open it?

Dear, understanding friend, you are my only slight link with him. I don't wish to take advantage of your good nature and I well understand that you are not able to write long letters . . . but you will not refuse your daughter a brief word or two, first to help her to keep up her courage and secondly to console her in her struggle. Goodbye, dear Madame, with my very deepest respect, your, etc.

109

Cécile Volanges to the Marquise de Merteuil
From the Château de ———, 10 October 17—

Dear Madame de Merteuil, I've only just given back today the letter you were so very kind to write to me. I kept it for four days although I was often scared in case it might be discovered, but I was hiding it very carefully and whenever I felt miserable I shut myself away in my room and reread it.

I can certainly see that what I thought was a great misfortune in fact isn't really one at all and it must be admitted that it gives a lot of pleasure so I'm not really upset any more. It's only thinking of Danceny which still worries me sometimes. But there are lots of times now when I don't think of him at all! And another thing is, Monsieur de Valmont is so nice!

I made it up with him two days ago. It was very easy as I'd hardly said two words before he said that if I had something to tell him, he'd come to my room that evening and I only needed to say that I was agreeable. And then once he was there he didn't seem any crosser than if I'd never done anything to him. He only told me off later on and so nicely . . . Just like you, which proved he felt very friendly disposed towards me, too.

I can't tell you how many funny stories he told me that I'd never have believed, especially about Mummy. I'd love you to tell me if it's all true. It certainly is true that I couldn't help laughing, so much so that once I actually burst out laughing so loudly that we were both quite frightened because Mama might have heard us and if she had come to look, where would I have been? I'm sure she'd have packed me off back to the convent on the spot!

As we have to be careful and as Monsieur de Valmont himself said he wouldn't like to risk compromising me for anything in the world, we've agreed that in future he'll just come and unlock my door and then we'd go to his room, where there's no danger. In fact, I went there yesterday and I'm waiting for him to come as I'm writing to you now. So I hope you'll stop telling me off, Madame.

But one thing in your letter which did very much surprise me was what you said about when I'm married, on the subject of Danceny and Monsieur de Valmont. It seems to me that one night at the opera you were telling me the opposite, that once I was married I couldn't love anyone but my husband and I'd even have to forget Danceny. Perhaps I didn't quite understand and I do prefer it to be the other way round because now I shan't mind getting married so much. In fact, I'm even looking forward to it because then I'll be much freer and I hope that I'll be able to arrange it so that I can think of no one but Danceny . . . I really do feel that I'll only be truly happy with him because at the moment thinking about him still worries me and I can only feel happy when I can stop thinking about him and that is very hard. And as soon as I do think about him I start being miserable again straight away.

What consoles me a bit is that you promise me that because of what has happened Danceny will love me all the more. But are you really sure of that? . . . Oh, you must be, you certainly wouldn't want to tell me something untrue. All the same, it's funny that it's Danceny I love but it's Monsieur de Valmont who . . . But as you say, perhaps it's a good thing! Anyway, we'll see.

I didn't quite understand your remark about my letter writing. It seems to me that Danceny likes my letters very much as they are. But I do realize that I mustn't say anything to him about what's happening between me and Monsieur de Valmont, so there's nothing for you to be afraid of.

Mummy still hasn't said a single word about my marriage. But I'll watch out and when she does mention it, as she's setting a trap for me, I promise you I'll be able to pretend to her.

Goodbye, dear, kind Madame, and thank you very much indeed, I promise you I'll never forget all your kindness towards me. I must stop now because it's nearly one o'clock and Monsieur de Valmont won't be long now.

110

The Vicomte de Valmont to the Marquise de Merteuil
From the Château de ——, 11 October 17—

Heavenly powers! My soul has tasted the pangs of love; teach it to savour its delights!* I think it is the tender-hearted Saint-Preux who voices this wish. I'm better off than he, I'm enjoying both states of mind simultaneously. Yes, dear lady, I am at one and the same time very happy and very unhappy; and since I have complete trust in you, I owe it to you to tell you my double tale of woe and joy.

I have to inform you that my ungrateful and pious judge's wife has still not relented. At the last count, four of my letters have been returned unopened. Four is perhaps misleading: guessing that once the first one had been rejected, it would be succeeded by lots of others and being unwilling to waste my time in this pursuit, I decided to turn my sad story into the standard rigmarole and leave them undated; so ever since the second one, it's been the same letter shuttling to and fro. I merely change the envelope. If one day my beloved grows tired of this shuttle service, she'll keep my epistle and then will be the time for me to bring it up to date. As you can see, with this new style of correspondence, I can hardly expect to make much progress or be any better informed than on the day it started.

I have however discovered that the flighty young body has changed her confidante; at any rate I have ascertained that since she left the château, no letter has come from her to Madame de Volanges whilst there have been two for old Rosemonde and since the latter hasn't mentioned this to me and is keeping completely mum on the subject of *her lovely friend* whereas previously she never stopped talking about her, I concluded that this revolution has been brought about on the one hand by the need to talk about me and on the other by the coyness she may feel with Madame de Volanges at reverting to a feeling she has so long disclaimed. I fear that here again I have lost in the exchange: the older women are, the more sour and strict they become. The first one would certainly have said far nastier things about me but Madame de Rosemonde will talk to her more of love and our susceptible puritan is much more scared of the feeling than of the person.

My only means of keeping myself informed, as you will have gathered, is to intercept this clandestine exchange of letters. I've already given appropriate instructions to my valet and I'm expecting him to put them into effect any day now. Until then I can only operate at random; so for the last week I've been vainly going over every known way, in novels* or in my secret memoirs, without finding anything to fit either the circumstances of this adventure or the character of the heroine. It wouldn't be difficult to slip into her house, at night indeed, nor even to drug her and turn her into another Clarissa;* but imagine having to resort to methods so foreign to my nature after more than two months of laborious and meticulous effort! To gain a victory without glory by following slavishly in someone else's tracks! . . . No, she's not going to enjoy *the pleasures of vice and the honours of virtue.** Just possessing her isn't enough; I want her to surrender willingly. And to do that, it's not only necessary to get into her house but for her to let me in herself; to find her alone and ready to listen to me; above all to close her eyes to any danger, for if she sees it she'll be able to overcome it or die in the attempt. But the more clearly I can see what's required, the more I realize how difficult it is and at the risk of exciting your hilarity once again I confess that the more I think about it, the more complicated it seems.

But for the pleasant diversions provided by our joint ward, I think I'd feel quite lost: if it wasn't for her, I'd have nothing better to do than write elegiacs.*

Would you believe it, that little girl was so scared that it took three whole days for your letter to take effect? See how one single mistaken idea can warp the most promising disposition!

Anyway, it wasn't until Saturday that the person concerned sidled up to me and stammered a few words, in such a low voice and so smothered in shame that they were impossible to understand. But the red face accompanying them allowed me to guess their meaning. Till then I'd remained on my high horse but mollified by such an amusing act of contrition, I relented and promised to call on the pretty penitent that very night; this gracious gesture of mine was received with all the gratitude appropriate to such a great act of charity.

As I never lose sight of either your plans or mine, I determined, in addition to speeding up her education, to use my opportunity to discover how gifted the child is. However, in order to have greater freedom to achieve this aim, I needed to change our venue because the small closet separating your ward's bedroom from her mother's was hardly calculated to offer her adequate security to display her talents free of any inhibitions. So I'd promised myself to make, quite *innocently*, some noise that would scare her enough to persuade her to find a safer haven for our activities; she herself spared me the trouble.

She's a jolly little girl and to keep her amused during the intervals, I took it into my head to tell her about all the scandalous adventures that came into my mind; and to make them more spicy and more likely to hold her attention, I gave the credit for all of them to her Mummy and took delight in painting a highly colourful picture of her vices and absurdities.

I wasn't doing this just for fun; not only did it arouse my coy young pupil more than anything else but at the same time I was filling her with the deepest contempt for her mother. I've long known that if this method may not always be necessary to seduce a girl, it's the indispensable and often most effective way of depraving her, for a girl without any respect for her mother won't have any self-respect either: a moral truth which I consider so useful that I was delighted to offer practical proof of the principle.

However, your ward had no concern for moral truths and was stifling her giggles all the time until finally she once nearly burst out laughing. I had no difficulty in persuading her that she'd made a *terrible din* and pretended to be dreadfully afraid, a feeling she easily came to share. To make sure she didn't forget, I declined to provide further pleasure and left her three hours earlier than usual, after we'd agreed that in future we would meet in my room.

I've already welcomed her there twice and in this short space of time the schoolgirl has become almost as adept as the teacher. Yes, indeed, I've taught her everything, even the more engaging forms of collaboration. The only thing I left out was how to take precautions.

Being busy all night allows me to have a good long sleep during the day and as the present company in the château is madly unexciting, I spend barely an hour in the drawing-room all day. Today I even decided to eat in my room and apart from the odd short walk, I intend to stay there. These vagaries are put down to my health: I've explained that I've been feeling *out of sorts* and also announced that I have a slight temperature. All I need to do is to speak in a slow, far-away tone of voice. As for any change in my face, you can safely leave that to your ward. *Love will provide.**

I spend my spare time wondering how to regain my lost advantage over my ungrateful judge's wife and also drawing up a sort of catechism of lechery for my pupil's use. I'm enjoying spelling everything out in strictly technical terms and chuckling as I imagine the fascinating conversation which this will provide for her and Gercourt on their wedding night. There's nothing funnier than her ingenuous way of using the few words of this sort she already knows! She thinks these are the only expressions. She really is such an attractive little girl! This contrast between her simple innocence and her shameless language manages to produce quite an effect; somehow, I don't really know why, these days I can only enjoy things that are off-beat.*

I may be indulging too much in this one because I'm making excessive demands on my time and my health;* but I'm hoping that my sham illness, apart from rescuing me from that dreary drawing-room, may also be of some use with my saintly puritan who combines tigerish virtue with a tender heart! I've no doubt that she has already been apprised of the great event and I'd very much like to know what she is making of it, the more so as I bet she won't fail to take credit for it. I shall adjust my state of health to the impression it's making on her.

So now, fair lady, you are as up to date with my affairs as I am myself. I am longing to have more interesting news for you soon and I ask you to believe me when I say that the major part of the pleasure I'm looking forward to is the reward I'm expecting from you.

III

The Comte de Gercourt to Madame de Volanges
Bastia,* 10 October 17—

My dear Madame de Volanges, everything now points to peace in this country and we are anticipating leave to return to France any day. I hope that you have no doubt how eagerly I still look forward to doing so and to forging the links that will bind me to you and to Mademoiselle de Volanges. However, my cousin the Duc de ——, to whom, as you are aware, I am under considerable obligation, has just informed me of his recall from Naples. He tells me that he is expecting to pass through Rome and in the course of his journey to visit that part of Italy with which he is still unfamiliar. He has invited me to join him on this excursion, which will last approximately six weeks to two months. I shall not disguise the fact that I should enjoy taking advantage of this opportunity, being fully aware that after my marriage it will be difficult to find time to be away, except as my military duties require. It may thus possibly be more appropriate to wait until the winter to celebrate our nuptials, since all my close relatives, and in particular the Marquis de —— whom I have to thank for giving me the privilege of making your acquaintance, will find it impossible to come together in Paris before then. In spite of these major considerations, my plans in this regard are entirely in your hands and should you for any reason prefer to maintain your earlier arrangements, I shall gladly abandon mine. My only request would be that you may let me know your intentions on this matter as soon as possible. I shall await your reply here and will act only in accordance with your wishes.

I remain, dear Madame de Volanges, with the devotion and respect due from your future son, your humble, etc.

The Comte de Gercourt*

112

Madame de Rosemonde to Madame de Tourvel
(*dictated and unsigned*)
From the Château de ――, 14 October 17―

My dear young friend, I have only this very instant received your gently reproachful letter of the 11th.* Admit that you were very tempted to use stronger words and that had you not again recalled that you are now my *daughter*, you would have given me a proper dressing-down! Yet that would have been very unfair of you. It had been my hope and desire to be able to reply to you myself which led me every day to postpone writing to you and you can see that even now I am obliged to employ the services of my maid. My tiresome rheumatism has again attacked me, this time in my right arm, rendering me completely one-armed. See what comes of a fresh young woman like yourself taking such an antique friend! You suffer from her disabilities.

As soon as I am offered a slight relief from my pain, I am most anxious to have a long chat with you. Till such time, let me merely say that I have received both your letters and that I shall always feel the keenest sympathy for everything that concerns you.

My nephew is also slightly indisposed but it is nothing serious and gives not the slightest cause for alarm, a minor ailment which seems to be affecting his moral rather than his physical well-being. We hardly ever see him.

His absence and your departure do nothing to contribute to the gaiety of our little society. The Volanges girl in particular has a serious bone to pick with you and sits all day long yawning her head off. She is paying us the compliment, especially during the last few days, of regularly dropping off to sleep after dinner.

Goodbye, dear friend. And as always, I am your friend, your mother, and even your sister, if my great age were to allow such a thing. In a word, I am, in every way, yours most affectionately.

Signed: Adelaïde, for Madame de Rosemonde.

113

The Marquise de Merteuil to the Vicomte de Valmont
Paris, 15 October 17—

I think you should know, Vicomte, that people here in Paris are beginning to talk about you; your absence is being remarked on and there's already surmise as to the cause. Yesterday, at a very large supper party, it was stated as a positive fact that you were detained in some village by a romantic and unsuccessful love-affair; immediately the faces of all the men envious of your reputation and of all the women you've been neglecting lit up with joy. If you take my advice, you'll not let these dangerous rumours gain currency and you'll return straight away to give them the lie by showing yourself.

Bear in mind that once you've allowed the suspicion to take root that you're not irresistible, you'll soon discover that women actually will find you easier to resist; that your rivals will lose their respect and will be encouraged to compete with you, for which of them doesn't think he's more than a match for any woman, however virtuous? Above all, don't forget that amongst all the women you've flaunted in public, all those you haven't had will attempt to reveal the truth while the others will try and hide it. In a word, you'll see yourself as much underestimated as you were previously overestimated.

So, do come back, Vicomte, and don't sacrifice your reputation to a childish passing fancy. You've accomplished all we wanted you to do with the Volanges girl and as far as your judge's wife is concerned, you're hardly likely to be indulging your fancy for *her* at a range of thirty miles or so. Do you imagine she'll be coming to look for you? Maybe she's stopped thinking of you altogether or remembering you only while she rubs her hands at having humiliated you. Here at least you'll have an opportunity of making a triumphant return—and that's what you need . . .

And even if you persist in your absurd adventure, I can't see how your return could adversely affect it, quite the opposite.

In fact, if your judge's wife *adores* you, as you keep on telling me so often, without providing much evidence, her only joy and comfort must be to talk about you, to know what you're thinking and even the slightest particulars of the things that interest you. Such trivial details become progressively more precious the more you're deprived of them; they're the crumbs from the rich man's table, which he despises and the poor man greedily picks up and feeds on. Well, at the moment Madame de Tourvel is gathering all those crumbs and the more she can find, the less of a hurry she'll be in to tackle the main course.

Moreover, since you know her confidante, you can be sure each letter contains at least one short homily and everything she thinks likely *to confirm her good sense and strengthen her virtue.** So why provide the means for one of them to defend herself and for the other one to do you harm?

Not that I share in the least your impression that you've suffered a setback through her change of confidante. In the first place, Madame de Volanges hates you and hatred is always more ingenious and clear-sighted than friendship. All your old aunt's virtue will never for a moment induce her to speak ill of her dear nephew because virtue, too, has its shortcomings. What's more, your fears rest on a completely misguided premiss.

It's just not true that *the older women are the more sour and strict they become.* Between the ages of forty and fifty, despair at seeing their faces going wrinkled, anger at being obliged to give up pleasures and privileges which they still expect to enjoy, make almost all women shrewish and prudish. They need this long period to come fully to terms with this great sacrifice but once it's complete, they all fall into two categories.

The major one comprises women who've had only their faces and their youth in their favour: they fall into a mindless apathy from which they can be roused only by certain devout practices and card-games; they are always dull, they frequently nag, sometimes they're mildly busybodyish but they're rarely malicious. Nor can it be said that such women are or are not strict: being spineless and empty-headed, they just repeat, indiscriminately and without understanding, anything they hear and will never be anything but utter nonentities.

The other category, much smaller but worth its weight in gold, contains those women of character who haven't neglected to enrich their minds and are capable of creating a life of their own when nature begins to desert them; these women are determined to decorate their minds, just as earlier they have decorated their faces. Normally they possess sound judgement and have lively, judicious, and cultivated minds. They replace physical attraction by an engaging kindness as well as by a sprightliness which grows all the more charming with age; in this way they somehow manage to come closer to being young by winning the affection of the young. But with such women, far from being *sour and strict* as you allege, their habits of tolerance, the many hours they spend pondering on human weakness, and finally their youthful memories which are now their only link with life would tend rather to make them almost too easy-going.

What I can tell you, finally, is that having always sought the company of older women, since I realized early in life the importance of obtaining their approval, I met a large number to whom I felt drawn as much by inclination as by interest. I shall say no more, for now that you catch fire on the slightest provocation, and so high-mindedly, I'd be afraid you might fall unexpectedly in love with your old aunt and allow yourself to be buried with her in the tomb where you've been spending so much of your life recently. So let's come back to the point.

In spite of the spell which your little schoolgirl seems to have cast over you, I cannot believe she has any part to play in your plans. She was available, you took her: bravo!—but you can't really fancy her. If the truth be known, you're not actually possessing anything but her body; quite apart from her heart which I'm pretty sure you've not got much interest in, she doesn't even have any room for you in her head. I don't know if you've noticed it yourself but I have proof of it in the last letter she wrote me,* which I'm enclosing so that you can judge for yourself. You can see that when she refers to you, it's always *Monsieur de Valmont*; all her thoughts, even when they've started off from you, always end up with Danceny; and she doesn't call him Monsieur Danceny, always just Danceny. This shows how different she considers him from everybody else; and even when she's giving herself to you, she only feels at home with Danceny. If you find such a conquest *attractive*, if the pleasures you enjoy with her are *delightful*, you really must be modest and undemanding! I'm not objecting to your keeping her on; actually it fits in with my plans. But it does seem to me that it's not worth putting yourself out for even a quarter of an hour if you can't also assert some authority over her, as, for instance, by not allowing her to go back to Danceny without first driving him out of her head rather more convincingly.

Before leaving your affairs and turning to mine, I should like to say that this bogus illness which you told me you're thinking of using seems to me trite and extremely old hat. You really do lack imagination, Vicomte. Actually, I do occasionally repeat myself, as you'll see, but I frequently redeem myself with a certain originality in the details and above all I'm justified by my success. I'm about to try for another one: I'm pursuing a new amorous venture. I agree it will hardly rank as difficult but it will at least provide some distraction: I'm bored stiff.

I don't know why it is but ever since my Prévan caper, I've found Belleroche quite unbearable. He's become so madly attentive, affectionate, and downright *adoring* that I just can't take it any more. At first I found his anger quite amusing, though I had to cool him down because had I let him go ahead I should have been compromised. But there was no way of making him see reason except by showing myself more devoted to him, which I proceeded to do so as to bring him to heel more easily. The trouble was that he took me seriously and ever since he's been driving me to distraction with his unending ecstasies of delight. In particular I notice the utterly outrageous trust he shows in me and the smug way he considers me his permanent property. It's positively mortifying! What a low opinion he must have of me if he thinks he's good enough to hold on to me for ever! Didn't he say recently that he'd be the only man I'd ever loved? Oh, when I heard that, I needed all my self-control not to undeceive him on the spot by telling him the truth. What a ludicrous oaf to claim exclusive rights! I concede that he's well-built and moderately good-looking but taken all round, in fact, as a lover he's no more than a hack. It's time for a break.

I've been trying to bring this about for nearly a fortnight: I've been successively cold, moody, sulky, cantankerous but the pig-headed man still clings on. I shall have to resort to more drastic measures: I'm going to cart him off to my country house. We're leaving the day after tomorrow. There'll be only a few other people there who'll be neither concerned nor discerning; we shall be pretty well as free as if we were on our own. Once there, I intend to stuff him with a surfeit of love and caresses and we shall be living in each other's pockets so much that I bet that he'll be longing for our little trip, which he's expecting to be marvellous, to come to an end even sooner than I shall and if he doesn't come back more bored with me than I am with him, then I'm perfectly ready to let you tell me I'm as ignorant in such matters as you are . . .

My pretext for this sort of retreat is to give serious consideration to my big lawsuit which is finally coming on at the beginning of the winter. I'm glad it is because it's not very pleasant having your entire fortune hanging in the air. Not that I'm worried about the outcome: for one thing, all my lawyers tell me I'm in the right. And even if I weren't, I'd surely have to be extremely inept not to be able to win a case where my only adversaries will be under-age girls, still children, and their guardian! Nevertheless, in a matter of such importance, one mustn't leave anything to chance and I shall in fact be taking two lawyers down with me. A jolly trip, don't you think? All the same, if it means winning my case and losing Belleroche it won't have been time wasted.

And now, Vicomte, guess who's designated as his successor? I'll give you a hundred to one you can't! But what's the point? I know you're hopeless at guessing, don't I? Well, it's . . . Danceny! That's a surprise for you, isn't it? Because after all, I'm not yet reduced to baby-snatching! However, he deserves to be an exception: he has the charm of youth without any of its frivolity. His discreet behaviour in society is admirably designed to avoid suspicion and when he lets himself go in private, he's all the more delightful. Not that I've as yet had any personal contact with him on his own, till now I've only been his confidante. But under this veil of friendship I think I can detect that he fancies me a lot and I can feel that I'm beginning to fancy him very much indeed . . . It would be such a pity if so much wit and delicacy of feeling were to be thrown away and desecrated with that cretinous Volanges girl! I do hope he's mistaken in thinking he's in love with her; she doesn't deserve him in the least. Not that I'm jealous of her but it would be sheer murder and I do want to protect Danceny. So while I'm away, Vicomte, I'm asking you to use your good offices to prevent Danceny from having closer contact with *his Cécile* as he still unfortunately persists in calling her. A first love is always stronger than we suspect and I should feel extremely unsure of my ground if he were to see her now, particularly while I'm away. Once I'm back, I can look after everything myself—and I guarantee the result.

The thought did, in fact, cross my mind of taking the young man away with me but I sacrificed that idea on the altar of my normal cautiousness; and I'd also be afraid he might become aware of something between Belleroche and me and I'd be devastated if he had the slightest suspicion of what's happening. I want to present myself at least to his imagination as chaste and immaculate, as indeed I should be to be really worthy of him.*

114

Madame de Tourvel to Madame de Rosemonde
Paris, 16 October 17—

Dear friend, while I have no idea if you can answer this query I am so uneasy in my mind that I cannot refrain from approaching you: Monsieur de Valmont's state of health which you describe as giving *no cause for alarm* does not seem as reassuring to me as it appears to be to you. It is not uncommon for melancholy and aversion to company to be preliminary symptoms of some serious disease; physical as well as mental disorders lead us to seek solitude and we often accuse people of being moody when we should sympathize with them for being ill.

It seems to me that at the very least he ought to consult someone. Since you are yourself not in the best of health, do you not have a doctor in attendance? My own doctor, whom I saw this morning and whom I make no secret of having consulted indirectly, is of the opinion that with naturally active persons this kind of sudden apathy should never be ignored; he added that certain disorders may fail to respond to treatment if they are not taken in time. Why let someone of whom you are so fond run this risk?

I am doubly anxious because I have had no news of him for the past four days. Dear Heavens! You are not hiding from me the truth about his health, are you? Why should he suddenly have stopped writing to me? If it is merely because I persist in sending back his letters, I think he would have adopted that course earlier. In any case, although I hold no brief for forebodings, I have for the last few days been alarmed by my feeling of depression. Ah, perhaps I am on the brink of a great catastrophe!

You would not believe, and I feel ashamed to tell you, how hurt I feel at not receiving any more letters from him. Even although I would still have refused to read them, at least I was sure he was thinking of me! And I was seeing something that had come from him . . . I never opened his letters but I looked at them and cried: my tears would flow more easily and gently and they were the only means I had of relieving some part of my depressed state of mind since I've been here. Dear, generous friend, I beseech you to write to me in person as soon as you are able and in the mean time do let me have news of yourself and of him every day.

I see that I have hardly spoken of you; but you know my feelings, my boundless affection for you, my deep gratitude for your sympathy towards me; and you will forgive me because you realize my confused state of mind, my appalling suffering, the dreadful torment I feel at the thought of the ills I may have caused. Dear God, that devastating thought never leaves me, it is rending my heart! Till now I had escaped such a misfortune but I can feel that I'm fated to endure them all!

Farewell, dear friend. Love me and pity me. Shall I be receiving a letter from you today?

115

The Vicomte de Valmont to the Marquise de Merteuil
From the Château de ——, 19 October 17—

Fair lady, it is incredible how easily misunderstandings arise as soon as two people are parted . . . All the time I was at your side, we felt as one, we looked at things through the same eyes; and now because we've not met for nearly three months, we can't agree about anything.

Who's to blame? I'm sure you wouldn't hesitate in your answer; but being wiser—or more polite?—I shan't offer a judgement but merely answer your letter and continue to describe my conduct.

But first, let me thank you for your warning of the rumours circulating about me, even though at this stage I don't feel concerned by them and I think I can be sure of being in a position to put an end to them shortly. Don't worry: I shan't re-emerge into society until I bear greater honours than ever before and have become even worthier of you.

I even hope that my adventure with the Volanges girl, which you seem to make light of, won't be entirely discounted: as if it were child's play, in the space of an evening to take a girl away from the man she loves; next, to do with her what I liked, for my own ends, like a piece of my own property, without let or hindrance; to get her to do things that you wouldn't dare to demand from professionals;* and all this without in any way upsetting her feelings towards her man, without making her waver in her love, even without being unfaithful—indeed she gives me hardly a second thought—so that after I've gratified my fancy, I'll deliver her back to her lover without her, as it were, ever having noticed anything. Is that an everyday occurrence? And what is more, having passed through my hands, the principles I've inculcated in her will still go on developing, believe me, and I predict that the bashful schoolgirl will soon be spreading her wings and becoming a credit to her mentor.

If, however, the heroic mode is preferred, I shall show the judge's wife, this legendary paragon of all the virtues, so greatly respected even by our libertines that the very thought of attacking her never entered anyone's head; yes, I tell you, I shall show her, oblivious of her duties and her virtue, sacrificing her reputation and two years of impeccable behaviour in pursuit of the happiness of pleasing me, intoxicated with the happiness of loving me, finding adequate reward for all her sacrifices in a word or a glance from me—which, indeed, she'll not always be granted. I shall go further: I shall abandon her and unless I'm very much mistaken in the woman, I'll not have any successor. She will fight against the need for consolation, against her new-found addiction to pleasure, against even the desire for revenge. In a word, this period of her life belongs entirely to me and whether it be long or short, I alone shall have dictated its start and its finish. Once I've achieved my victory, I shall say to my rivals: 'See what I have done and ask yourselves whether you know of a similar achievement in our age!'

You'll be anxious to know the reason for my supreme confidence? It's because for the last week I've known all my lovely lady's secrets. Not that she has told me them herself: I'm intercepting them.* Two of her letters to Madame de Rosemonde gave me all the information I needed and I shall continue to read the rest purely out of curiosity. In order to reach my goal, I've absolutely nothing further to do except to arrange for us to meet and I know how to do it. I intend to start at once.

Your curiosity's aroused? Well, as a punishment for not believing in my inventiveness, I shan't tell you. Actually, by rights, I ought to stop trusting you altogether, at any rate in this particular adventure; indeed, but for the delightful reward offered for my success, I wouldn't tell you any more at all. As you can see, I'm cross. However, in the hope that you'll mend your ways, I'm prepared to let you off with that minor punishment. So, in a spirit of forgiveness, let me put aside my grand designs for the moment and discuss yours.

So there you are down in the country, as boring as a pastoral novel and as bored as its reader. And poor little Belleroche! Not content with making him drink the waters of forgetfulness, you're using them to torture him!* How's he taking it? Is his surfeit of love making him sick of it? What fun it'd be if the treatment makes him keener than ever! I'd be curious to see what other remedies you'd have to resort to. I'm really sorry to see you've had to fall back on to that one. In my life only once did I ever make love merely to oblige a lady. I certainly had an excellent motive, since she was the Comtesse de ——. A dozen times or more while lying in her arms I was tempted to say: 'Madame, I withdraw my application for the position I've been trying for, so please let me vacate the one I'm in at the moment.' And that's why she's the only woman of all those I've ever had about whom I really enjoy saying nasty things.

As for your reasons, I must honestly say that I find them manifestly absurd: you were right in thinking that I shouldn't be able to guess his successor. So you're actually going to all that trouble for Danceny? O dear lady, do let him go on adoring *his virtuous Cécile* and don't become involved in these children's games. Let schoolboys learn the facts of life from *housemaids* or play *innocent little games* with convent girls. What a burden you'll be taking on with a novice who'll not know either how to take you or leave you. I must tell you in all conscience how much I disapprove of your choice and however well you managed to keep it dark, it would lower your reputation, in my eyes at least—and in your own.

You tell me you've developed quite a fancy for him: come, come, dear lady, you're surely mistaken and I think I know the source of your error. This elaborate dislike for Belleroche has come over you in the dry season * and since Paris had nothing to offer you, your mind, always over-active, settled on the first object it met. But do remember that on your return there'll be hundreds and hundreds of candidates to pick from; and in any case, if you're scared of the possible danger of enforced inactivity, should you delay your plans, I can volunteer to fill any spare time agreeably . . .

Between now and your return, my main concerns will have been settled one way or another and neither the Volanges girl nor your judge's wife will be taking up enough of my time to prevent my being at your disposal as much as you want. By then I may even have restored the little girl to her discreet lover; while in no way agreeing, despite what you say, that she's failing to provide me with *delightful pleasures*, since I plan to leave her for the rest of her life with an impression of me as a man superior to anyone else, I've adopted a tempo that I'd be unable to maintain for long without damage to my health and from this moment on, my interest in her is purely a family one . . .

You don't grasp my meaning? . . . In fact I have to wait for one more period to confirm my hopes and be sure that my plans have reached full fruition. Yes, fair lady, I already have a first inkling that the husband of my young pupil runs no danger of dying childless and that the future head of the house of Gercourt will be a scion of the house of Valmont. But let me finish off this adventure—undertaken purely at your earnest instigation—as the fancy takes me. Don't forget that if you make Danceny untrue to his love, you'll remove all the spice from this story. And finally, do remember that by volunteering to substitute for him, I have, methinks, acquired some claim to preferential treatment.

I'm relying on this so implicitly that I've ventured to go counter to your advice and made my own small contribution to increase this diffident suitor's tender passion for this first and most deserving object of his affection. Yesterday I discovered your ward writing to him and after interrupting this pleasant pursuit by one even more pleasant, I asked to see her letter and finding it cold and clumsy, I pointed out that this was no way to comfort a lover and prevailed on her to write another one, dictated by me, in which, while imitating to the best of my ability her style of girlish drivel, I tried to foster the young man's love by holding out the promise of more tangible benefits. The little lady was utterly thrilled, in her words, to discover she could write so well and henceforth I have been put in charge of the correspondence. The things I'm doing for Danceny! I'll have been his friend, his confidant, his rival . . . and his mistress! And at this very moment, I'm even doing him the favour of rescuing him from your dangerous clutches as well. Yes, dangerous indeed: for possessing you only to lose you means paying for a moment's bliss with everlasting regrets . . .

Goodbye, fair lady. Be brave and give Belleroche his marching orders as soon as you can. Leave Danceny to his own devices and get ready to enjoy once more the pleasures of our first association—and to let me enjoy them again as well.

I wish you good luck for the imminent success of your lawsuit and I shall be delighted for this happy outcome to take place under my regime.

116

The Chevalier Danceny to Cécile Volanges
Paris, 17 October 17—

Madame de Merteuil left this morning for the country, so depriving me, now that my dear, charming Cécile is no longer here herself, of my only remaining pleasure, which is the chance of talking to someone who's your friend as well as mine. For some time now she's been letting me consider her as such and I was all the keener to take advantage of this as it seemed a sort of way to be nearer to you. My goodness, what an agreeable woman she is! And what a charming and gracious friend! With her, friendship, such a gentle feeling, seems all the finer and stronger because she excludes any thought of love. If you knew how fond she is of you, how much she enjoys hearing me talk about you! . . . This must be what makes me so attached to her. How happy it makes me to live only for you both, to switch all the time from the delights of love to the gentler joys of friendship, to devote every moment of my life to them, to be in a sense the link between your mutual affection, to have the constant feeling that when concerning myself with the happiness of one of you, I'm contributing equally to the happiness of the other! Cécile, charming, charming Cécile, you must grow to love this adorable woman and love her very much. You must strengthen my fondness for her by sharing it. Ever since I realized the charms of friendship, I have wanted you to experience them too. It seems impossible for me to enjoy anything properly if you aren't sharing it. Yes, my darling, I should like to surround your heart with all the most delightful feelings, so that every emotion is pure joy—and even then I should feel that I was giving back only part of the happiness I owe you.

Why must all these wonderful plans be merely a figment of my imagination and reality offer me only pain and frustration everywhere I look? I can see that I shall have to give up any hope of seeing you in the country, as you had led me to think. My only comfort is to convince myself that it really is impossible. Yet you've never mentioned it to me yourself, you've never commiserated with me. And I've written to you twice about it and you've never said anything about your own regrets . . . Ah Cécile, I feel sure you love me, heart and soul, but you don't feel the same burning passion as I do! Why is it always I who's required to remove the obstacles? Why can't I give some consideration to my own interests instead of yours? I'd soon prove to you that for love there's no such word as impossible . . .

And you haven't let me know either when our cruel separation can come to an end; if you were in Paris, I could be seeing you now and again. Your charming eyes would revive my dejected spirits; their tender look would reassure my heart, which sometimes needs to be reassured. Oh, I'm sorry, dear, dear Cécile, don't imagine that my misgivings mean I'm suspicious, I do believe in your love, you're not inconstant. Ah, if I doubted that I'd be too utterly miserable! But there are so many obstacles! And they never seem to come to an end! Dear, dear, dear Cécile, I'm sad at heart, so sad. Madame de Merteuil's departure seems to have revived all my feelings of unhappiness . . .

Goodbye, Cécile, goodbye, my dear love. Never forget that your lover is utterly miserable and that you're the only one able to make him happy again.*

117

Cécile Volanges to the Chevalier Danceny
(*dictated by Valmont*)
From the Château de ——, 18 October 17—

Do you think, dear love, that, knowing how miserable you are, I need you to tell me off in order to make me sad? And do you have any doubt that when you're suffering, I feel it just as much as you do? I even feel it as much when I'm the deliberate cause of your suffering; and it's even worse for me because I can see you're being unfair. Oh, that's really not nice of you. I can certainly see what's annoying you, it's because the last twice you've asked to come and see me here, I didn't reply. But is it all that easy to reply? Do you think I don't know that what you want to do is very wrong? Yet if I find it so hard to refuse you at a distance, what would it be like if you were here? And then, because I'd wanted to offer you a moment's consolation, I'd be miserable for the rest of my life!

Look, here are my reasons, I've nothing to hide: judge for yourself. I might perhaps have done what you want except for what I told you: this Monsieur de Gercourt who's the cause of all our troubles won't be coming back for some time yet and as Mama has recently been much friendlier and I for my part am being as nice as possible to her, who can tell what I'll perhaps be able to get her to do? And if we can be happy without me having done anything wrong, wouldn't that be much better? If I'm to believe what people often say, men don't even love their wives as much when they've shown their husbands too much love before they got married. Well, that's what I'm afraid of and it's that more than anything else which is holding me back. Dear love, aren't you sure of my heart and won't there always be plenty of time later on?

But I must say goodnight, dear love, I started writing to you very late and have spent part of the night on it. Now I shall get into bed and make up for lost time. Here's a kiss from me but please don't go on telling me off.

118

The Chevalier Danceny to the Marquise de Merteuil
Paris, 19 October 17—

If I can trust my calendar you have been away for only two days, adorable lady, but to my heart it seems like two centuries. And as you told me yourself, one must always trust one's heart . . . So it is high time for you to come back; all your business must surely have been settled by now. How can you expect me to take an interest in your lawsuit if, win or lose, I have to pay the costs by the tedium caused by your absence? Oh, I'd really like to lodge a complaint against you myself. Isn't it a shame that with such a good case for being cross with you, I haven't the right to show it?

And isn't it being really faithless, a treachery of the deepest dye, to leave your friend far away after you've got him so used to being unable to be without you? You may consult your lawyers as much as you like, they'll never find a way of providing you with any justification for such unfriendly conduct and in any case such people only deal in arguments and arguments can never be a satisfactory response to feelings.

As for me, you kept telling me so often that your trip was motivated by reason that you've completely turned me against it and even when it's telling me to forget you, I refuse to listen to it any more. Yet that voice of reason is certainly eminently reasonable and it wouldn't be as difficult as you might think: all I'd need to do is to break my habit of thinking of you constantly, for I can assure you that nothing here would remind me of you.

Our prettiest women, the ones said to be the most deserving of being loved, are still so vastly inferior to you that they could never provide more than a very pale image of you. I even think that for a practised eye, the greater the similarity might appear at first glance, the greater the discrepancy afterwards. Try as they may and using every means at their disposal, they are still not *you* and that's where the charm positively lies. Alas, when the days seem so long and there is nothing to do, we start to dream, to build castles in the air, the castles begin to take shape, our imagination catches fire, we try to make them more beautiful, bring in everything we find attractive and finally produce our ideal woman; and having done that, we compare our picture with the model and we're greatly surprised to see that it's you we had in mind all the time.

At this moment I'm victim of an almost similar error. Perhaps you think I started writing to you in order to talk about yourself? Not at all: it was to take my mind off you. I have a hundred and one things to say, not concerning you but which, as you know, touch me very closely, and it is those which completely flew out of my head. And since when has the charm of friendship put the charm of love out of someone's head? . . . Ah, if I were to probe deeply into that question, I should feel a trifle guilty! But shush! Let's put that little weakness aside in case we're in danger of starting to fall into it again; and my dear friend must overlook it, too.

So why aren't you here to answer me, to bring me back to the proper path when I stray from it, to talk to me about my Cécile, to make me even happier, if that were possible, at the thought— and what a charming thought it is!—that the girl I love is your friend? Yes, I must confess that the love she inspires in me has grown even more precious since you were kind enough to let me tell you about it. I take such pleasure in opening my heart to you, in involving yours in my emotions, in pouring them out to you without restraint! And they seem all the more precious now that you have condescended to show an interest in them. And then I can look at you and say to myself: 'All my happiness is contained in her!'

I've nothing new to tell you concerning my situation with Cécile. Her last letter renewed my hopes and removed my doubts but it still means postponing my happiness. However, her reasons are so honourable, so full of love, that I cannot blame her or complain. It is perhaps quite possible that you do not completely understand what I mean by that: but why aren't you here? Although we tell our friends everything, we don't dare to put everything down on paper. Love's secrets especially are so delicate that we can't let them out just like that, because they are so sincere. If we sometimes do so, at least we must never let them out of our sight; we have, so to speak, to see them safely into their new home. Oh, adorable friend, do come back, you can see that you positively must. So forget all the *thousand and one* reasons keeping you down where you are or else let me have one good reason to teach me how to live when you are not with me.

Most sincerely, etc.

119

Madame de Rosemonde to Madame de Tourvel
From the Château de ——, 20 October 17—

Dear child, although I am still in considerable pain I shall none the less make an effort to write to you myself so that I may talk to you of the matter which concerns you. My nephew remains as misanthropic as ever. He enquires after my health regularly every day but he has not once been to call on me himself, although I've sent a message asking him to do so. In fact I see as little of him as I should if he were in Paris. However, I did meet him this morning in a place where I didn't expect to: in my chapel when I went down there for the first time since I have been so drastically incapacitated. I learned today that for the last few days he has been going regularly to Mass. May it be God's wish for him long to continue in that way.

When I went in he came up to me and offered me his most affectionate good wishes on the improvement in my health. As Mass was about to begin I cut short our conversation, fully expecting to resume it afterwards, but he disappeared before I could catch him. I won't conceal the fact that I found him

somewhat changed. But you must not make me regret the trust
I have placed in your good sense by showing excessive concern.
Above all, you may rest assured that I should even prefer causing
you pain to misleading you.*

If my nephew remains adamant, as soon as I'm better, I shall
make a point of calling on him myself and try to solve the
mystery of his peculiar behaviour which I think must be partly
attributable to you. I shall let you know what I discover. But I
must leave you now since I can no longer hold my pen properly.
Indeed, were Adelaïde to know that I had been writing, she'd be
cross with me for the rest of the evening. Goodbye, dear, dear
friend.

120

The Vicomte de Valmont to Father Anselme
(*a strict Bernadine in the Convent in the Rue Saint-Honoré*)
From the Château de ———, 22 October 17—

Reverend Father, I do not have the honour of being known to
you; but I do know the implicit trust that Madame de Tourvel
places in you and I know moreover how worthy you are to bear
that trust. I believe therefore that I may approach you without
risk of being thought indiscreet to ask a favour of vital importance, one truly appropriate to your holy office and in which
the interests of Madame de Tourvel and myself are equally
concerned.

I have in my possession important papers concerning her
which can be entrusted to no one else and which I must, and
intend to, hand over to her in person. I have no way of informing
her of this matter since, for reasons of which you may have been
apprised by her but which I think I have no warrant to reveal, she
has decided to refuse to have any sort of correspondence with
me; a decision for which at this time I readily confess that I am
unable to blame her since she could not have foreseen certain
events which I was myself far from anticipating and which have
only come about through a more than human agency whose hand
in this matter it is impossible not to recognize.

I ask you therefore, Reverend Father, to have the great kindness to inform Madame de Tourvel of the new resolves I have

made and to request her to grant me a personal interview so that I may offer her my apologies which may in part at least make amends for my transgression; and as a final penance destroy before her own eyes the sole remaining vestiges of an error or fault which I have committed against her.

Only after this preliminary sacrifice shall I dare to place at your feet my humiliating confession of my lengthy moral aberration and implore your mediation to assist me to make an even more important and unfortunately more difficult act of atonement. May I be allowed to hope, Reverend Father, that you will not refuse your invaluable and indeed indispensable help? And that you will deign to support me in my infirmity and guide my footsteps in this new path I aspire most sincerely to follow but with which I blush to confess I am as yet far from familiar.

I await your reply with all the impatience of a repentant sinner eager to reform and ask you to believe me, in gratitude and veneration, your very humble, etc.

PS Should you think fit, I authorize you to communicate this letter in its entirety to Madame de Tourvel whom I consider myself in duty bound to respect for the rest of my days and whom I shall honour for ever as Heaven's instrument to lead my soul back to the path of virtue by the touching example of her own.*

121

The Marquise de Merteuil to the Chevalier Danceny
From the Château de ——, 22 October 17—

My very youthful friend, I have received your letter but before thanking you for it, I must issue a reprimand and warn you that if you don't mend your ways, you will receive no further letters from me. So take it from me, give up this cajoling tone which, if it's not an expression of love, is nothing but sheer jargon. Is this how friends should talk? No, my friend: each feeling has its own appropriate language and using any other falsifies the idea you are expressing. I realize, of course, that our smart young women can't understand a word of what someone's trying to tell them unless it's translated into the fashionable idiom but I confess that I thought I deserved rather more discriminating treatment at your hands. I'm truly sorry, perhaps sorrier than I ought to be, that you have taken such a poor view of me.

So in my letter, you'll only find what is missing from yours: sincerity and forthrightness; I shall tell you, for instance, that it would indeed give me great pleasure to see you and that I feel frustrated at being surrounded by people who bore me instead of people whom I like; that same statement would, however, be transcribed by you as: *teach me how I can live when you are not with me*, so I presume that when you're with your beloved you wouldn't be able to live unless I were there to make up a threesome! How sad! And those women who *still aren't me*, do you perchance consider *your* Cécile as *still not me*? Yet that is precisely the kind of statement you're tricked into making by that misuse of language so prevalent today, which doesn't even reach the level of fashionable compliment but turns into a mere form of words, just as unconvincing as your most humble obedient servant!

When writing to me, dear friend, do so in order to tell me what you are thinking and feeling, not to trot out all those things which, without any help from you, I can find expressed, more or less well, in any old novel in vogue. I do hope you won't be offended by what I'm saying, even if you may detect that I'm in rather a bad temper, because I don't deny that I am; but to avoid even the semblance of being guilty of the offence which I'm accusing you of, I shall not tell you that this temper is perhaps made somewhat worse by the distance separating us. All things considered, it seems to me that you are better value than a lawsuit and two lawyers and perhaps even than the assiduous Belleroche as well.

You can see that instead of deploring my absence, you ought to be pleased, for that is the nicest compliment I've ever paid you. I'm afraid your example is catching and I'm trying to flatter you, too; however, it mustn't be, I prefer to stick to sincerity and it's for that reason alone that you can be sure of my affectionate friendship and the interest in you which it has inspired. It is most pleasant to have a young friend whose heart is committed elsewhere. That's not the way all women operate but it's my way. It seems to me that there's more pleasure in indulging in an emotion which gives no cause for fear and so perhaps from quite early on I went over to being your confidante. But you pick your girls so young that you made me realize for the first time that I'm starting to get old. So you have only yourself to blame for launching yourself on to a long career as a constant lover and I wish, wholeheartedly, that your feelings are reciprocated.

You are perfectly right to fall in with her reasons, *so honourable and so full of love*, which, from your account, are *deferring your happiness*. For women who don't always resist, a protracted defence is their sole remaining asset and I should consider it unforgivable in anyone but a child like little Volanges not to know how to steer clear of a danger of which she must be sufficiently forewarned when she admits she's in love. You men have no conception of virtue and the high price of sacrificing it! But even the least sensible of women must know that, quite apart from the moral lapse, any weakness spells disaster for her and I can't for the life of me understand how anyone could ever let herself fall into that trap if she's given it a moment's thought.

And don't start trying to argue against that view because it's the main reason why I feel attracted to you. You'll save me from the hazards of love and though up to now I've managed to defend myself against them quite well without your help, I'm prepared to feel grateful and I shall like you all the better for it, and all the more.

So hereupon, dear Chevalier, I pray God keep you safe in His august and holy care.*

122

Madame de Rosemonde to Madame de Tourvel
From the Château de ——, 25 October 17—

I had been hoping, my dear daughter, to be able finally to allay your anxiety but I am distressed to find that on the contrary I shall be adding to it even more. But you must calm yourself: my nephew is in no danger; he cannot even be said to be actually ill. But certainly he is in the throes of some extraordinary inward change. I cannot understand what it is but I left his room with a feeling of sadness, perhaps even of dread, which I am sorry to have to share with you but which I cannot refrain from mentioning. Let me tell you what has been happening: you may rest assured that he is faithful, for were I to live another eighty years I should never forget the impression made on me by his sorrowful face.

So, I called on him this morning. He was writing, surrounded by a host of piled-up papers which seemed to be the subject of his work. He was so busy that I was halfway into the room before he even turned his head to see who had come in. As soon as he caught sight of me, I noticed very plainly that as he stood up he was making an effort to compose his features and perhaps it was that which made me scrutinize him more closely. It is true that his hair was unpowdered and that he was not yet dressed, but I could see his face was pale and drawn and above all his expression was very different: his eyes, previously always so jolly and lively, looked sad and dejected. In fact, between ourselves, I'm glad you weren't there to see him because he had a very touching look, most likely, I think, to arouse that feeling of tender pity which is one of love's most dangerous pitfalls.

I was somewhat shocked by all this but I still began the conversation as if I hadn't noticed anything. First I asked after his health and although he didn't say he was well, he didn't state categorically that he was ill either. Then I scolded him for being so unsociable, saying that it almost looked as if he was becoming crotchety; but as I was trying to soften my little rebuke with a touch of humour, he merely replied very emotionally: 'Yes, that's one more bad thing I've done, but I shall put that right, together with all the others.' Even more than his words, his look rather warned me not to joke and I hastily added that he was taking what was just a friendly reproach too seriously.

We now started talking again more calmly. After a moment, he mentioned that he might soon be called back to Paris by some business, *the most important of his whole life*. But as I was afraid I could guess what that business was and afraid too, dear girl, that such a beginning might lead me to make an admission that I was anxious to avoid, I didn't question him any further and merely replied that more amusement might be good for his health. I added that for this once I wouldn't plead with him since I loved my friends purely for what they are. On hearing this extremely simple comment, he grasped my hands and said with a vehemence which I cannot convey to you: 'Yes, love your nephew, aunt, love him well, he respects and reveres you; and love him, as you say, for what he is. Don't fret about his happiness and don't disturb the eternal peace he hopes soon to enjoy by having regrets. Just say that you love me and forgive me . . . Yes, you do forgive me, I know how kind you are. But how can I expect those whom I've treated so badly to be equally forgiving?' And he bowed his head, I think to hide from me how much he was suffering, although his voice was betraying it despite himself.

More strongly moved than I can say, I hurriedly stood up and no doubt noticing how startled I was, he immediately made an effort to pull himself together. 'I'm sorry, aunt, forgive me,' he said. 'I realize I've been talking wildly but I can't help myself. So forget what I've said and remember only how much I respect you.' And he added: 'I shan't fail to come and pay my respects to you again before I leave.' That remark seemed to me to be an indication that my visit had come to an end and so I then left.

But the more I think about it, the less I can work out what he was trying to say. What is this business which is *the most important in his whole life*? What is he asking me to forgive him for? What can have caused his involuntary emotion while he was talking to me? I've been asking myself these questions over and over again without being able to find the answers. I can't even discover anything connecting them in any way to you but as the eyes of love are more discerning than those of a friend, I didn't want to leave you unaware of anything that transpired between my nephew and me.

I've had to have four shots at this long letter which would have been even longer if I wasn't feeling so tired. Goodbye, dear girl.

123

Father Anselme to the Vicomte de Valmont
Paris, 25 October 17—

My Lord, I have the honour to acknowledge receipt of your letter and in accordance with your wishes, at once proceeded to call on the person concerned yesterday to inform her of the reasons for the step you wish to take in her regard. Although I found her strongly inclined to persist in the wise course of action she had first chosen, when I pointed out that by refusing she might perhaps be placing in jeopardy your gratifying contrition and thereby in a sense impeding the merciful intentions of divine Providence, she agreed to your visit on the one condition that it be your last.* She has asked me to inform you that she will be at home next Thursday, the 28th. If for some reason this day proves unsuitable, will you please be so good as to inform her accordingly, suggesting an alternative. Your letter will be received.

Nevertheless, my Lord, may I venture to invite you not to delay without very cogent reasons, in order that you may be in a position to comply more completely and expeditiously with the praiseworthy intentions of which you spoke. Consider that he who delays accepting the gift of Grace incurs the risk of seeing it withdrawn; that if God's goodness is infinite, its dispensation is subject to divine justice and a moment may come when a God of mercy can be transformed into an avenging God.

Should you continue to honour me with your trust, I beg you to believe that my pastoral care will be entirely at your disposal as soon as you so wish: however pressing my other occupations, the duties of my holy ministry to which I am particularly devoted will always have precedence; it will be my finest hour to see my efforts, under the blessing of Almighty God, crowned by success. Miserable sinners that we are, we can do nothing by ourselves! But God who is calling you to Him can accomplish all things and we shall both be equally indebted to His goodness, you for your steadfast desire to return to the fold and I as His instrument to lead you thither. It is with His help that I hope soon to persuade you that even in this world, holy religion alone has the power to offer that solid and lasting happiness vainly sought in the blind pursuit of human passions.

I have the honour to be, my Lord, your most respectful, etc.

124

Madame de Tourvel to Madame de Rosemonde
Paris, 25 October 17—

Although still utterly bewildered by news which I received yesterday, I shall not forget the satisfaction which it is bound to cause you and I am writing to inform you straight away: Monsieur de Valmont has ceased to concern himself either with me or with worldly love and his only wish henceforth is to make amends by a more edifying life for the faults or rather the errors of his youth. I have been informed of this great event by Father Anselme to whom he has turned for the future direction of his conduct, as well as with the request to arrange a meeting with me, the main purpose of which I imagine will be to hand me back my letters which, despite my urgings, he has till now been refusing to return.

Certainly I can only approve this happy transformation and be glad if, as he maintains, I have in some way contributed to it. But why did it fall to me to be the instrument of this change of heart at the cost of destroying the serenity of my life? Could Monsieur de Valmont achieve happiness only through my unhappiness? O dear, kind friend, forgive me this cry of distress! I know that it is not for me to fathom God's inscrutable decrees but while I have been praying Him endlessly, and always to no avail, to give me strength to overcome my unhappy love, He gives that strength in full measure to the man who was not even asking Him for it and leaves me helpless, at the mercy of my frailty.

But we must stifle these sinful complaints. Do I not know that on his return the prodigal son received more favours from his father than the one who had never gone away? Who are we to call God to account? He is answerable to us for nothing. Even if it were possible for us to claim some rights in His eyes, what rights could I claim? Am I to be proud of my virtue when I in fact owe it entirely to Valmont? He saved me, yet I presume to complain because I'm having to suffer. No, I must not complain! If the price of his happiness is my own suffering, I shall accept it gladly. No doubt it was time for him to return to the bosom of the Father of us all. The God who had shaped him must surely hold His handiwork dear. He had not created that charming being in order to turn him into a reprobate. It is I who must suffer the penalty for my foolhardiness. Shouldn't I have realized that, since it was forbidden to love him, I ought not to have allowed myself to see him?

My fault or my misfortune is to have failed for too long to face this truth. You are witness, dear, kind friend, that as soon as I recognized that this sacrifice had to be made, I accepted it; but to fill my cup of bitterness, one thing was lacking: that Monsieur de Valmont was not sharing it. Shall I confess that it is this which is now tormenting me most? Ah, what insufferable pride to allay our own sufferings by the thought of those we're inflicting on others! But I shall crush that rebellious heart, I shall teach it to live with humiliation without end!

This is the prime reason for my finally agreeing to receive Monsieur de Valmont next Thursday. It will hurt me, I shall hear him tell me that I now mean nothing to him, that the pale, fleeting impression I made on him has completely evaporated! I shall see him looking at me impassively while I shall have to lower my eyes for fear of revealing my own feelings. How many times has he refused to return my letters, despite my repeated requests! And now he doesn't care—I'll be getting them back because they're useless, of no further interest. As I take them back, full of shame, my hands will tremble and his will be calm and steady! And as I see him leaving, leaving for ever, I shall follow him with my eyes but he will not turn round to look at me!

This was the humiliating fate reserved for me! Oh, let me at least use it to achieve a full realization of my weakness. He's no longer interested in keeping my letters but I shall treasure them. I shall set myself the shameful task of rereading them every day until my tears have blotted out every last trace on the paper; his letters I shall burn because they're infected with the deadly poison that has corrupted my soul. Oh, what is this love if it makes us pine even for the dangers to which it exposes us? And above all if we are still afraid of feeling it even after we've ceased to arouse it? We must cast aside this fatal passion which gives us only the choice between unhappiness and shame. If we can't be virtuous, at least let us remain prudent.

How far away Thursday still seems! Why can't I perform my painful sacrifice at once and forget both its cause and its object here and now! This visit is preying on my mind; I'm sorry that I agreed to it. After all, why does he need to see me again? What do we mean to each other now? If he has wronged me, I forgive him. I even appreciate his wish to make amends and I commend him for it. I'll go even further; I'll imitate him and since I've been led astray by the same errors, his example will bring me back to the path of duty. But since he's intending to have nothing more to do with me, why is his first action to come and see me? Isn't the most urgent thing for both of us to forget each other? Oh, that's surely the case and from now on that will be my only concern.

Dear, honourable friend, if you will let me, I should like to start on that hard task in your house. If I need help or even perhaps comfort, I want to receive them only from your hands. You are the only person capable of understanding me, of speaking to me heart to heart. My whole existence will centre round your precious friendship. I shall put myself entirely in your hands to do anything you care to propose. I shall owe you my peace of mind, my happiness, and my honour and the fruit of your many acts of kindness will be to have at last made me worthy of them.

I am afraid this is a very disjointed letter, at least I assume it must be from the bewildered state I've been in while writing it. If it happens to contain any expressions of my feelings which might make me blush, you must hide them under the kindly veil of your friendship on which I so much depend. I shall certainly never wish to conceal any of the emotions of my own heart from you.

Goodbye. Once again, let me tell you of my deep respect for you; I hope to announce the date of my arrival in a few days' time.

PART IV

125

The Vicomte de Valmont to the Marquise de Merteuil
Paris, 29 October 17—

Well, fair lady, take a look now at that haughty woman who was rash enough to imagine she could resist me! There she is: I had her yesterday; I've conquered her, she's mine, completely mine, she has granted me everything I want . . .

I'm still too overcome by my good fortune to be able to appreciate it; but I am amazed by the strange charm which I felt. Could it be that a woman's virtue makes her more rewarding to have at the very moment when she's losing it? No, that's puerile nonsense, just another old wives' tale. Don't we almost always meet a more or less faked resistance the first time we have any woman? And haven't I felt the charm I mentioned with other women? Yet it's not the charm of love either, because after all, if I did experience with that astonishing woman a few moments of weakness with some apparent similarity to that anaemic passion, I was always able to overcome them and be true to my principles. Even if during yesterday's events I was, as I believe, carried away rather further than I'd anticipated and for a moment shared the ecstasy and turmoil which I'd aroused, that passing illusion would have evaporated by now. Yet that same charm still lingers on and I confess I should find it rather agreeable to go on enjoying it if it didn't make me feel rather uneasy. Am I going to be overpowered at my age, by an involuntary and unfamiliar emotion, like some schoolboy? Certainly not! I must first of all fight it and analyse it more closely.*

And in any case, I have perhaps already got some dim notion of the reason! At any rate, I like to think so and it would be nice if it's true.

Well, amongst the host of women with whom I've performed the role and function of lover, up till now I'd never had one who wasn't at least as keen to give herself to me as I was to persuade her to do so; I'd even got into the habit of describing as prudish those who'd only go half-way, as opposed to so many others whose resistance is just provocation and nothing but a poor attempt to cover up the fact that it was they who made the first moves.

Here, on the contrary, was a woman with an initial prejudice against me, later reinforced by the advice and information of a poisonous but perspicacious woman; with an extremely timid nature which strengthened her clear-sighted sense of modesty; a love of virtue based on religion and which had already staunchly survived two years of marriage; finally, as a result of these varying motives, she was deploying a series of most impressive stratagems, all directed towards one goal: evading my pursuit.

So, unlike my previous adventures, this isn't just a more or less expedient capitulation, something to enjoy rather than brag about, it's a crushing victory achieved by a hard-fought campaign and clinched by clever manœuvres. So it's not surprising that my success, due entirely to my own efforts, should be all the more gratifying and that my extra pleasure at my conquest, which I can still feel, is the sweet taste of a famous victory. I find this thought particularly attractive since it saves me from the humiliating feeling that I might somehow be dependent on the very slave whom I've just subjugated; or that my great happiness lies anywhere but in myself; or that my ability to extract enjoyment out of it is restricted to one particular woman to the exclusion of any other.

At this important juncture, I intend to let my conduct be guided by these sensible conclusions and you may be sure that I shall not allow myself to be so constricted by these new bonds as to be prevented from breaking free, effortlessly, whenever I see fit. But here I am, talking of breaking free and you still don't know how I've come to be in a position to do so. So read on and discover the perils facing a chaste and reasonable woman when she tries to save a wild and foolish man. I kept such careful note of all I said and of her replies that I hope to give you a meticulous verbatim account of both which I'm sure you'll enjoy hearing.*

You'll see from the enclosed copies of two letters* which go-between I'd chosen to restore relations with my beloved and with what zeal the holy father set about achieving our reunification. You also need to know something which I'd gleaned from a letter intercepted in the usual way: namely, that the fear and the minor mortification of being abandoned had somewhat upset the pious young woman's prudishness* and filled her heart and head with feelings and thoughts which, however nonsensical, were still quite intriguing. It was after making these vital preparations that yesterday, Thursday, the 28th, the day already suggested by the ungrateful wench, I presented myself as a timid and penitent slave at the house which I was to leave crowned in the laurels of victory.

It was six o'clock when I arrived at the residence of the lovely recluse—since her return her door had remained closed to everybody. When I was shown in, she made an effort to stand up but her knees were trembling too much for her to remain on her feet and she immediately sat down again. The servant who had shown me in stayed to do a few things in the room and while we exchanged the normal civilities, Madame de Tourvel showed signs of impatience. However, not wishing to waste time when every second counted, I was carefully reconnoitring the terrain and straight away selected the field for a successful operation. I could have chosen a more comfortable one because she even had an ottoman in her room; but I noticed that there was a portrait of her husband hanging opposite and I admit that with such an odd woman a single glance in that direction might destroy in a second the result of all my labours. Finally, the servant left and I launched on my preamble.

After a few words explaining that Father Anselme must have informed her of the reasons for my visit, I protested at the harsh way I had been treated, with particular emphasis on the *contempt* I'd been shown. As I expected, this statement was contested and as you certainly also expect, I justified it by pointing out the suspicion and fear I had inspired; her scandalous ensuing flight; her refusal to answer any of my letters or even to receive them, etc. etc.* As the lady now started to exonerate herself—which was all too easy—I felt it incumbent on me to interrupt and in order to excuse my brusqueness, I immediately glossed it over with flattery. 'Such irresistible charm had made a deep impression on my heart but your virtue had made an equally strong impression on my soul. No doubt carried away by my longing to draw nearer to such a paragon, I was foolhardy enough to imagine that I deserved such a privilege. I do not blame you for thinking otherwise but I am punishing myself for my mistake.' As my little piece was followed by an embarrassed silence, I went on: 'Madame de Tourvel, I wanted either to justify myself in your eyes or else receive your pardon for the wrongs you think I've committed, so that I might at least end my days in some sort of peace, since now that you have refused to enrich them, they no longer have any value for me.'

At this point, however, an attempt was made to reply: 'But my duty wouldn't allow me . . .' The difficulty of completing the lie that duty required prevented her from finishing the sentence, so I started again in my most loving voice: 'So it's true that I was the person you were escaping from?' 'It was necessary to leave.' 'And that now you're going away and leaving me?' 'There's no other course.' 'And for ever?' 'I must.' I don't need to tell you that during this brief exchange the tender-hearted prude was speaking in a strained voice and not daring to look up. Things were hanging fire and I decided to liven them up. With an offended look I sprang to my feet and said: 'You're very determined but two can play at that game. Very well, Madame, we'll each go our own way and we'll be even further apart than you think. And you will have all the time in the world to feel proud of what you've achieved.' Somewhat taken aback by my accusatory tone, she tried to reply: 'The decision you've taken . . .' she began. 'Was taken through sheer despair,' I retorted heatedly. 'You wanted me to be unhappy and I'll prove to you that you've succeeded beyond your wildest hopes.' 'I want you to be happy,' she replied, in a voice that was beginning to be quite emotional. Thereupon I flung myself at her knees and exclaimed, in that theatrical voice you know so well: 'Oh, how cruel you are! As if there can be any happiness for me if you don't share it! Never! Never!' I confess that having let myself go so energetically, I was relying heavily on tears to help me out but either because I wasn't in the mood or else because my excessive concentration was proving a strain, my tear-ducts failed to respond.

Luckily once again I recalled that to bring a woman to heel anything goes, and that to create a deep and favourable impression I needed only to do something striking to dumbfound her. Since sentiment was not available, I decided to resort to terror and without changing my position but merely my tone of voice, I continued: 'Yes, here at your feet, I swear that I shall either possess you or die!' As I spoke these last words, our eyes crossed; I don't know what the frightened woman saw or thought she saw in mine but she stood up with a scared look and slipped out of my arms which I had placed round her. It's true that I made no attempt to hold her back because I'd frequently noticed that scenes of despair, when they are too intense and protracted, can become ridiculous or capable of being resolved only by tragic means, which I was very far from wishing to resort to. All the same, as she was slipping out of my arms, I muttered in a sinister voice, but loud enough for her to hear: 'Ah, then the answer is death!'*

Then I rose to my feet and stood there silent for a second, casting fierce glances at her, seemingly at random, but although they looked wild, I was observing her closely and carefully. Her body was swaying, her breath coming in gasps, her muscles contracted, her trembling arms half-raised: everything told me well enough that I'd achieved the desired effect; but since in love nothing can be brought to a conclusion except at close quarters and we were quite far apart, it was first necessary to get nearer to each other. To achieve this as quickly as possible, I adopted an attitude of apparent calm likely to allay the effect of my violent outburst but without weakening the impression it had created.

This was my transition: 'I'm very unhappy. I had been intending to devote my life to making you happy and I've made you miserable. I want to give you peace of mind and I am destroying that as well.' Then, as if struggling to remain calm: 'You must forgive me, Madame, I'm not used to the storms and stresses of passion and I am finding it difficult not to be swept away by them. If I was wrong to give way to them, please remember that it was for the last time. Oh, please compose yourself, be calm, I beg you.' In the course of this lengthy pronouncement, I kept stealthily approaching her. 'If you want me to be calm,' replied my frightened beauty, 'you must please calm down yourself.' 'Very well, then, I promise,' I said, adding in a weaker voice: 'It will be a great effort but it won't be for long.' Then I went on, with a frantic look: 'But wasn't my real purpose in coming to give you back your letters? For pity's sake, please, please take them back. It's one more sacrifice that I still have to make. Don't leave me with anything which may weaken my determination.' And pulling the precious bundle out of my pocket, I said: 'Here they are! Here are the false promises of friendship you placed in my keeping. They gave me something to live for. Take them back and that will be your signal that I must part from you for ever.'

At this the timorous lover gave way completely to her tenderness and anxiety: 'But what is the matter with you, Monsieur de Valmont? What do you mean? Are you not doing this now of your own free will? Isn't it the result of having thought things over which has led you to take this necessary decision, one I have taken myself out of a sense of duty?' 'Well,' I replied, 'it was your decision that led to mine!' 'And what is your decision?' 'The only one possible for me, to put an end to my suffering now that I have to part from you.' 'But you must answer my question: what have you decided?' Thereupon I clasped her in my arms while she offered not the slightest resistance. Realizing how overpowering her emotion must be to lead her so to forget her sense of propriety, I said: 'Oh, how adorable you are!' (I thought it worth while to risk a little enthusiasm) 'you have no idea of the love you have inspired, you never realized how I worshipped you and how much stronger that love was than my love of life! May peace and happiness go with you for the rest of your days! And may they be enriched by all the happiness you have stolen from me! Won't you at least reward this sincere wish of mine with a tear or a regret? And you may be sure that this last sacrifice of mine will not be the one my heart finds most painful. Farewell!'

As I said this, I could feel her heart pounding, I noticed her contorted features, and I could see that her tears, though flowing slowly and painfully, were choking her. It was only now that I made a pretence of moving away from her but she clung hard on to me and said abruptly: 'No, listen to me!' 'Let me go!' I retorted. 'I insist that you listen to me!' 'I've got to leave you, I must!' 'No!' she cried. As she said this, she flung herself or rather collapsed fainting in my arms. Being still not quite sure of a successful outcome, I pretended to be greatly alarmed; but in the course of my alarm, I steered her or rather carried her over to the place I'd earlier selected as the field of my triumph;* and in fact when she came to, her capitulation was complete: she had already succumbed to her gratified conqueror.

Till now, fair lady, you will have recognized and appreciated the classic purity of my methods and seen how scrupulously I adhere to the essential principles of this sort of warfare which, as we've often acknowledged, is extremely similar to the real thing. So look upon me as a Turenne or a Frederick.* I'd forced an enemy who was using delaying tactics to join battle; by clever manœuvring, I had chosen the ground and the battle order; I had lulled the enemy into a sense of security so as to penetrate more easily into her defences; before launching my attack, security had been replaced by terror; I had left nothing to chance since, while aware that success would bring me indubitable advantages, if repulsed I had other resources ready; and finally, I went into action knowing that my retreat was covered and I would lose none of my earlier gains. I don't think anyone can do better than that; but now I'm afraid that like Hannibal surrounded by the luxuries of Capua,* I have grown effete. This is what happened.

I was of course prepared for the despair and tears normally attending such major events; and the first thing I noticed was slightly increased confusion and a sort of inner withdrawal, which I attributed to a prudish nature, and so without paying further attention to these variations which I imagined to be purely local, I simply pursued my course along the main avenue of consolation, convinced that, as usual, the senses would come to the help of sentiments and that a single action would speak louder than any words, although I didn't neglect those either. But I met a resistance truly terrifying, not so much for its extravagance as for the form it took.

Picture to yourself a woman sitting rigidly still, with set, frozen features, apparently neither thinking, listening, nor hearing anything, from whose wide, staring eyes tears were pouring almost without pause and without effort. This was how Madame de Tourvel looked while I was speaking to her; but each time I endeavoured to attract her attention by a caress, by even the most innocent gesture, this apparent apathy was immediately replaced by a look of terror, gasps, convulsions, sobs, and occasionally by completely inarticulate cries.

These spasms recurred a number of times, each time more violently; the last one was even so violent that I completely lost heart and for a moment I feared I'd achieved a hollow victory. I fell back on the usual platitudes, one of which happened to be this one: 'And so you're in despair because you've made me a happy man?' At these words, the adorable woman turned towards me and though still looking haggard, her face had already recovered its heavenly expression. 'Happy?' she said. You can guess my reply. 'So I've made you happy?' I repeated my assurances. 'And happy through me?' I provided the additional compliments and words of love. While I was talking, her whole body relaxed and she sank gently back into her armchair, even letting me take her hand. She murmured: 'I feel relieved and comforted by that thought.'

You'll understand that once launched on that course, I took good care not to leave it: it was certainly the correct and perhaps even the only one. Indeed, when I tried to repeat my first successful attempt, I met with some initial resistance and my previous experience was making me wary. But when I again appealed to that same idea of my happiness to help me, I soon felt the beneficial effects. 'You are right,' said the tender-hearted woman; 'I can bear to go on living now only as long as it serves to make you happy; from now on I shall devote myself entirely to that, I shall give myself to you and you will never hear any regrets or meet any refusal from me again.' And so, with an innocence which was either naïve or sublime, she abandoned herself to me in all her beauty, sharing my pleasure until it ended in simultaneous ecstasy. And for the first time, mine outlasted my pleasure. I left her arms only to fall at her feet and swear eternal love.* I don't wish to hide anything: I meant what I said. Indeed, even after we'd parted, I kept thinking of her and had to make a great effort to put her out of my mind.

Ah, why aren't you here to match my glorious action by an at least equivalent reward? But I shan't lose anything by waiting, shall I? And I hope that I can assume your agreement with the happy arrangement which I suggested to you in my last letter. As you see, I'm fulfilling my obligations and, as I promised, I shall be sufficiently far advanced in my business to be able to give you part of my time. So do hurry up, send the ponderous Belleroche packing and leave the soppy Danceny, so that you can devote yourself entirely to me. What on earth are you up to down there in the country, not even answering my letters? Do you know that I've a good mind to give you a thorough telling-off! But happiness makes us forbearing. And in any case I'm not forgetting that by rejoining the ranks of your admirers I have once again to submit to your little vagaries. But do remember that the new lover doesn't want to lose any of his long-standing rights as a friend.

Goodbye, as in the good old days. *Yes, goodbye, my angel! With all my loving kisses!**

PS Do you know that at the end of his month in gaol, Prévan has been forced to resign from his regiment? It's the talk of the town today. He really has been cruelly punished for a wrong he didn't commit! Your triumph is complete!*

126

Madame de Rosemonde to Madame de Tourvel
From the Château de ——, 30 October 17—

I should have answered you earlier, dear girl, if writing my last letter hadn't brought on my aches and pains and denied me the use of my arm these last few days. I was anxious to thank you for the good news you gave me of my nephew and not less so to offer you my sincere congratulations on your own behalf. In this matter we are truly forced to recognize the hand of Providence which by blessing one of you has also offered salvation to the other. Yes, dear child, He who wished merely to put you to the test has lent His aid at the moment when your strength was exhausted and, despite your slight misgivings, you owe him, I think, some measure of thanksgiving. Not that I fail to recognize that it would have been more agreeable for you to have made this decision first and for Valmont's to have followed as a result. Humanly speaking, it seems that the claims of our sex would have benefited thereby and we don't wish to forgo any of those! But what are these minor considerations compared to the important objects that have been achieved? Does someone rescued from shipwreck ever complain about not having been consulted as to the way he was saved?

You'll soon find, my dear daughter, that the sufferings you dread will start to cure themselves and even should they continue to persist in all their virulence, you'll still feel that they would be easier to bear than self-contempt and remorse for your crime. To have addressed you in this seemingly harsh tone earlier would have been pointless: love is an independent spirit; being cautious may help us to avoid it but can never enable us to overcome it; once it's born, it can only die of natural causes or complete hopelessness. The latter is what has happened to you and gives me the chance and the courage to give you my honest opinion. It's cruel to scare people who are mortally ill; they need soothing and comforting; but it's sensible to inform a convalescent of the risks he's been running in order to make him understand how wary he must be and of his need to accept advice which may still prove necessary.

Since you've appointed me your doctor, I'm talking to you like one and I can assure you that the minor pains you're suffering at the moment are nothing compared to the dire disease you've just recovered from. And speaking now as a friend, the friend of a sensible, virtuous woman, I shall take the liberty of adding that this passion which you've overcome, however unfortunate in itself, was becoming even more so because of its object. If I am to believe what I am told, my nephew, whom I admit to loving—perhaps to the point of weakness—and who has indeed a great number of admirable as well as many charming qualities, is neither harmless nor blameless in his relations with women; he's almost equally interested in seducing and in ruining them. I feel sure that you would have reformed him;* there was certainly never anyone more qualified to undertake that task; but so many women who have nursed that fond hope have been disappointed that I am far happier for your sake that you've not been reduced to that resort.

But now, dear friend, you must reflect that instead of all the dangers you were incurring, you will enjoy not only a clear conscience and peace of mind but the gratifying feeling of having been the main agent of Valmont's contrition. As for me, I have no doubt that this is in large measure the result of your courageous resistance and that a moment of weakness on your part might have left my nephew in an eternal state of profligacy. For me this is a happy thought and I hope you will share it, for it will provide you with your initial consolation and I shall cling to it as a reason for loving you even more.

I shall expect you here in a few days' time, dear daughter, as you have announced. You shall come back here and again find peace and quiet in the house where you had lost them; above all, come and rejoice with your affectionate mother at having so successfully kept the promise you made her never to do anything unworthy of either her or yourself!

127

The Marquise de Mertcuil to the Vicomte de Valmont
From the Château de ———, 31 October 17—

If I haven't replied to your letter of the 19th, Vicomte, it's not for lack of time but quite simply because it made me cross and I thought it contained a good deal of rubbish. So I thought the best thing was to let it fall into oblivion; but since you've brought it up again and seem attached to the ideas it puts forward, indeed take my silence as consent, I shall have to speak my mind plainly.

On occasion, I may well have laid claim to being able to replace a whole harem on my own but I've never felt the slightest inclination to form part of one. As you will henceforth have no further excuse for being ignorant of this fact, you will easily grasp how ludicrous your suggestion must have appeared to me. I, the Marquise de Merteuil, am supposed to drop someone I fancy—and someone new, too!—to concern myself with you! And to concern myself in what way? Awaiting my turn, like a humble slave, for the sublime favours of Your Royal Highness. When, for instance, you are kind enough for a moment to dispense with the strange charm which only the adorable, the divine Madame de Tourvel seems capable of providing you with or when you're alarmed at the thought of compromising in the eyes of the *endearing* Cécile the impression you are very glad to leave her with of yourself as a man superior to all the rest, you'll deign to come down to my level and try to find pleasure there, less exciting, of course, but of little consequence anyway; and your precious favours, albeit distributed somewhat parsimoniously, will be more than adequate to make me happy.

You certainly have a plentiful supply of self-conceit; but it would seem that modesty is less plentiful with me because however hard I look at myself, I fail to see that I'm such an utter wreck as that . . . The fault may lie in me; but I warn you I've got lots of others.

In particular I have the fault of thinking that the schoolboy, the *soppy* Danceny who is concerned only with me, who's sacrificing his first great love, without claiming any credit for this and even before it's reached its consummation, loving me in fact in the way men do at that age, might, for all his twenty years, be a more efficient instrument for my happiness and pleasure than yourself. I shall even take the liberty of adding that, should I fancy providing him with a deputy, it wouldn't be you, at least not at this moment.

And what are my reasons, you will ask? Well, in the first place, there might well not be any reason: the whim which could have led you to be preferred might equally well exclude you. All the same, since I'm a polite young woman, I'm prepared to let you know my motives: it seems to me likely that while you'd be giving up so much for me, I myself, instead of feeling the proper gratitude you would certainly expect, would be quite capable of considering that you owed me still more! So you can well understand that since our ways of thinking are such miles apart, we can't possibly find any point of contact; and I fear it will take me a long time, a very long time indeed, to feel differently. I promise to let you know when I have mended my ways. Until then, believe me, press on with other arrangements and keep your kisses to yourself, you have so many better targets for them!

Goodbye, as in the old days, you say? But in the old days you used to think rather more highly of me; you hadn't yet relegated me completely to supporting roles; and above all you were prepared to wait until I said yes before being sure I'd agree.* So please allow me, instead of saying to you also 'goodbye as in the old days', to say 'goodbye as of now'.

Your servant, sir.

128

Madame de Tourvel to Madame de Rosemonde
Paris, 1 November 17—

I did not receive your delayed reply till yesterday. If my life were still mine to call my own, it would have killed me on the spot: but my whole existence belongs to someone else and that other person is Monsieur de Valmont. You see that I am hiding nothing from you. Even if you are bound to think of me as no longer worthy of your friendship, I'm still less afraid of losing it than keeping it fraudulently. All that I am able to tell you is that having been faced by Monsieur de Valmont with the dilemma of choosing between his death or his happiness, I opted for the latter. I take no pride in this, nor am I accusing myself: I am merely stating facts.*

You will thus have no difficulty in understanding the effect your letter must have had on me with the stern truths it contains. But do not imagine it was able to arouse in me any regrets or that it can ever affect my feelings or my conduct. Not that I do not find myself suffering abominably at times, but when my heart is most cruelly distressed, when I become afraid that I can no longer bear my anguish, I tell myself: Valmont is happy and that thought drives everything else out of my mind or rather it makes everything a pleasure.

So I have dedicated myself to Valmont; I have ruined myself for him, he has become the centre of all my thoughts, feelings, and actions. As long as my life is necessary for his happiness, I shall treasure it and consider myself a lucky woman. If some day he has other views, he will never hear a word of protest or blame from me. I have already faced up to this possibility and made my decision.

You can now see how I am bound to be unaffected by the fear which you seem to have that Valmont may ruin me since, before trying to do that, he will inevitably have stopped loving me and in that case how can futile reproaches have any importance for me if I shan't be hearing them? Since I shall have been living purely for him, he will be my sole judge, my memory will be in his hands and I shall be sufficiently justified if he is forced to recognize that I loved him.

Now I have given you, dear Madame de Rosemonde, an insight into my heart; I'd sooner suffer the misfortune of losing your esteem by being frank than prove unworthy of it by debasing myself with lies. Your kindness to me has been so precious that I felt that I owed you this complete confidence; if I say more now, you might suspect me of thinking I can presume on that kindness whereas on the contrary I am accepting my fault by renouncing any further claim on it.

I am, Madame, with deep respect, your humble and obedient, etc.

129

The Vicomte de Valmont to the Marquise de Merteuil
Paris, 3 November 17—

Do tell me, fair lady, what induced that sour, teasing tone which was so obvious in your last letter? What is this crime I've committed, apparently unawares, which has made you so cross? You accuse me of appearing to take your consent for granted; but I thought that what might be taken for presumption in someone else could never be viewed, between us, as anything but trust; and since when has trust been an enemy of friendship? By combining hope and desire I was merely giving way to that natural impulse which makes us want to be as near as we can to the happiness we're seeking; you are mistaking my eagerness for pride. I know that in such cases it is usual to show a certain respectful doubt; but you know too that this is purely a matter of form, nothing but protocol; and it seems to me that I had the right to think that this sort of extreme wariness was no longer necessary between us.

It even seems to me that when it is based on a long-standing relationship, a free and honest approach is far more preferable than the bland flattery which so often removes the zest from love. And perhaps my liking for that way of dealing merely springs from my liking for the sort of happiness which it reminds me of and for that very reason I should be even more sorry to see you taking a different view.

Yet this is the only fault I can discover in myself, since I can't

think that you can seriously have imagined that any woman exists
in our world whom I might prefer to you and even less that I can
have had such a poor opinion of you as you pretend to think. You
have looked hard at yourself, you say, and you did not find
yourself such a wreck. I can well believe that and this merely
proves how truthful your mirror is. But wouldn't it have been
easier and fairer for you to have come to the conclusion that I had
certainly not thought of you in such terms?

I'm still vainly trying to work out the reason for such an odd
idea. However, it does seem to me that it is in some way or other
related to the fact that I took the liberty of praising another
woman. At any rate, I infer as much from your apparent fondness
for picking on such adjectives as *adorable*, *divine*, and *endearing*
which I used when speaking variously of Madame de Tourvel or
the little Volanges girl. But don't you realize that those words,
chosen more often than not at random rather than for any purpose, don't necessarily reflect our good opinion of someone so
much as our own situation at the time we express it? And if, at
the moment when I was so keenly affected by one or other of
those two women, my desire for you was in no way reduced and
in fact I was showing a marked preference for you over those
other two, since after all I couldn't renew our earlier relationship
except at their expense, I can't see how that can be seen as a
reason to blame me.

Nor is it any harder for me to justify my use of *strange charm*
which seems to have rather shocked you too, since, in the first
place, being strange doesn't imply that it's stronger. Ah, what
could be more delicious than the pleasures you alone can give,
pleasures that are always new, always more intense! All I meant
was that it was a kind of pleasure I had never experienced before.
I had no intention of assessing it; and I had added a comment
that I shall now repeat: whatever it is, I shall resist and overcome
it. And I shall do that all the more vigorously if I can see that the
slight effort involved will count as a tribute to you . . .

As for our little Cécile, I think there's absolutely no point in
arguing about her with you. You'll remember that it was at your
request that I took her on and I'm only waiting for the word from
you to drop her. I may have remarked on her ingenuousness and
freshness; I may even, for a moment, have thought her *endearing*
because we're always more or less pleased with our own handi-

work, but she's certainly too insubstantial in every way to hold anyone's attention for long.

So now, lovely lady, I appeal to your sense of fair play and to your earlier favours for me, as well as to the long and perfect friendship, the complete and utter trust which has brought us ever closer to each other: have I really deserved that carping tone you've recently been adopting towards me? But how easily you can make amends whenever you like! Just say the word and you will see whether all the *charming* and *endearing* qualities available here will detain me, not just one day but even one minute: I shall fly to fling myself at your feet and into your arms and prove to you a thousand and one times in a thousand and one ways that you are and always will be the true queen of my heart.

Goodbye, fair lady. I eagerly await your reply.

130

Madame de Rosemonde to Madame de Tourvel
From the Château de ——, 4 November 17—

And why, dear friend, do you not want to be my daughter any longer? Why do you seem to be announcing that all correspondence between us is to come to an end? Are you trying to punish me for not having guessed at something which was beyond all probability? Or do you suspect me of having deliberately caused you distress? No, I know your heart too well to think that it would believe me capable of that. So the distress your letter caused me relates far less to me than to you!

O dear young friend, it hurts me to have to say it, but you are far too worthy of being loved ever to be happy in love! Is there any truly sensitive and fastidious woman who hasn't been let down in the very feeling that gave promise of such happiness! Do men appreciate the women they possess?

Not that there aren't a number who are honourable in their conduct and constant in their affections; but amongst those, how few are in tune with our hearts! Never think, dear girl, that their love is like ours. They certainly experience the same intoxication of the senses, indeed they are often more carried away by it; but they know nothing of that restless eagerness, that tender solicitude, which produces in us that continuous loving concern uniquely centred on our beloved. A man enjoys the pleasure he feels, a woman the pleasure she bestows. This difference, so essential and so unnoticed, has however a very marked effect on their respective general behaviour. The pleasure of one partner is to satisfy his desires, that of the other is primarily to arouse them. For the man, pleasing is merely a means to succeed whereas for her it is success itself. And feminine flirtatiousness, for which she is so often blamed, is nothing but an abuse of this way of feeling and for that very reason proves it is true. And so this exclusive fondness for someone, which is a particular characteristic of love, remains, for a man, purely a preference which is, at the most, useful for him to assess the extent of his pleasure and which some other affection might weaken but not destroy, whereas for women it's a deep emotion which not only abolishes all desire for anyone else but, being more powerful than nature and outside its control, causes them to feel nothing but repugnance and disgust even in situations which ought apparently to provide them with extreme pleasure.

It is easy to quote numbers of exceptions to these general principles but you mustn't think that they invalidate their truth! They have the support of public opinion which has drawn a distinction—for men only—between being unfaithful and being inconstant; it's one they are delighted to take advantage of, instead of considering it disgraceful, as they ought; but it's one that has never been accepted except by depraved women who are themselves a disgrace to their sex and who'll clutch at any straw to avoid having to face the unpleasant reality of their own ignominy.

I thought, dear friend, that it might help you to hear my reflections and compare them with those illusions of perfect bliss in love that we never cease to dream about; false hopes which we still try to cling to even when we're forced to abandon them; and whose loss aggravates and increases the strains and stresses, already only too real, inherent in any intensely passionate love! This attempt to calm or reduce your sufferings is the only one I want or am able to make at the moment. When ills are incurable, advice can only hope to try to alleviate them. All I ask you to remember is that feeling pity for someone who's ill doesn't mean blaming them. Who are we to cast the first stone? Let us leave the right to judge to Him who alone can read in all our hearts; and I venture to think that in our Father's eyes, a single weakness can be redeemed by a host of virtues.

But I do beseech you, dear, dear girl, above all to resist those violent resolutions which indicate not so much that you are strong but that you are utterly dejected. Aren't you forgetting, that if, in your own words, your existence belongs to someone else, none the less you may not deprive your friends of that part of your life which they already had and which they will never agree to give up.

Goodbye, my dear, dear daughter. Think sometimes of your loving mother and never doubt that you will always be first and foremost in her thoughts and her affection.

131

The Marquise de Merteuil to the Vicomte de Valmont
From the Château de ——, 6 November 17—

Bravo, Vicomte! You get much better marks this time than last. But now let's settle down to a friendly chat and I hope to convince you that the arrangement you seem to want would be madness for both of us.

Haven't you yet realized that pleasure, which is indeed certainly the one and only reason for the two sexes to come together, is nevertheless not enough to establish a relationship between them? And that though this pleasure is preceded by desire which draws people together, it is however followed by aversion which pushes them apart? It's a law of nature which only love can change. Can we feel love whenever we want? Yet love is always needed, which would be a dreadfully tiresome thing if it hadn't fortunately been realized that it's enough for just one of the partners to feel it, thereby halving the problem, and without even incurring any great loss; in fact, one party is happy to love, the other to please, which is actually a bit less exciting but which can be combined with the pleasure of deceiving and that evens things out, so everyone's happy.

But tell me, Vicomte, which of us two will undertake to deceive the other? You know the story of the two card-sharpers who spotted each other when they were playing together: we're not going to get anything from each other, they said, let's split the proceeds; and they stopped playing. Believe me, let's follow this wise example and not waste our time together when we can spend it so profitably elsewhere.

To prove to you that my decision is prompted as much by your interests as my own and that I'm not acting out of malice or caprice, I shan't withhold the reward we agreed on: anyway, I feel that for a single evening we'll hit it off together fabulously; I even have no doubt that we can embroider on it sufficiently well to make us sorry when it comes to an end. But don't forget that this regret is necessary for happiness; and that however pleasant the illusion, let's not imagine that it can last.

You will see that I too am fulfilling my obligations—and before you've yet settled up with me; after all, I was to be given the heavenly prude's first letter, yet either because you're reluctant to part with it or else because you've forgotten the terms of our bargain (which maybe you find less interesting than you want me to believe), I've received nothing, nothing whatsoever. Nevertheless, unless I'm very much mistaken, your tender-hearted and pious conquest must be a great letter-writer. What else could she do when she's alone? She's certainly not sensible enough to look around for amusement. So I have a small bone to pick with you, if I have a mind to: but I'll hold my peace on the subject, to make amends for the slightly acrimonious tone I allowed to creep into my last letter.

Now, Vicomte, the only thing left for me to do is to make a request, as much for your sake as mine: it is to postpone an event which I am perhaps looking forward to as much as you but which it seems to me must be held over until I come back to town. For one thing, we wouldn't find the requisite freedom here; for another, I'd be running a certain amount of risk because a little touch of jealousy is all that's required for that dreary fellow Belleroche to grow more attached to me again than ever, even though he's on his last legs. As it is, he's making such desperate efforts to love me that at times I'm continuing to smother him with caresses as much out of mischief as of prudence. But all the same, as you can see, it could hardly be described as making a sacrifice for you! Being unfaithful to each other will add a lot more spice to a charming occasion.

Do you know, I'm sometimes sorry that we've been reduced to these expedients? In the old days, when we loved one another—for I think it was love—I was happy. How about you, Vicomte? But why concern ourselves with a happiness that can never return? No, whatever you may say, it's not possible to turn the clock back. First of all, I'd demand sacrifices from you which you'd be unable or unwilling to accept and which I may not even deserve. And then, how could I hold on to you? No, I don't want such a thought even to come into my head and although at this moment I'm enjoying writing to you, I'd better break off quickly now . . . Goodbye, Vicomte.

132

Madame de Tourvel to Madame de Rosemonde
Paris, 7 November 17—

I am overwhelmed by your kindness, Madame, and the only thing which somehow holds me back from throwing myself on that kindness is fear of profaning it. At a time when your help is so precious, why do I feel so unworthy of it? Ah, at least I shall not be afraid to show how grateful I am for it and, above all, how greatly I admire the way in which a virtuous woman can forgive and feel only sympathy for the weaknesses she perceives; who can cast such a powerful spell over our hearts with a strong yet gentle authority which prevails even over the spell of love.

But am I still worthy of your friendship now that it no longer has any power to make me happy? And I feel the same with regard to your advice: I value it yet I cannot follow it. And how could I fail to believe in perfect happiness when I am enjoying it at this very moment? Yes, indeed, if men are like you say, they must be shunned, they are odious; but if that is the case, how different from them Valmont is! If like them he feels that impetuosity of passion which you describe as 'being carried away', how he manages to transcend it by his exquisite delicacy of feeling! Dear friend, you talk of sharing my sorrows; why don't you enjoy the happiness my love is bringing me and which is all the more rewarding because of its object? You say you are fond of your nephew, perhaps to the point of weakness? Ah, if you only knew him as well as I do! I idolize him but far less than he deserves. No doubt, as he himself admits, he may have been led astray; but who ever understood the meaning of true love better than he does? What more can I say? He feels it as strongly as he inspires it.

You will be thinking that this is one of *these illusions of perfect bliss in love that we never cease to dream about*: but in that case, how is it that he has become more loving, more attentive since he has nothing more to gain? I must confess that earlier on I used to think he almost always had a reserved and brooding look which in spite of myself often reminded me of the false and cruel impressions of him which I had been given. But ever since he has been able to surrender unreservedly to the dictates of his heart, he seems to be able to see into my own. Who knows if we weren't made for each other? Or if my happiness wasn't fated to be necessary for his? Oh, if that's an illusion, may I die before it's destroyed. No, that's wrong: I want to live and cherish him, to adore him. Why should he ever stop loving me? What other woman could he make happier than me? And I can feel it myself: the happiness we inspire is the strongest link, the only link that really holds two people together. Yes, it's that delightful feeling which uplifts love, which somehow purifies it and makes it really worthy of a loving and generous heart such as Valmont's.

Goodbye, my dear, my honourable, indulgent friend. I cannot hope to write to you at greater length at this moment; this is when he's promised to come and that is the only thing I can think of. Forgive me! But you do want me to be happy and at the moment my happiness is almost greater than I can bear.

133

The Vicomte de Valmont to the Marquise de Merteuil
Paris, 8 November 17—

Fair lady, what pray are these sacrifices which you consider me incapable of, though their reward will be to give you pleasure? Oh, just let me know what they are and if I hesitate one second, I authorize you to reject my offering. How have you come to change your view of me so much recently that, indulgent as you are, you still doubt my energy and my feelings towards you?

Sacrifices that I couldn't or wouldn't make? So you think I'm in love and helpless? And you suspect me of thinking that the person is as important as the success? Ah, I've not yet been reduced to such straits, thank Heaven, and I hereby volunteer to prove it. Yes, I'll prove it even if it has to be at Madame de Tourvel's expense. After that, you'll surely have no further room for doubt.

I don't think I've compromised my reputation in setting aside some time for a woman who has at least the merit of being something of a *rara avis*. Perhaps it was also the close season when this adventure turned up that made me rather keener; and even now when the open season is getting into full swing, it's not surprising that I'm still giving it most of my attention. After all, if you think of it, it's barely a week ago that I started enjoying the fruits of three months' hard work. I've so often spent more time than that over something that was far less worth while (and didn't require anything like as much effort!). You didn't draw invidious conclusions about me then.

Would you like to know the real reason for the sort of enthusiasm I'm showing? Here it is: this woman is naturally timorous; in the early days, she still felt permanently doubtful of her happiness and this doubt was enough to upset it, so that I'm only now beginning to be able to realize the full extent of my power over this kind of woman. However, this was something I was curious to find out and the chance of doing it doesn't occur as often as people think.

First of all, for lots of women, pleasure is always just pleasure and nothing more; and with such women, whatever high-falutin title we may be given, we're just ciphers, stand-ins whose only assets are our performance and the most vigorous man is always the best.

In another category, perhaps these days the largest, the lover's prestige, the pleasure of having taken him away from a rival, the fear of subsequently seeing him taken away from them, absorb almost the entire attention of women; so while we certainly play some part, more or less, in the sort of happiness they enjoy, it's more related to the circumstances than the person. They achieve it through us, not from us.

So for my investigation I needed a woman with a delicate,

sensitive nature, who would devote herself completely and utterly to love and who, in that love, had eyes only for her lover; whose emotions would reverse the normal route and always start from the heart to arrive at the senses; one whom I've seen, for instance (I'm not referring to the first day), emerge in tears from her pleasure and a moment later be again plunged into delight by a word which struck a chord in her heart. Finally, all this still needed to be combined with a natural candour which, having become an inveterate second habit, never allows her to conceal any of her innermost feelings. Well, you'll agree that such women are exceptional and I'm tempted to believe that but for her I might never have found one at all.

So it wouldn't be surprising if she does hold my attention longer than any other woman, and if the research I wish to carry out on her requires me to make her happy, completely and utterly happy, why should I refuse, particularly when that suits my purpose rather than hindering it? But because the mind is absorbed, does it follow that the heart is infatuated? Certainly not. And any importance which I am bound to attach to this adventure won't prevent me from embarking on others nor even from sacrificing it to other, more congenial, ones.

So free do I feel that I've even not been neglecting the Volanges girl, though she doesn't mean very much to me. Her mother's taking her back to town in three days' time; and yesterday I made sure of keeping my lines of communication open: a small tip to the porter and a little soft soap to his wife did the trick. Can you conceive how Danceny couldn't even manage to find such a simple solution? And then they say that love sharpens your wits! On the contrary, it merely makes the love-sick more stupid. And I'm supposed to be incapable of resisting it? Ah, don't worry. Very shortly, in a few days' time, I'm going to weaken the perhaps over-favourable impression I had by bestowing part of it on someone else and if one woman isn't enough, I'll find more.

However, I shall be ready to hand the little convent girl back to her discreet lover as soon as you think fit. It seems to me that you've no grounds for any further delay and as for me, I've no objection to doing poor Danceny this signal favour. In fact, it's the least I can do in return for all those he's done me. At the moment he's terribly worried as to whether Madame de Volanges will admit him to her house. I'm calming him down as well as I can by assuring him that, one way or another, I'll make him a happy man on the very first day he comes;* meanwhile, I continue to look after his correspondence which he wants to take over as soon as *his Cécile* arrives. I've already got six of his letters and I shall certainly have a couple more before the happy day. That young fellow really doesn't know what to do with his spare time!

But let's leave these two children and come back to us, so that I can concentrate exclusively on the marvellous hope your letter gave me. Yes, of course you'll be able to hold on to me and I shan't forgive you for doubting it. Have I ever failed to be constant to you? Our relationship may have been strained but it was never broken; our so-called separation was never anything but a figment of our imagination: our feelings and interests have always remained united. Like the returning traveller who has seen the light, I shall acknowledge that I had deserted the substance of happiness to pursue its shadowy hope and, like d'Harcourt, I shall say:

*Plus je vis d'étrangers, plus j'aimai ma patrie.**

So stop struggling against your thoughts, or rather your feelings, which are drawing you back to me and after having, in the course of our different careers, tried out every pleasure, let us appreciate our good fortune and realize that none of them can match those we used to enjoy together and which will prove more delightful than ever!

Goodbye, charming lady. I agree to wait until you come back: but do make it soon and don't forget how much I'm longing for the day.

134

The Marquise de Merteuil to the Vicomte de Valmont
From the Château de ――, 11 November 17—

Really, Vicomte, you're just like those children whom you can't say anything in front of or show anything to without their wanting to lay hands on it straight away! A simple thought crosses my mind which I even tell you I've no intention of pursuing and you take advantage of my mentioning it not only to remind me of it but to focus my attention on it—even although I'm doing my best to move on to other things—and make me somehow connive at your ridiculous desires in spite of myself. Is it very nice of you to put the responsibility for being cautious on to my shoulders alone? I must tell you again, as I continually tell myself even more often: your proposed arrangement really is out of the question. Even were you to continue to display your present magnanimity, don't you think I also have my own scruples about accepting sacrifices that would stand in the way of your happiness?

Now, is it true, Vicomte, that you are so deluded as to your feelings for Madame de Tourvel? It is love or I don't know what love is. Certainly, you've been denying it in hundreds of ways—and proving it in thousands. Take, for instance, this deception you're practising on yourself—because I do believe you're being sincere with me—which has led you to describe as a need to observe your longing, which you're unable to conceal or resist, to keep your hold on that woman. One would think you'd never before made any other woman happy, perfectly happy!* If you're uncertain about that, you must have a very poor memory! But it's not like that at all. Quite simply, it's your heart misleading your head and letting it fob itself off with very bad reasons. But I, myself, have a considerable interest in *not* being misled and I'm not going to be fobbed off so easily.

Thus, while I noticed that, for politeness' sake, you carefully excluded all those words which you imagined displeased me, I saw that, perhaps without realizing it, you still stuck to the same ideas. So now it isn't the *adorable*, the heavenly Madame de Tourvel, it's an *astonishing woman, a delicate, sensitive woman*, absolutely different from other women, an *exceptional* woman in fact and you might *never have found another one like her*. It's the same thing with the strange charm which doesn't imply that it's *stronger*. All right: but since you'd never found it up till then, it's very unlikely that you would find it in the future either and your loss would be equally irreparable. And if these aren't infallible symptoms of love, Vicomte, we'll have to give up all hope of ever discovering them.

And this time you may be sure I'm not talking crossly. I've made a vow never to be cross again: I recognized all too plainly what a dangerous trap that might lead me into. But take my word for it, let's just be friends and leave it at that. Only do give me credit for having the courage to defend myself: yes, courage, because sometimes we need it even to avoid taking a decision which we know is the wrong one.

So I'm going to answer your query about the sacrifices I'd demand of you (and which you wouldn't be able to make), though not in any attempt to persuade you to share my views. And I'm using the word demand deliberately because I'm well aware that you're going to find my attitude too demanding: all the better! Far from being vexed by your refusal, I'll be grateful for it. Look, I'm not going to start pretending to *you*: maybe I need you to refuse.

So let me reveal to you the full extent of my cruelty: I should demand that you cease to consider that *rara avis*, that astounding Madame de Tourvel, as anything other than an ordinary woman, which is what in fact she is, because, let's face it, this charm we find in other people is all in the mind; it's only love which makes the loved one appear so wonderful. Now, you may well be able to make the necessary effort to promise to do what I'm asking, impossible though it is, and even swear to do it; but I must confess that I wouldn't accept mere words. I could only be convinced by your whole behaviour.

And that's not everything: I'd be capricious. You most graciously offer to give up Cécile: I couldn't care less about the girl. On the contrary, I'd be asking you to continue to struggle on until further notice from me, either because I enjoy exploiting my authority in this way or else because when I'm in a more forgiving or fairer frame of mind, I'm content to control your feelings without wanting to thwart your pleasures. In any case, I'd insist on being obeyed and my orders would be very strict!

It's true that I'd then feel obliged to thank you; who knows, perhaps even reward you . . . For instance, I'd certainly cut short my stay here; I shouldn't be able to bear being away any longer.

So I'd finally be meeting you again, Vicomte; and when we met, how would that turn out? But you remember, this is just a little chat we're having, all about an impossible plan; I don't want to be the only one to forget that.

Do you know, I'm a bit worried about my lawsuit? I finally decided to find out what my position actually is. My lawyers keep quoting a few laws and above all lots of leading cases as they call them; but I can't see much reason or justice in them. I'm almost beginning to regret having turned down an out-of-court settlement. However, when I reflect that the public attorney is shrewd, my advocate glib, and the plaintiff pretty, I feel more confident. If these three qualifications were no longer to carry any weight, we'd need to change the whole system and where would our respect for ancient custom be then?

At the moment, my case is the only thing that's keeping me down here; Belleroche's has already been heard: case dismissed, costs shared by both parties. He's even reached the stage of regretting this evening's ball: the typical frustration of someone who doesn't know what to do with his time. As soon as I'm back in town, I'll let him off the hook completely. I shall make this painful sacrifice for his sake and console myself with the thought that he will be thinking how noble I am.

Goodbye, Vicomte. Keep writing to me: the details of your pleasures will at least be some compensation for my current vexations.

135

Madame de Tourvel to Madame de Rosemonde
Paris, 15 November 17—

I'm not yet certain whether I shall be able to write this letter to you but I shall try. Dear God! When I think that I was too overwhelmed by happiness to finish my last letter and now I am overwhelmed by despair, barely strong enough to feel the full extent of my suffering and too weak to find words to express it.

Valmont . . . Valmont no longer loves me, he has never loved me. Love doesn't just vanish like that . . . He is deceiving me, betraying me, debasing me. I am being subjected to every imaginable humiliation and misfortune and he is the perpetrator!

And don't imagine that this is mere suspicion; suspicion had never even entered my head! And I can't even hope to give him the benefit of the doubt! I saw him with my own eyes: what could he possibly say to justify himself? . . . But what does he care? He won't even bother to try . . . Ah, poor me! What effect can your reproaches have on him? You're the least of his concerns! . . .

So he has sacrificed me, even thrown me into the clutches of . . . of whom? A vile creature . . . But how can I say that! I've even lost the right to despise her. *She* hasn't broken faith with so many of her duties; she's less guilty than I. Oh, how dreadful it is not just to suffer but to feel your suffering exacerbated by remorse. I can feel my anguish weighing on me more and more. Goodbye, dear, dear friend. I hardly deserve any pity from you now but you will still spare some for me if you can have some idea of the torture I'm enduring . . .

I've just reread my letter and realized that it tells you virtually nothing, so I shall try to pluck up courage enough to tell you what has happened to cause me such terrible distress. It was yesterday: for the first time since my return I was going out to supper. Valmont called on me at five o'clock; he had never seemed more loving. He gave me to understand that he was put out by my plan to go out to supper and you can imagine that I quickly changed my mind so as to stay at home. Two hours later, however, and all of a sudden, his tone and attitude changed markedly. I don't know if I had blurted something out which he might have taken amiss; in any case, shortly afterwards he claimed to have remembered a matter which demanded his urgent attention and he left, not without expressing considerable regrets in what seemed very loving terms which at the time I took to be sincere.

Left to my own devices, I thought that as I was now free, it would be only right of me to fulfil my earlier commitments. I dressed and got into my carriage. Unfortunately my driver took us past the Opéra: as the performance had just ended we were held up in the crush of carriages. Four yards ahead of me in the line next to mine I caught sight of Valmont's carriage. My heart gave a sudden leap but not from fear; my only wish was for my carriage to move up. Instead his was forced to move backwards and ended level with mine. I at once leaned forward; imagine my surprise to see a woman sitting beside him, a notorious prostitute! As you may well understand, I drew back. This sight alone cut my heart to the quick; but you will find it hard to believe that, having apparently been let into my secret by some odious informant, she sat glued to the window of the carriage staring at me all the time and creating a scene with her loud ribald laughter.

With death in my soul, I still went on to the house where I was to have supper but feeling that I might faint any minute, I found it impossible to stay; above all, I could not hold back my tears.

When I got home I wrote Monsieur de Valmont a letter and sent it off to him immediately. He was not at home. Being anxious to be relieved from my devastating situation at all costs or at least to know the worst, I instructed my man to go back and wait for him; but before midnight he had returned with the news that the coachman had come back and told him that his master wouldn't be coming home that night. This morning I came to the conclusion that my only course now was once again to ask for the return of my letters and request him to cease calling. I gave the appropriate instructions but no doubt they were futile: it is now after noon and he has not yet appeared nor have I even received any word from him.

Now I have nothing more to add, dear friend: you know all and you know my feelings. My one hope is that I shall not be a burden on your friendship and sympathy much longer.

136

Madame de Tourvel to the Vicomte de Valmont
Paris, 15 November 17—

After what happened yesterday, Monsieur, you doubtless no longer expect nor indeed have any great wish to be admitted to my house! This note is thus intended not so much to request that you cease calling on me as to ask yet again for the return of those letters which should never have been written and which, if they may briefly have aroused your interest as proofs of the blindness which you set out to create, can only be a matter of indifference for you now that my eyes have been opened and that they have come to express nothing but feelings which you have destroyed.

I recognize and admit that I was wrong to offer you the trust which had led to the downfall of so many of your other victims. For this I blame only myself but I did at least think that I had not deserved to be subjected by you to obloquy and contempt. I thought that in sacrificing everything to you and forfeiting purely for your sake my rights to the respect of others as well as of myself, I might nevertheless have expected not to be judged by you more harshly than by public opinion, which still acknowledges the immense gap between a weak and a depraved woman. I am here referring only to those wrongs which everybody would feel; I shall say nothing of those committed against love: your heart would not understand mine . . . I wish you farewell, Monsieur.

137

The Vicomte de Valmont to Madame de Tourvel
Paris, 15 November 17—

Your letter has only just been handed to me, Madame. I shuddered as I read it and hardly have strength enough to answer it. What an atrocious image you have of me! Oh, no doubt I have shortcomings, and ones that I shall never forgive myself even were you prepared to throw a kindly veil over them. But how could those of which you accuse me have ever, even remotely, crossed my mind? *I* humiliate *you*? Debase you? I, who respect you as much as I adore you? I, who only learned the real meaning of the word pride when you considered me worthy of you. You have been misled by appearances—and I admit that they may have seemed against me; but did not your heart give you the means to refute them? Was it not shocked at the mere thought that it might have cause to complain of mine? Yet you believed that! So not only did you think me capable of such an abominable lunacy but you were even afraid that you had been exposed to it as a result of the favours you have shown me! Ah, if you think yourself so debased by my love, then I myself must be a vile creature in your eyes.

And I am so dejected by this appalling thought that here I am wasting the time refuting your idea of me which should be spent demolishing it. I shall speak frankly: there is still one further consideration holding me back. Do I have to go back over actions which I should prefer to consign to oblivion and draw your and my attention to a moment of weakness, that I should like to redeem by all my remaining years, whose cause I can still recall and the meaning of which will for ever fill me with humiliation and despair? Ah, if these self-accusations arouse your anger, at least you will not have far to seek for your vengeance: you need only leave me to suffer the pangs of my own remorse.

However, incredible as it may seem, the main cause of this unfortunate incident is the charm of your company. It was this that drove an important matter of business completely out of my mind, a matter which brooked no delay. I was too late in leaving you to meet the person concerned, went on to the Opéra in the hope of being more successful but in vain. However, I did there meet Émilie whom I used to know in a period of my life when I was very far from having any knowledge of love or of you. She was without her carriage and asked me to give her a lift to her house, only a few yards further up the street. It seemed a trivial request and I agreed. But it was then that I met you and I immediately sensed that you would be inclined to condemn me.

I am so appalled at the thought of incurring your displeasure or causing you distress that my fear was bound to be and indeed soon became obvious. I confess that it even made me attempt to persuade this abandoned creature not to show herself; but this solicitude itself misfired at the expense of love. Like all her sort she was used to asserting her authority—never legitimately acquired—only by shamelessly abusing it and Émilie took good care not to miss such a heaven-sent opportunity. The greater and more evident my embarrassment, the more she delighted in making an exhibition of herself; and her extravagant hilarity—and I blush to think that you imagined even for a second that it was directed at you—was motivated purely by my own anguish of mind, itself the result of my love and respect!

Till now I had been no doubt unfortunate rather than guilty; and as you *were referring only to those wrongs* such as *everybody would feel* and these wrongs are non-existent, you cannot blame me for them. But as for *saying nothing about the wrongs committed against love*, I cannot agree and I shall not remain equally silent: I am too closely affected not to speak out.

Not that I find it anything but extremely painful to bring myself to revive memories of such unimaginable profligacy which still leaves me ashamed. I am so strongly convinced of my errors that I would be ready to pay the penalty for them or wait for the passage of time, my eternal devotion, your forbearance, and my repentance to bring forgiveness. But how could I keep silent when what I have still to say is a matter of such delicacy for you?

Do not imagine that I am trying to find some devious expedient to justify myself or mitigate my fault: I admit my guilt. But I do not and never shall admit that this humiliating error can be considered a wrong committed against love. Ah, Madame, what can a turmoil of the senses, a momentary loss of self-control, quickly followed by shame and regret, really have in common with a pure feeling which can only arise in a sensitive soul, be based on respect, and whose ultimate outcome is happiness? Oh, you must not profane love in that way! And above all, beware of profaning yourself by bringing together things which are so distinct. Those depraved women who are tormented and humiliated by the pangs of jealousy, and feel under threat despite all their efforts, may well keep an anxious eye on their rivals; but you will spurn such creatures, their sight alone would defile your eyes; as a pure image of the Divinity, you must, like Him, punish the sin while shunning it.

But what greater penance could you impose on me than the one I am now suffering? What can be compared to my regret at having displeased you, my despair at distressing you, to the devastating thought of having made myself less worthy of you? You are thinking of ways of punishing me! But I shall ask you to comfort me, not that I deserve to be comforted but because I need it and it can come only from you.

But if on the other hand you suddenly choose to forget my love and yours, to consider my happiness of no further interest, to wish to condemn me to suffer for ever, you have the right: strike me down. If, however, you choose to show more forbearance or more feeling; if you can still recall those tender sentiments that bound our hearts together, those raptures of our souls, ever renewed and ever more deeply felt, those sweet, blissful days for which we were beholden to each other: all those treasures of love which love alone can provide; then perhaps you may prefer to use your power over me to bring them back rather than to destroy them?

So now what is left for me to say? I have lost everything, lost through my own fault . . . But through your charitable heart, may I not yet win everything back? It is for you now to decide; I shall say no more. Only yesterday you swore that my happiness was in safe hands as long as it was with you! Ah, Madame, will you condemn me today to everlasting despair?

138

The Vicomte de Valmont to the Marquise de Merteuil
Paris, 15 November 17—

I still can't agree, fair lady: no, I'm not in love and it's no fault of mine if circumstances are forcing me to act as if I am. So accept the fact and come back: you'll see for yourself how sincere I am. I passed my test with flying colours yesterday and that cannot be destroyed by what happens today.

Well then: there I was with the tender-hearted prude and without anything else on my mind whatsoever: the Volanges girl, in spite of her condition, was off to spend all night at the pre-season ball at Madame V——'s. Having nothing else to do, I felt tempted to stay on and to do so, I'd even prevailed on her to make a small sacrifice; but hardly had she done so than the pleasure I'd been promising myself was soured by the thought of that love which you persist in attributing to me or at least accusing me of; my only wish now was to be able to convince myself and you that it was a pure libel on your part.

So I decided to take stern measures and on rather a slim pretext at that. To her great surprise and no doubt to her even greater distress, I took leave of my beloved and calmly went off to meet Émilie at the Opéra; and she could confirm that throughout the whole time until we parted this morning our pleasures were quite untroubled by the slightest regrets . . .

All the same, had I not been feeling completely unconcerned, I had a pretty sound reason for being worried, for I have to inform you that barely had I gone four houses along the street from the Opéra with Émilie in my carriage beside me than the saintly prude's own carriage drew up level with us and we were held up for a good ten minutes or so side by side; and it was as bright as day and there was no way of escape.

Nor was that all: I took it into my head to tell Émilie that she was the woman in the letter—you may remember that crazy idea I had when I used Émilie as my writing desk? She had certainly remembered and as she's fond of a laugh, she couldn't rest until she'd taken a good long look at this *paragon of virtue*, as she called her; and what's more, she kept bursting into fits of laughter in a most irritating and scandalous way.

And that was still not the end: didn't the jealous woman send round a message to me that very night? I wasn't at home; but she insisted on sending a messenger again with instructions to wait until I returned. But having decided to spend the night at Émilie's, I had sent my carriage away, merely instructing the driver to come back and pick me up this morning; and when on arriving at my house he found the messenger of love waiting, he thought the simplest thing was to tell him that I wouldn't be home that night. You can well imagine the effect of this news and that on my return I'd been given my marching orders with all the solemnity appropriate to the circumstances!

So this affair which you regard as love eternal could, as you see, have been brought to an abrupt end this morning and even if it hasn't, it's not because, as you may be tempted to think, I attach the slightest importance to prolonging it but because, on the one hand, I don't think it proper for someone to leave me* and, on the other, because I wished this sacrifice to be a tribute to you.

So I answered the stern note with a sentimental missive on the grand scale. I gave lengthy explanations and relied on love to make them appear convincing. I've already succeeded: I've just received a second note, still very stern, confirming, as was to be expected, that we must part for ever; but it's not in the same tone. Above all, I'm never to show my face again; this decision is repeated four times in the most categorical manner. I therefore concluded that I must present myself forthwith. I've already sent my man to get hold of her major-domo and in a moment I shall myself go and get my pardon signed, sealed, and delivered: when we're guilty of such grave transgressions as these, there's only one formula for general absolution and that can only be received in person.

Farewell, dear charmer. I'm leaving forthwith for this grand occasion.

139

Madame de Tourvel to Madame de Rosemonde
Paris, evening of 16 November 17—

Dear, dear friend, how guilty I feel at having told you, in such detail and without waiting, of my short-lived worries. You'll have been distressed by them and still be upset while I myself am happy. Yes, all is forgiven and forgotten, or perhaps it would be better to say that everything has been explained. Oh, how can I find words to express the joy in my heart! Valmont is innocent: how can anyone be guilty when he feels such love! Those horrible, insulting actions of which I was accusing him so bitterly were not true and if on just one point I have needed to make allowances, I did, after all, owe him some redress for certain unfair actions of my own, did I not?

I shan't give you all the facts and reasons to explain this in detail; it may be difficult to understand them rationally; they can only be appreciated properly by the heart . . . But if you suspect me of being weak, I shall appeal to your own judgement to support mine: you said yourself that for men, infidelity is not the same thing as inconstancy.

Not that I don't feel that this distinction doesn't offend our susceptibilities, even if public opinion tries, unsuccessfully, to justify it; but why should my feelings be hurt if Valmont's are even more greatly offended? You mustn't think that he himself is easy in his mind or ready to forgive himself for his wrongdoing, which I am prepared to overlook; yet how completely he has atoned for that peccadillo by the abundance of my happiness and his love!

Ever since I was afraid I had forfeited all my happiness it has either actually increased or else I am appreciating it more. What I can tell you is that if I still felt I had strength enough to bear yet again the cruel sufferings I have been through, I should not consider I had paid too high a price for the supreme happiness I've since enjoyed.* O my dear affectionate mother, scold your thoughtless daughter for having distressed you by being so hasty; scold her for having made a rash judgement and slandered a man whom she would continue to adore. But while recognizing her foolishness, see how happy she is and make her happiness even greater by sharing it!

140

The Vicomte de Valmont to the Marquise de Merteuil
Paris, 21 November 17—

How comes it, fair lady, that I've received no reply from you at all? Yet my last letter seemed to me rather to deserve one; meanwhile I'm still waiting, even though I should have received it three days ago! I'm irked, to say the least, so I'm not going to tell you anything about my own important affairs.

That the reconciliation produced the desired effect; that instead of reproaches and distrust there were new effusions; that now it's I who's receiving amends and apologies for the suspicions cast on my sincerity . . . No, I'm not going to say a single word on that subject. And but for last night's unforeseen incident I shouldn't be writing at all. But as this last concerns your ward and she'll probably not be in a fit state to tell you about it herself for quite a while, I'm undertaking to do so myself.

For reasons that you may or may not be able to guess, for the last few days I've not been bothering myself with Madame de Tourvel and as those reasons couldn't possibly apply to the little Volanges girl, I'd been seeing more of her.* Thanks to the obliging porter I'd not met any obstacles and your ward and I were leading a cosy, orderly life. But familiarity breeds contempt: from the first we'd never taken adequate security precautions; we still felt apprehensive behind bolted doors. Yesterday, as a result of an incredible oversight, there occurred the incident which I shall now tell you about, and though I managed to escape myself with nothing more than a scare, the little girl wasn't quite so lucky.

We weren't asleep but in that relaxed and drowsy state induced by the delights of love when we suddenly heard the door open. I immediately sprang up to get my sword to defend myself—and our joint ward. I went towards the door but saw no one, though the door was open. As we had some light, I went to explore, without finding a soul. Then I recalled that we had omitted our usual precautions and the door, having been merely pushed to or not properly closed, had come open by itself.

When I returned to reassure my frightened companion, I found her no longer in bed: she'd fallen or slipped down between the bed and the wall and in fact was lying there unconscious and jerking convulsively. You can imagine my embarrassment! However, I managed to lift her back on to the bed and even succeeded in reviving her; but she had hurt herself in her fall and the effects soon became apparent.

The violent pains in her back and stomach as well as even more obvious indications quickly told me what was amiss but in order to inform her it was necessary first of all to tell her what her previous condition had been, because she had no idea; perhaps never before has any girl preserved such innocence while doing her damnedest to lose it. Ah me, that little girl doesn't waste much time using her head!

Meantime she was spending a great deal of time weeping and wailing and I realized the need for decisive action. I arranged with her that I would go off straight away to the family doctor and the family surgeon, give them notice that they were going to be called in, and tell them everything under the seal of secrecy; for her part, as soon as I'd left, she was to ring for her maid, pleasing herself whether or not to let her into the secret, but sending her to fetch help and above all giving instructions that on no account was Madame de Volanges to be woken up: a perfectly natural and considerate action by a daughter anxious to avoid giving her mother cause for concern . . .

I completed my two errands and confessions with all possible speed and then came home. I've not stirred since, but the surgeon—whom I knew, incidentally—called on me at noon to report on the state of the patient. My assumption was correct; but he hopes, if there are no further complications, that nobody in the house will notice anything wrong. The maid is in on the secret; the doctor has thought up a name for the illness and, like so many others, this business will turn out all right—unless it suits us for people to talk about it at a later date.

But do we still have any interests in common, you and I? Your continued silence makes me doubtful and I'd even give up believing it altogether if I didn't want to so much that I'm exploring every possible avenue in order not to lose hope.

Goodbye, fair lady. I embrace you, hard feelings notwithstanding . . .

141

The Marquise de Merteuil to the Vicomte de Valmont
From the Château de —, 24 November 17—

My goodness, Vicomte, your pigheadedness is really getting beyond a joke! What can it matter to you if I don't write? Do you think it's because I'm short of reasons to defend myself? Ah, if only that were the case! The truth is I find it painful to let you know them.

Now, out with it: are you fooling yourself or are you trying to fool me? The discrepancy between what you say and what you do leaves me with no choice but between those two alternatives. Which is the right one? So, what do you expect me to say when I don't know what to think myself?

You seem to be rather pleased at your last scene with that judge's wife; but what does it prove as between your system and mine? I certainly never said you loved that woman so much as not to be unfaithful to her and to grasp every opportunity to do so that seemed agreeable or easy. I never had the slightest doubt that for you it was more or less a matter of indifference to satisfy the desires aroused exclusively by her with someone else—the first woman handy; nor am I surprised, in view of your open-mindedness, which nobody would ever dare deny, that once in a while you would do out of calculation something that you've already done countless times previously out of convenience.

Who doesn't realize that that's the way things are and the normal conduct of all you males from the villains to the small fry? Nowadays anyone who refrains from doing it is considered a romantic and I'm hardly likely to be accusing you of being that.

But what I did say and think—and still do—is that nevertheless it is love that you feel for your judge's wife, not, indeed, very pure nor very devoted love but the sort you're capable of; the sort, for instance, that leads you to discover qualities or charms in a woman that aren't there; which sets her in a class of her own and all the others in second place; which binds you to her even when you're treating her abominably; in a word, the love I can imagine a Sultan feeling for his favourite Sultana, which doesn't prevent him from frequently preferring a simple concubine from his harem. My comparison seems to me all the more apt because, like him, you are never a woman's friend or lover but always her tyrant or her slave. And this is why I'm very sure that in order to creep back into the good books of this fair object of your affections you must have eaten very humble pie and in your delight at having succeeded, as soon as you think the time is ripe to be granted your pardon, you take leave of me to set out for *this grand occasion*.

Even in your last letter, if you don't talk exclusively about that woman, it's only because you don't want to tell me about your *own important affairs*, which you seem to find so important that you imagine you're punishing me by not saying anything about them. And it's after revealing these countless proofs of your marked preference for another woman that you calmly ask me if you and I still have any *common interests*! Watch out, Vicomte! If I ever once give an answer to that question, I'll not take it back! And the fact that I'm afraid to give an answer here and now may perhaps be too much like giving it already. . . So I positively refuse to discuss the matter further.

What I can do is tell you a story. Maybe you won't have time to read it or pay careful enough attention to understand it properly. It's up to you: at the very worst, I'll only have wasted a story.

A man I know became, like you, entangled with a woman who did him little credit. True, he did have the good sense to feel, sporadically, that sooner or later this affair would damage his reputation; but despite being ashamed of it, he hadn't the guts to break it off. He was all the more embarrassed because he'd boasted to his friends that he felt completely free and he knew full well that the more you deny being a fool, the bigger fool you look. So he spent his life doing stupid things and afterwards saying each time: 'It's not my fault.' This man had a woman friend who for a moment was tempted to publicize his besotted state, thereby branding him as a figure of fun for all time; but being rather more kind-hearted than spiteful, she decided to make one last attempt so that whatever happened she'd be able to say, like her friend, 'it's not my fault'. So without any comment, she sent him the following letter as being something he might find useful to cure his ills.

'We get bored with everything, my angel, it's a law of nature: it's not my fault.

'So now if I'm bored by an affair which has completely absorbed me for four solid months, it's not my fault.

'If, for instance, the extent of my love has exactly matched the extent of your virtue—and that's certainly saying a great deal—it's not surprising that they have both run out at the same time. It's not my fault.

'The result is that I've been deceiving you for some time now; but in fact it was your dogged devotion which somehow forced me to! It's not my fault.

'And now a woman whom I desperately love is insisting that I give you up. It's not my fault.

'I'm well aware that this gives you an excellent opportunity to cry foul; but if Nature granted men only constancy while endowing women with stubbornness, it's not my fault.

'Take my advice, do like me and get yourself another lover. This is good advice, in fact, it's very good advice: if you don't like it, it's not my fault.

'Farewell, my angel. I've enjoyed having you and I've no regrets at leaving you. I may come back to you. That's the way of the world. It's not my fault.'*

It's not the time or the place to tell you the effect and the upshot of this last attempt; but I promise to let you know in my next letter, in which you'll also find my *ultimatum* for the renewal of the pact which you're proposing. So for now, it's just goodbye.

By the way, thanks for the details on the Volanges girl: it's a nice little article to be kept in reserve for the Gossips' Gazette the day after the wedding. Meanwhile, my sincere condolences on the loss of your progeny . . . Goodnight, Vicomte.

142

The Vicomte de Valmont to the Marquise de Merteuil
Paris, 27 November 17—

Well now, dear lady, I don't know if I misread or misunderstood your letter as well as the story with its little illustrative note. But I can tell you that the latter seemed to me highly original and likely to be effective. So I quite simply copied it out and equally simply sent it off to the divine judge's wife. I didn't waste a second: the tender epistle went off yesterday evening. I preferred to do that, first, because I'd promised to send her a letter yesterday anyway and, secondly, because I thought that she would need a whole night to collect her thoughts and ponder over *this grand occasion*—I realize I risk being told off again for repeating this expression.

I was hoping to send you my beloved's reply this morning but it's nearly twelve and I've not yet received anything. I'll wait until three and if by then I've still not heard anything I'll go and find out for myself because, particularly in such matters of common courtesy, the first step is the hardest.

And now as you may well imagine, I'm all agog to hear the end of the story of that man whom you know who was so violently suspected of being incapable, when it came to the point, of giving up a woman. Didn't he mend his ways? And wasn't his friend generous enough to pardon him? I'm equally keen to hear your ultimatum, as you put it so diplomatically! I'm particularly anxious to know whether, in this last action, you'll still discern traces of love. Of course there certainly are—lots and lots of them! But love for whom? However, I'm not trying to stake any claims, I'm merely relying on your good nature.

Goodbye, charming lady. I'll wait until two before sealing this letter, in the hope of being able to enclose the desired reply.

2 p.m.

Still nothing: I'm very pressed for time and can only add a short word. But this time, will you still reject love's fondest kisses? . . .

143

Madame de Tourvel to Madame de Rosemonde
Paris, 27 November 17—

My fool's paradise has been shattered and the fateful truth revealed, which leaves me only shame and remorse on a path leading to a quick and certain death. And if my sufferings can cut short my life I shall bless them. I am sending you a letter which I received yesterday; I need add no comment, it speaks for itself; the time for complaining is over, all that remains for me is to suffer! I don't need pity, I need strength.

This is my last, my farewell letter to you, Madame de Rosemonde, and I beg you with all my soul to forget me completely, to count me no more in the land of the living. There is an ultimate stage of misfortune when even friends are incapable of healing our pain and can only make it more excruciating. When someone is fatally wounded, it is cruel to offer help. I can feel nothing but despair, I am fit only to bury my head in the bottomless pit of night. If I can still find tears to shed, it will be over my errors; but ever since yesterday I have shed not one single tear: the mainsprings of my heart are dried up.

Farewell, Madame. Do not reply to this; I have sworn on this cruel letter of Valmont's never to open another one.

144

The Vicomte de Valmont to the Marquise de Merteuil
Paris, 28 November 17—

Well, fair lady, I lost patience at not hearing anything from the forsaken beauty so yesterday, at five, I appeared at her door only to be told that she was out. I interpreted this as meaning that she was refusing to see me, which neither surprised nor annoyed me.

I took myself off hoping that such an action on my part would perforce lead such a courteous woman to honour me with at least a brief note of reply. Hoping to receive it I went back expressly to my house at nine o'clock but there was nothing. Surprised at this unexpected silence, I sent my man round to make enquiries and to ascertain if the sensitive lady was dead or dying. When I eventually returned home he told me that Madame de Tourvel had indeed left her house with her maid at eleven o'clock that morning; that she had driven to the Convent of —— and that at seven she had sent her carriage and her servants away, stating that she was not to be expected home. She's obviously putting her affairs in order: a convent is the proper haven for a widow and if she persists in such a praiseworthy resolve I shall be able to add to my already considerable indebtedness to her the fame which will accrue from this particular adventure.

As I was indeed telling you quite recently, despite your concern I shall not make any reappearance on the social scene unless I am crowned with fresh laurels. So I'd like to meet those carping critics who were accusing me of feeling a hopeless romantic love and see if they can manage to put an end to an affair more suddenly and brilliantly. No, they'll have to do more than that: they must volunteer to take on the role of comforter, there's nothing standing in their way. So just let them set out on the course which I've succeeded in pursuing all the way to the winning post and if any one of them achieves the slightest success I'll willingly concede them first place. But they will all discover that when I'm prepared to take the trouble, the mark I leave is indelible. Ah, there's no doubt at all that this one will be the same and I would consider all my other triumphs dust and ashes if I were ever to see that woman prefer one of my rivals.

The step she's taken flatters my self-esteem, I admit; but I'm vexed to see that she's had the strength to part from me so decisively. Can there actually be any other obstacles holding us apart than those I've chosen to set up myself? If I wanted to become reconciled with her, would she really not agree? Or rather: not long for it? Not still consider it the supreme happiness? Is that really the way to love? And do you think, fair lady, that I have to put up with that sort of treatment? For instance, why shouldn't I—indeed, wouldn't it be better if I did—try to lead this woman back to the point of foreseeing the possibility of a reconciliation, something people always want as long as hope still remains? And I could set about this without attaching any importance to it and thus without offending you; on the contrary, it would be a joint venture and even if I succeeded, it would only be a way of re-enacting, at your good pleasure, a sacrifice which you seemed to enjoy. And so, dear lady, all that remains is for me to receive my reward and all that I now long for is your return. So do come back soon and rediscover your lover, your pleasures, your friends, and the latest goings-on . . .

That business with the Volanges girl has turned out quite splendidly. Yesterday I was fidgety and uneasy and in the course of my wanderings I even called on Madame de Volanges. I found your ward already down in the drawing-room, still dressed as an invalid but fully convalescent and looking all the fresher and more interesting. In similar cases you women would have spent a month stretched out on your *chaises-longues*: thank God for little girls! This particular one really did make me keen to find out if she's completely cured!

In addition I have to inform you that the little girl's mishap nearly drove your soppy young Danceny out of his mind. First, it was with grief; now it's with joy. *His Cécile* was ill! You can imagine how the head reels at such a calamity! He was making enquiries three times a day and insisted on calling in person at least once. In the end, he despatched a splendid missive to *Mummy* to ask leave to call and congratulate her on the recovery of the object of such deep affection; Madame de Volanges gave permission, so I found the young man enjoying the same status as previously, minus a few liberties which he didn't yet dare to take.

I learned all these details from the young fellow himself as we left together and I got him chatting. You've no idea of the effect that visit had had on him: a joy, a fervour, an ecstasy impossible to describe. With my weakness for violent emotions, I succeeded in whipping him up into a frenzy by promising him that in a very few days' time I'd put him in even more intimate contact with his beloved.

I have in fact decided to hand her back to him as soon as I've concluded my research. I intend to devote myself entirely to you; after all, would it have been worth all the trouble for your ward to have been my pupil as well if she was going to deceive no one but her husband? The masterstroke is deceiving your lover and in particular, your first lover, for as far as I'm concerned, my conscience is clear: I never once mentioned to her the word love.

Farewell, dear lady: do come back very soon to enjoy your absolute power over me, to receive my most sincere respects and to let me have my reward.

145

The Marquise de Merteuil to the Vicomte de Valmont
From the Château de —— , 29 November 17—

Seriously, Vicomte, have you really left the judge's wife? You sent the letter I wrote for you to send? You really are charming and you've exceeded all my expectations. I frankly admit that I find this victory of mine more flattering than any of my previous ones. You must be thinking that I may be rating that woman, whom I used to have rather a poor opinion of, far too highly? That's not the case; the point is that it's not her that I've got the better of, it's you: that's what makes it such tremendous fun. Delicious!

You know, you did love Madame de Tourvel a great deal, Vicomte; you're still in love with her, even; in fact, you're madly in love with her but because I thought it amusing to make you ashamed of your love you heroically gave her up. You would have given up a thousand women like her rather than be teased. Ah, to what lengths does vanity lead us! It was a wise man who described it as the enemy of happiness.

Where would you be now if I'd just been trying to play a trick on you? But as you well know, I'm incapable of deception; and even if you were to reduce me in my turn to despair—and to a convent—I'll take the risk and submit to my conqueror.

Yet if I do capitulate, it's really sheer weakness on my part because what mischief I could still think up if I wanted! And perhaps you'd deserve it? For instance, I'm amazed at your subtlety—or clumsiness—when you calmly suggest that I let you take up with your judge's wife again. That would suit you down to the ground, wouldn't it, to claim the credit for discarding her without having to forfeit the enjoyment she provided? And since in that case this sacrifice wouldn't be any sacrifice at all, you offer to repeat the performance whenever I like! Under this convenient arrangement, this divine and pious lady would still be able to think that she was the sole queen of your heart whereas I could feel proud of being the favoured rival; we'd both be wrong but you'd be happy and what else matters?

What a pity that with such a gift for planning, you carry out your plans so inefficiently that, with one single rash act, you have, of your own accord, placed an insurmountable obstacle between yourself and what you most desire.

So when you wrote that letter, you still imagined that there was some possibility of a reconciliation! You must have thought that this time it was I who was being terribly clumsy! But when one woman stabs another to the heart, Vicomte, she rarely misses the vital spot and the wound can never be healed. When I was stabbing that woman, or rather, guiding your hand, I didn't forget that she was my rival and for a time you'd preferred her to me, in fact, had ranked me below her. If I've bungled my revenge, I'm willing to pay the penalty: so, Vicomte, I'm happy for you to try your hardest, I even challenge you to try, and I promise not to be annoyed when you succeed—if you do succeed. My mind is so completely at rest on this score that I've no desire to go on talking about it. Let's change the subject.

For example, let's talk about the Volanges girl's health. You'll be letting me have definite news on my return, won't you? I'll be very glad to hear it. After that, it'll be up to you to decide whether it suits you better to hand the little one back to her lover or to have a second shot at founding a new branch of the Valmonts under the name of Gercourt. That idea seemed quite fun to me and although I shall leave the choice to you, I'd still ask you not to take a final decision without having discussed it with me. It won't mean too great a delay since I shall be in Paris almost immediately. I can't say for certain the exact day but you can be sure that as soon as I'm back, you'll be the first to be told.

Goodbye, Vicomte; in spite of my quibbles and teasing and telling you off, I'm still very, very fond of you and I'm getting ready to prove it. Till we meet, dear man.

146

The Marquise de Merteuil to the Chevalier Danceny
From the Château de ——, 29 November 17—

I'm on my way at last, dear boy, and I'll be back in Paris tomorrow evening. With all the fuss of moving, I shan't be at home to anyone but if you have some special secret to confide in me urgently, I've no objection to making an exception for you. But as you'll be the only exception, I ask you not to let anyone else know that I'm returning. Even Valmont won't be told.

If anybody had said to me a little while ago that I would have such unique trust in you, I should never have believed it. But your trust has inspired mine; I'm inclined to think that you've been rather artful and perhaps even been trying to lead me astray... That would be very naughty of you, to say the least! Anyway, at the moment there's no danger; you've really got so much else to do! When the heroine's on centre stage, the confidante doesn't get much of a look-in...

And you haven't even found the time to tell me about your latest exploits. All the time *your Cécile* wasn't there, you spent all day and every day bemoaning your fate; if I hadn't been there to listen to your lamentations, you'd have been left talking to the echoes... And later on, when she was ill, you still honoured me with your tale of woes, you needed a sympathetic ear. But now she's recovered and back in Paris and particularly now you can see her occasionally, she fills your whole life and you've no longer any time for your friends. Don't think I'm blaming you; your only trouble is that you're twenty years old. Don't we know that, from Alcibiades onwards—and including you—young men are only interested in friendship when they're miserable? When they're happy, they may sometimes become indiscreet but never confiding. I can well say like Socrates: *I like my friends to turn to me when they're unhappy;** but he was a philosopher and could perfectly well do without them when they didn't come. However, I'm not quite so wise as he and being the weak woman that I am, I've felt your silence deeply.

But you mustn't think I'm a demanding woman: far from it? The same feeling which makes me realize that I'm being left out enables me to bear it undaunted when it's the result or proof of the happiness of my friends. So I shan't count on seeing you tomorrow evening unless your love leaves you free and unoccupied, and I positively forbid you to make the slightest sacrifice for my sake.

Goodbye, Chevalier. I'm looking forward to seeing you again so much. Will you be coming?

147

Madame de Volanges to the Marquise de Rosemonde
Paris, 29 November 17—

You will surely be as distressed as I am, dear friend, to learn of Madame de Tourvel's condition: she fell ill yesterday with such suddenness and displaying such disquieting symptoms that I am really alarmed.

The only outward signs are a high temperature, violent and almost continuous delirium, and an unquenchable thirst. The doctors say that they cannot as yet offer any prognosis and that any cure will be made all the more difficult as the patient stubbornly refuses treatment, so that force had to be used to bleed her; and it was even required twice more, to replace her bandage which she keeps continually trying to tear off in her delirium.

We both know how very gentle and timid she was, and not very strong; can you imagine, it took four people, with some difficulty, to restrain her and when anyone tries to explain something to her, she falls into a raging fury impossible to describe. For my part, I fear that she is not just delirious but actually mentally unhinged.

My fears on this score have been strengthened by something which happened the day before yesterday.

This was the day she arrived at the Convent of —— about eleven o'clock in the morning. As she had been brought up there and since that time had been in the habit of staying there sometimes, she was welcomed as usual and everyone thought she looked calm and well. About two hours later she enquired if the room which she used to occupy as a girl was free and when told that it was, asked to go and have a look at it. The Prioress took her there, with a few other nuns. It was then that she announced her intention of coming back and staying there, adding that she should never have left it and that she would depart only *when she died*; that was the expression she used.

At first they hardly knew what to say but once they had recovered from their amazement, it was pointed out to her that as a married woman she could not be accommodated there without a special dispensation. But neither this nor countless other reasons had any effect; from that moment onwards she stubbornly refused to leave, not just the convent but her room. Finally, tired of arguing, at seven o'clock they agreed to let her stay the night. Her carriage and servants were sent home and any decision was left until the following day.

Everybody then went away except her maid who fortunately was going to have to sleep in the same room since no other accommodation was available.

According to this girl's account, until eleven o'clock her mistress was relatively calm; but before undressing completely, she started pacing excitedly up and down in her room, waving her arms. Julie had been present at the day's events and did not dare to make any comment, merely waiting in silence for nearly an hour. In the end, Madame de Tourvel called out to her twice in quick succession and she barely had time to rush to her aid before her mistress collapsed into her arms saying: 'I can't go on!' She allowed herself to be put to bed but refused to take anything or to let any help be fetched. She merely asked for some water to be placed by her bedside and told Julie to go to bed herself.

The girl states that she remained awake until two o'clock in the morning and that during that time heard no movement or moaning. But she says that at five o'clock she was woken by hearing her mistress speaking in a loud, strident voice and that after asking her if she needed anything and receiving no reply, she picked up a light and went over to her bed. Madame de Tourvel failed to recognize her but suddenly interrupted her incoherent ravings and cried out: 'I want to be left alone, alone in the darkness, that's where I belong.' I myself noticed yesterday that she often uses that phrase.

In the end Julie, taking advantage of what seemed a sort of order, left the room and fetched help; but Madame de Tourvel flew into a fury of rage and refused any assistance; and she has continued to fall into similar states of delirium frequently ever since.

In view of the highly embarrassing situation created in the whole convent, at seven o'clock yesterday morning the Prioress decided to send for me. It was not yet daylight. I hurried round at once. When they told Madame de Tourvel that I was there, she seemed to come to herself and replied: 'Yes, let her come in.' But when I reached her bedside, she stared at me, took my hand, squeezed it, and said in a strong but sombre voice: 'I am dying because I failed to believe you.' Immediately after that, she covered her eyes and went back to her usual phrases: 'I want to be alone, etc. etc.' and her mind started wandering again completely.

Her remark and a few others which she blurted out in her delirium make me fear that this cruel illness may have an even crueller cause. But we must respect our friend's secrets and be content to pity her misfortune.

During the whole of yesterday she remained in a similar state of wild confusion with appalling fits of delirium alternating with moments of sheer prostration—the only time when she takes any rest and allows others to relax. I stayed by her bedside until nine o'clock that night and I shall go back to spend the whole day with her. I certainly do not intend to desert my unfortunate friend but her obstinate refusal to accept any help or treatment is most distressing.

I'm sending you last night's report on her which I've just received: as you see, it's anything but reassuring. I'll make sure that you receive all of them from now on.

Goodbye, dear, kind friend, I'm going back to the invalid. My daughter, who is fortunately almost completely recovered, sends you her kindest regards.

148

The Chevalier Danceny to the Marquise de Merteuil
Paris, 1 December 17—

Oh, how I do so love you! No, I do so positively *adore* you! You have taught me the meaning of true happiness! My cup of bliss is overflowing! You are so sensitive, so loving! A friend and a lover in one! Yet why does the memory of your distress have to cast a cloud over the charm I feel? Ah, Madame, set your mind at rest, I beg you as your friend! Dear friend, be happy! Your lover entreats you!

Tell me, what reason can there be to blame yourself? Believe me, your scruples are mistaken; they are causing you misgivings and accusing me of wrongs which are all equally imaginary. I feel in my heart that it was love alone which seduced us both. So forget your fear of surrendering to the feelings you inspire, surrender to the burning passion which you have aroused. Are our hearts really any less pure because they took so long to be stirred? Certainly not! On the contrary, it is the seducer who plots everything in advance and works out his campaign, looking ahead to anticipate events.* But true love doesn't accept that sort of calculation and premeditation; feelings of love are too powerful to give us time to think and its power is never greater than when it works underground, in silence, unrecognized, binding us in shackles which are as impossible to foresee as they are to break.

So even yesterday, excited though I was by the thought of your return and in spite of the prodigious pleasure I felt at the prospect of seeing you, I still thought that I was being moved and spurred on by a peaceful feeling of friendship; or, to put it differently, being entirely involved in the gentle feelings of my heart, I was paying little attention to analysing their cause or origin. So like me, dear, loving friend, you did not realize the power of that soft, tender charm which was carrying our hearts away;

we only recognized it as love once we had recovered from the blissful ecstasy into which this divine passion had plunged us.

But that doesn't condemn us, in fact it vindicates us. No, you haven't been any more untrue to friendship than I have been guilty of abusing your trust. It's true we were both unaware of our real feelings but it was merely a delusion and one which we were not deliberately trying to create. Ah, far from complaining, let us remember only the happiness that those feelings have brought us; and instead of spoiling them by unfairly blaming ourselves, let us strive to make them even more charming by our trust and faith in our love. O dearest friend, how my heart treasures that hope! From now on, having finally banished all fear and with only love in our hearts, you will share my raptures, my desires, the wild intoxication of my senses, the elation of my soul, and every blissful moment of our days will be marked by new delights.

Farewell, my adorable beloved! I shall see you this evening! But will you be alone? I hardly dare to hope . . . Ah, you do not long for it as keenly as I do!

149
Madame de Volanges to Madame de Rosemonde
Paris, 2 December 17—

For most of yesterday, dear friend, I had hopes of being in a position to let you have better news of the health of our dear invalid; however, yesterday evening those hopes were dashed and I am left only with the regret that they have vanished. An apparently trivial event but with the direst consequences has caused her to relapse into a state at least as bad as before and perhaps even worse.

I should have been completely at a loss to understand this sudden deterioration if our unhappy friend had not opened her heart completely to me yesterday. As she also gave me to understand that you were equally aware of her misfortunes, I need conceal nothing as to her sad situation.

When I arrived at the convent yesterday morning, they told me that the invalid had been asleep for more than three hours

and indeed sleeping so deeply and peacefully that for a moment
I was afraid that she was in a coma. A short while later she woke
up and opened her bed-curtains herself. She gave us all a surprised look and as I stood up to go towards her, she greeted me
by name and invited me to come nearer. She gave me no time to
ask any questions but enquired where she was, what we were
doing there, if she were ill, and why she was not in her own
home. At first I thought her mind was wandering again, even if
rather less wildly; but I saw that she understood my reply perfectly well. In fact, she had recovered her senses but not her
memory.

She questioned me closely as to everything that had happened
to her since her arrival at the convent. I replied frankly, leaving
out only anything likely to disturb her; and when in my turn I
asked her how she felt, she replied that she was not in any pain
at that moment but that she had been suffering a great deal
during her sleep and that she felt tired. I urged her to rest and
not to talk too much. Then I drew her curtains, leaving them
half-open, and sat down beside her bed. The nuns offered her a
bowl of broth which she accepted and enjoyed.

She remained like this for half an hour during which time her
only words were to thank me for my concern and care, expressing her thanks in her usual friendly and gracious manner with
which you are familiar. Then for a while she remained quite
silent and then said: 'Ah, yes, now I remember coming here'; and
a moment later she exclaimed in an agonized voice: 'O dear
friend, dear, dear friend, pity me! I can feel all my sorrow returning . . .' And as I went towards her, she grasped my hand and
resting her head against it, she cried out: 'O dear God, can I not
be allowed to die?' Even more than her words, the look on her
face moved me to tears. My voice betrayed my emotion and she
said to me: 'You're pitying me . . . Ah, if you only knew . . .'
Then she broke off and said: 'Send the others away and I shall
tell you everything.'

I think I have already hinted that I had some suspicion of the
secrets she was about to confide, and fearing that our conversation, which I foresaw would be long and painful, might perhaps be detrimental to her health, I at first refused, on the
pretext that she needed rest. But she insisted and I yielded to her
pleading. As soon as we were alone, our unhappy friend told me

everything which you have already heard from her and which I therefore do not need to repeat.

Finally, as she was telling me of the cruel way in which she had been deserted, she added: 'I was so certain that I would die and I felt that I had the courage to do so; it will be impossible for me to survive my shame and my misfortune.' I tried to help her combat her dejection or rather her despair by recourse to the comforts of religion, which till now had had such power over her but I quickly realized that I lacked competence for such an exalted mission and confined myself to the suggestion of calling in Father Anselme in whom I knew she had every confidence. She concurred and seemed even to be eager for this to happen. They sent for him and he came at once. He stayed with the invalid a long time and as he was leaving he said that, if the doctors were of his opinion, he thought he could delay administering the sacraments. He will call again tomorrow.

This was at about three o'clock and our dear friend remained relatively calm until five, so that all our hopes started to revive. Unfortunately at that moment a letter arrived for her. When they tried to give it to her, she said that she did not want to receive any letters. They did not insist. But after that, she seemed more agitated. A short while later, she asked where the letter had come from. It wasn't stamped. Who had brought it? Nobody knew. On whose behalf had it been handed in? The sisters at the gate hadn't been told. She fell silent for a while and then began to talk again but so incoherently that all it told us was that she had once again become delirious.

However, this was followed by another period of calm until finally she asked to see the letter which had come for her. As soon as she set eyes on it, she cried out: 'It's from him! Dear God!' and then in a loud voice she gasped: 'Take it away! Take it away!' She immediately made us close the curtains of her bed and forbade anyone to come near her; but almost at once we were in fact forced to go back to her as her delirium started again more violently than ever, made even worse by truly terrifying convulsions. She continued to be so afflicted for the whole of that evening and the doctor's report this morning informs me that this frenzied state lasted all night. In fact, her condition is so serious that I am surprised that she has not already succumbed. I cannot conceal my fear that I see very little hope of recovery.

I presume that this unfortunate letter came from Valmont but what can he still have the audacity to say to her? Forgive me, dear friend, I shall forbear to make any comment: but how cruel it is to watch a woman hitherto so happy, so deservedly happy, now doomed to such an unhappy fate.

150

The Chevalier Danceny to the Marquise de Merteuil
Paris, 3 December 17—

Waiting with joy in my heart to see you once again, my lovely, lovely lady, I shall indulge in the pleasure of writing to you and by thinking of you, try to beguile my regrets at not yet being with you . . . It is truly a heartfelt joy to tell you yet again of my feelings for you and to recall those you have for me; and even now, when I am deprived of your company, this joy is still a cornucopia of love's treasures . . . However, if I am to believe you, I shall not receive any reply from you and this letter will even be my last. We shall have to refrain from a form of communication which, so you say, is so dangerous and *which we do not need*. If you insist, I shall of course comply because what can you want that, by the same token, I do not also want? But before you finally make up your mind, won't you give permission for us first of all to have a tiny chat about it?

On the question of danger, you must be the sole judge: I cannot form any opinion and can only beg you to take care of your own safety since I can never be at ease if you are uneasy. In this matter it is not that we think as one but that you think for both of us.

It is not quite the same thing where the *question of need* arises; here, we can only think as one and if our opinions differ it can only be because we have failed to understand or explain ourselves properly. So here is what I think I feel.

Naturally, there seems hardly any need for letters when we can meet freely. What would we write that couldn't be expressed a thousand times better with a word, a glance, or even by silence?

That seems to me so true that when you mentioned to me not writing to each other, the thought simply brushed the surface of my soul, worrying it perhaps but not making any real impact, rather as when my lips try to place a kiss on your heart and encounter a ribbon or a piece of muslin, which I merely push to one side and have no impression of having met an obstacle.

But since that time, we have been separated and as soon as you were no longer there, the thought of this letter returned to plague me. I asked myself: why this additional frustration? Have we really nothing further to say to each other merely because we are parted? Supposing for instance we had the good fortune to spend a whole day together: shall we spend any of that time talking rather than in the ecstasy of love? Yes, beloved, an ecstasy because when I am with you, even moments of calm are ecstatic. And ultimately, however much time there is, we have to part and then how lonely one feels! It is then that a letter is so precious! If one doesn't read it, at least one can look at it . . . Oh, surely one can look at a letter without reading it, in the same way as it seems to me that even at night I should still take pleasure in touching your portrait . . .

Did I say your portrait? But a letter is the portrait of the soul. Unlike a cold image, it hasn't that stagnancy so far removed from love: it lends itself to all our emotions; it can move from excitement to ecstasy and then to calm. Your feelings are so precious to me! Will you deprive me of a means of hoarding them?

And are you really so sure that you will never be tormented by an urge to write to me? If in your loneliness your heart swells or sinks, if a movement of joy penetrates to your very soul, if it is distressed by a moment of involuntary sadness, won't you pour out your happiness or your sorrow into the bosom of your friend? Are you then capable of feeling some emotion that he ought not to share? Will you let him wander, a lost and lonely dreamer, far away from his beloved? O my friend . . . my dear love! But it is for you to say, I've merely tried to express a point of view, not to coax you . . . I've only reasoned with you and I am foolhardy enough to hope that my case would have been stronger had I pleaded with you . . . So if you persist, I shall make an effort not to be too sad, I shall try to tell myself the things that you would have written to me . . . But that's the trouble: you would have expressed it better than I can and above all, it would have given me greater pleasure to hear you say it.

Farewell, my charmer, my beloved. The time is fast approaching when I shall at last be meeting you again: I shall break off very quickly now to make it all the sooner . . .

151

The Vicomte de Valmont to the Marquise de Merteuil
Paris, the evening of 3 December 17—

You surely can't think, Marquise, that I have so little worldly wisdom as to be taken in by the *amazing coincidence* which resulted in my finding Danceny alone with you in your house tonight! Not that your long training failed to produce an admirable expression of imperturbable composure nor that you betrayed yourself by any of those words which sometimes slip out when people are flustered or guilty. I will even admit that your meek glances produced a prodigious effect and if they had been as convincing as they were understandable, far from feeling or remaining in the least suspicious, I should have had no doubts whatsoever as to the extreme distress occasioned by that *tiresome interruption*. But to avoid wasting your remarkable histrionic talents and achieve the success you were anticipating—in a word, to produce the illusion you were attempting to create—you really should have subjected your apprentice to a more thorough preparation.

Since you are embarking on an educational career, you really must teach your pupils not to go red in the face and become confused at the slightest teasing, to be less eager to deny in the case of one particular woman the very same things they show far less enthusiasm in repudiating for all the others. Furthermore, do teach them to be able to hear their mistress being praised without feeling obliged to join in too warmly; and if you let them look at you in the presence of other people, they should at least be able to conceal that possessive look which gives the game away so transparently and which they are too clumsy to distinguish from a look of love. Then will be the time to allow them to appear with you in the course of your social commitments without any danger of their behaviour bringing discredit to their teacher's reputation . . . And since I'm only too ready to contribute to your prestige, I promise to draw up and publicize on your behalf the curriculum of this new school for lovers.

But until such time, I confess to being amazed that you tried to take me for a schoolboy. Ah, how quickly I should have retaliated against any other woman but you! And how I'd have enjoyed doing it! And how much more enjoyable it would have been than any pleasure she might have imagined she would be depriving me of! Yes indeed, it's only because it's you that I feel I'd prefer amends to revenge; and please don't imagine that I'm being held back by the slightest doubt, even a shadow of uncertainty. I know everything.

You've been in Paris four days and you've been seeing Danceny—and only Danceny—every day. Even today, your door was still barred to everyone. Your major-domo failed to prevent me from gaining access to you only because he lacks your effrontery. Yet I was certain, you assured me, to be the first to be informed of your arrival—the exact date of which you couldn't say, though you were writing to me on the eve of your departure. Are you going to deny these facts or try to explain them away? You cannot possibly do either of those things: yet I'm still restraining myself! See the power you have over me; but take it from me, be satisfied at having put it to the test and don't abuse it in future. We know all about each other, Marquise; that thought should be enough.

Tomorrow, you tell me, you'll be out all day? That's fine—if you actually are going out; and rest assured, I shall find out. But in any case, you'll be home that evening and since our reconciliation will be a tricky one, we shall certainly need every available minute until next morning. So let me know whether we shall be performing our numerous acts of expiation at your house or at your *little place*. Above all, no more Danceny. In your wrongheadedness you've become obsessed with him and my jealousy doesn't prevent me from overlooking this temporary imaginative lapse; but please reflect that from now on, something that was just a passing fancy would have turned into a distinct preference. And I don't think I'm the sort of man to accept such a humiliation . . . and I'm not expecting to receive it at your hands.

I even have the hope that in this particular case you won't feel that you're making any sacrifice. And even if it is something of a wrench, it seems to me that I've set you rather a fine example: a woman as beautiful as she is sensitive, who lived only for me and perhaps even at this very moment is dying from love and regret, is surely as good as a young schoolboy who, I grant you, may be witty and not bad-looking but who still lacks sophistication and substance.

Goodbye, Marquise. I shan't say anything about my feelings towards you. The only thing I can do at the moment is to avoid peering too closely into my heart. I shall look forward to your reply. When making it, consider carefully, and above all don't forget that the easier it is for you still to make me overlook the offence you've given me, the more deeply any refusal on your part, a mere hesitation, would engrave it indelibly in my heart.

152

The Marquise de Merteuil to the Vicomte de Valmont
Paris, 4 December 17—

Do be careful, Vicomte. An extremely timorous woman must not be handled too roughly! How can I possibly bear the dreadful thought of incurring your wrath, and in particular not blanch with fear at your threat of vengeance—the more so since, as you know, were you to play some nasty trick on me, I would have no possible redress? However much I should reveal, your brilliant career would pursue its course unperturbed. What indeed is there for you to fear? Being forced to leave the country, assuming you had the time? But can't you live abroad in exactly the same style as you do here? And all in all, provided the French court left you in peace at the court where you decided to settle, it would only mean that you'd have a new stage for your triumphs. So having made this attempt to restore your peace of mind, I suggest we come back to business.

Do you know why I never remarried, Vicomte? Certainly not for lack of attractive offers; it was purely so that no one should have the right to criticize my actions. It wasn't even because I was afraid of not being able to continue behaving as I liked, because ultimately I should certainly have managed to do that; but it would have irked me for anybody even to have the right to complain of my behaviour; and finally because if I was going to deceive anyone, I preferred to do it for my own good pleasure and not because I had to. And yet there you are, writing me the most husband-like letter possible! You keep talking all the time of my wrongdoing and your forgiveness! But I can't see at all how anybody can fail in their duty to someone to whom they have no obligation . . .

Let's examine the matter: why all this fuss? You found Danceny at my place and you didn't like it? Fine! But what conclusions could you draw from that? Either that, as I said, it was coincidence or else it was deliberate, as I didn't say. In the first case, your letter is unfair; in the second case, it's ridiculous. What was the point of writing? But you're jealous and jealous people are incapable of reasoning properly. Very well: I'll do the reasoning for you.

Either you've got a rival or you haven't. If you do have one, you need to make yourself agreeable; if you haven't got one, you still need to be agreeable, to avoid acquiring one. So in either case, you've got to behave in the same way; then why plague yourself? And in particular, why plague me? Have you lost the art of being the most amiable of men? Have you lost confidence in your all-conquering ways? Come now, Vicomte, you're being less than fair to yourself! But it's not that: the truth is that in your eyes I'm not worth all that trouble on your part. You're less interested in gaining my favours than in exercising your power. You're an ungrateful man . . . But that remark comes, I think, from the heart and if I continue much longer, this letter might become very loving and you don't deserve that.

Nor do you deserve to expect me to justify myself. To punish you for your suspicions, I shall leave you to live with them: I shan't tell you anything at all either about the date of my return or about Danceny's visits. You took an immense amount of trouble to find out everything about them, didn't you? Well, where did it get you? I hope it gave you great pleasure; it didn't spoil mine in the least.

All that I can say in reply to your threatening letter is that it succeeded neither in pleasing nor in intimidating me and at the moment I couldn't feel less inclined to grant your request.

In fact, to take you back in your present frame of mind would really be tantamount to being unfaithful to you. It wouldn't mean taking up again with my old lover, it would be like taking a new one and one who's by no means as good as the earlier one. And I haven't forgotten the old one yet enough to make that mistake. The Valmont I loved was charming; I'm even ready to admit that I've never met a more agreeable man. Oh, Vicomte, if you can find that Valmont again, do bring him along to me: he'll always be most welcome.

But you must warn him that in no circumstances would it be for today or tomorrow. His Menaechmus* has rather spoilt his chances and if I were to make too hasty a decision I'd be afraid of mistaking one for the other. Or maybe I've promised to spend the next two days with Danceny? And your letter taught me that for you, breaking one's word is no joking matter. So you'll have to wait.

But what does waiting matter for you? You'll certainly still be getting your own back on your rival. And he won't treat your mistress any worse than you'll treat his! And after all, isn't one woman just as good as any other? Those are your principles. Even one who was *loving and sensitive*, who would finally *die of love and regret*, would still be sacrificed to any passing fancy, to the fear of being teased a little. And then you expect us to put ourselves out for you? Tut, tut, that's not fair.

Goodbye, Vicomte. Do try and recover your amiability... Look, I ask nothing better than to find you charming and as soon as I'm convinced, I promise to prove it. I really am so kind-hearted.

153

The Vicomte de Valmont to the Marquise de Merteuil
Paris, 4 December 17—

I'm answering your letter straight away and I'll endeavour to make myself clear, which in your case isn't easy once you've taken it into your head not to listen.

It was hardly necessary to indulge in long explanations to establish that since we both have the means to ruin each other, we have an equal interest in not provoking each other; consequently, that is beside the point. But between the drastic option of ruining each other and the doubtless better option of remaining united as we used to be and becoming even more closely united by resuming our earlier relationship, between these two options, I am saying that there are countless others. So it was in no way ridiculous for me to tell you nor is it ridiculous to repeat that, as of today, I shall be your lover or your enemy.

I realize perfectly well how embarrassed you are at having to make this choice, that you'd prefer to dilly-dally, and I'm aware that you've never enjoyed being faced by the necessity of saying yes or no. But you must realize, too, that I cannot allow you to escape from this dilemma without running the risk of being fooled; and you must already have understood that that's something I wouldn't tolerate. It's for you to decide; I'm prepared to leave the choice to you but I'm not prepared to be left in any uncertainty.

I merely warn you that you won't sidetrack me with your arguments, be they good or bad; nor will you fob me off with any endearments you might employ to dress up your refusal. In a word, we've reached the moment of truth. And I'm more than happy to set the example: I am pleased to inform you that I prefer peace and alliance; but if they are both to be shattered, I think that I have the means and the right to do so.

Let me just add that the slightest prevarication on your part will be regarded by me as an outright declaration of war. So you see I want a straight answer; it doesn't need to be long nor elaborately phrased; a couple of words will do.

The Marquise de Merteuil's reply written
at the foot of this letter:

Very well: it's war!*

154

Madame de Volanges to Madame de Rosemonde
Paris, 5 December 17—

These medical reports will give you a better idea of our invalid's deplorable state of health than I can. Being constantly in attendance on her, I can only afford to break off to write when there are other events to relate than her illness. Here is one which I certainly never expected. It is a letter to me from Valmont who has chosen to make me his confidante and even to ask me to act as his go-between with Madame de Tourvel, for whom he also enclosed a letter. I have sent this letter back, together with my answer to him. I'm passing this letter on to you and I imagine that you will share my view that I neither could nor should have done anything he asked me to do. Even had I been prepared to do so, our unhappy friend would have been in no state to listen to me. She is permanently delirious. But what do you think of this 'despair' of Valmont's? And first of all, is he to be believed or is he merely trying to mislead everyone to the bitter end?* If for once he is being sincere, he can certainly say that he brought his misfortune down on his own head. I suspect he'll not take kindly to my reply but I confess that the more I learn of the details of this unhappy affair, the greater my indignation against the man responsible.

Now I shall go back to my sad task as nurse which is becoming all the sadder as I can see little hope of a successful outcome. Goodbye, dear friend: I do not need to tell you again of my feelings for you.

155

The Vicomte de Valmont to the Chevalier Danceny
Paris, 5 December 17—

My dear Chevalier, I've twice called on you but ever since you have abandoned your role of swain for that of philanderer you have been, quite rightly, impossible to find. However, your valet assures me that you will be returning home this evening and that you have instructed him to expect you. Knowing your plans, I realized perfectly well that you would be staying only long enough to dress for your part before gallivanting off on your victorious adventures without delay. Well done! I can only applaud you! But tonight, perhaps, you may be tempted to alter your venue: you only know half of your options and I must acquaint you with the other half, when it will be up to you to make up your mind. So please spare a moment to read this letter, Chevalier. It won't be diverting you from your pleasures; on the contrary, its sole purpose is to provide you with a choice.

If I had been completely in your confidence and you had told me about that part of your secret life which I could only guess at, I should have known in good time, been less clumsy in my well-meaning efforts to help you, and not be interfering in your plans now. But let's start from where we stand at the moment. Whatever you may decide, even your second-best choice would make someone happy.

You've got a rendezvous with a woman tonight, haven't you? And a delightful woman, too, whom you adore? At your age what woman do we not adore, at least for the first week! The scene of the encounter must also enhance your pleasure: a ravishing *little house, taken especially for you*, will add the charms of mystery to the exquisite delights of love, no holds barred. It's all laid on, you're expected and you're raring to go! This is something we both know although you omitted to say anything about it to me. But now here's something you don't know and which I have to tell you.

Ever since I came back I've been devoting my time and energy to finding ways and means of bringing you and Mademoiselle de Volanges together, as I had promised, and even when I last spoke to you on this subject I had reason to think from your reaction—I'm tempted to say your rapturous delight—that I was actively promoting your happiness. I was unable to complete this rather difficult task on my own but having prepared the ground, I left the rest to the enthusiasm of your mistress. Her love enabled her to find solutions that my experience had overlooked; and the unfortunate thing for you is that she has succeeded. For the last two days, so she informed me this evening, every obstacle has been removed and your happiness is now entirely in your own hands.

For the last two days also she has been longing and hoping to tell you all this in person and even though her mother is not there, you would have been admitted to the house. But you didn't even call! And since I wish to hide nothing from you, the young lady, rightly or wrongly, seemed to me a trifle put out by your lukewarmness. Anyway, she found a way for me to meet her too and made me promise to let you have the enclosed letter as quickly as possible. From the urgency she displayed, my bet would be that there's some question of a rendezvous for tonight. However that may be, I promised on my honour as a friend that you should receive this loving epistle this very day and I cannot and do not wish to break my word.

And now, young man, what are you going to do? What's your choice between a flirtation and love, pleasure and happiness? If I were talking to Danceny three months or even a week ago, I'd have had no doubt where his heart lay and what he would do; but today Danceny is in such demand by women, flitting from one adventure to the next and, as would be expected, becoming something of a rogue. So will he prefer a timid young girl whose only assets are her innocence, her beauty, and her love to the attractions of a woman of infinite sophistication?

For my part, my dear friend, it seems to me that even according to your new principles, which I admit I rather share, in these circumstances I'd be inclined to opt for the young lover. First, it's another name to add to your list: a brand-new woman. And if you don't cull her now there's the danger of losing the fruit of your efforts, for after all, in her case, it really would be missing a golden opportunity and they don't always turn up twice, particularly when it's a first lapse. In cases like that it often needs only a moment of irritation, a touch of jealous suspicion or even less, to thwart the most brilliant victory. When it's sinking, virtue often clutches at straws and once it's been salvaged, it remains on its guard and is never so easy to take unawares again.*

And in any case, what do you risk from the other side? Not even being shown the door, at worst a tiff which, with a little care and attention, can be patched up, very pleasurably. What other choice is open to a woman when she has already surrendered, except to forgive? What would she gain by turning nasty? She'd forfeit her pleasures and do nothing for her prestige.

If, as I assume, you go for love, which also seems to me the reasonable thing, I think you'd be well advised not to send any apologies in advance for having to miss your rendezvous: simply fail to turn up. If you tempt fate by giving some reason, the party may try to discover whether it's true. Women are nosy and persistent; anything is liable to come out—as you know, I've just provided a good example of that! But if you leave her in hopes, which will be buoyed up by vanity, she will continue to hope until it's far too late for her to find out what has happened and this will give you time until tomorrow to decide what insurmountable obstacle stood in your way: whether you were ill—dead if need be—or anything else which has reduced you to despair. And all will be forgiven!

Incidentally, whichever way you decide, I'll ask you just to let me know and as I'm completely indifferent in the matter, I shall always approve any choice you may make.

Goodbye, dear friend, and good luck.

Let me finally add how badly I miss Madame de Tourvel; the truth is that being parted from her has left me in despair. I would happily give up half my life to be able to dedicate the other half to her. Ah, believe me, love is the only thing that can bring happiness!

156

Cécile Volanges to the Chevalier Danceny
(enclosed with letter 155)
Paris, 4 December 17—

Dear friend, how is it that I've stopped seeing you recently, even though I've never stopped wanting to? Don't you still long to see me as much as I do? Ah, that makes me really sad! Even sadder than when we weren't able to meet at all . . . It used to be other people who made me miserable but now it's you and that hurts me much more.

For the last few days, Mummy has been out all the time, as you know, and I'd been hoping that you would try to take advantage of this opportunity. But you don't even think of me; oh, I'm so miserable! You used to keep on telling me that I was the one who didn't love you as much as you loved me but I knew it was the other way round and I've been proved right. If you had called to see me, you would in fact have been able to because I'm not like you, I think of nothing else but ways for us to come together. You don't deserve for me to tell you all the arrangements I've been making and which have given me a lot of trouble. But I'm too much in love with you and I'm longing to see you so much that I can't help telling you. And then afterwards I'll be able to see whether you really do love me!

I've even managed to get the porter on our side and he's promised that any time you come, he'll let you through as if he hadn't seen you; and we can certainly rely on him because he's a very nice man. So we just need to be careful that you are not seen in the house and that's very easy if you come only at night-time and then there'll be no danger at all. For instance, ever since Mummy's been away all day, she goes to bed at eleven every night. So we'd have lots of time.

The porter told me that any time you might be coming like that not to knock on the door but to tap on his window and then you'll have no difficulty in finding the back stairs. And as you may not have a light I'll leave the door of my bedroom a little bit open and that will help you to find the way at least. Be careful not to make any noise, especially as you go by Mummy's side-door. As for my maid's room, you don't need to worry because she's promised not to wake up; she's very nice, too. And it'll be the same when you leave. So now we'll see if you're going to come.

My goodness, I wonder why my heart is beating so fast while I'm writing to you? Is something dreadful going to happen to me or is it the hope of seeing you that's making me so excited? One thing I do know I'm feeling is that I've never loved you so much and never felt such a longing to tell you that I do. So do come, my love, my dear love, so that I can tell you over and over again how much I love you, that I adore you and shall never love anybody else, ever.

I've managed to let Monsieur de Valmont know that there's something I'd like to tell him and as he's such a nice kind friend he'll certainly come tomorrow and I'll ask him to let you have my letter straight away. So I'll be waiting for you tomorrow night and if you don't want your Cécile to be really and truly miserable, you won't let me down.

Goodbye, my dear. I hug you and love you from the bottom of my heart.

¹57

The Chevalier Danceny to the Vicomte de Valmont
Paris, 5 December 17—

You need have no misgivings, my dear Vicomte, concerning either my heart or my actions. How could I fail to respond to any desire of my Cécile's? Ah, she is indeed the woman, the only woman I love and always shall love! Her simple innocence, her tender devotion have cast a spell that, in my weakness, I may have allowed myself to forget but which will always remain anchored in my heart. When I launched out on another adventure, almost as it were without noticing, even in my moments of greatest pleasure, the thought of Cécile often loomed up to disturb me and perhaps my heart never paid her a more sincere tribute than when I was being unfaithful to her. However, dear friend, we must spare her feelings and never reveal the wrong I've done her, not in order to mislead her but so as not to distress her. I have such a longing to make her happy and I should never forgive myself if she even once had to shed a single tear through any fault of mine.

I realize that I deserve your teasing when you pointed to what you called my principles; but believe me, I'm not letting them govern my conduct at the moment and I've decided to prove it by tomorrow at the latest. I shall call on the lady herself who has caused and participated in my dissolute conduct and I shall accuse myself: 'Look into my heart,' I shall say, 'and you will see there the great affection and friendship I feel for you; and when friendship is combined with desire, it seems so similar to love! We were both deceived. But although I may make mistakes, I'm never insincere.' I know my friend: she is as forgiving as she is straightforward; not only will she forgive me, she will approve of what I've done. She even frequently used to blame herself for having been untrue to the demands of friendship; her scruples often caused her distress in her love. She is wiser than me, she will reinforce those proper fears which I felt in my own heart and which I so unwisely tried to stifle in hers. Through her I shall become a better man and through you, a happier one. O my two good friends, you must share in the gratitude I owe you both!

And the thought of owing my happiness to you makes me value it all the more.

Goodbye, my dear Vicomte. However much I rejoice, I'm not unmindful of your own troubles and I sympathize with them. Oh, why can't I help you! Is Madame de Tourvel as hard-hearted as ever? People are also saying that she is very ill. Heavens, how sorry I am for you! We must hope that as her health improves, so will her compassion and that she will make you happy for ever! I am sending you these wishes as your good friend and I dare hope that love will find a way.

I should like to continue our talk, but time is pressing and my Cécile will be already waiting for me . . .

158

The Vicomte de Valmont to the Marquise de Merteuil
(on waking)
Paris, 6 December 17—

Well, Marquise, how do you feel after last night's revels? A trifle tired, maybe? You must admit that Danceny is a real charmer! He's a phenomenon, that lad! You didn't expect that from him, did you? Look, I must admit defeat: a rival of that calibre certainly deserved to oust me. But speaking seriously, he's got all sorts of good qualities. What constancy! What delicacy! What love! Ah, if he ever comes to love you as much as he loves his Cécile, you'll never need to fear any rivals: he proved that last night. Perhaps some flirt might snatch him from you, momentarily: a young man finds it hard to resist exciting and provocative offers; but don't worry, one single word from the real object of his affections is enough to dispel his illusions, as you can see. So all you need do now is to become such an object and you will be perfectly happy.*

I'm sure there's no chance of your going wrong there; you've got too sure a touch for there to be any fear of that! But our close friendship, as sincere on my part as it is well recognized on yours, induced me to offer you last night's little trial. It sprang from my eagerness to please. And it succeeded; but don't bother to thank me, it's not worth it. It was as easy as falling off a log.

In fact, what effort did it involve? A minimal sacrifice and a little skill. I agreed to share his mistress's favours with the young man, but after all, he had as good a claim on them as I did and I could hardly have cared less! The young woman's letter to him was certainly my handiwork but that was purely to save time because we had better ways of spending it. My covering letter? Well, it was really nothing, nothing much at all: a few friendly tips to put the new lover on the right track. But the truth is that they were hardly necessary; to put it bluntly, he jumped at the chance.

And now this ingenuous young fellow is going to call on you today and tell you all. And what he has to say is sure to please you greatly. He'll be saying: *Look into my heart*—he's already announced that to me himself; and you'll surely understand that this means: all can be forgiven. And I do hope that, while looking into this heart of his to see everything he'd like you to find there, you may perchance also discover that such very young lovers do have their dangers; and also that it's better to have me as a friend than as an enemy.

Goodbye, Marquise. Till our next opportunity...

159

The Marquise de Merteuil to the Vicomte de Valmont
(*a note*)
Paris, 6 December 17—

Shabby behaviour followed by a shabby joke leaves me cold. It's not to my taste and it's not my style. When I have a grudge against someone, I don't try to be funny. I do better: I hit back. No doubt you're frightfully pleased with yourself at the moment; but don't forget it wouldn't be the first time you started celebrating a victory that misfired. Goodbye.

160

Madame de Volanges to Madame de Rosemonde
Paris, 6 December 17—

I am writing to you from our unhappy friend's bedroom; her condition remains more or less stationary. There is to be a consultation between four doctors this afternoon. Unfortunately, as you know, this often betokens danger rather than any hope of a cure.

However, it seems that her head was a trifle clearer last night. The maid informed me this morning that about midnight her mistress called for her, asked to be left alone with her, and then dictated quite a long letter. Julie added that while she was preparing to write the address on the envelope, Madame de Tourvel's mind again started to wander so that the girl didn't know what address to put. At first I felt surprised that the contents did not provide sufficient indication but when she replied that she was afraid of making a mistake but that her mistress had urged her to send the letter off without delay, I took it on myself to open the envelope.

In it were the sheets I am enclosing; they are indeed not addressed to anyone but at the same time addressed to far too many people. I would, however, be inclined to think that our unhappy friend started by wanting to write to Monsieur de Valmont but without realizing it, fell victim to her disordered mind. However that may be, I took the view that this letter should not be delivered to anyone. I am sending it to you because you will be able to see what sorts of ideas were running through the sick woman's head better than I could explain to you. As long as she remains so deeply disturbed, I feel there is little hope. When the mind is so unsettled, the body will find it difficult to recover.

Farewell, my dear, kind friend. You are indeed fortunate to be so far away from this sad spectacle which I have constantly under my eyes.

161

Madame de Tourvel to ———
(dictated to and written down by her maid)
Paris, 5 December 17—

Will you never grow tired of persecuting me, you fiend, you devilish creature? Are you not satisfied at having tormented me, debased me, defiled me? Do you wish to rob me of peace even in the grave? In this dark underground world into which I have been driven so ignominiously, is there not a ray of hope? Is my torment never to end? I am not begging for forgiveness, I do not deserve it, I am asking only for my sufferings not to go beyond my endurance. I shall suffer in silence, without complaint, but do not make my sufferings too great to bear. You can leave me with my pain but help me to forget the precious joys I have lost. Now you have torn them away from me, why continue to torment me by conjuring them up in my mind? I was innocent, at peace with the world; it was meeting you which destroyed me; through listening to you I have become a criminal. You made me do wrong, what right do you have to punish me?

Where are my friends who loved me so dearly, where are they? They are appalled at my misfortune, not one of them dares approach me. I am crushed, yet they leave me helpless! I am dying and there is no one shedding tears over my plight. I am denied any consolation. The criminal plunges into the abyss and pity halts at the brink! He is torn by remorse and his cries remain unheard!

And you whom I have so grievously wronged and whose esteem only makes my anguish greater, you who indeed are the only person who has the right to seek revenge, what are you doing so far away from me? Come to me and punish a faithless wife. Let me finally pay the dire penalty which I deserve. If I had not lacked the courage to inform you of the shame I have brought down on your head I would have already submitted to your vengeance. It was not because I wished to hide it from you, it was because of my respect for you. May this letter at least tell you that I am repentant. Heaven has taken up your cause and avenged you for the wrong of which you never knew. It was God who tied my tongue and stifled my words, fearing that you might forgive a fault that was to be punished by Him. He placed me beyond the reach of your forgiveness, for it would have offended His sense of justice.

But His vengeance is pitiless. He has delivered me into the hands of the man who has ruined me. I am being made to suffer both for him and by him. I keep trying to escape from him but it is useless, he is pursuing me, he is always there, always obsessing me. But how different he seems now from himself. His eyes are full only of hatred and contempt. His lips utter only abuse and reproaches. He takes me into his arms only to tear me to pieces. Who will rescue me from his barbaric fury?

But who is that? Oh, there he is, no, it's no mistake, he's here again, I can see him! O gentle friend, take me into your arms, hide me in your breast! Yes, it's you, it is really you! What fatal illusion was it that made me not recognize you? Ah, how I have suffered while you've been away! We must never part again, never! I can breathe once more. Feel how my heart is pounding! And it's not from fear now, it's from the sweet emotion of love! Why are you spurning my tenderness, my caresses? Let me see the gentle light of love in your eyes! What are these bonds which you are trying to break? For whom are you preparing that funeral pomp and ceremony? What can have caused that changed look on your face? What are you doing? Leave me alone! I'm trembling. Dear God, it is that fiend again!

Dear ladies, my friends, don't desert me. You were urging me to flee from him, help me to fight him; and you who were more forbearing and promised to relieve my suffering, come to my side. Where are you both? If I am no longer allowed to see you, at least answer this letter so that I may know that you still love me.

Leave me alone, you cruel monster! What new fury has possessed you? Are you afraid that my heart will be filled by gentle feelings of love? You are making my torments more and more unbearable and forcing me to hate you. Oh, hatred brings such pain, it corrodes the heart that secretes it! Why do you persecute me? What can you still have to say to me now? Haven't you already made it impossible to listen or reply to you? Do not expect anything more from me. Farewell, Monsieur.

162

The Chevalier Danceny to the Vicomte de Valmont
Paris, 6 December 17—

I have become aware, Monsieur de Valmont, of your conduct towards me. I also know that, not content with having so odiously tricked me, you have not scrupled to brag about it and congratulate yourself on your behaviour. I have proof of your double-dealing written in your own hand. I confess to being devastated and even rather ashamed at having myself contributed so considerably to the disgraceful abuse which you have made of my blind trust. However, I do not envy you the despicable advantage you have gained over me; I am merely curious to see whether you can maintain it indefinitely. This I look forward to discovering when, as I hope, you are good enough to be at the gate of the Bois de Vincennes in the village of Saint-Mandé tomorrow morning between eight and nine o'clock. I shall ensure that everything necessary to clear up all the matters outstanding between us is available.

Chevalier Danceny

163

Monsieur Bertrand to Madame de Rosemonde
Paris, 7 December 17—

Dear Madame de Rosemonde, it is with the deepest regret that I perform my sad duty of apprising you of an event that will grievously distress you, and I hope I may take the liberty of reminding you of your pious submission to God's will which we have so frequently admired and which is the only means given to us to bear the ills that beset us throughout the course of our wretched lives.

Your nephew—dear God, why does it have to be me who must cause such grief to so respected a lady!—your nephew has suffered the misfortune to receive fatal injuries in a duel with Monsieur le Chevalier Danceny this morning.* I know nothing of the subject of their disagreement but from a letter which I later found in Monsieur le Vicomte's pocket and which I am enclosing herewith, it seems that he was not the aggressor; yet it was to be he whom Heaven saw fit to allow to perish.

I was waiting to see Monsieur le Vicomte at his house at the very time when he was brought back. You can imagine my great dismay on seeing your nephew carried in by two of his servants, bathed in his own blood. He had received two sword thrusts in the body and was already very weak. Monsieur Danceny was

there and he was even in tears. Ah, indeed, well may he weep, but
it is too late to shed tears when you have already caused an
irreparable calamity.

As for me, I was beside myself and despite my humble position remonstrated with him over his conduct. But it was
now that Monsieur le Vicomte showed his real greatness of
heart: he ordered me to be quiet and taking the hand of his
murderer, called him his friend, embraced him in front of us all,
and said: 'I order you all to show the Chevalier Danceny all the
respect due to a fine and gallant gentleman.' He also, in our
presence, had a large bundle of letters handed over to him; I do
not know what they are but I do know that he attached considerable importance to them. After that, he asked to be left alone
with him for a moment. Meanwhile I had immediately sent for
help, both spiritual and temporal but, alas, his injuries were
beyond mortal aid. Less than half an hour later the Vicomte lost
consciousness and barely had time to receive the last rites before
breathing his last.*

Dear God, when I received this precious mainstay of such an
illustrious family into my arms as he came into this world,
how could I have foreseen that it would be in my arms that he
left it and that I should have to mourn his death? And so prema-
ture and so unfortunate a death! Despite my efforts, I cannot
control my tears. I must ask you to excuse me, Madame, for
mingling them with yours but in every walk of life people
have their own hearts and feelings; and it would indeed be ungrateful of me not to mourn for the rest of my life his lordship,
who has shown me so much kindness and honoured me with
such trust.

Tomorrow, after the removal of the body, I shall seal up
everything where necessary; you may rely on my most careful
attention.

You will be aware, Madame, that this sad event puts an end to
the entail on your estate and leaves you free to make any provisions that you may wish. If I can be of any assistance, I would
ask you to be so kind as to let me have your instructions which I
shall be only too glad to carry out most meticulously.

With deepest respect, Madame, I am yours etc.

                                                        Bertrand

164

Madame de Rosemonde to Monsieur Bertrand
From the Château de ——, 8 December 17—

My dear Bertrand, I have just received your letter informing me of the dreadful calamity which has befallen my poor unfortunate nephew. Yes, I certainly do have instructions for you and it is only because I am eager to deliver them that I can bring myself for a brief moment to put aside my immense grief.

Monsieur Danceny's letter which you enclosed is convincing proof that it was he who provoked the duel and my intention is for you to have charges laid against him without delay, in my name. When forgiving his enemy, his murderer, my nephew may have been satisfying his generous instincts; but I must avenge not only his death but humanity and religion.* It is impossible to invoke the full rigour of our laws too energetically against this relic of barbarism which remains a blot on our customs; nor do I think that in such a case any talk of forgiveness of sins is relevant. I therefore expect you to prosecute this matter with the vigour and zeal of which I know you to be capable. You owe it to the memory of my nephew.

In the first instance, you must take particular care to call on the presiding judge Monsieur de —— and consult with him; at the moment my grief is too great to make it possible for me to write to him myself, so make my apologies to him and show him this letter.

Goodbye, my dear Bertrand. All my thanks and good wishes; I shall always rely on you in all things.

165

Madame de Volanges to Madame de Rosemonde
Paris, 9 December 17—

I know, dear friend, that you are already aware of your recent sad bereavement. I knew how fond you were of Monsieur de Valmont and I deeply sympathize with the grief which you must be feeling. I am very sad to have to add to the sorrows which you already suffer, but, alas, our dear unhappy friend Madame de Tourvel is no more and we can only mourn her: she passed away at eleven o'clock last night. Fate seemed set on thwarting any effort of human foresight and it dogged her to the end: though she survived Monsieur de Valmont for so short a time, it was still long enough to hear news of his death, so that as she herself said, she was not finally allowed to die without draining her cup of bitterness to the dregs.

I believe you knew that she had been completely unconscious for two days, and even yesterday when her doctor arrived and we went over to her bed, she did not recognize either of us and we were unable to obtain a single word or sign from her. Well, hardly had we gone back to the fireplace and the doctor was informing me of the sad death of Monsieur de Valmont when this unhappy woman completely recovered her senses, either through some sudden natural agency or else by the repetition of the words 'Valmont' and 'death' which may have reminded the sick woman of the only thoughts that had been going through her head for such a long time.

Whatever the reason, without warning she flung open her bed-curtains, exclaiming: 'What was that you were saying? Is Monsieur de Valmont dead?' I tried to persuade her that she was mistaken and that she had misheard what we were saying; but far from being convinced, she insisted on the doctor's repeating his grim tale; and when I again attempted to persuade her otherwise, she called me over to her and whispered: 'Why do you try to deceive me? In my eyes, wasn't he already dead?' So we had to do as she asked.

At first, our poor friend listened fairly calmly but she soon cut the doctor short and said: 'That's enough, that's all I wanted to know.' She immediately asked for her curtains to be closed and when the doctor later tried to attend to her, she refused to allow him near her.

As soon as he had left, she similarly sent her maid and her sick-nurse out of the room and once we were alone, she asked me to help her to kneel up in bed and support her. She remained like that in silence for a while, with no expression on her face but with tears pouring down her cheeks. Then, clasping her hands and lifting them up to Heaven, she said in a weak but fervent voice: 'Almighty God, I submit to Thy just punishment; but forgive Valmont. May my misfortunes, which I acknowledge are well-deserved, not be a cause of blame for him and I shall bless Thy merciful grace!' I have taken the liberty, dear friend, of going into these details, while realizing that they are bound to renew and exacerbate your sorrow, because I feel sure neverthe-less that this prayer of Madame de Tourvel will bring great comfort to your soul.

After uttering these few words, our friend collapsed into my arms and hardly had she been laid down on her bed than she fainted but was revived by the usual methods. As soon as she came to herself, she asked me to send for Father Anselme, add-ing: 'He is the only doctor I need now. I can feel that all my ills will soon be at an end.' She complained of having great difficulty in breathing and was finding it hard to speak.

A short while later she asked her maid to let me have a small casket which she said contained some of her papers and re-quested me to pass it on to you immediately after her death. I am sending it to you herewith.* After that she talked with me about you and your friendship with her, as well as her condition al-lowed, with much emotion.

At about four o'clock Father Anselme arrived and spent nearly an hour with her alone. When we came back into the room the expression on the sick woman's face was calm and peaceful but it was easy to see that Father Anselme was very tearful. He stayed to witness the last rites. This ceremony, always so painful and so impressive, was made even more so by the contrast be-tween the calm resignation of the sick woman and the deep distress of her venerable confessor who was sobbing beside her, so that the only person not crying was the one for whose sake we were all in tears.

The rest of the day was spent in appropriate prayer which was interrupted only when the sick woman frequently lost con-sciousness. Finally, towards eleven o'clock that night she seemed to me to be in greater pain and finding it harder to breathe. I stretched out my hand to feel for her arm; she barely had the strength to take it and place it on her heart. I could not feel it beat and indeed at that very moment our dear, unhappy friend breathed her last.

Do you recall during your last visit here less than a year ago how we chatted together about the few people whose happiness seemed more or less secure and with what pleasure we dwelt on the happy lot of that very woman whose misfortunes and death we are now mourning? She was so virtuous, with so many admirable and agreeable qualities, with such a gentle, easy-going nature; a husband whom she loved and who adored her, the darling of a society which she enjoyed; she was young, beautiful, wealthy; yet this combination of so many advantages has been utterly destroyed by one single imprudent relationship! O Providence, your decrees must no doubt be respected but how unfathomable they are! I must stop: I am afraid of causing you greater sadness by giving way to mine.

I shall leave here and go back to see my daughter who is a trifle indisposed. This morning, when I told her of the sudden deaths of two people with whom she was acquainted, she felt unwell and I had to put her to bed. However, I hope that this slight indisposition will have no further consequences. At that age, they are still not used to such upsets and they react all the more sensitively and violently. This sensitivity is no doubt an admirable quality but everything we see all the time warns us to beware of it! Goodbye, dear friend; with my kindest regards, yours, etc.

166

Monsieur Bertrand to Madame de Rosemonde
Paris, 10 December 17—

Madame, following the instructions which I had the honour of receiving from you, I myself had the further honour of calling on the presiding judge Monsieur de —— and communicating your letter to him, informing him also that, in accordance with your wishes, I was to take no action without first consulting him. His Honour directed me to draw your attention to the fact that the charge which you propose to lay against Monsieur le Chevalier Danceny would equally compromise your nephew's memory, that his own honour would of necessity be impugned by any judgement of the court, and this would certainly be most unfortunate. His advice therefore is that we must take care not to proceed in this way and were any action to be contemplated it should rather be to endeavour to prevent the Public Prosecutor from enquiring into this unhappy affair which has already aroused excessive scandal.

These observations seemed to me full of wisdom and I shall therefore await your instructions before proceeding further in this matter.

May I also beg you, Madame, when you send these instructions to add a word on the state of your dear health which I greatly fear may have suffered from the trials to which it has been subjected. I hope that you will excuse this impertinence on my part which springs wholly from my eagerness to serve you and from my affection for you.

With due respects, I am, Madame, yours etc.

167

Unsigned note* to Monsieur le Chevalier Danceny
Paris, 10 December 17—

I have the honour to inform you, Monsieur, that the matter of your recent affair with Monsieur le Vicomte de Valmont was considered by the King's Officers in the Public Prosecutor's office this morning and it is to be feared that charges may be laid. I thought that this warning may be of some help to you, either to enable you to alert your friends in court to find means of countering these unpleasant consequences or, if you are not in a position to do this, to take measures to remove yourself to a place of safety.

If indeed I may be allowed to offer you a word of advice, I think that you would do well to make fewer appearances in public than you have recently. Although in general these sorts of affairs are viewed leniently, the Law must none the less always be treated with respect.

This precaution becomes all the more necessary inasmuch as a certain Madame de Rosemonde, who, we have been told, is Vicomte de Valmont's aunt, was proposing to lay charges against you, in which case the Public Prosecutor would be unable to refuse her demand. It might perhaps be appropriate if you were able to have a word placed in that lady's ear.

Private reasons prevent me from signing this letter; but though you do not know from whom it has come, I hope I may rely on you to give due weight to the feeling which lies behind it.

I have the honour to be your obedient humble servant.

168

Madame de Volanges to Madame de Rosemonde
Paris, 11 December 17—

Dear friend, there are some most surprising and extremely un- pleasant rumours circulating here concerning Madame de Merteuil. You may be sure that I am far from believing them and would stake a great deal on their being nothing but wicked slander but I know so well how easy it is for such mischievous reports, however implausible, to gain credence and how hard it is to stifle them, not to be very much alarmed, even if I think they may be easy to squash. Above all, I should like them to be stopped early on before they can spread. I only heard yesterday of these dreadful things which people are beginning to hawk around; and when I sent someone round to Madame de Merteuil's this morning, she had just left for the country where she will be spending a couple of days. They weren't able to say exactly where she will be staying. I sent for her second maid to come and talk to me and she told me that her mistress's only instructions were to expect her back next Thursday; and none of the servants she has left behind here knows anything more. As for me, I can't suppose where she may be; I don't know anybody amongst her acquaintances who stays on in the country as late as this.

However that may be, you will, I hope, be able to obtain between now and her return further information that may be helpful to her. These odious rumours are based on the circum- stances surrounding Monsieur de Valmont's death; you will ob- viously have been told if these are true or it will at least be easy for you to find out if such is the case and I would ask you, as a favour, to do so. What people are saying or rather, as yet whisper-

ing—but it won't be long before it becomes a hue and cry—
is this:

The quarrel between Monsieur de Valmont and the Chevalier
Danceny was brought about by Madame de Merteuil and she
was deceiving the pair of them, so that, as almost always happens, the two rivals started by fighting each other and didn't
discover the whole story until afterwards, whereupon they were
completely reconciled; and in order to give the Chevalier
Danceny a full account of Madame de Merteuil as well as to
justify himself beyond any shadow of doubt, Monsieur de
Valmont also produced a large number of letters representing a
regular correspondence which he had been conducting with her
in which she recounts, in the most abandoned terms, the most
scandalous anecdotes concerning herself.

It is also alleged that in his first moment of anger, Danceny
released these letters to anyone who wanted to see them and that
they are currently circulating throughout Paris. Two in particular are being quoted;* one in which she gives a full account of her
life and principles and which is said to be the abomination of
abominations; the other one contains a complete justification of
Monsieur de Prévan, whose story you will recall: it proves that,
contrary to the general belief, all he did was to yield to Madame
de Merteuil's flagrant advances and that their rendezvous had
been concerted with her.

Fortunately I have the strongest possible grounds for thinking
that these imputations are as false as they are odious. In the first
place we both know that Monsieur de Valmont was certainly
never involved with Madame de Merteuil and I have every
reason to believe that Danceny wasn't involved with her either. It
seems to me that this proves that she cannot have been either the
subject or the instigator of the quarrel. Nor can I understand
what possible interest Madame de Merteuil, supposedly in
agreement with Monsieur de Prévan, could have had in causing
a scene which was bound to lead to a great scandal and indeed
might have proved dangerous for her, since she would be making
an irreconcilable enemy of a man who knew part of her secrets
and who had at that time large support. However, it must be
noted that since that affair not a single voice has been raised on
his behalf and that even he has made no claims.

These considerations incline me to suspect that he is the source of the current rumours and to view these foul insinuations as the product of his hatred and vengeance, hoping at least to raise some doubts and perhaps provide a suitable diversion. But wherever these vicious reports may be emanating from, the most urgent thing is to demolish them. They would collapse of their own accord if it turns out, as is likely, that Monsieur de Valmont and the Chevalier Danceny did not speak to each other at all after their unfortunate encounter and that no letters had changed hands. Being anxious to get to the bottom of this matter as soon as possible, this morning I sent over to Monsieur Danceny's but he's not in Paris either. His servants told my man that he left last night, acting on advice which he received yesterday, and that his whereabouts are being kept secret. He is obviously alarmed by the consequences of his duel. So, dear friend, I am entirely reliant on you for the details that interest me and which may become so necessary for Madame de Merteuil. I do beg you once again to let me have them as soon as possible.

My daughter's indisposition has had no further consequences;* she sends you her regards.

169
The Chevalier Danceny to Madame de Rosemonde
Paris, 12 December 17—

Madame, you may perhaps think it very strange of me to approach you in this manner but I earnestly beg you to listen to me before condemning me and not to regard my action as impertinence or presumption; it springs purely from my trust and my respect. I am fully conscious of the harm which I have inflicted on you and I should feel guilty for the rest of my life were I for one moment to think that I might have been able to avoid doing so. You may even rest assured that while I consider myself free from blame, I am not free from regret; and may I further add, in all sincerity, that a great deal of my own grief comes from the thought of the grief I have occasioned you. In order that you may be convinced of the sincerity of these feelings which I am making bold to express, it will be sufficient for you merely to do yourself justice and to realize that, though not having the honour of being known to you, I nevertheless have the honour of knowing you.

However, whilst I am bewailing the cruel fate which has caused you such grief and me such misfortune, I have been led to fear that you yourself are intent solely on revenge and were looking to satisfy it even by recourse to the rigours of the law.

I ask you to allow me to observe that in this you are being misled by your grief, since in this matter my interests and those of Monsieur de Valmont are closely linked, and that he himself would be implicated in any condemnation that you succeeded in obtaining against myself. I should think, therefore, that instead I may be able to rely on you, Madame, to assist rather than oppose any efforts I may have to make to ensure that this unfortunate incident never sees the light of day.

However, my conscience will not be appeased by mere collusion, which suits innocent and guilty alike; so while I do not want you as my plaintiff, I appeal to you to be my judge. The esteem of those whom we respect is too valuable for me to allow yours to be taken from me without defending myself and I think I have the means to do it. Indeed, if you share with me the belief that revenge is legitimate, in fact a duty when our love, our friendship, and particularly our trust have been betrayed, then you will cease to think I have done anything wrong. You do not need to trust what I say; if you have the courage, then read this correspondence that I am passing over to you herewith.* The large number of original letters seems to guarantee the authenticity of those which are copies. Moreover, I received them in exactly the same state as I am handing them over to you from Monsieur de Valmont himself. Nothing has been added and I have retained only two letters which I have taken the liberty of making public. One of them was necessary for Monsieur de Valmont's and my revenge; we both had the right, and he expressly requested me, to do this. I also thought that I should be doing society a real service in unmasking such a positively dangerous woman as Madame de Merteuil who, as you will see, is the true cause of everything that transpired between Monsieur de Valmont and myself.*

It is this same sense of justice which has impelled me to publish the second letter to justify Monsieur de Prévan whom I scarcely know but who in no way deserved the harsh treatment inflicted on him nor the even crueller public condemnation which he has been enduring ever since without any chance of vindicating himself.

So you will find only copies of those two letters; I owe it to myself to keep the originals. As for the rest, I think I could not place this collection in safer hands since it is important for me that it should not be destroyed, though I should be ashamed to take unfair advantage of it. In entrusting these papers to your care, Madame, I believe I am serving the best interests of all those involved as well as I should be in handing them back to the persons concerned; I shall spare them the embarrassment of receiving them from me and thus of knowing that I am familiar with episodes in their lives which they are anxious never to be disclosed.

In this regard I think I should warn you that the enclosed are only part of a much larger correspondence from which Monsieur de Valmont extracted them in my presence and which you will find when the seals are lifted, under the heading, as I saw, of: *Account opened between the Marquise de Merteuil and the Vicomte de Valmont*. On those letters please take any decision you think appropriate.

I remain, Madame, with deep respect, yours, etc.

PS Following certain warnings and advice from friends I have decided to remove myself from Paris for a while and seek refuge in a place which I intend to keep secret from everybody but yourself. Should you be honouring me with an answer to this letter, please send it to the Commandery of ———, near P———, addressed to the Knight Commander of ———.* It is from his residence that I am writing to you.

170
Madame de Volanges to Madame de Rosemonde
Paris, 13 December 17—

I am being jolted, dear Madame, from surprise to surprise and faced by one problem after another. Only a mother can have any idea of what I have been through in the course of this morning and if my most urgent fears have been allayed, I am still terribly worried and I can see no end to my miseries.

Yesterday morning at about ten o'clock, surprised at having seen nothing of my daughter, I sent my maid up to discover the reason for her lateness. After a moment she came back looking very alarmed and scared me even more by announcing that my daughter was not in her rooms and that her maid hadn't seen her all that morning. Imagine my situation! I summoned all my servants and in particular my door-keeper: they all swore they knew nothing and couldn't give me any information about what had happened. I immediately went up to my daughter's bedroom. It was so untidy that it was plain that she had certainly left only that morning but apart from that I was unable to deduce anything. I went through her wardrobes and secretaire; everything was in order and all her clothes were there except for the dress she had put on to go out. She hadn't even taken the small amount of money which she keeps in her room.

As she had heard the gossip about Madame de Merteuil only yesterday and is very fond of her, so much so that she had spent the whole evening in tears; and as I remembered too that she didn't know that Madame de Merteuil had gone down into the country, my first thought was that she intended to call on her friend and had foolishly gone there unattended. But as time passed and she did not return, I once again became as alarmed as ever. But while I was growing more worried every minute and extremely anxious to obtain information, I was afraid to do so because I dreaded the thought of arousing too much attention as to her actions which I might later regret not having kept to myself. I really never have been so upset in all my life.

In the end it wasn't until after two o'clock that I received a letter from her at the same time as one from the Mother Superior of the convent of ———. My daughter's letter merely said that she was afraid that I might have prevented her from doing what she had decided to do; that she felt she had a vocation, wanted to take the veil, and hadn't dared to tell me. The rest of the letter consisted of excuses for having taken this step without my permission but which, she added, she was sure I would not disapprove were I to know her motives, which she begged me however not to ask her to disclose.

The Mother Superior reported that, seeing a young person arriving alone, she had first refused her admission and then after questioning her and discovering who she was, she thought that she would be doing me a service by initially offering her shelter so that she would not need to continue her wanderings as she seemed bent on doing. The Mother Superior naturally offers to send my daughter back to me if I ask for her but, as was her duty, urges me not to stand in the way of a vocation which she describes as very positive; she adds that she had not been able to inform me earlier of this incident because it had been difficult to persuade the girl to write to me, as my daughter was anxious, so she says, for no one to know where she had sought refuge. Ah, the dreadful foolishness of children!

I immediately went to the convent, saw the Superior, and asked to see my daughter; she was very reluctant to come and very scared. I spoke to her in front of the nuns and then alone; the only thing I could get out of her, apart from floods of tears, was that she could only feel happy in a convent; I decided to let her stay there but not yet as a postulant, as she wanted. I am afraid that the deaths of Madame de Tourvel and Monsieur de Valmont have been too great a shock for her young head. However much I respect the religious vocation, I should feel sorry and indeed apprehensive were she to embrace it. It seems to me that we already have enough duties to perform without adding to them; and moreover, she is hardly likely to know what suits her at her age.*

My embarrassment is made all the greater by the imminent return of Monsieur de Gercourt: will it be necessary to break off this most attractive match? How can we provide for our children's happiness when it is not sufficient for us merely to wish to secure it and devote all our efforts to achieving it? I should be so grateful if you could tell me what you would do in my place. I can think of nothing more frightening than having to make a decision that will settle the fate of other people and in this case I'm equally afraid of acting either too sternly as a judge or too weakly as a mother.

I keep reproaching myself for adding to your troubles by talking about mine; but I know how kind-hearted you are: any comfort you could bring to others would be of equally great comfort to yourself.

Goodbye, dear, valued friend. I am looking forward most eagerly to hearing your answers to my two questions.

171

Madame de Rosemonde to the Chevalier Danceny
From the Château de ——, 15 December 17—

Now I have read what you tell me, Monsieur, I can only take refuge in silence and tears. When we learn such monstrous things, we can only regret still being alive; when we see a woman capable of such enormities, we blush for our sex.

For my part I am only too ready to consign to silence and oblivion everything connected with these events, now or in the future. I even hope that you will suffer no further distress through them than that inevitably resulting from having had the better of my poor nephew. In spite of his wrongdoing which I cannot but acknowledge, I feel that I shall never be able to reconcile myself to his loss; but the only revenge I shall allow myself to take on you will be to mourn him for ever and I shall leave it to your heart to appreciate how deeply that will be.

If you will permit an old woman to pass a reflection rarely made to the young, I would say that if we truly understood where our happiness lies, we should never look for it outside the bounds laid down by law and by religion.

You may rest assured that I shall keep strict guard over the letters you have entrusted to me but I ask you to authorize me not to hand them over to anyone, not even to you unless you require them to justify yourself. I venture to hope that you will not refuse my request, and that you no longer feel that seeking revenge, however justified, often leads to remorse.

I am so convinced of your generosity and delicacy of feeling that this is not the last of my requests: these two qualities would be even more admirable if they made it possible for you to let me have Mademoiselle de Volanges's letters which you seem to have kept, though they doubtless have no further interest for you. I know that this young person has wronged you badly but I do not imagine that you are thinking of punishing her for that; and if only out of self-respect, you will not want to blacken the character of someone whom you loved so much. So I do not need to point out that while the daughter doesn't deserve any consideration, at least her mother certainly does; she is a most respectable woman to whom you perhaps owe considerable amends since, however much someone may delude himself by parading his delicate feelings, none the less when he is the first man to try to seduce a simple well-bred young girl, he is by that very action starting her on the downward path and must be held responsible for her later moral aberrations and dissolute behaviour.

You must not be surprised, Monsieur, at the stern note I am sounding: it is the best proof that I can offer you of the extremely high regard in which I hold you and you will stake further claim to it by agreeing to my wish to maintain secrecy in a matter which, should it become public knowledge, would not only harm you but be a death-blow to a mother's heart which has already suffered through you. This is a service, Monsieur, which I wish to render to my dear friend Madame de Volanges and if I were to have the slightest doubt that you would refuse this request of mine, I would ask you to reflect beforehand that this is the only consolation that you have left me.

I have the honour to be etc.

172

Madame de Rosemonde to Madame de Volanges
From the Château de ———, 15 December 17—

If, as you asked, I had been obliged to send, and wait, for the further details about Madame de Merteuil to arrive from Paris, it wouldn't yet have been possible to let you have them and they would certainly have been vague and indefinite; however, I have received information which I did not and had no reason to expect and this information is all too definite. Ah, dear friend, how grievously has that woman deceived you!

I am reluctant to go into any details of this revolting story but you may be sure that whatever you hear on this subject is still short of the truth. I hope, my dear, that you know me well enough to take my word for it, that you'll not ask for any corroboration and that it will suffice for me to tell you that there is plenty and I am holding some of this evidence in my hand at this very moment.

And it is not without the deepest regret that I am similarly asking you not to force me to give any reason for the advice which you request concerning Mademoiselle de Volanges: I urge you not to oppose the vocation which she has in mind. There is certainly no reason for anyone to be allowed to follow that vocation who doesn't feel called to it; but sometimes it is a great boon when someone does feel this call; and you have heard your daughter tell you herself that if you were to know her motives, you would not disapprove. The One who inspires our feelings knows better than we do, with our futile wisdom, what is right for each of us and often what seems harsh turns out to be merciful.

In a word, my advice, which I well understand will distress you and for that very reason must make you realize that it is not given lightly, is for you to leave Mademoiselle de Volanges in the convent, since that is her choice; to encourage rather than oppose the plan on which she seems set; and, in the anticipation that she will carry it through, to have no hesitation in breaking off this marriage which you had arranged.

Now that I have fulfilled these painful duties as your friend and am powerless to offer you any comfort, there remains just one favour that I ask of you: I beg you never to question me further on any matter relating to these sad events. We must allow them to sink into the oblivion where they belong, realize how futile and distressing it would be to attempt to throw more light on them, place ourselves in the hands of Providence, and accept the wisdom of God's laws, however impenetrable. Goodbye, dear, dear friend.

173
Madame de Volanges to Madame de Rosemonde
Paris, 18 December 17—

Ah, dear friend, what a terrifying veil you have drawn over my daughter's fate! And you seem to be afraid that I might attempt to lift it! What can it be hiding more likely to cause a mother greater distress than the terrible suspicions that you have left me with? The longer I reflect on your friendship and your tolerant nature, the more tormented I feel; since yesterday I have been tempted a score of times to be relieved of my cruel uncertainty and ask you not to spare me, to tell me the unvarnished truth; and each time I shuddered as I remembered that you had begged me not to question you. So in the end I have decided on a course which still leaves me some hope; and as my friend I expect you not to refuse to answer my request, which is for you to tell me whether I more or less correctly understood what you would have to say to me and not to be afraid of informing me of something which a mother can forgive and which it is not impossible to remedy. However, if your information would be adding to my burden even more heavily, then I agree that you should give me no further explanation other than remaining silent. So let me tell you how much I already know and how much more I can bear.

My daughter showed some liking for the Chevalier Danceny and I have been informed that she went so far as to receive letters from him and even to answer them; but I thought I had managed to prevent this childish mistake on her part from having any serious consequences; now that I fear the worst, I imagine it is conceivable that my vigilance has been circumvented and I must have the dreadful thought that my daughter has sunk so low as to be seduced.

Looking back, I can recall a number of incidents that may perhaps strengthen this fear. I informed you that my daughter fainted on learning the misfortune that had overtaken Monsieur de Valmont: may she possibly have been so strongly affected merely by the thought of the danger to which Monsieur Danceny had been exposed in this encounter? Later on, when she cried so bitterly on hearing of all the things that people were saying about Madame de Merteuil what I took to be distress for a friend was perhaps nothing more than a feeling of jealousy or sorrow at her lover's unfaithfulness. Her most recent action may also, it seems to me, be similarly explained. Women often feel called to God for other reasons than disgust with men. Anyway, assuming these facts are correct and that you are conversant with them, you may no doubt have thought them sufficient to justify your uncompromising advice to me.

All the same, in such a case, whilst still blaming my daughter, I should consider that I owed it to her to save her from the torments and dangers inherent in following an erroneous vocation. If Danceny is not devoid of all sense of decency, he will not refuse to right a wrong which is purely of his making and I think I may say that marrying my daughter is a sufficiently attractive match for him and his family to feel flattered.

So that, dear friend, is my last remaining hope and I beg you not to delay in confirming it, if that is possible. You can well imagine how greatly I need you to let me have a reply and the appalling shock for me if you say nothing.

I was just about to close this letter when a gentleman of my acquaintance called and told me of a humiliating incident involving Madame de Merteuil. As I have not been seeing any people recently I have only now heard of it; according to an eyewitness this is what happened.

On her way back from the country last Thursday, Madame de Merteuil called in at the Comédie-Italienne where she has a box; she was sitting alone and not a single man visited her throughout the whole performance, something which she must have found extraordinary. After the performance, following her usual custom, she went into the little salon which was already full of people; immediately there was a great stir which she did not seem to connect with herself. Noticing a vacant space on one of the seats, she went over and sat down, whereupon all the women sitting on it stood up as if of one mind and left her completely isolated. This pointed indication of the general indignation was applauded by all the men and added even further to the buzz which people are saying even reached the point of hissing.

To complete her discomfiture, unfortunately for her at that very same moment Monsieur de Prévan, who had not been seen in public since the incident involving him, came into the room. As soon as they noticed him, everybody, men and women, flocked round him to congratulate him and he found himself, as it were, propelled directly in front of Madame de Merteuil by the throng of people surrounding them. It is asserted that Madame de Merteuil continued to look as if she was blind and deaf to all this and that neither did her expression change! But I think that must have been an exaggeration. However that may be, she remained in this truly ignominious situation until her carriage was announced and as she was leaving, once again there was even louder hissing. It is appalling to have that woman as a relative! That very evening Monsieur de Prévan was warmly welcomed by his follow-officers and there is no doubt that he will soon be given back his rank and reinstated in his post.

The same man who gave me these details told me that the following night Madame de Merteuil fell ill with a very high fever which was at first thought to be caused by the savage treatment she had received; but last evening we heard that it was smallpox, of the confluent variety* and extremely virulent. It would in fact, I think, be a blessing for her to die of it. People are saying, too, that this whole escapade may well do her a great deal of harm in her lawsuit which is about to be judged and in which people allege that she badly needed all possible support.

Goodbye, dear, dear friend. In all this I can certainly see the hand of retribution against the wicked but I can see no comfort at all for their unhappy victims.

174

The Chevalier Danceny to Madame de Rosemonde
Paris, 26 December 17—

You are right, Madame, and I shall surely not refuse you something that is in my power to do and to which you seem to attach some importance. The bundle which I have the honour of enclosing contains all Mademoiselle de Volanges's letters. If you read them you will perhaps not fail to wonder that so much ingenuousness can be combined with such duplicity.* At least, that was what struck me most the last time I read them recently.

But in particular can we possibly resist a feeling of outrage towards Madame de Merteuil when we recall the loathsome pleasure she took in her unrelenting effort to exploit such innocence and sincerity?

No, my love is dead. I no longer have the slightest vestige of that feeling which she basely betrayed and it is not love which is my reason for trying to justify Mademoiselle de Volanges. But surely such a simple-hearted girl, with such a sweet and pleasant nature, would have been even more easily attracted towards goodness than the evil into which she allowed herself to be inveigled? Would any young girl who had just left her convent, lacking experience, with hardly any ideas at all and flung into society, as is almost always the case, equally ignorant of good and evil, yes, would any girl at all in similar circumstances have been strong enough to stand up to such diabolical trickery? Ah, to be forgiving we need only reflect how many circumstances beyond our control affect the terrifying choice between decent or dishonourable conduct. So, Madame, you were judging me fairly in saying that the harm Mademoiselle de Volanges has done me and which has certainly caused me much suffering has nevertheless not given me any desire for revenge. It was painful enough for me to have to give up loving her! Having to hate her would have been excruciating.

I never had the slightest hesitation in deciding to make every effort to keep everything concerning her, and which might be likely to hurt her, secret from everybody for all time. If I seemed somewhat tardy in carrying out your wishes in this respect, I think I am allowed not to conceal the reason from you: I wanted to wait in order to be sure that I should not suffer any ill effects from my unfortunate encounter. At a time when I was requesting your indulgence and when I even thought that I had some right to it, I should have felt afraid of seeming in some way to be trying to buy it by complying with your request, and since I was convinced of the purity of my intentions, I confess that I was arrogant enough to want not to leave you with any possibility of doubting them. I hope that you will forgive my scrupulous, perhaps over-scrupulous, behaviour as springing from the veneration which I feel for you and which causes me to attach so great an importance to your good opinion of me.

It is this same feeling which leads me to ask you for one final favour: to have the kindness to tell me if you consider that I have fulfilled all my obligations regarding the unhappy situation in which I was placed. Once I am reassured on that point, my mind is made up: I shall leave for Malta where I shall gladly take and religiously observe vows which will set me apart from a society which has treated me, young as I am, so badly; I shall finally attempt to expunge from my mind every memory of this accumulation of horrors which could only sadden and mortify my heart.

I am, Madame, most respectfully yours, etc.

175

Madame de Volanges to Madame de Rosemonde
Paris, 14 January 17—

Dear friend, Madame de Merteuil's fate seems finally to have been sealed and in such a way that her worst enemies are hesitating between rightful indignation and pity. I was surely correct when I said that it would be a blessing for her to die of smallpox. It is true that she has recovered but she is terribly disfigured; in particular, she has lost one eye. As you may imagine, I haven't seen her again but I have been told that she is absolutely hideous.

The Marquis de ——, who never misses a chance to say something unkind, when talking of her yesterday said that her illness had turned her inside out and that now her soul was showing in her face. Unfortunately everyone thought that the remark was apt.

There is something else which has just added to her misfortunes and misdeeds: the day before yesterday they pronounced judgement on her lawsuit: a unanimous verdict against her: costs, damages, and the return of all past revenues; the infant plaintiffs were awarded everything, so that any small amount remaining after meeting her legal expenses will be more than swallowed up by the costs.

Although she was still unwell, as soon as she heard the news, she made arrangements to leave that very night, post-haste and alone. Her servants were saying that no one was willing to go and join her. It's thought that she was making for Holland.*

Her departure has caused more of an outcry than anything else because she has taken her diamonds with her which were extremely valuable and part of her husband's estate; her silver and jewellery as well, in fact everything she could lay hands on; and has left behind nearly 50,000 francs' worth of debts. She is completely bankrupt.

The family is holding a meeting tomorrow to see how to come to some agreement with the creditors. Though I'm only distantly related, I offered to take part but I shan't be able to attend that particular meeting as I have to be present at an even sadder occasion: tomorrow my daughter will be taking the habit of a postulant. I hope you will not forget, dear friend, that the only reason that I feel obliged to make this great sacrifice is your reluctance to break your silence on the question which I put to you.

Danceny left Paris nearly a fortnight ago. He is said to be going to Malta and planning to settle there permanently. Would there perhaps still not be time to keep him here? O dear friend! . . . Is my daughter really so guilty? . . . I feel sure that you will forgive a mother for finding it hard to accept the thought that this is truly the case.

What a dreadful fate has overtaken me recently and attacked me through the people I held most dear! My daughter and my friend!*

Who can fail to shudder at the thought of all the disasters which can result from one single dangerous acquaintance! And what trials and tribulations would we not avoid by being more careful! What woman wouldn't take flight the very first time a seducer approached her! But all these reflections come too late, always after the event; and one of the most important truths, perhaps even the most universally recognized, is stifled and ignored in the frantic turmoil and folly of our morals.

Goodbye, dear friend. At the moment I feel that our reason, inadequate as it is to warn us of impending disasters, is even more inadequate to offer us any comfort for them.

Publisher's Note*

Special reasons and considerations which we shall always feel it our duty to respect oblige us to stop at this point.

For the moment we cannot inform the reader of Mademoiselle de

Volanges's later adventures* nor of the grim climax to Madame de Merteuil's misadventures and her final retribution.*

We may perhaps one day be permitted to conclude this work but we cannot give any firm assurance on this point; and even were we able to do so, we should consider it our duty first to consult the taste of the general public who have not the same reasons as ourselves to be interested in such matters.

APPENDIX

1. *This letter,* originally intended by Laclos as letter 155, was replaced in the published edition by the note to letter 154.*

The Vicomte de Valmont to Madame de Volanges
Paris, 4 December 17—

I am well aware, Madame, that you do not like me and equally aware that you have always tried to turn Madame de Tourvel against me. Nor have I any doubt that you still harbour the same feelings towards me, indeed more strongly than ever. I even concede that you may consider them well-founded. I am nevertheless approaching you and am not only undeterred from asking you to pass on to Madame de Tourvel the letter which I am enclosing for her but I even request you to persuade her to read it and to encourage her to do so by assuring her of my repentance, my regrets and, above all, my love. I feel that my gesture may seem strange to you; it surprises me myself; but a desperate man does not calculate, he seizes on any means he can; and in any case, such a great, such a precious concern, one shared by us both, makes all other considerations irrelevant. Madame de Tourvel is dying, she is wretched: we must bring her back to life, to health, and to happiness. This must be our aim and any means of ensuring and expediting that end is right; if you reject the one I am offering you, the responsibility for the outcome will rest on your shoulders: her death, your remorse, and my everlasting despair—they will all have been your work. I know that I have abused, abominably abused, a woman who deserved only to be adored; I know that the only cause of her present sufferings are the appalling wrongs I have committed against her. I am not trying to hide my faults or excuse them but should you, Madame, prevent me from redressing them, then beware of becoming my accomplice. I stabbed her to the heart; but I am the only person who can staunch that wound, only I have the power to cure it. And if I can be of use, what does it matter if I'm guilty? But save your friend, you must save her! It is your help she needs, not your vengeance.

2. *An undated, unnumbered, and unpublished rough draft of an unfinished letter from Madame de Tourvel to Valmont. Various positions have been suggested for it: immediately after letters 125, 126, or 128 seem the most likely.*

Dear, dear man, why, ever since you left me, am I so upset? I have such a need for a little peace! How is it that my agitation is even turning into pain and making me positively frightened? Would you believe me if I told you that I needed to summon up all my strength and appeal to my reason even to write to you? Yet I tell myself, I keep telling myself, that you are happy; but this thought, so precious to my heart and which you so rightly described as the gently soothing effect of love, has turned instead into a ferment and I feel overwhelmed by an excess of happiness; whereas when I try to tear myself away from this blissful meditation, I immediately relapse into the cruel anguish which I solemnly promised you to avoid and which I must indeed take care to guard against since it spoiled your own happiness. You have not found it hard, dear friend, to teach me how to live apart from you . . . No, that's not what I meant to say, it's really that when I'm away from you, I'd rather not live at all or at least I should like to forget the sort of life I was living. Left all to myself, I can't stand either my happiness or my pain, I feel that I need rest but there is no way for me to find it. I've appealed to sleep but sleep seems so far away; and I can neither occupy myself nor remain idle. I am consumed by a passionate, burning fire and shivering with a deathly chill. I feel too tired to move and yet I can't stay still! How can I express it? I would suffer less if I was burning with fever and though I realize that my suffering stems purely from my inability to control or direct a whole host of emotions, at the same time I should still be happy to be able to surrender to their charm, heart and soul.

At the time when you left me, I was less tormented; true, I was rather agitated as well as full of regrets but I attributed that to my impatience at the presence of my maids who came in just as you were leaving. They always take too long for my liking to attend to me and this time it dragged on far, far longer even than usual. Above all I wanted to be alone; I was sure that with such sweet memories all around me, once I was on my own I should enjoy the only sort of happiness I could expect to find in your absence. How could I have foreseen that though, whilst you were there, I was strong enough to bear the turmoil of such a rapid succession of shifting emotions without faltering, I couldn't bear to go over them again now that I was by myself . . . My error was soon brought cruelly home to me . . . And now, dear heart, I find myself hesitating whether to tell you everything . . . Yet aren't I yours, all yours? Ought I to hide any of my thoughts from you? Ah, that would surely be impossible; only I must beg you to forgive my involuntary weaknesses, none of which come from my heart . . . Following my usual practice, I had sent my women away before getting into bed . . .*

3.

Epistle to Margot*

Why be afraid of admitting it? I've taken up with Margot. Yes, Margot! Do you think that's funny? What's in a name? It's the thing itself that counts. Margot's not well-born, no empty, grand, fancy titles; like her humble forebears, she's poverty-stricken. As for wit, to tell the truth, even at her wittiest, I'd sooner she kept her mouth shut. But Margot has such lovely eyes that one single glance is worth more than riches, wit, or birth. Good God! Am I to submit to our peculiar society's crazy notions and pathetically crawl along to consult a d'Hozier* to discover whom I'm supposed to like? No, Cythera's amiable son* isn't afraid of marrying beneath him: often the mysteries of love lead this God, with his common tastes, to show a preference for a shepherdess over the lady with sixteen quarterings of nobility.* Anyway, who knows what the uncertain future has in store for my girl? Margot's still young, just learning the game. Only give her time to turn into a trollop and maybe Fate will soon make her a Marquise or a Comtesse;* a pretty face, a heart that's fancy-free, make fine titles of nobility. Margot's poor, agreed: why would she need to be rich? Aren't plump curves and a warm heart treasures enough? She has a wealth of love, what else does she want in the way of riches? They're a source of trouble, a nuisance, and those who try to enjoy them fritter them away, and those who keep them don't enjoy them. So I think all those people are wrong and Margot proves to me every day that you can be happy in love without high birth or money.

And what about wit? . . . I can hear our fine talkers, our clever dicks exclaiming: 'What's that? No wit? What sort of enjoyment is that? What about all those sweet nothings, the chit-chat, the puns, which a lover skilfully trots out to fill the boring gaps between lovemaking? If you're prevented from talking, what can you do once you've done all you can? Ah, our clever dicks aren't very well up in this particular matter. What's the problem? Once you've done it all, you just start again. And even if you don't, there's an easier form of pleasure which you can enjoy without the effort of thinking: sleep helps to give your senses and your heart more of a rest than all that soft soap from people who are full of fine words, swearing a hundred times to love you for ever but never proving it more than once.

O mistress mine, whom I love so fondly, who holds me so fast, the time spent writing these verses is probably wasted; you'll never read them, because . . . you can't read; but bear with an old foible of mine: try as I may, I can't break myself of my inveterate habit of thinking; but at least, I make a point of thinking only of you. Come here beside me: Pleasure is awaiting your return. Come to me and on that day, I'll exchange the thankless laurels of Parnassus for the myrtles of Love.

The Procession
A Tale*

Dear friends, 'twas a festive day, a holy day! As you know, on such occasions, all good Christians devoutly make ready to prove with zeal their love of God. What you may not know—but you must take my word for it—is that at times of such religious fervour the Devil also increases his malice and boldly challenges God's omnipotence! He spares no mischievous trick to inflame our senses and our heart. More often than not God wins the day but sometimes the Devil does triumph: listen to this tale which proves my point.

Liza was in the flower of her youth: simple, modest, as lovely as she was virtuous; rather pious; what's more, contrary to normal custom, she'd reached her sixteenth birthday and still kept her virginity. Satan's aware of this and on this holy day intends to play some trick on her— that's his job. You know our ancient custom and that, on this solemn day, so dear to the people, when The Eternal reveals himself in public, He walks the earth like an ordinary mortal . . . Now, our young virgin has been specially chosen by the parish priest to accompany her God in the procession, carrying a candle in honour of her virtue.

Everything's been arranged: that morning, at the appropriate time, her cousin is to come round and lead her on his arm to church. This cousin, my informant tells me, was a well-built lusty lad; mild-looking but dangerous, a wolf in sheep's clothing. At first light, already in her best mob-cap, Liza started dressing; her other finery, as simple as herself, was lying all around; a piece of brown boulting cloth would drape her divinely lissom figure which invited love; the thick muslin must hide the curves of her lovely bosom: this was how Liza dressed for holy days.

In comes Lubin; teasing and full of flattery, the first thing he wants from his cousin is a kiss; but daunted by Liza's blushing innocence, he restrains his ardour. Audacity is forced to respect true modesty. He strikes a more serious note (he's already twice apologized) and reluctantly begins to chat: girls are never tired of prattling. They chat, they laugh, the Devil lends a hand to keep the charming conversation flowing along so smoothly that they forget how time is flying. But now she really must get properly dressed because, like Sunday, this special day demands a ceremonial white shift. Liza goes off into a closet but at the very moment when she's more or less naked, there are sounds in the street outside. What's happening? Do take a look, cousin. Lubin takes a look and to his surprise sees the godly cortège coming down the street! 'It's too late now to get to the church; come and look, Liza, do come, there's nothing else you can do.' Urged on by curiosity, forgetting that by itself a shift is not enough to cover her many precious charms, Liza rashly runs over to look. And the cousin? He too takes a look but without saying a word as he runs a discreet eye over these manifold attractions.

Liza however is looking at the banners and the canopy, then says her prayers. And as she modestly lowers her eyes, gazing down over her lovely bosom, her snow-white tits, needing no support, rise and fall as she breathes; their movement is enticing . . . Liza sees them, takes fright, goes pale and then, overcome by shame, turns a bright pink; in her confusion she hastily bundles up the folds of her scanty garment. The Devil laughs. O gullible girl! He it was who'd caused her sudden qualms. The result is that Lubin can now see lots of other lovely things! His blood boils, he endeavours to calm himself: in vain! What could he do? The Devil has got into him: he feels bold, then scared, then confident again. Satan is tempting him and Liza is tempting, too. So much, indeed, that, to finish off the adventure, he tries to take advantage of her devout posture; and the Devil shows him the way to do it . . . At first, Liza wants to escape but is hemmed in against the window. 'Ah, you Judas, cousin,' she said to him. 'Aah!' Then, to push Lubin off, she makes a move: how clever the Devil is! The effort she made was his real masterstroke. Unwittingly, she's helping her cousin; her firm resistance is making things easier for him. Still trying to escape, still pushing him away, quietly protesting, the pretty girl, without quite knowing how, lost her virginity. But Lubin is still not satisfied, not he! My author tells that she is said to have lost her virginity three times to his hot pursuit before his tempestuous love abated; so much so that Liza, a novice in this sort of fight, stopped struggling and kept still, resigned to wait until he'd had his fill; such is the force of habit over us. However, Lubin now has thoughts of withdrawing; the splendid cortège has already moved on. And Liza too, tired by her defeat, is beginning to feel she needs a nice rest. Lubin perches the pretty lass on his lap, comforting her, praising all her charms and promising to love her for ever. Liza was crying and made no reply. Flattery, lover's vows, gentle caresses, were all to no avail. Finally the doleful beauty said: 'What's the good of promises? Give me back what you've just taken away.'

EXPLANATORY NOTES

Square brackets are used to enclose Laclos's original notes to his text.

3 *francs*: interchangeable with *livre*; it was worth roughly the English shilling of the day; there were 24 livres in a *louis*, worth about a guinea or 21 shillings (there were 20 shillings to the pound). 60,000 francs was thus a very considerable sum.

4 *chronological order*: the manuscript shows, however, that Laclos played about with dates, often to produce dramatic or ironic effects.

this work: [I must also inform the reader that I have deleted or changed the names of all concerned and should any name happen to belong to any living person or persons, this is sheer coincidence from which no conclusion can be drawn.]

quite unconnected matters: Laclos is teasing; he achieves many dramatic and ironic effects by these means.

5 *Academicians*: a sly dig at the French Academy; passages from well-known writers were used as models of good letter-writing in fashionable anthologies. Laclos had a healthy disrespect for too much authority.

title: *Les Liaisons dangereuses* has the subtitle: 'or a compilation of letters from one social set and published for the edification of some others'. Laclos wisely refrained from specifying either from which social set the letters purport to have been taken or which they are intended to edify. The title is complemented by an epigraph from the preface to a work adored by Laclos, *La Nouvelle Héloïse*; it reads: 'I saw the morals of my times and published these letters.' Laclos thereby proclaims his own virtuous intentions, no doubt hoping to ward off accusations of immorality. He didn't succeed; he may not even have expected to.

diversity of styles: this diversity represents not only the individual voices of the correspondents but the particular tone of a voice (indignant, cajoling, gushing, malicious, etc.). Rendering this diversity is, of course, essential in an epistolary novel and Laclos's skill is unparalleled.

6 *observations*: Merteuil's and Valmont's letters in particular contain many such maxims and apophthegms about moral and social conduct, in the French moralizing tradition of La Rochefoucauld

(1613–80), or of Laclos's contemporaries Chamfort (1741–94) and
Rivarol (1753–1801).

9 *Ursuline Convent*: Ursulines were a teaching order. In his Pléiade
edition Versini says there was one of their convents in Grenoble
which had no better a reputation than their Parisian establishment
in the Rue Saint-Jacques.

Tanville girl: [a co-boarder in the convent]; she will be mentioned
again.

in fiocchi: all dressed up. Cécile is already fashion-conscious and
knows the smart Italian expression.

dinner-time: taken at midday; the evening meal is supper.

Joséphine: [a sister allowed outside the convent.]

11 *rakery*: [fortunately good society is beginning to give up these
expressions which were very current at the time these letters were
written.] The expressions were *rouerie* and *roué*, from *rouer*, to
break on the wheel, an extremely painful form of judicial execution
reserved for such heinous crimes as treason. The roués were the
licentious companions of the debauched Philippe, Duke of
Orléans, nephew of Louis XIV and Regent from 1715 to 1723
during the minority of Louis XV, and were considered so depraved
as to deserve this ignominious death. Laclos is probably attempting to obscure the dating of this correspondence and thereby mol-
lify his contemporaries by situating the depravity of his characters
in this more remote period; we shall see other evidence proving
that it was far closer. Nor is Valmont strictly a Regency roué
interested only in sensual debauchery; his approach to women is
more psychological, even intellectual. See also note to p. 14 on
destiny.

memoirs: memoirs, either authentic or fictional, were very popular
reading in France at this time. Writing someone else's memoirs is
a typically impertinent notion of Merteuil's. See also note to p. 100
on Céladon.

intendant: a provincial governor or other very senior administrator
of the Crown; but see note below, where she's described as a judge's
wife.

monster: [to understand this passage, the reader must know that the
Comte de Gercourt had deserted the Marquise de Merteuil for the
wife of the presiding judge Monsieur de ——; she had given up
Valmont for Gercourt and it was then that the Marquise and the
Vicomte had become attached to one another. As there was nothing
extraordinary in all this and it took place long before the events

related in these letters, we saw no point in reprinting any of that correspondence.]

12 *sixty thousand a year*: but Gercourt is even wealthier; he can be absolved of the charge of marrying beneath him to *fumer ses terres* (manure his land) as one aristocrat is said to have put it.

the rosebud: the exact expression used by Lovelace to describe one of the female characters in Richardson's *Clarissa*.

tomorrow evening: the increasing reliability of the postal service was important for the epistolary novelist. Laclos uses it to achieve very ironic effects (e.g. letters 125, 126, and 128).

13 *pretty*: Laclos uses italics in a variety of ways: to render fashionable jargon (e.g. '*rakery*'); to point the occasional neologism; for quotation from other writers; and most particularly when the correspondents quote from each other's letters.

14 *constancy*: the first mention of an important concept which recurs throughout: it is possible to remain constant and still indulge in passing infidelities.

follow our destiny: an early indication that this libertine's prime interest is the exercise of male authority, even if violence is required (*conquerors*). As the aim is to achieve notoriety, vanity is a great spur and too easy a prey is spurned as unworthy of a practised seducer.

myrtle and laurels: the myrtle was sacred to Venus; a wreath of laurels was the crown for a conqueror or a poet. Such classical allusions are commonplace to these cultivated aristocrats.

15 *a great poet*: [La Fontaine.] These two lines, a slight misquotation from La Fontaine's Dedication of his first book of Fables, translate as: 'And if I do not win the prize, I shall at least have the honour of having tried.' In letter 10 we shall find Merteuil reading another work by La Fontaine, his erotic *Contes*, verse tales drawn from, amongst other sources, Boccaccio's *Decameron*. Some of Laclos's youthful versifying has a very similar erotic quality. See *The Procession*, pp. 376–7.

16 *No hard feelings*: in the manuscript, this and numerous other letters of Valmont end with a special sign ∠, which Laclos used regularly in his own correspondence. Versini sees this sign as indicating Freemasonry. However, since these signs do not appear in the text, it must have been decided not to attribute any Masonic associations to Valmont. In eighteenth-century France any suggestion of Freemasonry would have carried a strong connotation of anticlericalism, which Laclos may have wished to avoid.

Saint-Roch's: a smart Paris church; Tourvel is no provincial rustic.

17 *a prude*: in the libertine's book, modesty counts as prudery and piety is ridiculed as inhuman. Laclos is beginning to draw attention to the relativity of moral standards.

18 *cruel*: Merteuil is on the road leading to other cruel females, e.g. Madame Clairwil in Sade's *Juliette ou les prospérités du vice* (1797), who is even more power-loving and, unlike Merteuil, physically cruel.

19 *corner of my eye*: cf. a similar passage in *The Procession*, p. 377.

taking the plunge: [we can recognize here that unfortunate taste for punning which was just starting and has since gone so far.]

pounding . . . fear: Valmont is vain; but he may be right.

21 *Sophie Carnay*: [in order not to try our readers' patience too sorely we are omitting many of the letters of this daily correspondence and reporting only those necessary for an understanding of the events involving this group of persons. We are similarly omitting all Sophie Carnay's letters and a number of those from other people concerned in these adventures.]

happy: the ingenuous and ignorant Cécile seems to think that Knights of Malta are celibates; this would be true only if Danceny were to take his final vows.

23 *in anyone's cap*: is Tourvel's hope of reforming Valmont entirely disinterested? It certainly has an ironic touch of over-confidence; but here as in many other passages Laclos implies rather than states motives. Richardson's Clarissa also speaks of reforming Lovelace.

reply: her formal reply to the invitation to Cécile's wedding.

24 *husband's death*: [Madame de Volanges's misapprehension shows that, like other scoundrels, Valmont did not betray his accomplices.]

in the neighbourhood: similarly, a friend of Clarissa Harlowe's warns her against Lovelace and Clarissa asks her to keep an eye on Lovelace's actions.

Corsica: Corsica was handed over to France by Genoa in 1760; in letter 111 we learn that Gercourt is no longer needed on the island. It would thus seem that, despite Laclos's other hints, this correspondence dates from the 1760s or later.

27 *little house*: an important adjunct to the high society of Paris at the time: a discreet, luxurious villa of assignation, usually nearby in the suburbs—Neuilly was much favoured—where couples could

couple at leisure and unobserved, thus, most importantly, creating no scandal.

27 *Le Sopha . . . La Fontaine*: *Le Sopha*, an erotic oriental fantasy by Crébillon *fils* (1707–77): a Brahmin's soul, imprisoned in a series of sofas, will be released only when two pure young lovers consummate their love on one of them; during his longish wait he hears the dialogues and associated sounds of various couples analysing their emotions and, in the main, manœuvring verbally and otherwise towards sexual congress. *Eloïsa's letters*: probably not a reference to Rousseau's novel so much admired by Laclos, but to the letters, easily available, from the unfortunate nun Eloïsa to her even more unfortunate lover Abélard (1079–1142), castrated by Eloïsa's uncle, a bishop, when their affair came to light—a fate which could appeal to Merteuil's cruelty. Some of the letters are very passionate. *La Fontaine*: see note to p. 15.

the cafés: coffee-houses had become enormously popular in Paris, as important as a sociable meeting-place for men as drawing-rooms were for both sexes; many cafés had become centres of discussion of 'enlightened' ideas.

romantic: such proceedings were indeed a commonplace in the romances, that is, the novels of the period.

28 *to part for ever*: Laclos does not tell us the reason for this decision. The use of 'joyous' may, of course, be ironical or merely untrue: Merteuil is certainly too proud to admit that the parting may have been painful; or she may have had another attractive man in mind; or become fed up with Valmont's bullying; or even suspected him of having his eye on another woman and wanted to ditch him before he ditched her? The extent of any residual 'love' of, or resentment towards, Valmont remains a mystery.

29 *knight*: this detailed account of her doings is clearly—and perhaps maliciously—intended to arouse Valmont's jealousy.

transformation: has Tourvel been reading Rousseau's *La Nouvelle Héloïse*, a central theme of which was the moral and physical salubrity of country life? Country life in *Liaisons* hardly supports this view.

32 *Belleroche*: [the knight mentioned in Madame de Merteuil's letters.]

34 *out of a comedy*: e.g. Figaro, the resourceful valet in Beaumarchais's *Barber of Seville*, first performed in 1775.

35 *writing*: [the letter referring to this party is missing. Presumably it is the party proposed by Merteuil and mentioned in Cécile's earlier

letter.] In these little notes, we see Laclos continually striving for plausibility.

37 *for ever*: a key phrase. This promise of eternal love was obligatory for any fashionable 'man of feeling'. Such sensitivity was considered proof of an all-embracing virtue, e.g. Valmont's 'feeling' act of charity in letter 21. However, the social requirement of delicacy of feeling can lead to hypocrisy (Valmont) or smugness (Danceny). It is easy to burst into tears or heave sighs; it can become a useful, self-indulgent party trick.

safe and convenient: we shall meet this apparently harmless phrase in a later very sinister context (see letters 89 and 93).

39 *make him glad*: Cécile is naïve but shrewd; her education has begun.

43 *ten louis*: extremely generous; Valmont spares no expense for his affairs.

drama: this is the eighteenth-century *drame bourgeois*, a blend of tragic and comic depicting ordinary domestic and social middle-class life as opposed to the royal or mythical heroes and heroines of classical tragedy; it could fall into sentimentality and pathos. Valmont obviously relishes the irony of his pretence.

44 *my trouble*: Laclos's original text—'worth ten louis'—was blunt and coarser. He clearly wishes to show Valmont in a less disagreeable, though hardly attractive light; and certainly not a tender lover.

45 *He would not*: the ironical implications of her mistake are plain.

46 *the Gazette*: the first French newspaper, founded as a weekly in 1631. It later became a bi-weekly called the *Gazette de France* and an official newspaper under the control of the Minister of Foreign Affairs.

48 *in my tears*: is Valmont pretending to be more cynical than he really is, in order to impress Merteuil?

49 *the keyhole*: in Richardson's *Clarissa*, Lovelace peeps though keyholes too; and enjoys Clarissa's tears.

50 *24*: Versini in his Pléiade edition notes the careful structuring of these six letters dated 20 August; they contain the start of not only the main love-affairs but that of Merteuil's involvement with Cécile and her crucial terms for letting Valmont go ahead, as well as the closer involvement of Volanges around which so much of the plot hinges; and Volanges's fruitless warning to Tourvel is matched by Sophie's equally fruitless warning to Cécile.

50 *hope or fear*: the relentless fraudulent campaign has been launched: appeals to female pity are followed by reproaches and accusations of cruelty; insinuation, equivocation, and obfuscation lead to downright lies; and pleas lead to insolence, threats, and blackmail—conduct to be accepted when the partner is a Merteuil, who knows the rules; but Tourvel neither knows nor would accept them. Cécile is equally disadvantaged; but is her convent education really to blame? What sort of education could teach her how to cope with a Valmont or a Merteuil?

52 *everything's in order*: for purposes of blackmail?

54 *which you wrote me*: but she fails to mention that she has taken a copy of it; however, taking copies of letters received was common practice.

60 *'I love you'*: Danceny is reading rather more into Cécile's letter than she wrote: a subtle pressure which soon persuades the naïve Cécile to utter the magic word which, in accordance with the unwritten rules of libertine love, means: 'You can have me.'

63 *the right moment*: another essential term in the libertine's glossary: the critical moment when the woman has been softened up and needs only to be attacked, sometimes roughly, in order to surrender.

give herself to you: Laclos again tones down his bluntness. Originally he had written: 'go to bed with you'.

64 *Héloïse*: Rousseau's *La Nouvelle Héloïse*.

65 *Comtesse de B——*: is she the Comtesse de B—— in letter 59 or even the Comtesse de —— in letter 47? It hardly matters: Valmont has had numerous, interchangeable, titled women, apparently all married. Cécile would appear to be something of a novelty and Tourvel certainly falls into a different category. But we must remember that for the libertine, all women in their heart are rakes.

68 *left the room*: this scene can hardly have failed to arouse the suspicion in Rosemonde that there is something afoot between Valmont and Tourvel.

two letters: Valmont here reveals something we suspected: letter-writing is for him an art form as well as an artful one.

77 *occupied*: the girls won't have learnt in the convent that in the smart jargon of the day, 'occupied' meant: having a lover. Contemporary readers would have taken the mischievous point.

write to you: [we are continuing to leave out Cécile Volanges's and the Chevalier Danceny's letters because they are uninteresting and give no information of any events.]

80 *could make*: [letter 35.]

86 *'Le bon sens . . . m'épouvante'*: [*Métromanie*, Piron.] A verse comedy by Alexis Piron (1689–1773), first performed in 1738. The word metromania means an urge to write verse, something which the young Laclos would have sympathized with. The translation reads: 'The rascal's good sense sometimes appals me.'

87 *Scipio*: Publius Cornelius Scipio showed clemency in 209 BC when he captured the southern Spanish city of Cartagena; in particular he allowed a beautiful girl-captive, whom he could have treated as a spoil of war, to go free and rejoin her pledged husband.

88 *to everything*: the manuscript contains here a passage omitted from the published work: she agreed to everything, 'as you might expect, and I was about to go when I noticed that my valet had taken my torch instead of his own, which gave me a chance for a bit of fun: I asked the pretty little thing to show the way with my torch. She wanted at least to slip on some clothes first but I assured her that in view of what had happened there was no need to stand on ceremony and she'd got to carry off this little joke as best she could. And so she came along just as she was and I then handed her over to her loving swain and left' the happy couple, etc. Laclos may have scrapped this passage, which throws further light on Valmont's cruel idea of *fun* with women, because its scabrous quality clashed somewhat with his claim to be writing a moral work.

mention of myself: in other words, she's hiding things from her husband.

91 *singing his praises*: in *Clarissa* Richardson gives Lovelace a fond uncle; Rosemonde is certainly a fond aunt.

92 *with my death*: this letter offers a fine (ironic?) example of the sentimental/passionate jargon demanded of a lovesick suitor to hyperbolize what was possibly quite a sincere feeling.

94 *of a tart*: Laclos doesn't shrink from being scabrous here; however, Versini in his Pléiade edition tells us that this situation was not invented by Laclos (p. 1237).

the Italians: one of the two main Paris theatres, formed in 1762 by a merger between the strolling fairground players (Théâtre de la Foire) and an Italian company. It was at the Comédie-Italienne that the comic opera *Ernestine*, with libretto adapted by Laclos from an edifying novel by Madame Riccoboni (see Introduction, p. ix) received a single ignominious performance in 1777.

96 *genuineness of my feelings*: this brilliantly suggestive pastiche of a Rousseauistic frenzy of passion clearly shows that whatever his feelings for Tourvel may be, Valmont is still a willing exponent of libertinism; and, of course, he's anxious to impress Merteuil (and make her jealous). Perhaps this scene is his counter to her story of her night with Belleroche.

100 *Céladon*: the chivalrous hero of the pastoral novel *L'Astrée*, by Honoré d'Urfé (1567–1625), a long-winded, idealizing sentimental romance in which members of high society, often recognizable to their contemporaries, appear as shepherds and shepherdesses. Such romances, a great vogue in seventeenth-century society, continued to be read even later; the spectacle of faithful, respectful heroes eventually united—after various mishaps, misunderstandings, and narrow escapes—with their true loves, had considerable appeal. Céladon was the epitome of such virtuous lovers.

reply: [this letter is missing.]

top of the list: presumably because of the reputed homosexual proclivities of members of orders of knighthood.

101 *all and sundry*: [the reader will have long since deduced from her morals Madame de Merteuil's scant respect for religion. We would have deleted the whole paragraph but we thought that when showing the effects, we ought not to omit showing the causes.] Once again Laclos is trying to cover himself against accusations of ungodliness; yet ungodliness continues to triumph.

104 *Versailles*: the seat of the court, where Valmont appears to have his entrée. He seems to be taking Danceny under his wing, with ironic consequences.

I promise: we shall be savouring the irony of this promise later.

109 *a shudder through me*: in typical fashion, Laclos leaves the reader to speculate on the possible moral and social motives for this shudder.

than Danceny: this letter of Valmont's is a reply to letter 54 in which Merteuil writes of being physically attracted to Cécile; his reaction—or lack of reaction—to her admission suggests that lesbian feelings raised no eyebrows in their circles—and perhaps that he is refusing to rise to Merteuil's bait.

110 *La Châtre's*: the Marquis de La Châtre obtained from his beautiful, witty, and notoriously promiscuous mistress Ninon de Lenclos (1620–1705) a written promise that she would not be unfaithful to him, a note she quoted gleefully each time she was. This *note* had become proverbial.

112 *A sage . . . their source*: [this is thought to be Rousseau writing in *Émile*: but the quotation is inaccurate and Valmont completely misapplies it here; in any case, had Madame de Tourvel ever read *Émile*?] *Émile*, Rousseau's treatise on how to educate boys, was first published in 1762. The sentence asterisked is an interesting foreshadowing of Freudian psychotherapy.

113 *instrumental . . . arietta*: *instrumental recitative* is recitative accompanied by the instruments of the orchestra rather than by a continuo instrument such as a harpsichord. Recitative is used as dialogue or to further the narrative whereas the aria or *arietta* (the diminutive may here be contemptuous) was emotional and lyrical. Valmont's operatic metaphor reminds us that this drawing-room society saw itself as being a stage on which a part had to be played to create an often deliberately misleading effect: being natural was not only unsmart, it could be dangerous. Valmont is such a notable actor, playing so many often hypocritical parts, that he must surely have difficulty in discovering his true identity; hence, perhaps, his uncertainty as to his true feelings or even whether he has any fixed feelings towards Tourvel.

occupied: see note to p. 77.

preserve: an untranslatable pun here: Laclos uses *bois*, meaning both a wood and the horns of a stag, deer, or cuckold.

114 *refuse me your help*: never-ending irony: Cécile trusts Merteuil, Danceny trusts Valmont; in a moment, Volanges will be appealing to Merteuil.

116 *Athenian architect*: a story told by Plutarch (and repeated in *La Nouvelle Héloïse*): the Athenians were interviewing architects for two big buildings; one came up with a superb prepared speech, the second said laconically: 'I'll do what he's just said.'

118 *'Les sots . . . plaisirs'*: [Gresset, in his comedy *Le Méchant*.] Gresset (1709–77), writer of light verse and of this satiric comedy (first performed in 1745) about a malicious and shameless trouble-maker whose activities reflect the cynicism of a scandal-loving and frivolous aristocratic society. The translation reads: 'Fools are sent to provide us with entertainment.'

120 *local post*: Merteuil's comment suggests that the internal Paris post, which started in 1760, had been recently introduced—a further hint as to the date of the action of the novel.

125 *for ever*: [Monsieur Danceny is not telling the truth. He has already confided in Monsieur de Valmont before this event. See letter 57.] In this close-knit society honesty seems impossible; but

we need to take into account the motives: Tourvel's and Danceny's minor hypocrisies are harmless compared to Valmont's and Merteuil's.

126 *two enclosed letters*: letters 64 and 65.

the Prince: [reference to a passage in a poem by Monsieur de Voltaire.] Voltaire's mock-epic poem *La Pucelle d'Orléans* (The Maid of Orleans), first published in 1755, contains considerable spicy and burlesque elements. Readers familiar with the poem would have realized that if Danceny represents the Prince, the Prince's *friend* would be Valmont. In Voltaire's poem this *friend* is a euphemism for a pimp; the Prince is the future French king, Charles VII.

127 *Some of them . . . daughter*: [the reader will not be in a position to judge the truth of this statement. We have preferred to leave the question unsettled rather than enlarge this compilation with a host of letters almost all badly written and which Valmont rightly describes as boring. In any case, the possibility of such misrepresentation is inherent in all love-letters.] This note exists only in the manuscript. Laclos, always striving for even-handedness, leaves the question of various responsibilities as open as possible.

130 *paper, pen, and ink*: Clarissa was similarly deprived.

132 *as we call it*: again, the theatrical image of life as a show.

133 *she adores me*: the plainest statement as yet of phallocentricity, i.e. absolute submission of women to male authority, to which belief Valmont adds his own touch of sadistic cruelty. He also clearly believes that male intelligence is superior to female, an attitude for which Jacques Derrida has coined the amusing barbarism of phallogocentricity.

135 *'dans le simple appareil . . . au sommeil'*: [Racine's tragedy *Britannicus*.] First performed in 1669. The translation is: 'in the simple attire of a beauty recently snatched from sleep.'

my performance: we note that Valmont fancies himself as a sexual athlete; we must not forget this.

140 *nothing . . . to me*: an ironical echo by Laclos of Terence's 'humani nil a me alienum puto' (nothing human is alien to me).

141 *gentlemanly treatment*: such catty malevolence suggests that Merteuil's feminist libertarian principles don't extend to other women, particularly if they've been to bed with Valmont so enjoyably. The reason she gives for her attitude must be a mere pretext.

142 *space*: [shortly afterwards, as we shall see, Mademoiselle de Volanges found a new confidante and we shall thus no longer be reporting the letters she continued to write to her convent friend since they would not be providing us with any new information.]

147 *all right*: this whole section is an object lesson in the rational application of principles of seduction based on experience. Valmont smugly believes that he has turned the whole matter into an exact science. Having analysed and labelled Tourvel to his own satisfaction, he intends to proceed with cold-blooded precision.

replied to Danceny: [this letter is missing.]

150 *Madame de Rosemonde ... to hear it*: another blatant untruth; Tourvel is employing desperate defensive tactics.

152 *apple of discord*: according to Greek myth, the golden apple inscribed 'for the fairest' was given by Paris to Aphrodite and not to the two other claimants, Hera and Athene; Paris got Helen in reward and the Trojan war resulted.

155 *goes for seven*: in the card-game faro, going for seven means raising your stake sevenfold.

157 *country estates*: in this story, the men are smug and get off scot-free; the women are strictly punished: the double standard is at work here, as elsewhere in *Liaisons*.

160 *Goodbye, Cécile*: despite the at times rather inflated tone, this letter shows an understanding of a lover's feelings very far removed from libertinism.

161 *Believe me ... do without*: one of the most acute of Merteuil's many witty aphorisms.

162 *those throneless tyrants ... our slaves*: [it is not known whether this line of verse, like the one above, *her arms still open though her heart is closed*, are quotations from little-known works or form part of Madame de Merteuil's prose style, as we would be led to believe by the host of such solecisms throughout this correspondence, except in Danceny's letters; as he sometimes wrote poetry himself, his better-trained ear made it easier for him to avoid this error.] It was considered bad form to incorporate verse rhythms into prose letters. This note shows the great care Laclos devoted to stylistic niceties. The whole of letter 81 reveals a powerful rhetorical drive indicative of Merteuil's strong feelings on the subject of female emancipation—particularly, even exclusively, her own.

165 *the pretext for them*: an exact summing-up of the hedonism of

the Enlightenment—that people are activated by purely selfish motives, of which the most basic is the desire for pleasure.

166 *the ones you think*: she is probably suggesting that Valmont may have Crébillon or more licentious authors in mind.

168 *humiliating*: Merteuil wields blackmail as freely as Valmont.

reckless one of us two: [later, in letter 152, we shall learn, not Monsieur de Valmont's secret but more or less what sort it was; and readers will understand why we could not further enlighten them on this subject.] Laclos, a master of suspense, skilfully introduces a tantalizing note of mystery: was the royal court—perhaps the Queen—involved? See letter 152, first paragraph.

169 *or die in the attempt*: she seems to be adopting a heroic stance which is traditionally virile; such hidden masculinity helps us to understand Merteuil's attraction towards the tender Cécile; it must also make her feel irked by any sensual dependence on men. However, her intellectual superiority always allows her effortless power over them; was Gercourt her only failure in this regard and thus so loathed?

Goodbye: this letter is central to our understanding of Merteuil's conduct and morality. Women who think men beastly have usually suffered some traumatic personal hurt; the 'enlightened' Merteuil uses reason and observation to reach the conclusion that male-dominated society is so unfair that the so-called fixed moral principles are an arbitrary convention. She therefore places herself beyond good and evil: it's legitimate to do anything you like in pursuit of your pleasure. Readers who find Merteuil's hatred of society inadequately motivated can be reminded that Stendhal—notoriously unreliable—claims that he knew Laclos's model for Merteuil: she had a limp, which would justify a certain discontent with life; but there is no mention of a *limping* Merteuil in *Liaisons*.

177 *announcement*: [see letter 74.]

lansquenet: a card-game introduced into France by German soldiers (*Landsknechte*).

Bishop of ——: a close acquaintance between a bishop and a notorious libertine is an intriguing note. A dangerous acquaintance—perhaps for both? Or birds of a feather? In any case, the hypocritical Valmont is well aware that, whatever his own belief or lack of belief may be, friendship with a high ecclesiastical authority can always come in handy; and a well-bred man observing the social code and avoiding openly outrageous scandal is accepted in all drawing-rooms.

179 *Their names*: [see letter 70.]

180 *prospect of failure*: once again we see the importance of the word *love* as an almost obligatory and, for the initiated, infallible talisman to lead to sexual intimacy.

181 *Zaïre, you are weeping*: Voltaire's tragedy *Zaïre*, first performed in 1732, concerns the love of Sultan Orosmane for Zaïre, a Christian raised in his seraglio. Thinking she loves someone else, he is ready to release her, but as he speaks, her tears reveal that she loves him. With typical impishness Merteuil uses a quotation from a tragedy to illustrate her comic situation.

182 *Cerberus*: in classical mythology this true hellhound guarded the entrance to the infernal regions; again Merteuil is being mock-heroic.

183 *'And that was all there was to it'*: a quotation from *Annette et Lubin*, a verse comedy by Charles-Simon Favart (1710–92), director of the Opéra-Comique. It was first performed in 1762. Annette is saying that love is just innocent pleasure; how can anyone think it wrong?

gallimaufry: [not everyone knows that a gallimaufry is a combination of various card-games from which each player may choose when it is his or her turn. It is one of this century's novelties.] A nice realistic and topical touch.

195 *more than one meaning*: we are reminded that Danceny, like Laclos in his youth, is a poet. This is one of Laclos's most brilliant letters: the impulsiveness and blindness of love; the attempt to explain away misgivings which, ironically have no basis—as yet; pathetic appeals to a false friend; fear at having lost his girl's love: all the cruel (for him; rather funny for the reader) uncertainties of a young, sensitive, and gullible man.

197 *safe, simple, and convenient*: [Danceny does not know what this method is; he is merely repeating Valmont's words.] A bitter irony here.

207 *anything else*: an excellent example of Laclos's clinical, deliberate, and perhaps mischievous impartiality in blurring moral issues: with Cécile's admission of semi-acquiescence, Valmont's violence (rape or near rape) appears less violent. Laclos's method of working largely by implication often leaves a whiff of moral anarchy.

208 *precious qualities*: precious indeed; but, ironically, sensitivity towards her daughter is not Volanges's forte. She has been too taken up with her social round, too dazzled by the prospect of a rich and aristocratic son-in-law.

209 *mother of his children*: perhaps the most savage dramatic irony of this relentlessly ironic novel.

212 *Achilles' spear*: on his way to Troy, Achilles had inflicted a spear-wound on Telephus, king of the Mysians. The king consulted the Delphic oracle, who told him that 'the wounder would also be the healer'. Telephus sought out Achilles and his wound was cured by the rust from Achilles' spear.

215 *'Je suis . . . pas galant'*: [Voltaire's comedy *Nanine*.] *Nanine* (1749), a sentimental verse comedy, deals with the common theme of persecuted innocence; an early example, though in verse, of the middle-class *drame bourgeois* (see note to p. 43). The translation is: 'I'm not being gallantly polite. I'm just being fair.'

216 *ruined*: Valmont uses the same word which he had already used to describe his own treatment of women: it's a case of the biter bit. His vanity (it is surely not his love) is particularly hurt because it is a basic principle of a libertine to be always the first to break off a relationship; here, not only has Tourvel left him first but, after his incautious anticipation of imminent surrender, he hasn't even succeeded in having her. Even more amusingly, now that his careful calculations have let him down, he's at a loss to know what to do; no sign of triumph here.

220 *if there are any*: this paragraph highlights Valmont's obsession with careful organization (we recall that his creator was an engineer) and his clear belief that rational analysis of Tourvel's external behaviour will infallibly lead to an understanding of her feelings. However Valmont, even if a rationalist, is clearly no *philosophe*; he shows no sign of deprecating his aristocratic privileges or of wishing to redress social injustice; and whether he is any sort of believer or not, he uses religion purely for his own egoistic and dastardly ends. It is ironical to see a rationalist becoming more and more obsessed, to the point of derangement, by his obsessive desire for Tourvel.

twenty-five louis: seduction of a virtuous woman is not a pursuit for the poor man; women such as Émilie certainly come cheaper.

221 *M——*: [a village half-way between Paris and Madame de Rosemonde's château.]

224 *nothing new*: but this wise and pious old lady did not warn this innocent young wife of Valmont's reputation (see note to p. 68); and like other victims of their sins of omission or commission, whether through weakness, self-delusion or even kindness, she will be tragically punished.

227 *Madame de Sévigné*: 1626–96, lived a good deal in the country, where life would certainly have been more spartan than in Paris. Merteuil is playing up to a perceived nostalgic affection of the conventional Volanges for 'the good old days' and perhaps for the imagined virtues of country life, *à la Nouvelle Heloïse*.

not found wanting: Merteuil knows very well Gercourt's special personal qualities, particularly in bed.

230 *friendship for you*: Merteuil's letter is a masterpiece of casuistry and hypocrisy. Laclos is pushing his irony to the point of impudence: Volanges, originally responsible for arranging this match, now has misgivings, and the defence of the system is placed in the mouth of a ruthless and mendacious woman using plausible arguments which Merteuil knows will flatter the suggestible and easily scared mother and appeal to her conservative instincts and religious beliefs, which Merteuil herself relentlessly subverts. The irony is compounded when we reflect that Merteuil may well be right: Cécile's love for Danceny may well be an infatuation; and Gercourt is a man of the world, with a good position in society and the wealth to maintain it. As Merteuil says, marriages made in heaven do not necessarily remain there.

none of its pleasures: Merteuil is again preaching the hedonism of the Enlightenment: the purpose of life is to seek pleasure and avoid pain; chastity is nonsense; we can understand the frowns of puritans.

233 *for having done so*: Merteuil's self-interested but comforting argument that 'everybody's doing it' (commonly used by predatory males) paradoxically does help to mitigate the harrowing effect of the violence enacted against Cécile by Valmont. Once again we see dishonesty seemingly the best policy.

235 *pleasure machines*: the use of this word suggests a view of men and women as pieces of machinery which, with appropriate stimuli, can be engineered to undertake any required action. Julien-Offray de La Mettrie, the most thorough-going behaviourist *philosophe* of all, wrote in 1747 a work entitled *L'Homme-Machine* which so shocked even the tolerant Dutch that he had to seek refuge with the 'enlightened' king of Prussia, Frederick II.

238 *at* ——: [still in the same village half-way to Madame de Rosemonde's château.]

239 *Clarisse*: a French translation of Richardson's *Clarissa* by the Abbé Prévost appeared in 1751. The predicament of Clarissa, who had imprudently entered into correspondence with a rake and then run

away to avoid his pursuit, was very relevant to Tourvel.

239 *servants' lodge*: an outbuilding in the grounds of the château to house the servants (and the horses) of visiting guests.

240 *judge's liveryman*: Azolan is a snob; he is the personal servant (and thus not wearing a footman's or groom's livery) of an authentic landed aristocrat by birth and looks down on the *noblesse de robe* granted to high legal and administrative officers by reason of their office. Azolan is a perfect Figaro, neither humble nor obedient but certainly matching his master in roguery.

244 *'Heavenly powers . . . . its delights'*: [*Nouvelle Heloïse*.] The situation of Tourvel, deeply in love but in duty bound to resist, bears a certain resemblance to Julie's, and Danceny's to Saint-Preux's. It is ironic to see the dissolute Valmont quoting from this overtly moralizing work from which he's probably borrowing his *standard rigmarole* (see this letter).

245 *in novels*: Crébillon's spring to mind; again, a mischievous reminder that, for Laclos, reading is a second education.

Clarissa: Lovelace drugs Clarissa to possess her; while Valmont rejects such methods, his own are hardly consistent with the willing surrender he had been so boastfully insisting on earlier.

'the pleasures of vice . . . virtue': [*Nouvelle Heloïse*.]

write elegiacs: perhaps a deprecating, ironical backward look at Laclos's own early versifying.

247 *'Love will provide'*: [Regnard, *Les Folies amoureuses*.] Regnard (1655–1709) was a very popular dramatist of his period. *Les Folies amoureuses* tells the rather trite story of a young girl foiling an old suitor and marrying her young sweetheart.

off-beat: Valmont is blasé and may be heading towards desperate boredom, perhaps even *taedium vitae*. Merteuil sometimes shows similar symptoms.

health: Valmont's not the sexual athlete he's been claiming to be.

248 *Bastia*: an important port on the north-east coast of Corsica.

249 *The Comte de Gercourt*: we can assess from this letter that Gercourt is something of a name-dropper, a trifle smug but mannerly.

11th: [this letter is missing.]

251 *to confirm . . . her virtue*: [*On ne s'avise jamais de tout*; a comedy.] In fact, a comic opera (*You can never think of everything*), by Michel-Jean Sedaine (1719–97), one of the principal practitioners of middle-class drama (see note to p. 43).

252 *wrote me*: [see letter 109.]

255 *worthy of him*: an outrageously mischievous letter, not only calculated to arouse Valmont's jealousy but impudently soliciting his help. Does she really fancy Danceny?

257 *from professionals*: Valmont is moulded in the line of Crébillon's heroes, circumspectly veiling scabrous situations in decorous language, easily decoded by the practised debauchee Merteuil and by any (enjoyably shocked and voyeuristic?) sophisticated readers of both sexes. It is now difficult to know, if tantalizing to speculate, what sexual practices might have been considered unreasonably demanding by eighteenth-century French tarts. Whatever they were, they must have been fairly outrageous and any familiarity with them by his 'virgin' bride would have been a rather nasty eye-opener for Gercourt on his wedding night. But perhaps Laclos was merely suggesting that, puffed up with vanity as always, Valmont was just bragging; a fact that would have not gone unnoticed by the alert Merteuil.

258 *intercepting them*: yet another trick Laclos could have picked up from Richardson's Lovelace.

torture him: funnelling a continuous flow of water into a victim tied-down face upward was one method of obtaining confessions.

259 *dry season*: smart people are all still away in the country and the season of plays, operas, and balls hasn't yet begun.

262 *happy again*: a brilliant pastiche of sentimental clichés, self-deception, and lover's pique, yet a genuine feeling of love withal; a comparison might be a similar blend achieved by Mozart in parts of *Così fan tutte*.

266 *misleading you*: Valmont is clearly using his fond aunt as a pawn, who is misled by her very piety: another irony.

267 *touching example of her own*: the profane duplicity of this letter shows Valmont's piety as a hypocritical shell; he is a *libertin* in both the eighteenth-century and seventeenth-century meanings of the word: a rake as well as a free-thinker.

269 *His august and holy care*: Merteuil is as blasphemous as Valmont.

272 *be your last*: to an aunt who is a sincere believer but, possibly through fondness for her nephew, an unwitting procuress, Laclos adds Father Anselme, an unwitting pimp, who displays an amusingly unctuous self-confidence: Laclos's irony at the expense of piety and established religion is pitiless.

276 *analyse it more closely*: Valmont's instinct or experience provides

him with the right solution: analysing feelings is often a way to destroy them—a permanent danger (or handy safeguard) for the professional rake.

277 *enjoy hearing*: Laclos is anxious to guarantee the plausibility of a story which Valmont is going to report in such, rather improbably, accurate detail.

two letters: [letters 120 and 123.]

278 *prudishness*: another reading has *prudence*; the reader can choose.

etc. etc.: the wily Valmont is using Tourvel's alleged infraction of the proper code of polite social intercourse to weaken her position whilst he, outwardly conforming to this code in public, ruthlessly ignores it in private; salon sociability hinged on the external forms of respectable conduct and the avoidance of scandal.

280 *the answer is death*: despite his proclaimed seducer's skills (and *Liaisons* has been called with some justification a manual of seduction), threatening to commit suicide is one of the most hackneyed tricks in the book. Later events in the novel give this threat of suicide an ironic twist.

282 *field of my triumph*: this turns out to be an armchair: Laclos accepts the convention of licentious writing that, lacking a bed or an ottoman (and always to strike while the iron is hot), the wide armchairs of the period were suitable for sexual intercourse, even when it occurs between two fully clothed persons of whom one is limply unconscious.

Turenne or a Frederick: Turenne (1611–75), Louis XIV's finest army commander, noted for his thoughtful approach to the art of war. Frederick II, the Great (1711–86), king of Prussia, a superb army commander as well as an 'enlightened' monarch.

Capua: in the course of his campaign against the Romans, the forces of the Carthaginian general Hannibal (247–163 BC), in winter quarters in the southern Italian town of Capua, became softened by luxurious living.

283 *eternal love*: despite his attempt to analyse away his feelings for Tourvel, Valmont's gesture in falling at Tourvel's feet to thank her, to swear eternal love *after* he has possessed her (and not falling at her feet *before* possessing her in order to persuade her to let him do so), offers a hint of genuinely tender feeling and an at least momentary relaxation in his desire to exert his phallic authority; but it may merely be gratitude and relief. Even if, as Merteuil, presumably an expert in such matters, asserts, his feelings towards

Tourvel may be described as 'love', they clearly do not involve abandoning his promiscuous habits, his libertine principles, and his male fatuity. Merteuil's pride must be badly jolted to learn that it was with Tourvel and not with her that *for the first time*, his ecstasy had not ended after possessing a woman.

284 *Yes, goodbye . . . kisses*: the italics suggest that Valmont is callously quoting from earlier letters written to Merteuil during their first love-affair.

triumph is complete: sour grapes from Valmont? The irony of the statement will appear later.

285 *have reformed him*: if this conviction of Tourvel's ability to reform Valmont was sincerely held, Rosemonde's blame in the seduction is greatly diminished, her possible status as the moral centre of the novel considerably enhanced—and her punishment the more tragic.

287 *But in the old days . . . agree*: does this seemingly affectionate mention of the past mean that, despite his involvement with Cécile and Tourvel, Merteuil's love for Valmont can be revived? Or is she hypocritically softening him up in order to deliver the *coup de grâce*?

288 *stating facts*: but not all of them. Modesty, shame, remorse, confusion—her first orgasm ever?—ignorance of the appropriate language, socio-cultural taboos, fear of the consequences, combine to make it impossible for her to refer to the intense sexual pleasure which is bound henceforth to colour, even unwillingly or unwittingly, her future relations with Valmont.

299 *I'll make him . . . he comes*: Valmont is speaking in Cécile's name, since it is he who's dictating her letters.

'Plus je vis . . . ma patrie': [Du Belloi, *Tragédie du Siège de Calais*.] This quotation from the patriotic tragedy by Du (or De) Belloy (or Belloi) (1727–75) clearly establishes the correspondence as post-1765, the date of its first performance. The translation is: 'The more foreigners I saw, the more I loved my native land.'

300 *perfectly happy*: again we may ask whether this dwelling on the past is a hint of genuine lingering affection or a lure to make him drop Tourvel.

309 *to leave me*: an application of the doctrine of a rake, such as Lovelace: once subdued, always subdued.

311 *I've since enjoyed*: we are reminded of Mademoiselle de Lespinasse, who ran a philosophical Paris salon from 1762 to 1776 and who

once wrote: 'there is a kind of ache so sweet and charming to the soul that one is willing to prefer this hurt to what people call pleasure.' The masochism of Tourvel makes her an appropriate victim for the sadist Valmont.

311 *For reasons . . . more of her*: an example of elegant social circumlocution to impart a blunt fact, with wit: Tourvel is menstruating.

315 *It's not my fault*: contemptuous dismissive letters were not a novelty; this one is brilliant.

323 *'I like . . . unhappy'*: [Marmontel, *Conte moral d'Alcibiade*.] Marmontel (1723–99), a talented and widely read man-of-letters, active in tragedy, comedy, and comic opera, an important contributor to the *Encyclopédie*, was particularly known for his moral tales, printed in the *Mercure*, whose editor he became; elected to the French Academy in 1763, he was a friend of Voltaire and a great frequenter of literary salons. Alcibiades (450–404 BC) was a brilliant, adventurous general and politician, who, as Socrates' favourite pupil, appears in Plato's Socratic dialogues. In the particular moral tale referred to by Merteuil, he is complaining that, despite his long list of conquests, he's not loved 'for himself'.

326 *the seducer . . . anticipate events*: we recognize Valmont's arguments, previously used against Tourvel.

336 *Menaechmus*: Plautus's play about amusing misunderstandings arising from the similarity of twin brothers of this name had been adapted by Regnard (see note to p. 247) in *Les Ménechmes*, first performed in 1705.

337 *war*: this declaration of war can be viewed as the happy conclusion of a long campaign of deceit by a contemptuous and resentful Merteuil confident of matching Valmont's male aggression. Why otherwise not persist in pursuing her proven policy of prudent dissimulation and temporization? But if she still genuinely hankers after Valmont, his brutal ultimatum could finally have caused an uncharacteristic but uncontrollable explosion of passion and rage.

338 *bitter end*: [as none of this correspondence appears to clarify this uncertainty, it has been decided to omit this letter.] Not a very convincing argument; Laclos leaves many other uncertainties unclarified. See Appendix 1, p. 373, and Introduction, pp. xxiii–xxv.

340 *unawares again*: the opposite view to Merteuil's (letter 33); but he may not really hold this view; he wants to manipulate Danceny.

344 *perfectly happy*: Valmont brutally reminds Merteuil of the words she used to describe their own earlier relationship in letter 134. See note to p. 300.

349 *this morning*: no sooner have we read Danceny's challenge than we very dramatically learn of the outcome of the duel; and yet again Laclos is content to leave any speculation to the reader. If Valmont has committed suicide (see Introduction, p. xxiv), we cannot exclude the possibility that his boredom already hinted at (see note to p. 247) may have led to downright accidie. He may even have felt momentary compunction at having so grossly wronged his opponent. There may even be the possibility that the greenhorn Danceny, although seemingly more interested in poetry and music than in fighting and generally despised by both Valmont and Merteuil, overcame Valmont in fair fight; his opponent is notoriously over-confident. However all this may be, in order to maintain even the pretence of writing a 'moral' work, Laclos had to ensure the punishment of such a scoundrel. See also the following note.

350 *breathing his last*: Laclos makes no comment; it is for the reader to surmise whether Valmont's edifying end is intended to indicate true repentance or to be a blackly humorous sham by Valmont, playing the part of a contrite sinner for reasons of social propriety, in support of his caste and his family. We note that in any case Laclos is here breaking with the heroic tradition of Molière's Dom Juan (to be followed also by Mozart's Don Giovanni five years hence) of being defiantly godless to the last. If Valmont is sincerely contrite, the reader will note that, ironically, Tourvel has achieved her hope of reforming her lover, albeit far to late to help any of his victims; and the double standard still flourishes: Prévan will continue Valmont's good work, to general applause.

351 *humanity and religion*: we must sympathize with this distraught rheumaticky old woman, tragically punished by the loss of her beloved nephew far more severely than she deserves; but it is not without irony that the immediate reaction of this forbearing and devout aristocrat is not Christian forgiveness but, in the name of religion, a desire for revenge. Is the future Jacobin inviting the reader to feel satisfaction that one member of the Valmont clan will survive to suffer for his misdeeds?

353 *herewith*: [this casket contains all the letters concerning her affair with Monsieur de Valmont.]

355 *Unsigned note*: the information contained in and the tone of this letter have led Versini and others to the view that it must have been written by Bertrand.

357 *being quoted*: [letters 81 and 85.]

358 *My daughter's . . . consequences*: poor Volanges! Her blindness to her daughter's plight persists until the end.

359 *herewith*: [this correspondence together with the letters handed over on Madame de Tourvel's death and also those which Madame de Volanges passed on to Madame de Rosemonde constitute the present work; the originals remain in the possession of Madame de Rosemonde's estate.] Laclos continues to make commendable efforts to achieve plausibility; but he does not tell us how the letters to Merteuil from Valmont, Cécile, and others find their way into the collection.

Valmont and myself: Danceny carefully omits any mention of his affair with Merteuil; he becomes even smugger when, in a later letter, he magnanimously forgives Cécile, to whom he had originally made the advances; see note to p. 60.

360 *Knight Commander of* ——: clearly the local Commander of the Knights of Malta.

362 *at her age*: precisely the argument her mother used to justify marrying her off to a man unknown to her.

368 *confluent variety*: the blisters run together to form one slimy mucopurulent surface; very nasty.

such duplicity: young girls are notoriously difficult to portray. In Cécile, Laclos has produced a plausibly complex blend of real innocence, lively sensuality, youthful resilience, and a resourceful shrewdness that is certainly not banal, though his picture of convent education seems to foster the indiscriminate view that if they do happen to stray, convent-bred girls do it rather thoroughly.

370 *Holland*: Amsterdam was a traditional haven for refugees from governmental and ecclesiastical intolerance.

371 *My daughter and my friend*: a tragic irony: Volanges may be selfishly misguided, snobbish, and self-deluded but her greatest misfortune comes from her clear-sighted and kindly warning to Tourvel.

Publisher's Note: not in Laclos's handwriting, this note may properly be seen as written by the real publisher Durand, anxious to leave his options open for a possible sequel.

372 *later adventures*: Cécile is clearly unsuited to convent life. Young, pretty, having tasted and enjoyed sexual pleasures, she is very likely to become the 'good time girl' prophesied by Merteuil and fit comfortably into the free and easy life of her class, where her money alone will guarantee her a husband.

final retribution: we must not however forget that in letter 113 Merteuil has already outlined a strategy for a way of life for intelligent women who feel their physical attraction fading. Merteuil is moreover an extremely resourceful woman, a born survivor: with her pockmarks covered in the heavy eighteenth-century fard and rouge, a dashing eye-patch over one eye, the financial resources from the family jewels she has stolen, and an inexhaustible supply of wit, spirit, and mendacity, this young, piquant, chic French marquise can still attract male attention for many years yet.

373 *This letter*: see Introduction, p. xxiv.

374 *into bed*: this uncompleted letter, seemingly written after Tourvel has just given herself to (or been taken by) Valmont, hints that, despite her violent sexual awakening, she has mixed feelings and even qualms of guilt. However, Laclos chooses to give his novel a different turn and Tourvel's piety will revive only after she feels definitively discarded. This would have been the 'first letter' required by Merteuil in letter 20 as proof that Valmont had 'had' Tourvel. The condition was, obviously, not met and Valmont has no right to claim his reward—a night with Merteuil.

375 *Epistle to Margot*: first printed in 1770 in a miscellaneous collection of occasional verse, this satirical poem was not attributed to Laclos until it was reprinted in 1776 in the *Almanach des Muses*, an annual publication launched in 1766 which printed such occasional verse, by amateurs as well as by professionals (including Voltaire); it also appeared, with other similarly light-hearted verse under the heading *Pièces fugitives*, in an edition of *Liaisons* published in Nantes in 1787. Informed contemporary critics (Grimm, La Harpe) as well as Versini consider it authenticated. Its subversive tone, the criticism of aristocratic society, and the political allusions gave its author something of a scandalous reputation.

d'Hozier: a distinguished family of genealogists.

Cythera's amiable son: Eros (or Cupid) was the son of Aphrodite, the goddess of love, who landed on the island of Cythera, according to legend, after being born out of the foam.

sixteen quarterings of nobility: a touch of sour grapes? Had he possessed these sixteen quarterings, Laclos would not have been barred, as he was at that period, from promotion to the highest ranks or entry to the crack regiments of the French army.

a Marquise or a Comtesse: this comment aroused particular scandal, as it was taken to be a reference to two of Louis XV's mistresses, the Marquise de Pompadour (1721–64) and her successor the Comtesse du Barry (1743–93), who died by the guillotine.

376 *A Tale*: an erotic tale, in the style of those of La Fontaine, which Merteuil consulted to get herself in the mood for a night with Belleroche (see letter 10). Known only in manuscript and dated by Versini from its handwriting and other evidence as an early work, it was not published until 1904. If the *Epistle to Margot* hints at a budding Jacobin, *The Procession* is not likely to have come from the pen of a devout believer; and both may be described as licentious; but we must not forget that such verse contains large elements of pure convention, including the final hackneyed image: cf. letter 4.

The Oxford World's Classics Website

www.worldsclassics.co.uk

- Information about new titles
- Explore the full range of Oxford World's Classics
- Links to other literary sites and the main OUP webpage
- Imaginative competitions, with bookish prizes
- Peruse the Oxford World's Classics Magazine
- Articles by editors
- Extracts from Introductions
- A forum for discussion and feedback on the series
- Special information for teachers and lecturers

www.worldsclassics.co.uk

American Literature

British and Irish Literature

Children's Literature

Classics and Ancient Literature

Colonial Literature

Eastern Literature

European Literature

History

Medieval Literature

Oxford English Drama

Poetry

Philosophy

Politics

Religion

The Oxford Shakespeare

A complete list of Oxford Paperbacks, including Oxford World's Classics, Oxford Shakespeare, Oxford Drama, and Oxford Paperback Reference, is available in the UK from the Academic Division Publicity Department, Oxford University Press, Great Clarendon Street, Oxford OX2 6DP.

In the USA, complete lists are available from the Paperbacks Marketing Manager, Oxford University Press, 198 Madison Avenue, New York, NY 10016.

Oxford Paperbacks are available from all good bookshops. In case of difficulty, customers in the UK can order direct from Oxford University Press Bookshop, Freepost, 116 High Street, Oxford OX1 4BR, enclosing full payment. Please add 10 per cent of published price for postage and packing.